From
The Women's Press Ltd
34 Great Sutton Street, London EC1V 0DX

Hannah Wakefield is the pen name for two women, both of whom were born and raised in America and settled in London in the early seventies. One is a former editor who now divides her time between writing and working in the field of co-op housing; the other, who collaborated on the story and characters, is a partner in a well-known firm of solicitors.

HANNAH WAKEFIELD

The Price You Pay

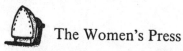 The Women's Press

First published by The Women's Press Limited
A member of the Namara Group
34 Great Sutton Street, London EC1V 0DX

Typeset by AKM Associates (UK) Ltd
Ajmal House, Hayes Road, Southall, London
Printed and bound by Hazell, Watson & Viney Ltd,
Aylesbury, Bucks

British Library Cataloguing in Publication Data
Wakefield, Hannah
   The price you pay
   I. Title
   823'.914[F]   PR6052.U7/

ISBN 0-7043-5027-0
ISBN 0-7043-4072-0 Pbk

With special thanks to Gwilym Owen, Helen English, Jane Battye, Pat Kavenagh, Sarah Dunant, Peter Busby, Sandra Gulland and Jen Green.

One

Celibacy had been my state for so long I'd practically lost track of the time. I suppose it must have been getting on for two years. And it was more or less my choice, made after my last affair had ended and I'd suddenly realised I didn't feel anything. Worse, I'd also had to accept that this wasn't the first time.

Dee, I'd thought, this is pointless. Who needs a second-rate sex life? Look: it's numbing you.

So I'd decided to pull back and wait.

It was, of course, a risk, but on the other hand I try to be pretty independent and I've taken risks before. If I hadn't I might have remained a typist in some office in the States instead of becoming a lawyer struggling to keep a small practice going in London.

Still, it *is* true that the older you get the fewer the possibilities. And it's true as well that my field was narrower than it might have been anyway because I refuse to get involved with men who are living with other women. To my shame I've already tried that (twice) and have proved that I'm not enough of a martyr to take the complexity. Besides, I've got too many wounded wives as clients.

When I left my flat that warm June morning, however, the state of my love life was hardly the foremost thing on my mind. I was late, for a start, and I was anxious. I needed desperately to find a psychiatric consultant to act as witness for one of my clients and all my usual contacts were either unavailable or wrong for the case. When I'd heard the previous day that there was to be a conference on the rights of the criminally insane at Conway Hall, I'd thought well, maybe: maybe, among the assembled experts, there'd be someone who could help.

I cut quickly across Red Lion Square and managed to slip through the doors just before they closed. Most people had found seats, but the coffee hadn't disappeared so I made for the queue of stragglers and reached for a cup. As I did this an unplaceable male voice spoke my name and, puzzled, I scanned the backs of the heads of the audience. After all, this wasn't exactly my milieu and if I'd known anyone who'd been planning to come I wouldn't have needed to change half a dozen appointments to get there myself.

'Dee – it *is* you,' the same voice called with more confidence. 'Over here . . . behind you.'

Disconcerted, I took a calming breath, put on my standard noncommittal courtroom smile, hoped I'd remember the face (never mind the name), readied a cliché and turned.

'Boing!' is a silly cartoonist's word, I know, but there's no other that describes the impact of that instant. I was so overcome by that sense of 'and their eyes met across the room' that I genuinely felt as if I'd been transported into the pages of one of the teen romance comics I used to secrete under my bed and read late at night by flashlight.

David Blake. Dr David Blake. He around whom I'd woven several hours' worth of romantic fantasy how many years was it before? Easily six. And as he came towards me, I tried to get the stupid grin off my face by recalling how that particular gauzy fabric, like the chiffon stuff of myriad other daydreams, had come to be relegated to the mental cupboard reserved for impossible imaginings.

I didn't have to search my memory very far. He'd been charged with obstruction after being arrested at a demonstration and I'd been the articled clerk assigned to prepare his defence. That alone would have been enough to cancel out whatever inclination to flirt with him I might have had. Involvement with clients was one of the firm's unwritten no-nos and I wasn't about to jeopardise the career I'd started later than most people do by transgressing it. On top of that I'd just extricated myself from my second role as the other woman and didn't have the emotional energy to consider other possibilities. Not seriously.

I always register attractive people though, and at the time I'd certainly registered David Blake. In so far as I've got a point system he'd earned a high score. He was personable. He was funny. He seemed sensitive and intelligent. He was committed to political causes I respected. And he had the lean, angular, slightly baggy looks that for some reason appeal to me. But once I'd indulged my fantasies and put them away – more to the point, once I'd got the charges dropped and sent him the final bill – I'd made myself forget about him. The real world, then, was problematic enough.

Now, as we stood a foot apart, all those old feelings rattled frantically against the door of the cupboard where they'd lain dormant for so long. In fact their din was so loud I nearly apologised. Instead I switched on to that automatic pilot that lets me, like most lawyers, act fairly normally even when I have no idea what's going on. And it worked. My feet moved; my hand accepted his; my cheek went forward for a friendly kiss; words passed between us, half of them mine. But all I remember from those first moments of our reunion is the extraordinary intensity of the signals coming from my gut – that and his suggestion that we have lunch together in the pub.

'What I can't get over is the coincidence,' he said three hours later as he set his lager and sandwich on the table and manoeuvred into the space beside me on the crowded bench. 'I've been on the verge of ringing you for the past month.'

'That tells me it's not another obstruction charge anyway.'

He touched the small scar on his right temple and smiled a smile that in other circumstances would have caused me to strip immediately. 'There are some things,' he said, 'which I don't have to go through more than once . . . No. My legal requirements this time are a lot more banal. I need a will.' He raised his glass. 'To this perfectly timed meeting, which has saved me a phone call to Samuelson Stevens.'

'Two phone calls. I'm not there any more.'

'No – really? God, I imagined you'd been made a senior partner by now. You seemed so happy there.'

'I was.'

'So?' He looked down at my left hand. 'Don't tell me – you've been enticed into indefinite maternity leave.'

I laughed. 'Are you kidding? After taking all those exams? No. I've gone into partnership. With my friend Suze. We started up three years ago – no, more than that, almost three and a half – and now there are six of us, all women. We can't seem to get people to stop writing to us as *Messrs* Aspinall Street but at least we've survived. We're even out of the red finally too.'

'Is that a political statement or merely a financial one?'

'Go on. Who do you think keeps Legal Aid in business?'

'Good. I'm relieved to hear it.'

'It doesn't cover wills I'm afraid.'

'No, I meant that you've stayed afloat working with grant-funded clients. That's what I'm hoping to do. A few of us have nearly organised the money for a new hostel. I only need a will because it goes with the life insurance policy I'm having to take out to satisfy one of the main funders.'

I sighed in sympathy.

'It's been a bit like that,' he said. 'And if we actually pull it off . . . God, I hate to think when any of us is going to have time to eat, never mind sleep.'

'You may count yourself lucky after you've had your first few nightmares about cash flow. And you can forget little luxuries like doing your laundry and reading books.'

'How about the occasional night out? You know, dinner, a film . . .' He was looking right into my eyes and I found myself hurriedly emptying my glass just to break the contact. I hadn't remembered what long lashes he had, or what deep blue, almost navy irises. Or perhaps they simply seemed more pronounced to me now because of the grey streaks that had appeared in his thick straight dark hair since I'd last seen him.

'People claim that such things do happen,' I managed. 'Another drink?'

As I waited at the bar I thought: go carefully, Dee. Stay calm. Take it easy.

When I'd sat down again I said: 'So. Tell me: what brings a GP like you to a specialist conference like this?'

He frowned. 'Has it been *that* long since we've met? I qualified in psychiatry about five years ago.'

'Really? . . . Have you testified at Mental Health Tribunal hearings?'

'Many times. Why?'

'Well believe it or not I didn't come to the conference because of your telepathic summons.'

'Damn,' he said. 'Another delusion, shot to hell.'

'Yup, 'fraid so. I'm trying to get one of my clients released from mental hospital. He's a young Chilean refugee named Carlos. He's been diagnosed schizophrenic. Been inside two years.'

'Fine. No problem.'

'You can help?'

'I specialise in working with young schizophrenics. That's why I want to open a hostel.'

'Wonderful! Well – look – maybe we can barter. The problem is time. There isn't much left.'

4

David reached into his jacket pocket for his diary. 'When is the hearing?'

'Three and a half weeks. But we'll have to arrange for you to interview him and meet with his barrister, so really . . .'

'And where is he?'

'Michelmore's, up in Norfolk. I know it's a long way . . .'

'Not as far as some. . . It's minimum security. He must be in reasonable condition. What did he do, have an outburst?'

'Yes. He destroyed the interior of a pub and broke the barman's arm. His sister Connie was so frightened that he'd be deported if he were convicted of assault that she'd had him committed before she'd even thought to call me. I was sorry of course but not surprised. Their parents were killed in Pinochet's coup and she somehow managed to get herself and her brother out *and* over to Barcelona, where they have relatives.'

'Jesus,' he muttered. 'All that to end up in a country where the treatment for schizophrenia is prehistoric.'

'That's why she brought him to London. As soon as he began taking lithium, he improved.'

'And then stopped taking the tablets I suppose.'

'Yes. When he moved into his own place.'

David sighed. 'Well, if he's been behaving himself there's no reason why they shouldn't let him out, though you never know for certain. How are you for next Wednesday? If we see him at five – well, there's an excellent seafood place not far from the hospital. We could have dinner together before we come back to town.'

I didn't even stop to think. 'Great,' I smiled. 'I'd love to. Now: about your will. How urgent is it?'

'Approaching very. *My* time's pretty flexible, the problem is . . . that is . . . I'm almost sure that . . .' He faltered and stared at the half-eaten sandwich on his plate. It seemed to me that something like uncertainty – angry uncertainty – crossed his face. Then he said: 'Hold on a minute, would you, Dee? I'd better just ring and sort this out.'

I knew then of course. I watched David's back disappear into the crowd, knowing. Shit, I thought. Shit shit shit.

When he came back, he took the now vacant seat opposite me. The lightness between us was gone.

'We can make it early morning either Monday or Tuesday,' he said with forced casualness. 'It's that or wait about a month.'

I nodded. My throat felt blocked, so when I finally managed to repeat 'We?' the word came out louder and squeakier than I'd intended. Then, embarrassed by the deflation that I was sure showed in my face, I turned away and began to rummage through my bag, where in among my keys and wallet and other paraphernalia I saw a phantom photograph portraying another anguished fantasy being led away, protesting, to its cubbyhole.

But I couldn't indulge my feelings, not here. I abandoned the search for my diary and looked over at him once more. '*Who* will you be bringing with you?'

Did he study my face? It seemed to me he did. In any case, I was conscious of a long moment, and of warmth rising from my neck.

'Amanda,' he said. 'Amanda Finch. My wife. She's going away on Wednesday and won't be back for a couple of weeks.'

A hook there, I grabbed it. 'Amanda Finch the journalist?'

He nodded, still watching my face.

'Great,' I said. It was a flat, hollow sound. 'I'll be interested to meet her.' Then, as I was in a grabbing frame of mind I grabbed my glass, drained it, reached for my bag, closed it, and stood up. I had absolutely no idea what my appointments were for the week ahead but I said: 'Monday. I'll expect you both at ten.'

He rose and with a slight move sideways blocked my way. My eyes were level with the button on the top pocket of his blue denim shirt and I was suddenly aware of his breadth and fitness, and of the faint smell of soap. 'Thanks,' he said softly. Then, holding out his hand to shake mine: 'Look – Dee. I don't quite know how to say this to you, but Amanda . . . she and I . . . we're not exactly . . .'

But I didn't want to hear it. I couldn't bear to hear it. It was too familiar.

'Shall we go?' I cut in.

He stepped aside.

'*Who*'s coming in?' Suze had been in court when I'd returned from the conference the previous Friday afternoon, so it wasn't until the Monday morning that I had a chance to tell her about it. For some reason (doubtless a desire not to be teased), I censored any mention of the emotional undercurrents I'd experienced. Besides, after a busy weekend weeding my allotment and visiting friends, my perspective had altered. My real problem, I'd decided, wasn't how I felt about David Blake, it was how I felt, period. For three years my life had been my work. I needed a change. But I didn't want to discuss that either.

I smiled and shook my head. 'Oh Suze, it's not that impressive. It's just a boring old will.'

'Of course. You're right. A film deal for Vanessa Redgrave, a three-book contract for Germaine Greer, even a tax rebate for Chris Lloyd would all be far more exciting. Forgive me.'

I was meant to chuckle and I did.

'But – failing those,' she went on, satisfied, 'Amanda Finch and her will could be good for a bit of flavour.'

I've known Suze a long time and I heard what she was really saying. 'Forget it,' I said. 'I don't even want to talk about it. The answer's no.'

'But Dee, for pity's sake . . .'

'No. It's pointless. In fact it's more than pointless. It would be positively counter-productive. We've got too much work as it is.'

'You just mistrust journalists.'

'Yes, of course I do. So do you – normally.'

Her palms went up. Her body bent over my desk. It was the appeal to reason. 'But Amanda Finch is different. Her women's page articles are bloody good. Hell, you even said so yourself the other day. What was that column about? A new clinic up in Oxford?'

'Cambridge.' I'm not usually pedantic. Suze made a prune face at me.

'It doesn't matter. She concentrated entirely on the work those women doctors are doing, not on their personal lives.'

'Then why do I remember that two of them are married and two come from medical families?'

'And you're single and come from a legal one. That's called fact.'

Her frown was so earnest that I laughed again. 'All right,' I said, 'out with it. What's the fantasy? No. Wait. Let me guess. Amanda – who, by the way, is due any minute – is so completely bowled over by my perspicacity about her assets that she pauses on her way out and says, "Gosh, golly, is this a feminist law firm? Shucks, I'll be darned. Why don't I whip up a lil' ol' article about you gals." '

'Something like that, maybe without the Americanisms.'

'Why? Didn't you read the piece about her a while back? She hails from the colonies too.'

'Does she now.' This was news and threw her into reverie.

The buzzer rang on the phone.

'This is probably them now,' I said. 'Hint hint.'

'Saved by the bell – as usual. But look Dee, if she does suggest a feature . . .'

'If.'

'. . . promise you'll bring it to the Monday morning meeting – discuss it with all of us – not dismiss it out of hand.'

'On punishment of what? Being held captive here, my hand poised over the phone?'

She stuck out her tongue. (We are so mature, Suze and I.)

I laughed again. 'If there's anything to bring to a meeting, I'll bring it. *As usual.* Now get out of here will you? I'll never even get to meet her at this rate.'

'Gone,' she said, bowing and shuffling, bum akimbo, backwards through the interconnecting door between our offices.

I ought to point out here I suppose that life at Aspinall Street & Co. is commonly punctuated by silly interludes. They're the oil that keeps us all functioning in the face of the endless dilemmas we're asked to disentangle; they're the fireproof lining on the door between us and despair; they're our sanity, in so far as we're sane for doing what we do at all. By rights, then, this particular silly exchange ought to have been as forgettable as any of our others. Yet it has stayed with me and I suspect this is partly because all trace of it evaporated so totally the moment its object entered my office.

It's true of course that the Amanda Finches of this world invariably throw me into sombre contemplation of the reason for my being. I know it shouldn't happen; I understand that I'm just reacting to thirty years' exposure to commercial art and that images of the ideal female form are subject to changes in fashion and that if I lived in ancient Greece or in Rubens' era or even in a modern Arab country, my body would be a near perfect match to the archetype. But despite all my careful rationalising, when I meet women who are of our time, it's small consolation that I am not.

Amanda Finch and I, in other words, were physical opposites. She was tall and slender where I am short and rounded. She was chic and sophisticated where I am casual and girlish. She had straight, shoulder-length blonde hair and I have dark curls. And while both of us were simply dressed, she looked as if she belonged in *Vogue* whereas I'd have had to argue to get into *Practical Self Sufficiency*.

But it wasn't only Amanda's appearance that erased my frivolous grin. For although she greeted me with charm, accepted my offer of a seat and a coffee with grace, and apologised politely for being a little early, there was a strained reserve about her manner that I realised, suddenly, I hadn't expected. She wasn't just composed, she was tense.

For a second, as I stood by the sideboard pouring milk into the cups, my hand froze. She knows, I thought. She knows and she's going to confront me.

But that, of course, was ridiculous, a panicky flicker of paranoia. There was nothing to know.

No, Amanda Finch was merely showing the anxiety symptoms typical of so many clients who come in about their wills. The prospect of talking about the wake of their own deaths simply does that to some people. And because it was such a common response I knew what to do: I made small talk, complimenting her on her articles and saying how pleased I was to meet her. This, however, elicited only diffident monosyllables and so, in desperation, I tried the 'expatriates together' tack.

'Where are you from?'

Now she had to have been asked this question as many hundreds of times as I had been, but when I asked it she looked over at me as if she'd only just realised where she was. Then, with a smile that invited me to forgive some unspecified lapse on her part, she sat back into the chair. She had decided, it seemed, that it was safe to relax.

'New York, California, you name it. And you?'

'California, Maine . . .' I said, pleased to have found this common strand.

She raised one brow. 'How long you been here?'

'Ten years,' I sighed. 'Over ten years. I came in early '71. What about you?'

'I feel as if I've been here forever.' She was smiling now.

'What brought you?'

She shrugged and reached into her bag for her cigarettes. 'In twenty-five words or less?'

I nodded.

She shrugged again. 'Curiosity. Wanderlust. Politics.' She lit up. 'I got disillusioned by politics. You?'

I laughed. 'Curiosity. Wanderlust. Politics. I felt the same.'

'And why have you stayed?'

It was my turn to shrug. 'I sometimes wonder these days. Friends. Gun control. It's home I guess. I can't imagine leaving any more.'

9

'Mmm,' she said, 'yes, and thanks to David and the Supreme Court, I've even got dual nationality.'

I started to remark that I supposed two passports must be useful to a journalist, but the words evaporated when I saw that her attention had once more lapsed. She was looking at her watch, frowning. I glanced at the clock. David wasn't late. What was this remoteness about? Why had she withdrawn again?

Eventually, after we had sat in the stillness for a long moment, Amanda stubbed out her cigarette and said: 'Dee – I hope you don't mind first names?' I shook my head. 'Look – Dee,' she went on, 'about these wills. Tell me, do husbands and wives have to draw them up together?'

God, I thought, so that's it.

'No,' I said, 'absolutely not. If you'd prefer to see me alone – separately –' The buzzer rang and I reached for the phone sure, as proved true, that David had arrived. 'Hold on, Pam,' I murmured to the woman who works in the front office. Then, my palm over the receiver, I said to Amanda: 'Why don't we make you another appointment?'

But she shook her head and stared past me, out the window, cool and self-controlled.

Now once a client says to me 'This is the way I want it' I'm bound to act (or to explain that I won't act) on that instruction. Amanda's apparent decisiveness, however, made me uneasy. Was she in the quandary I felt she was in? Or were my perceptions distorted by who she was? I didn't know and there was only one solution. I had to get her to say it again.

David had obviously rushed and strode in speedy, apologetic and breathless. He greeted us both with garrulous enthusiasm, accepting a mug and a chair, commenting on the greenhouse atmosphere of my small plant-filled office and asking Amanda about her tickets all in the same sentence. When he'd sipped and settled, he gave me one of his disconcerting smiles and said:

'Right then. Let's get down to it.'

I cleared my throat (my authoritative throat-clearing, Suze calls it), conscious that Amanda was again staring out the window. I was also conscious that he was watching me, not her.

'David,' I began, 'I was just saying to Amanda that if either of you would prefer to talk to me alone about your will, it's easily done. There's no requirement on married couples to do it together, so if you thought . . .'

'I suppose I did,' he said. 'Personally, though, I'm happy to carry on. After all, we're both here now.' He turned to Amanda. 'What do you think? Would you rather . . .' Then he realised she was only half listening. 'Amanda?' he said, touching her lightly on the arm.

At this she shook her head and forced a distant smile.

'I didn't mean to rush you into anything,' David said. 'If I did, I'm sorry. I mean . . .'

'No,' she said, the word bursting out with such vigour that the force of it seemed to startle her, as though she'd called out from a dream and woken herself. 'No,' she repeated with more control. 'I'm the one who's sorry. It's this trip. I've got so much on my mind. Why are we sitting here? As you said, let's get down to it.'

Well, I thought, there it was. She'd said it twice. And her excuse made sense of her distraction. I was being too careful, looking too hard for nuances, because of my own guilty feelings. It was me, not her.

And the brief, straightforward session that followed confirmed this conclusion. Her attention engaged, Amanda became quick and light and the two of them slipped into what seemed an easy rapport. Even their one disagreement was jocular, a routine they'd practised before.

We'd dispensed with the flat they'd bought together in Kentish Town, and with the small family keepsakes, when David turned to me and said: 'Now for the important items. About *my* Bruce Springsteen poster.'

'Hold it,' she said, 'hold it right there. That is *my* poster and you know it David Blake. Who bought it in New York, hmmm? Who had it framed?' She shook her head at me, her eyes wide with mock exasperation. 'This guy,' she confided, pointing towards him sideways with her thumb. 'In my high school we'd have called him a ratfink.'

'In mine he'd have been called a nerd,' I laughed.

'Wonderful,' she clapped. 'I'd forgotten that one. It's better. I like it.'

'I'm not sure I do,' David muttered.

Amanda, pretending to ignore him, continued: 'The next thing you know, he'll try to say that the collection of forty-fives I've been carrying around since I was seventeen belongs to him.'

'Doesn't it?' he said. 'I thought it was your dowry.'

They got up to leave a moment later and I was thinking with a mixture of relief and resignation that I was glad I'd seen them together when Amanda turned back to me. 'Oh,' she said, 'I almost forgot. David tells me that Aspinall Street is an all woman firm.'

Please, I thought, no.

'I'd like to do a feature on you,' she went on, 'when I get back. I'll call you, okay?'

My motives for seeing David Blake half a dozen times during the next two weeks seemed to me to be honourable and very straightforward. All but one of our meetings concerned Carlos' hearing and that one was about the wills.

We had already arranged the first meeting – the visit to Michelmore's Hospital. And while I now had misgivings about my agreement to have dinner with him afterwards, how could I have backed out? (Me, who loves seafood.)

On the other hand, I knew that if we were to work together the ground would have to be swept clear. The ambiguities that had enlivened our reunion could not go on muddying the friendship between us, nor slurry the potential friendship between Amanda and myself.

It struck me on the drive up to Norfolk that David had reached the same conclusion: there was nary a hint of flirtatiousness in his manner. But then, it's not easy to flirt during conversations about how the National Health Service might be decentralised (the subject of an article he was writing) and how various pieces of legislation had helped or failed to help ensure women's rights (the subject of a pamphlet I was helping to assemble). Still, I cautioned myself to remain wary, stay alert and look for an opportunity to let him know my position.

After two hours in Carlos' company, we inevitably spent most of the early evening reviewing his case. One of David's main concerns was that the hospital had put my client on too strong a tranquilliser following an angry outburst ten days earlier. So far as he could see they'd just done it 'for their own bloody convenience'. But what disturbed him even more was that not one of the hospital staff seemed to appreciate that Carlos really *had* been tortured. They'd actually been treating him almost as if his political past were some kind of hallucination. As David said, 'The poor lad should have been so lucky.'

Automatically we found ourselves discussing American policy in Latin America. How, we wondered, could the United States, itself born from revolution, suppress groups who were trying to achieve the same thing? Had they not learned from Vietnam? What possible justification could they have for supporting right-wing military dictators?

Neither of us was naive: we knew the answer was economics. We knew about the oil interests and the multinationals. But still we went through it, discovering more about each other's views and values as we talked.

David sighed and shook his head. 'I hope Amanda will be all right out there.'

I nearly choked on my mouthful of wine. 'Is *that* where she's gone? But I thought – I mean, doesn't she usually do Continental human interest pieces? My God, she hasn't gone to El Salvador has she?'

He nodded. 'Phil Knight who owns the news agency where she works caught malaria out there and had to come back a couple of weeks ago. He asked Amanda to organise his replacement and she decided to go herself. He wasn't what you'd call thrilled. She did spend a lot of her childhood in that part of the world and she speaks fluent Spanish, but she's hardly an expert on the recent political history of the area and she didn't have much time for research. They compromised. Her brief is to report on "the women's angle".'

'But for two weeks?' I was appalled. 'Isn't that a dangerously long time?'

'Her attitude is, two minutes, two weeks, the risk's the same, and no worse than some of the floods and earthquakes she's covered. She's hoping to travel into Nicaragua as well.'

'What about Cuba? Surely that's the place to go if . . .'

'For you or me perhaps; not for her. Her parents were killed in an accident there when she was twelve or thirteen so it doesn't hold much attraction for her.'

I whistled. 'What happened?'

'I believe it was a car crash though I wouldn't swear to it, and I think it must have happened just before Batista was thrown out. What I know for certain is that she got shipped home to her brother Craig, who fortunately is about ten years older and had moved back to New York.' He paused and smiled. 'Amanda is a very private woman. You'll discover that when you get to know her – or rather, try to get to know her. Coffee?'

After we'd caught the waiter's attention and ordered, David went on: 'I'll tell you one thing though – not that you might not

13

have noticed. Amanda and I met going in opposite directions on the class ladder. My father died of lung cancer after being a miner for twelve years. My grandfathers on both sides went the same way. Her family has its own oil company. . . It went to her brother needless to say.'

'Needless to say.'

He shrugged. 'It *was* twenty or twenty-five years ago. It wasn't customary to leave small girls multi-million-dollar businesses. And even though her brother's the worst kind of capitalist, to be fair to him, he gave her a generous allowance for several years. He'd be happy to give her a stake in it all *now* if she'd go and work for him. She refuses. She wants to "make it on her own".' He smirked. 'Just my luck.'

'Spoken,' I said, 'like a typical white male London socialist.'

'Ouch,' he winced.

'Go on,' I said, 'get yourself out of that.'

That gauntlet led us somehow into a long conversation about British politics since the war, which in turn led us, on the journey home, into an equally long conversation about the women's movement. There the opportunity I'd been waiting for arose at last.

'What I like,' I said, 'is how much more value women put on each other's friendships now. When I was a kid your girlfriends were second best, good only for discussing the magic day when you'd be rid of each other's company. And when it came and you found out that "life after" wasn't the idyllic fantasy you'd imagined, they were still second best – the ones who offered comfort and a cup of tea and sent you back for the next round.'

I hesitated, sensed imminent nerve failure and rushed on. 'And God help you if you found some man another woman believed she'd found first . . .'

David replied too quickly and too casually. 'Wasn't that called survival?'

I sighed. 'Was – and still is where a man is the only meal ticket. But for me and women like me, grabbing another woman's partner is nothing more nor less than betrayal.'

We met the next two times at Carlos' sister Connie's flat in Willesden and it really was totally coincidental that we finished the first meeting in time for lunch and the second at pub opening. And as for the day I stopped in at the hospital where David worked, well, there was nothing untoward about it. I was in the area and I knew he'd spoken with the director of Michelmore's that morning. So what if we adjourned to the Prompt Corner for a snack?

Similarly, David only dropped by my office one night as we were closing because he knew I'd spoken with the barrister. It was sheer chance that neither of us had any plans and ended up going for a light supper.

Okay – yes – the sixth meeting *could* be construed as gratuitous: I usually do put will documents in the post rather than have the person come in. But believe me, all our conversations were elaborations on our first, a mixture of business and politics with only the most occasional personal references. We were friends – colleagues – who simply enjoyed each other's company.

Suze, however, took a different view and as her Yorkshire upbringing can make tact as difficult for her as my American one can make it for me, she finally said so.

It was three fifteen and I'd just returned from lunch with David.

'Spinning this out aren't you?' she said, following me into my office.

'What?' I said. 'Spinning what out?'

'Don't play games with me Dee. You know what I'm talking about. You've been seeing David Blake a lot.'

'I'm trying to get Carlos out. He's helping.' The defensive edge to my voice surprised me, but when I tried to mute it by smiling, the effect felt like one of those wriggly lines cartoonists use to show embarrassment. I reached self-consciously for the post in my in-tray. For some reason which I preferred not to examine, I was eager to change the subject.

Suze wasn't and squinted at me, the inquisitor. 'The hearing's when? Next week?'

'A week tomorrow. I've marked it in the book. It's the same day as you're in court with the Thomas woman, so we'll have to make sure we're covered here. We seem to have the same problem coming up next Friday and again on the . . .'

'When is your conference with Counsel?'

'Monday.'

'So – when? Friday? I suppose you'll have a run-through with Connie and David.'

'Yes,' I said, sounding more irritated than I'd meant to. It annoyed me that she was trying to hold my eye as if I were in the witness box. It annoyed me even more when I looked away first.

And it annoyed me most of all that I was annoyed. Suze, after all, isn't merely my business partner. She's one of my closest friends.

Her hands had moved to her hips. 'And that will be that, eh? The end of a useful series of meetings with an amusing client.'

'*Yes*.'

She just looked at me, her eyes wide and full of doubt.

That did it. 'Why are you coming on with these stupid innuendos?' I snapped. 'David Blake is *married* for heaven's sake. And his wife is a talented, attractive, independent woman whose friendship I'd be pleased to have. God Suze, even if I had some uncontrollable lust for the guy and no sense of loyalty to other women, I could hardly hope to compete. But I don't and I do and I wouldn't. Bingo: three red lights. And there's nothing wrong with my sight thanks very much.'

But in the pause that followed, I heard a tiny little inner voice whisper, 'Oh yeah?'

Suze was its echo. 'Is that so?' she said, pushing some files aside and perching a blue-jean-wrapped thigh on the corner of my desk. 'I wish I had your confidence, but I'm happy to discuss your feet if you'd prefer. I look at the ground and they're simply not there.'

I thumped her on the leg, but she wouldn't let up. 'No, I've started playing mummy and I'm going to finish . . . You're kidding yourself, Dee. David Blake and his cute bum have insinuated themselves where no man and no bum have insinuated themselves in ages. Which I think is great! I mean, he's probably almost worthy of you . . . What's getting to me is that I see you doing what women are forever being accused of doing, which is putting over a double message, "talking out of both sides of your mouth" as you'd put it.'

'But that's not true,' I protested. 'He knows my position. I've been completely straight with him.'

'Yes, but *where*? Over dinner in some candlelit restaurant? During some tête-à-tête in an atmospheric little pub?'

'Oh for . . . what do you want me to do? Have the message printed on my T-shirt?'

She leaned over and placed her hand over mine. 'No. I want you to stop pussyfooting. I want you to face up to how you feel and either seduce him or stop seeing him. He deserves at least that, and so do you.' She glanced at her watch. 'I'm late for a meeting. See you later.'

Left alone again, my immediate impulse was to dismiss Suze's

16

admonitions as her problem. After all, she'd always loved love and she was forever trying to pair me up. Then my eyes strayed to the clock. *Quarter to four? How could it be quarter to four?* I reached for a file and as I did so knocked the rest of the pile to the floor. And it was in stooping to pick them up that I suddenly realised with something approaching humiliation that my partner had been right about my feet – and more tactful than I'd appreciated. I only ever got this far behind when I was working on some really large case.

Which I wasn't.

But I had been letting the two small pieces of work involving David take up the same amount of time.

I sighed and stacked the pile neatly. I'd duped myself. Somehow I'd duped myself. Yet even as I bemoaned the fact, I caught myself using the past tense. I wouldn't be doing it any more.

The test came three days later, as we were leaving Connie's. 'Drink?' David said.

Now, I thought. Now. 'Sorry,' I said. 'Babysitting.'

He nodded. 'Fine. Another time.'

Whew.

Then, unexpectedly, he said: 'Look, Amanda phoned the other night to say she's tacking on a few days' break and I'd booked theatre seats for tomorrow. Would you like to come?'

Unprepared for a double temptation, I felt overwhelmed by choice. I could have said, 'What? A Saturday night? Is this a declaration of intent?' Or I could have said, 'I'm sorry that in kidding myself I fooled you too: No.' Or I could even have said, 'Yes'.

Instead I looked down at my shuffling feet and, just barely containing a 'Gee whiz, gosh, golly', shook my head again. 'It's kind of you, but I'm afraid that I'm . . . that is, I mean . . .'

'I thought you'd have plans by now,' he smiled. 'I should have rung you. Don't worry. See you Monday.'

Okay, so I'm a chicken-hearted goody-goody lacking the courage of my passions. I called myself much worse things right up until curtain time that Saturday as I steadfastly resisted the fantasy which would have seen me lift the phone. Come Sunday morning, in fact, the urge to invite him over for tea was so insistent that I ignored the grey rain, donned my wellies and yellow slicker and went and tore into some weeds, a study in muddy masochism.

17

As the rows between the lettuces and the carrots and the radishes clarified, I calmed enough to appreciate that, really, I was suffering from a classic 'damned if you do, damned if you don't' dilemma. It was true that I was abusing my feelings now by not following them – the ache in my chest, heightened by the certainty that David Blake probably did fancy me every bit as much as I fancied him, was a symptom of that. But when I imagined the consequences of letting those feelings lead me, the images evoked just as much pain. Two months, six months, a year from now I'd be standing here, slinging the mud around with tears in my eyes, cursing my own stupidity. Sure, there was the chance that three would be lucky. But as a two-time loser it seemed unlikely to me that I could endure another wound: I had enough scars around the heart.

In my early twenties I might have gambled. Now, in my early thirties, I had too much invested in peace of mind.

For all my angst, by half past twelve on Monday I felt so vindicated that I could nearly have organised a demo on behalf of chicken-hearted goody-goodies. And the agent of my redemption was – yes, who else – Amanda Finch, who was waiting, sickeningly tanned, in our office reception when I returned from court.

Instantly fearing that she'd dropped in about the threatened feature article, I pointed to my bag of sandwiches and made my excuses.

She said she'd wait.

I shrugged, continued into my office, closed the door, thought 'Why are you hedging?', turned around, went back out and said: 'Look, I'll be blunt with you. I don't think this firm *needs* publicity.'

She said, 'But I've come for some advice.'

I ushered her in.

'When did you get back?' I asked as I gestured for her to sit.

'Saturday night,' she said as she tamped out her cigarette and immediately lit up another.

I thought of David's invitation and the excruciating moment that might have been and felt queasy. I even grabbed at the corner of my desk for support. But Amanda, now poised on the edge of a chair, appeared not to notice.

She pressed her palm against her forehead. 'I'm still out in the middle of the ocean so you'll have to excuse me. I can't decide if what I want will put you in some kind of invidious position or whether . . .'

'Ask me.'

'Yes – yes – but just in asking . . . I mean the question itself will tell you . . . Oh hell. It's about my will.'

'Was there something wrong with the draft?' I was concerned but puzzled by the build-up for such a simple thing.

'No,' she said hastily. 'That is, you put in everything we said. It's just that – well – there were a few things I didn't say. Couldn't say – not with David there. I'd have had to explain – so much. And it seemed such an unnecessary complication, you know? I mean, all the poor guy is really after is an insurance policy. The will's secondary, so it didn't seem important – not at the time – to . . . to . . .'

She stopped and looked down at her hands. When she spoke again it was more to herself than to me. 'I should have arranged to see you alone. I never thought, though . . . I hadn't expected we'd get the appointment with you so fast.'

So: my perception of Amanda that day hadn't been totally distorted after all. She *had* been lying. And now her effort to undo her mistake had her close to tears.

Feeling my way I said: 'Do I take it you still don't want to speak to David about the – ah – omissions?'

She started as though I'd tapped her on a bruise; her eyes filled. (So much for my sensitivity.)

'Shit,' she said, trying to force her trembling mouth into a smile and failing. 'I don't know what's the matter with me. I never do this. You must be wondering . . . you must be thinking . . .'

I shook my head sympathetically, aware that there was nothing I could say. I wanted to hug her, and grabbing a tissue, I stood up and went around to her. But then, seeing her tense up, I merely placed my hand on her back and rubbed up and down a few times.

For a moment this seemed to make things worse, and she hunched into a mute sob. Before I could say anything to her, though, she drew away from my hand and literally, visibly, pulled herself together. By the time I'd returned to my side of the desk, the redness on the lower rims of her eyes was the only sign of her distress.

She obviously wanted to carry on as if nothing had happened and I went with her.

'To answer your question,' she said, 'yes – I can't. You have to understand. Feelings like love and trust have never come easily to me, or not since my childhood. But if I love and trust anyone, it's David. He'd probably say I've had a funny way of showing it and he'd be right, but it's still true. And while it may sound like nonsense to you, it's also true that it's because I care for him that I can't tell him about the changes I want made to my will.'

The problem was clear. 'And you would of course expect me to refrain from telling him as well.'

She nodded. 'Do you think it would be impossibly awkward?'

Not as awkward as it might have been, I thought. Then, subtracting my emotions, I threw my mind into the future, trying to anticipate what might arise.

What I saw was the high likelihood of a conflict of interest. And what was worse, only one of them would know there was a risk of it.

I told her this and told her as well that my first obligation should probably be to David. I sighed at the irony of it. 'I'm sorry,' I said. 'I wish . . .'

'Don't,' she said. 'This was the difficulty that worried me, but I didn't want to go elsewhere without finding out.' She smiled. 'Can you recommend anyone to me?'

'Done,' I nodded, scribbling Samuelson Stevens' number on a piece of paper and sliding it over to her. 'I used to work there. Ask for Mike Samuelson and say I told you to ring.'

She rose. 'That's wonderful. I can't thank you enough.'

I stood up and extended my hand. 'My pleasure. If there's ever anything else you need . . .'

She gave me a strange look then and I saw in her eyes, or thought I saw, a woman in need of a woman friend yet leery of following up openings to such friendship. My bad conscience constrained me. I could hardly ask for her trust.

The expression passed. 'All I need now,' she said, 'is a nice fat miracle. I have about two hours to discover everything there is to know about the historical use of torture against political prisoners in Latin America.'

'No problem. I have a good friend at Amnesty. In fact I was just about to ring her about this young Chilean man whose hospital review hearing David's been helping me prepare for. I have her . . .'

'A Chilean man?' she repeated, looking as startled as she sounded. 'David's been helping you with a *Chilean* man?'

'Yes. The case is coming up the day after tomorrow and David's been closely involved all along – so closely that, well, I guess I'm surprised he hasn't told you.'

'*You're* surprised!' she laughed, inexplicably giddy. Then: 'You must think I'm deranged. I come in here asking you not to tell David I've seen you and end up hearing his news from you. Honestly, we do talk to each other. He may have even mentioned it and I didn't hear – I've been so disoriented since I got back. I must get him to tell me all about it –' She glanced at the phone and I nodded, but she shook her head again. 'No. I'll see him tonight. But I will speak to your friend if you don't mind.' And afterwards, the call completed, Amanda thanked me profusely and left.

I collapsed into my chair, feeling drained by her brief visit. Partly, of course, it was the way her mood had swung; but mostly I was just painfully conscious of the contrast between her ex-hilaration and my depression. What had she said? 'If I love anyone, it's David.'

I sighed. Yes. There was no doubt about it. I'd made the right decision. There was only one slight problem: I didn't like it.

On Wednesday the hospital review panel which heard Carlos' case rejected his application for immediate release – stupidly, cruelly rejected it because of one recent aggressive outburst. Owen the barrister, normally the epitome of control, was so disgusted I thought for a moment he might burst out himself, but instead he threw the papers into his case and offered to buy us all doubles at the nearest pub.

The clear sunshine of the early evening felt like an insult – only a gloomy corner would do – and when we'd found the gloomiest one we stayed there for nearly two hours going over and over the whys and hows and what ifs and how could theys, looking all the while for the wrinkle, the hook that would allow us to go to the High Court. And there were, indeed, one or two technicalities, slippery grounds for hope though they seemed to me, and out of them a strategy of sorts began to form. Owen, at least, recovered his usual optimism and started spelling out for Connie the possibilities he saw.

I was half listening, partly worried that he would build up too many expectations in her, partly trying to think what else we might do, when David spoke close to my ear.

'You've gone quiet.'

'Mmm,' I frowned. 'I was just wondering about outside

pressure. If Owen's ideas don't pan out, we might need some.'

'Well I'm certain Amanda would help. She was asking me about Carlos the other night. She thinks a story about him would tie in with her features about her trip. Trouble is, she hasn't finished those, so it couldn't be right away.'

'It couldn't be right away in any case. Owen's research will take him at least ten days, and if it doesn't lead anywhere I'm sure Connie will have her own ideas for organising publicity. She's so active in the Campaign for Socialist Chile and they've got lots of lobbying contacts. Tell her about Amanda though: I'm sure she'll be pleased . . .'

But David was shaking his head. 'I'll leave it for now.'

I shrugged wearily. 'Whatever.' The thought of my bed, my duvet, sleep was almost overpowering. Few cases really make me want to cry when I lose. This was one of them.

'And to think I'd planned to invite you for a celebratory meal tonight,' he said quietly.

'Oh, ugh,' I groaned, dimly sensing that the moment for 'other things' might be approaching and uncertain that I had the energy to face them as they should be faced. I tried evasion: 'I think I've drunk my caloric intake anyway. The thought of food . . .'

'I know how you feel,' he murmured. Then, smiling that smile of his: 'On the other hand, we've got to have one of our marathon conversations soon. I mean, look at me . . .' He displayed a shaking hand. 'I'm already suffering from withdrawal symptoms. I'm tied up till the end of the week, but if you're free Sunday or Monday night, we could go for dinner then. How does that sound?'

I looked at him, too tired to hide my sadness. His alluring smile wavered uncertainly then disappeared as he read the meaning of my expression. He averted his head and ran his fingers through his hair a couple of times before looking up again.

Holding his eyes I took a breath and said very carefully: 'I'd love to have dinner with the two of you.'

His gaze steady, his tone just as careful, he replied: 'I had in mind just you and me.'

Aware that my voice sounded like a forty-five playing at thirty-three and a third, I said: 'No, David. I don't think that would be a good idea.'

He nodded. 'I see.'

Both of us reached simultaneously for our glasses, lifted them, drained the last nearly invisible drops. He set his down and watched his fingers turn it around for several seconds. Then, addressing the glass, he said: 'Would you . . . I mean, if my circumstances were different . . . that is, if I weren't married . . .'

'But you *are*,' I said.

He sighed and hung his head.

His dejection (or was it my own?) animated my hand, which reached over and settled on his wrist. 'I like Amanda,' I said. 'I'd like her friendship.'

'Of course,' he said, 'of course.' Then he straightened, forced the semblance of a grin and shrugged. 'I understand, I really do, and I'm sorry if I –'

'Don't,' I cut in. 'It's not your fault. And I'll – well . . .' I smiled. 'I'll suffer from withdrawal myself.' I put out my hand and made it shake. 'See?'

His grin became genuine. 'So it will be all right to ring you for legal advice? You won't turn away my business?'

'Are you kidding?'

'Good,' he nodded. 'Good. In that case you may be hearing from me soon.'

23

Two

Another romantic fantasy interred, I recalled my earlier resolution: I needed a change. Various daydreams beckoned: about lying covered in oil on a white sandy Mediterranean beach; about touring the museums of Florence or Paris; about carrying a sleeping bag and tent into the Welsh mountains. But none of them inspired me until I realised that what I really wanted to do was go back to California. I wanted to see my old friend Paula whom I hadn't seen since my last trip over to America three years earlier, and I wanted to see my mother who'd made it plain after her fourth journey in a row to London some months before that she'd love it if I came home to her the next time. (I no longer even bother to argue that I am 'home'.)

I checked my diary and discussed it with the others, then pencilled in two weeks' leave and wrote to say I'd be arriving at the end of the month. Within days I'd begun to feel better.

In fact it was my lightened mood of anticipation which led me, on the morning of that now memorable Monday, to obey the impulse that urged me to have my hair cut and restyled. More, when the new me hankered after a bikini in a shop window, it encouraged her to give in *and* to purchase a matching beach robe as well. All in all I was about an hour and a half late getting into the office.

Suze was waiting for me, obviously agitated.

'Bathing suit,' I shrugged, holding out the bag. 'Couldn't resist. Like my hair?'

She shook her head with impatience as she grabbed my elbow and steered me out of the reception area into my office. It wasn't my time keeping, that was clear enough.

'What is it?' I asked. 'Not the Home Office again? Oh God, they haven't gone and deported Mrs Patel in the middle of the night have they?' Suze had been working for nearly a year to prevent the separation of this young Bengali woman and her British-born husband and children and it was the one case capable of riling her to the degree she now seemed riled. 'Look,' I said, 'maybe it's time we got in touch with . . .'

'Dee, it isn't Mrs Patel. Sit down . . . Where's the whisky? Don't tell me we're out.'

'Whisky! Suze Aspinall are you out of your mind? It's ten thirty in the morning. For heaven's sake, *you* sit down. I've never seen you like this.' Then I had a sudden thought. 'You're not pregnant are you?'

She made a dismissive grimace, then took a deep breath, opened her mouth, waited, closed her mouth, looked at me imploringly, and walked out of my office.

Bemused, I sat down at my desk and stared at the door. A moment later she came through it again, carrying the answerphone machine which she proceeded to set on a chair and plug in.

'I'm sorry,' she whispered. 'I wanted to soften it but I can't.' She reached over to the start button. 'Prepare yourself.' Then she pressed down.

'Dee,' the tape began, 'this is David Blake. I'm ringing from the police station in Little Yarmouth and I need to talk to you. Amanda . . .' His voice faltered and there was the sound of throat clearing. 'Amanda is dead. Murdered.' There was a scratchy pause. 'And – well – there's more.' Another pause. 'I find this very hard to say, but – well – she wasn't alone. That is, there were two bodies and the other one – God help us – the other one was Carlos.

'I don't understand this and I have been saying so all night. I wish I could think that the police believe me. They have certainly been civil, but the questioning did take an uncomfortable turn, to put it mildly. And I have been "advised" to stay around until the preliminary laboratory reports are finished later this afternoon.

'I'm leaving now for a hotel called the Metropole to try to get some sleep and while I can't give you the number – what? is it there? – just a moment, the officer is getting it – yes, it's Little Yarmouth 0695. If you could ring me there around half past twelve or one, I'd be grateful to you. Thank you very much.'

I've wondered since, when reflecting on that attenuated moment, whether Suze's being there wasn't somehow the catalyst to the calmness of my response. Looking back, it's as though her own extreme anxiety threw me in the opposite direction, distanced me from the horror and panic that might have overcome me as well.

And I suppose the stiff formality of David's enunciation, the sense of strained yet somehow detached exhaustion behind his words, also contributed, jolting me upright like an icepack on the lower spine. Whatever the cause, grit, iron, metal arose from some nether region. I rewound the tape and listened to it again carefully. I knew what I had to do.

'Can I leave my work for the rest of you to handle?'

Suze took her hand away from her mouth and nodded. Her face seemed to regain its colour. 'Annie and Beth are going to divide it between them. We talked about it when we heard the message and figured you'd want to go straight there. Annie even checked the trains. There's one every hour on the quarter from Liverpool Street.' She checked her watch. 'You ought to make the eleven fifteen. Shall I ask Pam to ring a cab for you?'

'Yes,' I said, 'thanks . . . Listen, are the morning papers here?'

'I've been through them all. Nothing. Same for the radio news.'

'Well that's something anyway.' Then, after thinking about this a moment: 'I wonder if it means that Connie hasn't been notified yet?' But on further reflection that didn't make any sense and I'm sure I frowned. 'She didn't *say* anything about going away.'

'When did you last talk to her?'

'Friday. I had to tell her that Owen's been forced to abandon the legal argument he thought might get Carlos' case into the High Court.'

'Oh dear,' Suze sighed. '*That* must have upset her.'

I nodded distractedly, suddenly hearing a fragment of that conversation replay in my mind. No, I thought listening to it; no. Connie had been distraught, just saying what anyone would have said.

Suze had been reading my face. 'Surely,' she whispered, 'not Connie . . . oh Dee, surely not . . .'

But I was still ruminating and still could only frown.

'What are you thinking?' Suze urged. '*Tell* me.'

I shrugged. It was ridiculous, and there was no point in giving an off-hand remark, spoken in heat, more weight than it deserved by repeating it. 'Look,' I hedged, 'Connie was disappointed, that's all. Owen had built up her hopes and now, the thought of waiting all those months for the next review –'

'For pity's sake, Dee,' Suze cut in, 'just tell me if she threatened to help him escape.'

'Not in so many words,' I demurred. 'She simply said something

26

like, "Who needs the High Court? I got him out of Chile, I can get him out of that hospital." '

Suze groaned melodramatically, but I carried on talking over her. 'Come on. It was obvious what she meant: she meant we'd have to get Parliament and the media to put pressure on the authorities. Christ Suze, Connie's not stupid. Apart from anything else, I've just submitted citizenship applications for her and her husband to the Home Office. She wouldn't jeopardise those. Anyway, she specifically mentioned that she'd be going into the Campaign for Socialist Chile office for an editorial meeting – they're working on a book about Allende – and would be sounding out the publicity worker. The real irony is that I should at that point have put Connie in touch with Amanda – David had told me she was interested in Carlos' story – but I completely forgot.' I shook my head. 'Connie wouldn't take such a huge silly risk. Neither she nor Carlos had anything to gain by his escape.'

'That seems pretty obvious now,' Suze murmured. Then: 'Don't you think it's curious, though, that David didn't say anything about Connie being with him at the station, or being on her way?'

'In his condition? I'm surprised he sounded as coherent as he did.'

'But does he know how to reach her?'

'Yes.'

'And he'd tell the police?'

'Why not?' I saw her expression and held up my hand to stop her. 'Don't ask. The answer is no. As far as I know there isn't a single reason why he shouldn't . . . What are you trying to do to me anyway?'

'Just testing,' she smiled.

'Thanks.' Then, as I reached for the phone: 'Would you ask Pam to do me another favour and ring David's hotel and say . . .'

But Suze had already nodded and was half way out the door.

I dialled Connie's work number slowly, preparing myself in case she hadn't been told, but my preparation was for naught: she was 'on sick leave'. Yet when I tried her home I got no reply.

I began to search through my file for her husband Juan's number, and I found it just as Pam came in to say the taxi had arrived. I stuffed the card into my bag and rushed outside.

David may have planned to sleep until I rang and woke him, but the plan clearly hadn't worked: when I stepped off the train he was there waiting for me on the platform. His eyes seemed to have retreated into dark pouches and his old baggy corduroys and cotton shirt were creased with overlong wear; his trainers were coated in a layer of crusty dirt. My feelings, heedless of circumstance, surged chaotically at the sight of him, then realised it was his lawyer he was smiling at with such obvious, if wan, relief. She resumed control as he leaned over and kissed me lightly on the cheek.

'I nearly asked you here,' he said, 'then thought better of it. It seemed a little alarmist when they're only keeping me for questioning.'

'And how's that gone?'

He shrugged and took my elbow, nodding towards the exit. 'Not too badly, all things considered.'

He guided me through the rows of parked cars to his old Renault, warning me as we approached to watch the still-wet spots on the thick mud that covered the wheels and underside of the chassis. My eyes asked, 'What is this? Is it . . .?' His replied, 'Wait – please. Just wait.' I slid quietly into the passenger seat and waited.

After he'd driven for a while he said: 'They were particularly curious about my marriage. Most of the questions were about that. They were also "intrigued" that I'd known Carlos in my professional capacity, and so recently. They couldn't resist trying to prise privileged information out of me, although they quite patently possessed the answers . . . I'm absolutely certain they don't believe that I had no idea Amanda had even met Carlos, never mind that she'd . . . well, that they'd . . .' Faltering, he glanced over at me, then swallowed as he returned his eyes to the road.

'They reminded me a number of times that most people who are murdered are killed by either a spouse, a relative or a friend. They claim that only some minute percentage of murder victims die by a strange hand. I'm clearly the – er – the prime suspect.'

'My God, David, I thought you said they'd been *civil*. They've been playing bloody head games.'

'Yes. They have. But I expected at least that. I just took it for granted that as I'd had nothing to do with it I could hold my own. The trouble is – well, the mere experience of being interrogated like that arouses all sorts of irrational guilt feelings, you know? Somehow the circumstance makes all your assumptions – your whole life – seem incredibly ambiguous. Some of *my* answers certainly rang hollow as hell anyway.'

28

I placed my hand on his shoulder and stroked sympathetically, sure there was another reason, too, why he felt so unnerved. He pulled over to the right and signalled to turn into the hotel car park. 'It must have upset you,' I said softly, 'having to identify the bodies.'

His hands gripped the wheel until his fingers were squeezed bloodless, then he swung the car too fast, so that it bucked as we cut across the traffic. He parked carelessly and switched off the motor, looking straight ahead. 'I didn't simply identify the bodies, Dee,' he said, hitting the rim of the steering wheel angrily with his palm. 'I found them. I found them together. In bed.'

To be near the phone we had to sit in the hotel coffee bar, a crowded, stuffy, salmon-pink and turquoise room where the electronic bleeping of Space Invader machines competed with orchestral versions of Beatles' songs and where instant coffee was served out of pots. David was too far away to notice any of it, and as he began to talk it gradually faded away for me as well.

Some time later, after I'd followed him through rambling spirals of incident and anecdote, pushed him out of guilty byways and waited when he broke under incomprehension or strain, this picture of events had emerged.

Amanda had had a huge row with her boss Phil her first morning back at work and although rows between them apparently weren't in themselves unusual – Phil was volatile and Amanda wilful and they habitually goaded each other – this one had been exceptionally bitter. It seems that when Amanda had 'abused her position of trust' by arranging to replace him in Latin America herself, Phil had made her swear to two things: that she'd be away at most two weeks, and that she'd return with completed articles. She'd broken both promises.

A freelancer had wandered in conveniently at around that point and Phil had hired him on the spot to do the work she'd been supposed to pick up. Then he'd instructed her not to come back until she'd finished the pieces.

David had learned about all this because Amanda had turned to him for help, as she so often did when she was having trouble with her writing. And despite all the things he needed to discuss with her – urgently needed to discuss with her – he'd put them to one side and helped.

Somewhere in the course of this she'd asked him about his own

29

work and been intrigued by Carlos' story. She'd even mused aloud about writing it up and adding it to the end of her series (headline: 'Memoirs of a Refugee') and David had offered to introduce her – later. After she'd finished.

Then, on the Friday night, he'd arrived home to find a note on the mantelpiece. 'Sorry,' it had said. 'Getting nowhere. Gone to get some peace and quiet. Will ring.'

He'd been irate. It was always like this – one thing when she had a problem and another when he needed to talk.

Nor had his resentment waned by the time she'd finally rung from a call box five days later.

But of course, all he'd done by being sharp with her had been to push her on to the defensive. She'd hedged about when she'd return and when he'd offered to drive to wherever she was, she'd hedged about the address. When the pips had started, she'd promised to send him directions.

They had never arrived.

The night he'd intended to go – the night when if he had gone things might have turned out differently – Amanda's brother Craig had phoned to 'confirm that he'd be getting in on Tuesday'. That had done it. David and Craig had come to terms with each other over the years for Amanda's sake. The thought of having to entertain him on his own – of having to make excuses for her – had been the last straw. David had told Craig he'd get her back there.

And once he'd set his mind to it, tracking her down hadn't been too difficult. Amanda after all had only one close friend, a woman who liked David, had met Craig and sympathised. It turned out Barbara had recently inherited a cottage in Norfolk. It even had a phone.

It was either broken or off the hook, however, for David was to find it engaged – frustratingly, infuriatingly engaged – every time he tried.

Sunday morning he'd read the papers and done odd tasks around the flat before going into his office at the hospital to work on an article. Again and again he'd tried the Norfolk number, his resentment growing anew. Finally, just after teatime, he'd slammed down the phone, cursed her for her games, cursed himself for playing along with them, got into his car and set off.

The cottage was at the end of a long and, that evening, muddy track. He'd got far enough down it before getting stuck to see

Amanda's Mini parked around by the side. As he'd walked the final stretch he'd wondered why the hell, if she was there, she hadn't come out. He'd gunned the engine loud enough.

At the door he'd sensed the stillness. Had she perhaps gone for a walk? He'd decided to look through the window.

He knew the signatures of madness – he'd been trained to read them – and he recognised them immediately in that sitting room: the broken furniture, the open drawers, the curtains pulled down, the cushions ripped, the knick-knacks and flowers and books strewn everywhere, the smell of urine.

Rushing through the unlocked front door, he'd hurriedly surveyed the ground floor before running up the stairs and opening the door at the top landing. The sight had stopped him on the threshold.

They had both been half sitting up in bed, their backs propped against pillows. Amanda had dyed her hair black and looked so different that for a moment he hadn't recognised her. He couldn't get over that: that he'd lived with her for five years and hadn't been sure it was her.

They'd been shot, Amanda in the heart, Carlos in the temple.

Overcome by this grisly vision, we both fell silent for a time. Then David said: 'I think they've eliminated Carlos as a suspect because they haven't found any trace of the weapon on the grounds. That's why they're so interested in me.'

'Mmm,' I sighed. 'They'll obviously try to prove that you were eaten up with jealousy and that you had the opportunity to act. We'll have to provide evidence to show that . . .'

'. . . I didn't care that much.'

I demurred. 'Not necessarily. We'll probably be better off simply establishing that you weren't at the scene of the crime at the time it was committed.'

David put his head in his hands and addressed the table. 'But Dee,' he said, 'I *didn't* care that much . . . You don't know – I've never told you – about me and Amanda. But now – now that I could end up asking you to defend me on a double murder charge, I *have* to tell you how things were between us. You can't do the job unless you know.'

Hesitantly he lifted his gaze and stared into my eyes. It was a brief look that in clock time I suppose lasted no more than half a second, yet while it went on clocks and their time seemed remote,

31

immaterial. My professional veneer buckled; my concentration on the pieces of the case slipped; my disgust for the crime itself was suspended; the tacky coffee bar shimmered. All that existed was his face; all I knew was that we were two sad people and that we needed each other in a tired, almost hopeless way.

Unnerved, I glanced away.

Softly he said: 'I drove to the cottage last night to tell Amanda I thought the time had come for us to split up again.'

Professionalism returned. I looked up. ' "Again"?'

He developed an interest in his spoon. 'After what's happened it's difficult ... I mean, I don't want you to get the idea that I blame her for all our problems, because I don't. But the fact is that she had other ... that Carlos wasn't the first ... that is ... oh *shit*.'

He reached for his cup of tepid coffee, sipped at it and set it abruptly aside with an expression of disgust. Then, clearing his throat, he began to tell me what had happened eighteen months or so before.

David had learned the signs: a rash of late-night 'interviews'; sudden weekend exclusives that never got written up; a certain distracted look; a don't-touch-me air; prickliness if he asked a personal question. And this time Amanda seemed to have got herself involved with an especially ardent type, the kind who couldn't resist ringing the flat every few days, only to hang up if David answered.

That night he'd stared at the receiver in his hand, heard the silence on the other end and thought: she can have them. I'm sick of being reasonable when I feel like I want to slap her face, break her arms, worse. It's not me. I'm opposed to violence. I'll get an ulcer or she'll end up in hospital – that's the choice.

By the time she came home an hour or so later he'd arranged to move to a friend's and was nearly finished packing.

'What's all this about?' she asked.

'I'm giving you a present. No more scenes. No more questions. No more need to think up excuses. I'm going.'

'Ha!' she snorted. 'That's cute. You just don't want to know what you've done to force me away this time.'

'No,' he agreed, 'I don't. But as I expect that you'll insist on telling me anyway, I suppose I should try to guess.' He feigned deep thought. 'Let me see. Presumably it isn't that I've been leaving you alone too much.' This was a reference to what she'd claimed the

32

first time. He suffered, she'd alleged then, from two stereotypical problems: he was the shrink who in striving to help other people through their difficulties neglected his own; and he was the political activist (male political activist) who in his determination to change 'the system' at large failed to see that his own home life needed attention.

He'd misled her, she'd added – she hadn't realised it would be like this – and he'd seen her point. When they'd met during that long hot summer nine months before, he'd just finished his psychiatry exams and had been between jobs. On top of that, he'd fallen out with the right-wingers in his local Labour Party and stopped going to meetings – had even stopped talking politics, which was unusual for him. But over the winter his old interest had revived and between that and evening and weekend clinic sessions, he hadn't been around much.

'And presumably,' he continued, 'it isn't that you still find me "suffocating".' When he'd cut back on everything in order to be with her, she'd gone off and had another affair anyway. This time she'd accused him of 'crowding her space' and 'threatening her independence'.

They stared at each other across his suitcases. 'As for our disagreement about having kids, I accepted your wishes and you know it.' How was he supposed to know that a few casual remarks about wanting to start a family would upset her so badly? He hadn't even realised they had until he'd read the signs of another affair and confronted her. 'You're a hypocrite,' she'd said. 'You condemn the idea of the "nuclear family" and then you ask me to be part of creating one.'

'No, I don't,' he'd protested. 'I'll be happy to work part time. We can share it. I didn't expect you to –'

'You expected me to *have* it, didn't you? Well listen buster, I won't. Got that? Won't – w – o – n – t – won't.'

He possessed one or two other grave character flaws as well, flaws that had driven her into subsequent affairs, though he couldn't, standing there, quite remember what they were. He shrugged. 'What is it now? The colour of my eyes?'

Amanda put her hands on her hips and glared at him. 'You don't have to get sarcastic,' she said coolly. 'No one's been forcing you to stay.'

'This is true,' he replied, giving each tired word equal weight. He might have added 'more fool I', but she cut him off.

33

'In fact,' she went on, 'you have consistently agreed that my criticisms of you were accurate.'

'And that is also true,' he nodded. 'But as I told you the last time, it's the way you put the message across that I object to.'

She sighed (his behaviour was *so* taxing). 'That's the crux of your problem right there,' she said. 'You're far too old fashioned. In case you haven't noticed this is the modern world, not fifties' Yorkshire. And you seem to forget that we only got married to make my visa situation easier.'

Well, his memories were different – of that summer, of their closeness and need for each other, of their impulsive decision to marry in that little chapel by the sea in Cornwall.

He could have said: 'You're not the only one who's felt misled.' Instead he said: 'Maybe I am old fashioned, if that's what it's called when you believe that caring about someone else means that you consider their feelings. And if it's "old fashioned" to believe that love is about both people making compromises so that the third thing that exists between them survives – well, that's fine by me. I suppose that sounds like "vulgar romanticism" to you . . .'

'You patronising prick,' she spat.

'Call me what you like,' he shrugged, surprised at his sudden indifference to her emotion. 'You know what I'm saying. You haven't a clue about love, Amanda. Your criticisms of me have been accurate – points for your insight – but blaming me has also been a convenient way of ignoring your own problems. It's taken me over two years to see it, and I guess you'd say that's another flaw in my character – but at least I *have* seen it, which is more than you can say. Love scares the hell out of you, that's the *real* truth, and you do everything in your considerable power to destroy it. You push the people who love you as far away as you can. You defy us to love you. *You* call it "liberation". *I* call it imprisonment. You're caught, Amanda. You're a novelty junkie on the run from yourself.'

'You can save the psychological crap for your patients,' she snapped; then she marched into the bathroom, slamming the door behind her.

'I will,' he called after her. He felt sad and exhausted. 'At least they know they need help.'

Two months later, just as he thought he'd reached the state where he felt nothing at all any more for Amanda, she rang. What's more, she did something she'd never ever done before: she sobbed into the phone. She *begged* him to come over. And despite himself, he immediately got into his car and went.

When she didn't answer the door after he'd pressed the bell several times, he let himself in with the key he still had, only to stop, incredulous, at the threshold. The shades were drawn though it was only late afternoon. Cups of cold coffee, overflowing ashtrays, plates full of abandoned meals, dead flowers were strewn all over the sitting room. And in the far corner, in an armchair surrounded by newspapers, sat Amanda, apparently asleep. She was wearing her old yellow towelling dressing gown and was clutching it around herself like a child gripping a favourite piece of tattered baby blanket.

David crossed the room, crouched down and felt for her pulse. Then he shook her lightly and spoke her name.

Amanda opened her eyes and, after blinking at him with confusion, threw her arms around his neck and groaned, 'Thank God'.

David stroked her back for a moment. 'Are you going to tell me what this is all about?' he asked.

'I'm going mad,' she mumbled into his shoulder. 'Isn't it obvious?'

'No, I mean seriously.'

She pulled herself away abruptly and squinted suspiciously into his eyes. But his expression evidently reassured her for she relaxed again and sighed. 'It's Phil. He refused a story. He said it was "hysterical journalism". So I quit. Last week. And I mean really quit. How can I do what he wants? How can I do what any of these editors want? It's wrong – all this . . .' She gestured contemptuously to the tabloids by her feet, then picked up the nearest one and handed it to him. 'Honestly, look at that crap.'

The headline was about the inquest into the death of a young black man who'd been killed during a riot the year before.

'This?' he asked.

'That,' she confirmed. 'I was at that inquest. I was only supposed to interview his wife, but I stayed. I listened to all the evidence. And the truth is . . . the truth is that the police murdered him themselves. I'm absolutely sure of it.'

Now if anyone else he'd known had said this in the same shock-horror tone David would have immediately taken it for sarcasm. Amanda, however, was different. For she, to his continual

35

frustration – no, no, to his continual disappointment – steadfastly resisted looking beneath the surface of political events. According to her, she'd 'had her fill' in America and had left largely to get away from 'that kind of thing'. Worse, he'd been unable to make her see that place makes no difference, that the escape she believed she'd made was a delusion created by her own refusal to look at what was going on around her in Britain and on the Continent. In other words, that statement she'd just made, coming from her, amounted to a major change of perception.

'Yes,' he nodded. 'Reading between the lines of the reports, I'm certain you're right. I can just imagine what . . .'

But she was suddenly on her feet, gesticulating angrily. 'Well if the truth is so obvious to you and to me and to hundreds of other people, what the *hell* was wrong with that jury? They heard the same evidence I did. Where is justice? Where?'

'*Whose* justice are you talking about, Mandy? The State's? Yours? Mine? Or are you going to insist, as I seem to remember you did the last time we had a conversation about this, that there's an absolute called "benign justice" that gets doled out as a matter of course by good democracies like Britain and America?'

She shook her head. 'No,' she said. 'I won't insist. I've seen your point now. When that verdict was read out I realised what you'd been driving at. For a lot of people, a lot of it must truly suck.' She went over to his old desk, opened the middle drawer and removed several sheets of paper. 'And for once that's what I've been trying to say.'

'I stayed on at the flat for a couple of days to help her rework the article but when it was finished and she'd sorted things out with Phil and generally begun to act like her old self, I said I thought I'd better push off back to my friend's spare room. We joked about that – very civilised we were – and she thanked me and I remember I went into the bathroom to get my shaving gear. When I came out, she was leaning against the front door, these big tears in her eyes.

'She said she'd realised that she'd been making herself even more unhappy than she'd been making me and had decided to see this therapist she'd heard of. She also said she wanted to try to write more think-pieces like the one about the inquest – with me, if I'd help. Then she asked me straight out to give her another chance.'

David sighed and looked down at his hands. 'Within about two months I think both of us were wishing we'd been a little less impulsive.' He frowned. 'I don't know what it was. I suppose I must have stepped back from her more than I'd realised while we were separated. When we began to bicker again it suddenly came to me that we were simply vastly different types of people. She needed dramas and crises all the time, you know? And sitting in her room fighting her way through her own woolliness wasn't quite exciting enough – especially when I couldn't be there to argue with her about the ideas. Phil dangled a couple of interesting Continental assignments and before long she was working to the most demanding, hectic schedule she'd ever had.

'Another separation began to seem to me to be inevitable back around Christmas – she took *one* day off – but the problem was getting her to sit down and talk about it. There was always something, some reason, why we couldn't. It seemed as if we couldn't keep the thing alive, but we couldn't quite bring ourselves to put it out of its misery either . . . Then – well, then, out of the blue, I ran into this woman I hadn't seen in years.' (He was talking now into the coffee cup.) 'It may sound crazy but just being with – her – made me remember what it was like to have easy conversations with an attractive woman. I'd forgotten how peaceful it could be and I felt – totally galvanised.'

I thought: play lawyer. But my voice still came out sounding small. 'Did you tell the police about – this woman?'

He shook his head. 'No. No, I told them the facts, not the fantasies.' He looked up. 'The only woman I mentioned was my solicitor. I told them you'd acted for Amanda and Carlos too. I assume that was all right.'

I nodded. It didn't seem quite the moment to tell him about his wife's second visit to my office. 'Well,' I said, 'I still think the quickest way to get you out of this is to keep on sticking to the facts – immediate facts – and simply establish that you couldn't have been there when it happened. Presumably they tested your fingers for gunpowder?'

'Yes, but the time of death hasn't been established. They're working on that now. The wounds didn't look fresh to me, so I'd say morning, but that's only a guess.'

'Right – well – let's go through your day again in more detail beginning with – '

'Dee – *no*body saw me all day yesterday.'

'*Some*body will have seen you. You've just got to . . .'

But he was shaking his head. 'How? Where? My upstairs' neighbours were away for the weekend; the people in the basement are on holiday; most of the regular Sunday floor nurses who know me in the hospital are on leave. Besides, I was trying to stay out of sight so I wouldn't be bothered while I was writing. I used the side entrance and didn't pass anyone going or coming. And I've got a direct outside line telephone.'

'Didn't you stop on the journey?'

'Once, outside Great Yarmouth: I picked up some fish and chips. I haven't a clue what the place was called, but it can't matter – it was so crowded that the girl who served me didn't even look up. So you see? My so-called alibi is all my say-so. I'm screwed.'

'Now look here,' I said, 'I may be the amateur when it comes to psychology, but you're definitely not "screwed". What you are, if you don't mind me saying so, is exhausted. You've had a rough time the past eighteen hours and you've kept your upper lip valiantly stiff about it all, but you obviously feel terribly guilty – about what you might have done, should have done and maybe shouldn't have done. And I do sympathise, believe me. But it's no reason to volunteer for punishment you don't deserve – especially when the police are going to have to go a pretty long way to mete it out to you.

'Really, David, think about it: they're going to have to prove that you went to that cottage, did the deed, drove away, removed the gunpowder from your hands, drove back, called to tell them about it and then denied any part in the whole thing. And they'll try to do this of course. It's bizarre and twisted and it assumes a cold calculation on your part, but it isn't wholly inconceivable as a scenario. I expect they're examining the pieces of it right now. My question is: what do you want me to do? Help them, or help you?'

He'd been staring at me and when I'd finished, he smiled. 'Good lecture,' he said.

'Sorry. It struck me that you needed it.'

'Unfortunately,' he nodded, 'I guess I did.'

Detective Superintendent James Henning, the officer in charge of the investigation, proved to be a portly, balding, dour-looking man of late middle age who seemed to have to search rather hard for the guarded smile which lifted his face when we were introduced. He was pleased to meet me, he said, as he understood that I had represented both of the victims. (I let this pass again.) Then, watching my eyes, he went on to say that as Connie had yet to be located – *pause* – he would be grateful if I would reconfirm Carlos' identity 'for the record'.

I had never been into a morgue and the prospect aroused immediate squeamishness. At the same time, I recognised that he was offering me another more important opportunity as well, and about that one I felt more certain. I reached into my bag, found the file card containing Juan's number and handed it to him.

It was, as I'd sensed, an appropriate gesture. Henning's smile softened and became more genuine. I thought: it's not an easy time for the police. Their powers and their accountability are being questioned with increasing openness, and like many of the older ones, this Henning is touchy because he doesn't know where he's standing any more.

I wasn't exactly overcome with sympathy. I believed then, as I do now, that such scrutiny is necessary. I also believed it was long overdue. We weren't there in his office to debate social policy and democratic principles, however, and I was relieved to see that he seemed as anxious to approach the situation co-operatively as I was.

'Well now, Dr Blake,' Henning began when we'd taken our seats, 'I've asked you here again, as I said I would, because I've at last received the preliminary lab reports. Our search of the grounds has still not produced the weapon, but we can now say with confidence what it was: a .38 pistol – a "hand gun" as you would say,' he added, looking at me. 'And the term is perhaps more appropriate as it seems to have been an older model Smith and Wesson.

'Mrs Blake would appear to have died instantly from a single bullet through the heart. Carlos de la Fuente was less fortunate: the head wound which killed him was not as accurately placed and it looks as if he moved around before dying. There are blood stains at the top of the stairs which are his type, so it is conceivable that he got up, wandered out of the room, then returned to bed. Alternatively, he may have been shot on the landing and placed in the bed . . . I asked you before, Doctor, did I not, whether you know much about guns?'

David had been listening intently and the sudden question obviously surprised him. It was an old tactic for catching someone off-guard, especially someone as tired as David, but to my eyes it worked in his favour.

'What?' he asked, looking confused. 'Me? Guns? No. Only what I know from watching TV.'

'Forgive me. I note from our computer that you had some connection with a certain Tommy Reilly who I understand has recently been charged with illegal possession of firearms.'

'Oh Christ,' David muttered, 'Reilly and I were busted at the same demo six years ago. I met him when we were booked. He belonged to a branch of the same political group I did, as did several thousand other people. Surely this is completely irrelevant – I mean, if you're going to . . .'

I placed my hand on his arm. 'I agree. With due respect I fail to see how my client's political affiliations have any bearing on this investigation.'

Henning gave a noncommittal shrug. 'At this point it is necessary for me to decide such things for myself . . . Now – to continue. It has also become clear that there are no fingerprints anywhere in the house – that is, with the exception of your own, Doctor. And yours do indeed correspond with your account of your entrance and dash up the stairs. In short, the place has been carefully wiped down.

'Next, there was a smudged but discernible set of glove prints in the dirt on the ledge of the sitting room window as well as a portion of a boot print on the ground nearby. The boot print matches an extremely popular type of Army surplus walking boot. Carlos de la Fuente himself had a pair of roughly the same size, and you were wearing a pair at the time we came for you, were you not?'

'I told you,' David answered, 'that I always keep them in the car, and I've given them to you. I daresay you've checked the size.'

Henning glanced at his notes. 'Ah – so we have. Well now, moving on, we have secured a rough inventory of the contents of the cottage from its owner, Miss Barbara Leigh, whom we naturally had to notify. What her statement made clear to us is that numerous valuables have been removed. In addition we found a plastic typewriter cover but no typewriter; nor did we find any typing paper, blank or written on. Strange, don't you think, for a journalist supposedly working there?'

David just sighed, very deeply, and shook his head.

'I'm almost finished,' Henning said. 'One or two more points and you'll be free to go, though I hope you'll understand that we must ask you to remain at your London address.'

'Fine,' David said tiredly. 'I expected you would.'

40

'Good. Now, in going through the young man's jacket we found these . . .' He held up a plastic bag which had what looked like an airline wallet inside. 'We also found this . . .' He displayed another bag which held a British passport.

'Tell me Doctor, were you aware that your wife and the young man were booked on a flight to Barcelona leaving at ten pm last night? . . . No. I see from your expression that you weren't. And I wonder if you might know how she secured a rather good, probably passable, forged passport for her companion? No again? Well, I suppose these media people have all manner of contacts, which a doctor, never mind a mental patient, are unlikely to have cultivated.'

The officer paused and studied David's face. 'Would you care for something to drink? Tea? Coffee? Juice?'

'No,' David replied. He looked pallid, ill. 'No. I'd really just like to hear the rest and go if you don't mind.'

'Not at all. I quite understand. The big question, of course, is when the deaths occurred, and our tests indicate the morning, between roughly nine and noon. Therefore, I'm bound now to ask you to provide me with a precise account of your movements from approximately six am until mid-afternoon, complete with the names of any and all witnesses.'

David just groaned.

Henning, sustaining his benign manner, went on: 'We should have liked the inquest to be later rather than sooner, but the coroner is going on holiday next week so we have booked him for Thursday at ten am in the police hall next door. I assume we may rely on you? Good. Now, Miss Street, if you would be kind enough to come with me, there is this small rather unpleasant task – that is, if neither of you has any further questions?'

'I do actually,' I said, rising. 'I noticed that there was nothing about the deaths in the morning papers. How long do you think it will be before word gets out? I assume you're waiting until you've spoken with Carlos' sister.'

'That is correct. She's the main immediate relative who hasn't been informed. On Mrs Blake's side I have only this afternoon finally contacted her brother at his hotel in Brussels, via the New York number Dr Blake gave us.'

'Jesus,' David swore softly. 'Craig. I'd forgot all about him. I suppose he's still coming?'

'Oh yes. He said to tell you he would see you tomorrow in

London.' Then, to me: 'As to your other question, about when the news will get out, we have of course had to inform Mr Philip Knight; some of my men were with him this morning.'

I glanced up at the ceiling.

'Quite,' he nodded. 'It was unavoidable I'm afraid. Perhaps you could help the doctor draft a statement.' He looked once more at his notes. 'Oh, yes,' he added, turning to David, 'there is one more point: your car. Could you leave it with us? It will be perfectly safe and you should be able to collect it on Thursday.'

This was, as we all recognised, a rhetorical question and at that point David didn't look capable of driving anywhere anyway. The Detective Superintendent and I left him slumped in his chair while we descended into the chill morgue and by the time we returned he was dozing.

He slept on the train too and for this I felt grateful to him, for it was only when his head fell against my shoulder and I became distracted by the smell of his hair that the after-image of Carlos' lifeless young face began to disperse.

*In*gratitude was to set in later, when we arrived back in London and he wouldn't fully come to. Getting him to place one foot in front of another demanded a mother's patience and once I'd finally manoeuvred him to the taxi rank I knew there was only one option: I pushed him into the first available cab, directed it to my place and then, with the driver's help, hauled his comatose form up two flights and deposited it on my sofa.

Three

I'd hit out at my alarm about three times and had finally picked it up to shake it when I realised the ringing was coming from the telephone. I squinted at the numbers on the clock: it was seven forty-five.

Damn, I thought, sliding out of bed and stumbling into the sitting room to silence the bloody thing. I hate being woken up this way – hate it, hate it, hate it. And such was my resentment that I'd grunted it down the mouthpiece before I'd noticed that the curtains were drawn back and the sofa was unoccupied. A bit of paper was propped against the vase on the coffee table.

'Christ,' David said softly, 'I really am sorry.'

'Ignore that woman,' I answered, struggling for a bit of graciousness and not quite attaining it. 'Where the hell are you?'

'Home. You won't believe what's happened.'

'Oh God.' (*They're pressing charges; someone else has been killed; he's being taken away at gun point by the murderer of his wife.*) 'Don't make me guess.'

'The flat's been burgled,' he said.

Suddenly I was wholly myself. 'What! Oh *David*. How awful! Is it bad?'

'If you mean bad as in turned over like Barbara's cottage, no. Whoever it was was into a quick in-out – cash, jewellery, small valuables. They did six of us on the terrace – everyone who was away on Sunday, when the caretaker wasn't around either. He had the police in yesterday but I've got to go round now and see them.'

'An experience you're looking forward to I'm sure.'

His cough said 'no comment'. He said, 'I just hope I'm not into one of those runs of three. I don't know what I'll do if I discover that my newsagent's suddenly been called back to Bangladesh.'

'I beg your pardon?'

'Sorry . . . you can't have had a chance to read my note I suppose.

I woke up about six thinking about the Sunday papers. I thought my newsagent might remember me picking them up.'

'And put a time to it.'

'And put a time to it.'

'You'll let me know?'

'Immediately. Will you be in your office?'

'From about one.'

'Good, I'll give you my temporary address and number at the same time. That's the other reason I risked waking you. I wasn't exactly thrilled by the prospect of coming back here anyway, but after this business – well – I'm going to check into one of the bed and breakfasts near the hospital for a few days. If you speak with Henning before I do, would you tell him? I don't want him to get the idea I've done a bunk.'

'He'll hardly think that when he hears what's happened.'

He sighed. 'Can you try to play it down? I really could do without wasting more of my time while more of his lads ask me more meaningless questions.'

'But if it's related, David, surely it's best to establish that as soon as possible.'

'Yes, of course, I agree – "if". I guess it just seems highly unlikely to me. And I've got so much else to do, you know?'

'I do, and if it begins to bear down on you, give me a call, okay?'

'Thanks. And thanks for yesterday too. I don't know what I'd have done.' He hesitated, then: 'Look, I was wondering: Amanda's brother and I are meant to be having a meal tonight. Would you join us? I must warn you before you say anything though – he does generally insist on dining at Claridges his first night in town and it can be damned off-putting eating a week's worth of wages – and seeing another week's worth thrown away.'

'Jeez,' I said, 'put so charmingly, how can I refuse?'

He laughed, and I think it made us both feel better.

David's day continued to improve.

His newsagent remembered seeing him between nine thirty and ten Sunday morning. His supervisor, indignant that 'one of his most valued staff' was under pressure to clear his name after such a dreadful experience, questioned every nurse, doctor and patient who'd been in the hospital while David had been writing and by teatime had located a handful of possible witnesses. Henning decided the local police report of the burglary would be adequate.

And then, when the murders were finally announced on the early evening news, the item was brief and understated. Carlos wasn't named, which confirmed what I'd learned from my further failures with phoning: Connie and Juan hadn't been located and still didn't know.

'The gods have certainly been smiling on you,' I remarked as I joined David in the taxi about eight.

'Maybe they reckon they owe me one . . . And there's a much more tangible explanation for one part of it: Phil. When I spoke to him this afternoon he offered to handle the media for me. He's even drafted a press statement, so there's one less chore for you too.'

'And one more "exclusive" for him.' It was a cynical comment and as soon as I uttered it I knew it was unfair. My own wariness of journalists had got mixed up with a lingering question about Phil Knight and his volatile relationship with Amanda Finch.

David's glance said he was mystified by my sarcasm. 'He hardly went looking for it. He *was* the first person they questioned after me. He could have published what he knew at once instead of sitting on it for twenty-four hours so that he could talk to me. God Dee, I hope I haven't given you the wrong impression of Phil. He feels absolutely miserable about this. Hell, how would you feel if the last time you saw someone you'd rowed?'

I nodded and apologised and pushed my suspicious thoughts aside and changed the subject. We'd begun to talk about his conversation with Barbara when the cab pulled up in front of the Connaught.

David said, 'I'm relieved to say that our host wasn't inclined to his usual first night ritual – the memories I expect. And thank heavens.' He slid out and offered me his hand in exaggerated gentlemanly fashion. 'I do hope you didn't have your heart too set on Claridges, my dear.'

Pouting and sighing, as if struggling to overcome this most profound dashing of my expectations, I gathered my skirt demurely, tucking the safety pin in the hem discreetly to one side. Then, unable to suppress a giggle, I profered my hand in return and adopted that version of an English accent that always makes Suze blanch: 'I shall, I suppose, just have to endure the disappointment.'

'If that's all you have to endure,' he smiled, 'you'll be lucky.'

I recognised Craig Asprey only because I'd twice seen the female version of his patrician face. Otherwise I doubt I'd have picked him out, for he wasn't at all the well-fed, cigar-smoking, shiny-skinned stereotype of the wealthy American tycoon which I had, for some reason, expected. On the contrary, his lean, greying, bespoke-tailored form blended totally into that olde-worlde, English upper-class milieu.

After the two men had exchanged brief condolences, David introduced me as 'my solicitor – the one I told you I'd be bringing', adding that I'd acted for Amanda as well. I started to upbraid myself silently – I had to correct him about my position with Amanda before he said this too many times – then noticed the look I was getting from Craig even as he shook my hand.

David clearly had not described me to his brother-in-law in any detail and Craig, I saw, was one of those men who can't hide their incredulity when they discover that the legal profession these days encompasses short, girlish beings, *sans* pinstripes.

Making a quick choice between humour and irritation, I emitted a knowing, tolerant laugh and sat down.

Craig recovered smoothly. A light aperitif wine had already been opened for us and he now filled my glass. 'Forgive me,' he smiled. 'I thought my sister used someone else. The family business, you understand, has employed a London firm for years.'

He tried the wine and nodded approvingly. 'It's preposterous of course that David requires legal services at all – even such charming ones as I'm sure you provide – may I call you Dee? – and I've said as much to that Detective Superintendent Henning. How on earth did you get yourself into such a predicament, David?'

He explained, tactfully censoring the role Craig himself had played in his impulsive drive to Barbara's cottage, and then, encouraged by his brother-in-law's questions, described his progress assembling an alibi. And watching them talk, it struck me that the behind-the-scenes conductor who regulated Amanda's brother's expressions was ever so slightly off tempo that evening. The beat was a trifle hesitant, so that before each change registered on his face, I fancied I could hear the baton tap against the podium. Click: concern. Click: politeness. Click: sympathy. Yet there was genuine emotion there; hard as he was striving to conceal it, I could see a distraction, almost a wildness, in his eyes.

What a shame, I thought, that both men were treating this encounter as if it were an endurance contest instead of doing what Suze and I, or any of our other women friends would have done:

gone to one of our houses, thrown our arms around each other and cried.

The menus had been placed before us and we stopped to order.

Afterwards, David leaned towards Craig and said: 'You know what gets me more than anything else about his whole thing? The way everyone's responded. The kindness . . .' He shook his head.

(Click: understanding.) Craig nodded. 'I'd like to do what I can too. In fact, if you'll let me, I'd like to take care of the funeral arrangements.'

'Oh, but I . . . but you . . .'

'No – I want to. I've already spoken with the Detective Superintendent about the timing and explained that you and I are very busy people – he appreciates the urgency. Besides, it's so undignified the way bodies are allowed to lie in those horrible basements.'

'But they can't release them,' I said, 'until there's been a satisfactory outcome to the investigation.'

Craig waved his hand dismissively. 'Naturally. But even Mr Henning agreed with me that if, by some quirk, the coroner decides that – ah – "she" needs to be re-examined, there is no reason why it can't be done by Friday afternoon. Therefore, the service can be held on Saturday. Now, Saint Margaret's Church at Westminster Abbey *is* available to us and the Bishop will – if you give the go-ahead David – preside. The choir, the flowers, the pall bearers, they're no problem. All *you* have to do is select the scripture and hymns.'

Craig looked pleased.

David looked uncomfortable. 'I don't mean to sound ungrateful,' he said after a pause, 'but in all the years I lived with Amanda, I never once knew her to set foot in church.'

The wildness glimmered. 'She was baptised,' Craig said firmly. 'And when she was my sister – that is, when she lived with me – she went to church every Sunday.'

The waiter arrived with the first course and David turned his reddening face downwards and dug into his avocado. What a curious turn of phrase, I thought, biting into a prawn: 'When she was my sister.'

David sighed and looked up. 'Okay,' he said to Craig. 'Okay.'

Who to invite? Where to hold the reception? What to serve? Which cemetery? The two men talked through the details and by the time the main course appeared, David looked as though he couldn't carry the thing any further. It was over to me.

After sampling the lobster thermidor, I turned to Craig. 'David tells me you were Amanda's guardian. I don't know if you feel like discussing it – I'll understand if you don't. But if it isn't prying too much, I wonder what she was like then. Was it a difficult time for you?'

Craig put his knife and fork down carefully and looked at me, the emotion in his eyes softening. 'My sister,' he said with earnest pride, 'was the sweetest kid you'd ever hope to meet. She was pretty, she was obedient and she was smart as a whip. She was even well mannered, which if you ask me was nothing short of a miracle.'

'Oh?'

'Our mother, may she rest in peace, had some pretty crazy ideas about raising girls. *I* got sent away to boarding school in Connecticut when I was seven. My sister on the other hand was allowed to go to local schools in whatever third-world backwater my parents happened to be in.' He shook his head and stared at his Châteaubriand for a long moment before resuming. 'When she arrived on my doorstep, I was worried, believe me. I didn't know if she could even read or write, and she was twelve.'

'She must have been in a – ah – "fragile" state as well.'

'Mmm,' he murmured, then began to eat again.

No, I thought, he doesn't want to discuss the death of their parents.

'But she could? Read and write I mean?' I prompted.

'Yes – in spite of it all. A month of remedial work and she went right into the eighth grade. I sent her to a private school on the East Side and she loved it. She fit into our household too. *That*'s what had really worried me. I was only twenty-three, married a year – long enough to know the honeymoon was over – and though I'd been working in the family firm since I'd finished at Harvard, I'd had no real responsibility. Then, suddenly, bang – I was in charge. *And* this adolescent girl I hardly knew came to live with me. It could have been a real disaster, but it wasn't.'

He frowned. 'Then . . . but no. I won't bore you with the subject of my first wife Claire. Besides, David's heard it all.'

But David, engrossed in his chicken chasseur and looking happy with the break, smiled and waved his fork. 'Carry on – don't mind me.'

'Yes,' I urged. 'Do.'

'Claire was – and if she hasn't drunk or drugged herself to death by now, probably still is – a very confused woman. Good family but – "disturbed". Needless to say, this wasn't evident when I married her – she was eighteen and very beautiful in 1957, so beautiful that I didn't care that her family no longer had money. Anyway, when my sister was sixteen or so, Claire took to meeting her after school so the two of them could go shopping – that was the story. The next thing was that they began "going to the movies" in the evenings and of course, come to find out, they were really sitting around in folk clubs in the Village. Then I discovered that Claire had gotten some quack doctor to give my sister the pill. Imagine! A seventeen year old! Naturally I confiscated them, but it didn't matter. Like so many young girls in that God-awful sixties period, she'd already acquired a taste for casual sex. They weren't even decent boys either; they were Puerto Ricans!

'She was cutting school – that's how I found out – but luckily she had a good grade point average so it didn't hurt too much. She still got into Radcliffe early admission.'

'Really?' I said, remembering how much that had once meant.

'But would she accept?' he continued. 'Unh uh. *She* wanted to go to Berkeley.' He wrinkled his nose. 'And once she got *there* her promiscuity became a "political statement", like the bare feet and unkempt hair and the articles she wrote for those "underground papers". She changed her name too. Finch is our mother's maiden name, and she used some ridiculous first name like Brook or Sunny . . .'

'I believe it was "Skye",' David said.

'Yes, that was it.' He sighed. 'I held my breath every time I saw a news story about arrests out there. Marches, bombings, drugs, nothing would have surprised me.'

He stopped abruptly and glanced at David. 'I'd better not go on. I don't want to argue, not tonight, and I know you were one of those new left hippy types yourself.'

David smiled. 'We could argue about whether "new left" and "hippy" should be strung together, just for openers, but I agree: let's not. You know what my politics are: they were the same in those days.'

'And *your* background?' Craig asked, addressing me.

'I was born and raised in LA,' I said, 'but I had friends at Berkeley and used to hitch up there for marches and concerts. I suppose it's

49

just possible that your sister and I actually jostled each other in some crowd somewhere.'

David squinted at me with interest. 'Did *you* get disillusioned with student politics and embark on the great European tour as well?'

I nodded. 'Only I got off at the first stop – and here I am still . . . But is that what she did? Travel?'

I glanced from one man to the other, but as Craig seemed happy to defer to David, he continued. 'She worked her way around Europe from what I gathered – mostly translation jobs with bits of English teaching thrown in. She met Phil in Paris and came over here with him when he decided to set up the agency. Is that about right Craig?'

'Sounds reasonable to me . . . And all I have to say is, thank God for the small blessings of age. Each of you would seem to have settled down since that aimless era too.'

'You mean, that's what you feel happened to Amanda?' I asked.

'I'd begun to *hope* it had happened – just to hope . . . Dessert? The profiteroles are excellent.'

My stomach in revolt, I declined.

When the final round of ordering was over, there was an uncertain lull which neither of my companions seemed able or willing to break, so I did it. 'When was the last time you saw your sister?'

Craig looked at David, who said, 'April? May? That was your last visit wasn't it?'

'Something like that.'

'Had you spoken to her since?'

'Yes, of course.'

'Didn't she speak to you during her last trip?' David said. 'I seem to recall her saying . . .'

'She was on her way back I believe.'

'Oh?' I said. 'Where was she?'

'Where? Why, I'm not sure. Barbados?' Again he looked at David, who this time shrugged. 'I think it must have been Barbados,' he repeated. 'Why? Is it important?'

'It's a loose end, that's all. She didn't tell David –'

'Didn't have a chance,' he muttered.

'– and Phil, it appears, doesn't know either. The police still have her effects. If her passports are there, which they –'

'Passports?' Craig interrupted. He looked startled. 'Did you say passports, plural?'

David gave him a sympathetic glance. 'She had two. I can't believe she didn't tell you. She took British citizenship a while ago – after that Supreme Court decision that made it legal for Americans to have dual nationality.'

Craig, obviously trying to restrain his turbulent emotions, gnawed at a knuckle for some moments. Finally the emotions won and banging his fist on the table he said: 'That woman – I don't want to speak ill of her, I really don't – she was my sister, my little sister, and I loved her – but her infuriating, wilful secrecy . . .' He stopped and just sat there shaking his head from side to side.

David raised a finger to the waiter. 'I think,' he said, 'we need some brandy.'

When it came, Craig took a large swallow, then said with great, but more even, feeling: 'Forgive me David. It's just such a godawful embarrassing mess, so unnecessary but so like her – so like her to get herself killed in this appalling, sordid fashion. I don't mean to go on. I just simply do not see why – I mean, that *boy* she was found with – a *patient* of yours, a schizophrenic – why would she run off with someone like that? You were good to her, decent to her – we have our differences, but you were patient, more patient than I would have been, so I just don't *see* . . .'

'It was ending, Craig,' David said gently.

'Oh but even so – there are ways and there are ways. Divorce is so cheap, so easy. But oh no, not her. She has to have melodrama, she has to let herself be swept away by impulse, she has to have these despicable, insufferable *boys* . . .' He stopped again, this time clearly because he'd remembered me.

'Dee knows about Amanda's affairs,' David said.

Craig gave me a shamefaced look. 'I thought she'd tamed her promiscuous urges years ago. I found out she hadn't when she forced David out of their home and moved in some Spanish car mechanic. I said to her then, I said: one day it will catch up with you. You'll be your own undoing.' He sighed. 'But I didn't think – I never really thought – it would be as bad as this.'

He drank again and I thought: I should make allowances. Grief makes people do and say irrational things.

I looked at David, who'd lifted his glass as if to say 'I'm not getting into this one'. As I caught his eye he shook his head at me. His look said 'Don't'.

My annoyance escalated. Isn't this how it's always been? That assumptions like Craig's are allowed to pass?

I turned to Amanda's brother and, choosing my words with care, said: 'Excuse me. I do appreciate how distraught you must feel. And I suspect that because you're upset you don't realise what you've just said.'

'Oh?' Although only one sound, it told. Here was a man unaccustomed to having his statements questioned.

David's foot touched my leg under the table.

I continued.

'I didn't, unfortunately, know your sister at all well. But even so I find it inconceivable – and I'm sure you don't mean it – that she was in any way responsible for her own death.'

Craig bristled. 'She didn't hold the gun, no, of course not. But she asked for what happened by doing what she did.'

'Just like rape victims "ask" to be raped?'

'Yes, most of them.'

A bad taste soured the rich meal I'd just finished. 'So it's a moot point to you who did hold the gun?'

'You're putting words in my mouth. It's a *vital* point. But it's a matter for the police, not for me . . . and not for you.'

'I disagree,' I said, reaching for my handbag. 'Until there is a named murderer behind bars, it's a matter for us all. And personally I intend to do everything I can to speed that day. Now if you'll excuse me . . .' And so saying I exited as gracefully as possible to the ladies where I fumed for several minutes. (*Thank God I'm an only child! No wonder Amanda rejected her brother's values and married a man like David; what if I were murdered and everyone judged me on the basis of* my *sexual history?*)

The men were standing by the table when I returned, and as I came up behind them, David was saying '. . . send you a copy if she ever signed it. I must say though, I was under the impression she'd written to you back around Easter or so, when we first talked about wills . . . ah, Dee . . .'

Here we go, I thought. Wrong place, wrong company and here we go.

But Craig merely acknowledged me with a stiff smile, then carried on. 'Perhaps she did. My secretary was sick over Easter and I had one hell of a time with the temp I got in – missing papers, that kind of thing.' He glanced at me. 'It's so hard,' he added, 'to find a reliable girl in New York these days.'

I turned and began to make for the door. 'Maybe,' I said over my shoulder, 'you should try a woman.'

'How did you manage to hold your tongue?' I asked David as we settled into the taxi.

'Practice. Long years of practice. That's what he's like. Certain things about her character have always wound him up.'

'Yes and that's what I couldn't take – the implication that she was somehow this innately flawed female *doomed* by her sex life. I mean, imagine for a start what being treated like that would do to you? And what about the effect of losing both your parents at the same time and finding yourself in the care of *that*?'

He was nodding, though his gaze was fixed on the back of the cabby's head. 'He's a Victorian,' he sighed. 'All he wants to do now, I'm sure, is forget all those things about her that disappointed him and concentrate on building the myth: his sweet, talented kid sister who died tragically abroad while pursuing her art.' The quick smile he gave me looked tired under the flicker of street lights and I thought I saw an appeal in his eyes before he broke the contact and stared out the window into the dark pockets of the night. 'The trouble is, I have this terrible feeling I'm going to do something similar myself when all this is over.'

My mouth was open to ask him what he meant (had I heard him right? did he sympathise with his brother-in-law's view?) when I noticed the slump of his shoulders and remembered the plea in his expression. I shut my mouth. There'd be another time, a better time, to call him on it.

We rode past the park and around Marble Arch in silence. The will drifted once more into my mind. David had to know about Amanda's second visit to me. My promise of confidentiality to her had been superceded by my duty to do my best for him – and that included giving him the truth. On reflection, in fact, we'd been lucky. Henning had been so preoccupied pursuing the jealousy motive that he hadn't yet examined any possible financial one. And there was still the coroner – who knew what he might ask?

I was just chastising myself for having forgotten to ring my old boss Michael to see if Amanda had contacted him when David slid his hand lightly over mine on the seat between us. From his side, and still staring out the window, he murmured: 'I'm glad you're here, Dee. I don't know how I'd have got through these past two days without you.'

My face went red and hot and I couldn't look at him. Suddenly I didn't feel very businesslike at all.

'Invite him in for coffee – the possibility of this other will's a perfect excuse,' a voice whispered. It was that voice I'd disobeyed in the name of principle all those weeks before.

'Tonight?' another voice replied, not a little shocked. It was the voice that won on the last round. 'But . . .'

'But what? His wife's dead now – blunt, I admit, but undeniable.'

'But she . . . but I . . . but he . . . it's so *soon*. It's so *crass*.'

'Crass? Crass? What's this *crass*? Who you trying to kid?'

'But there's plenty of time . . . besides, what if he doesn't want . . .'

There was a derisive cackle. 'Look at him. Go on.'

Sort of tentatively, I turned my head towards David. He was studying me. And he was smiling that smile of his.

'See?' the voice said. 'See? Isn't it obvious?'

I sighed.

It was.

The shocked voice is my inheritance from my New England grandmother, the one with whom I spent so many of my childhood summers. The Depression had reduced her first from indulged married leisure to the poverty of bankruptcy and then to a widowhood spent running a little guest house for tourists in Maine. Her original genteel values, however, had endured and, in insidious ways, she had passed some of them on to me.

Countering this were echoes of the voice of my mother – my mother who (to her own mother's shame) had gone west in search of work; my mother who'd ended up half the reason for the success of my father's law practice but had collected only a minute percentage of the credit; my mother who had had an affair with my father for nearly twelve years before deciding to have me; my mother who by then didn't see any need – despite her mother's pressure – to get married and so didn't. ('Why?' she'd say to me when I'd ask her about it. 'This is LA. Here it's the marriages that don't work out. Look – I know. I process most of the damn divorce petitions.')

As the taxi pulled up in front of my block of flats that night, I listened to my grandmother calling to me down the generations: one does not get involved with a widower of two days – and he a murder suspect at that. It's common. It looks bad. His name must be cleared. A decent interval must be allowed to pass. There is no choice. Knees together, you must slide out in a ladylike fashion on to the pavement, alone, and bid him adieu. After that you must wait nine or ten months, at which time you will let only the closest of friends suspect. 'Going public' in less than a year will be a grave breach of good taste.

Then I listened to the echo of my mother's voice.

'Why?' it said. 'Who cares? You acted on principle, demonstrated your integrity and did various other high-minded things several weeks ago. Now it's your turn.

'Can you really pass up a second chance? Can you bring yourself to kiss him on the cheek and tell him to have a cold shower and open the hotel room window? Can you actually do that to this poor tired man?

'Can you do it to yourself?'

Well, in this as in other things I'm my mother's daughter, so she won. I invited David in. And he accepted.

But my gran wins on another point – on the issue of discretion.

I'm not going to describe our night together.

I can't. It had too much of that magic sense of 'here's something real'; too much of that feeling of rightness people talk about; too much of that yearning to grow old (or at least older) together.

If I put that into sexual terms, I'd diminish it.

And that's because of soft porn, not because of my gran.

The moment I walked into her office the next morning, Suze sensed what had happened and, grinning, shook her head and remarked that I would choose this particularly complicated moment at which to end my celibacy. She also jibed that she'd thank me to keep it quiet or we'd have people ringing us up to inquire about our 'complete customer services'. I stuck out my tongue and accused her of being riven with jealousy because she'd never slept with a murder suspect.

The joke, however, sobered us both. David's situation might make a good story in time, but unless various details were sorted out, that time might never come.

I returned to my jungle cubbyhole and rang Michael, who claimed to have been waiting for me to offer him lunch for months. Then, more out of habit than expectation, I dialled Connie's house where, to my surprise, her husband Juan answered on the first ring.

He'd been that very moment searching for my number, he said. I wouldn't believe what had happened: he and Connie had returned home from a long weekend away and been greeted by a squadron of police officers, one of whom had announced bluntly that Carlos had been murdered. Connie had collapsed, been given a sedative and was now resting, yet even while he'd been carrying her inside and waiting for the doctor to come, they'd been asking him questions. *Him*.

What business was it of theirs, he wanted to know, that Connie had been so depressed by my news about Carlos' case (far more depressed than I had realised) that she had wanted to get away? What concern was it of theirs that they had decided to take up a friend's open invitation to borrow his holiday bungalow? And why should he tell them who this friend was? The person was a wealthy patron of the Campaign for Socialist Chile – a person whose contributions were generous and private.

'Did you explain that?' I asked him.

'Explain? That is all I have been doing for the past hour. And do you know what? They have threatened me – me, Juan Miguel Jesus Diego, a taxpayer of this country – with *obstrucción* if I do not tell them these things.'

'Are they still there?'

'No, but they are coming back at two o'clock. Connie will want you here and I think it will be good if you are with us. When I feel so angry like this, my English – it goes very bad and I want to use my hands, you know? I want to hit at . . .'

'Hold on to yourself,' I said. 'I'll be there by two.'

My mother says that my father's early cases weren't in fact accurately reported. She says that it was only when he was older and well known that he could afford to take on one major case at a time and dedicate himself to it. At the beginning, when he was starting out, he was always juggling dozens of clients at once.

That was (and is) my position: I'm a juggler, and I spent *that* morning shifting my other cases around to clear the next morning so that I could attend the inquest. Then I rushed over to the Samuelson Stevens' office.

When I got there, however, Michael was still in a meeting, so I sat in the waiting room talking with Maggie, the receptionist. Somewhere between her telling me that the old place wasn't the same since I'd left (she told me this every time I saw her) and our usual conversation about her daughter's progress at school, she said: 'Well, I suppose Michael's told you all about our excitement here.'

'The big union case? I heard he'd won – saw him on "Newsnight" too.'

'Yes, wasn't he impressive? But I didn't mean that. I meant our break-in. It happened Sunday night. Do you believe it? After all that hoo-ha about moving the offices to this respectable part of town! It's wicked of me, I know, but honestly, you do have to laugh.' As she gave a high-pitched snort, savouring the irony, I felt myself go cold.

Maggie looked at my face and stopped laughing. 'Oh damn, I *am* sorry. I forget that if you were here, you'd be upstairs helping sort through all those papers. But at least all the money had been banked Friday afternoon, so there wasn't anything in the safe except a load of wills . . . Listen Dee, are you all right? You look terribly pale. Shall I get you some water?'

'I'm fine,' I said. 'I just keep hearing about break-ins over the weekend and I guess I . . .'

'You're jealous,' Michael said as he strode through the door. I rose to accept one of his usual over-affectionate, arm-bruising hugs and, when the ritual was accomplished, he held me by the shoulders at arm's length and gave me a facetious look. 'Poor Dee – she hasn't quite gained our reputation for antagonising the right, nor does she represent such a sterling array of villains. Well, never mind – I've got more than enough contacts. I'll put the word around, shall I? "Burglar wanted for break-in at Aspinall Street – only women need apply." '

'Thanks,' I said, 'but I've got enough excitement for the moment.'

He squinted at me. 'I thought you'd given up on my half of the species . . . Or is that a sexist presumption? God, us men have to watch every word these days.'

'Quite right too,' Maggie muttered. 'Two thousand years is long enough.'

'Help!' he cried, throwing his arms in the air. 'And here was I, thinking that when *you* left I'd get some peace. Fool that I was, I didn't see that the rot had already set in. *Everyone* talks back to me now.'

'Rubbish,' said Maggie, with a wink at me. 'He loves it.'

'See what I mean?' he appealed.

'Well,' I began, assuming my most pontifical tone, 'subservience costs more these days; I mean, you get what you pay . . .'

'No,' he groaned. 'Not that. Not on an empty stomach.' And he took my elbow and steered me out.

On the short walk through Hatton Garden, I asked him how serious his analysis of his break-in had been.

'I don't actually believe it was politically motivated,' he said. 'There'd have been graffiti at least and probably a fire bomb. Besides, no one's claimed credit. No, while I hate to say it, I suspect it was some dissatisfied customer – you can see some of them sizing us up when they first come in. And I particularly think so because Ian's office was the worst mess.'

My stomach moved. Ian did probate. 'Ian? That's pretty . . .'

'. . . strange? I know. That's what got me thinking. He and John swapped offices about two weeks ago because John needed more space. Do you know John? He's our new criminal man. He's brought us a lot of work.' He smiled. 'Though on reflection . . .'

Once we were inside the Nosherie, our pink glasses of bortsch before us, Michael said: 'You didn't say so, but I got the feeling you wanted to sound me out about Amanda Finch. I'd intended to thank you for sending her along – bit late now. What an ugly-sounding mess, even if it *has* all been played down. The press protecting its own I suppose. How's David Blake taking it?'

'Okay considering he found the bodies.'

'Jesus. Good alibi?'

'Getting better.'

'Suspects?'

'No one really yet. The inquest's tomorrow. Random burglary looks likely.'

'Ah hah, so that's what you meant about burglaries. Who was the other victim?'

I told him about Carlos and about his links with David and Amanda; then, at his urging, I described the circumstances.

'I hadn't realised there was any mystery about where she was,' he remarked. 'I'm certain Ian had the address and number – I turned her over to him. You know how fond I am of wills.' He grimaced. 'I expect your main concern is whether she got around to signing the bloody thing. Well, needless to say, if she did, you know who has to get first peek. Who's the officer in charge by the way?'

'Henning – Norfolk.'

'Don't know him. What's he like?'

58

'Old school. Not very concerned about coincidental funny business.'

'Such as?'

'David's flat being broken into. With others in the terrace, but still . . .'

He whistled. 'And now our place . . . your pallor begins to make even more sense.'

I shrugged. 'I can't help it.'

'Indeed,' he murmured thoughtfully. Then: 'Look, why don't I ask Ian to check his log and ring you? He should at least be able to tell you if she returned the signed copy.' He checked his watch. 'Damn, I've got another meeting. Why don't you come back with me and ask him yourself?'

From my years working with Ian I know too well his longstanding grievance against Samuelson Stevens: he has to share a typist, which means that whenever there are important criminal briefs, his work gets postponed. No one, he reminded me, regards anything to do with dead people as urgent. And Amanda Finch happened to be a case in point. She had been willing to pay extra for early preparation of documents, yet – as usual – it hadn't mattered. Now, with everything in such chaos, he couldn't be certain . . .

His sigh was full of martyrly forbearance. 'I shall have to look in my book. I'll check the safe too – I haven't done that – for the letters she asked us to hold. Wait here –' He was in temporary space in the clerks' room – 'or have a look in my office if you want. It's your old room. You won't believe it.'

I'm ashamed to admit that I know an opportunity when I am handed one and so, nodding, I went upstairs to Ian's, rationalising as I went. What I had in mind – just a quick peep at the copy – was unquestionably a flagrant breach of trust, a wholly unethical act, yet my moral conscience lost in the face of my desire to know Amanda's last wishes before they were made known to the police.

The sight of Ian's office did almost make me waver: there were open folders spilling papers all over the floor and the filing cabinet drawers looked empty. Still, or so I reckoned, the contents of folders stay more or less together.

Kneeling hastily, I scrabbled around and found the section without too much difficulty. Fa – Fe – Fi: there. A label saying 'Finch, A'.

There was nothing in the folder.

I rose. This meant . . . this could mean . . .

But no. There wasn't time to ponder. There was one more place . . .

Glancing around my feet, I saw the corner of a red folder, *the* red folder where he kept the hand-written notes of his interviews with clients. They would be in date order – if they were there and in any order at all.

When had I seen her? Two weeks before? No. Three weeks. The sixth or seventh of July.

I stooped once more. Yes. The file was intact. And there it was: 'Notes on Amanda Finch' – one page. I started deciphering Ian's spiky little handwriting, concentrating hard, then jumped at the sound of voices coming down the hall. In a panic, I shoved the file back under the heap of papers and stood up, then realised I still held the page of notes in my hand. Shit, I thought – and stuffed it in my pocket.

Ian, however, was too agitated to notice either my standing position or the flush on my face. He had bad news – very bad. It was not simply that the signed will had not come back. The letters meant to accompany it were not in the safe. And not only that: his entire sack of D–E–F–G material had completely disappeared.

It seemed a good time to leave.

The pilfered notes calling to me from my pocket, I walked with self-conscious casualness along Holborn towards the tube, half certain that Ian or Michael would come running after me. I needed to get out of the area, examine my stolen goods, think, but every cab that passed was full.

Then, suddenly, from behind me, salavation emerged: not just one but two number 8 buses, both going to Willesden and the second nearly empty. For once actually grateful to London Transport for its unfathomable scheduling, I ran wildly along the kerb, caught the emptier one at the light, paid as I got on to assure myself of an uninterrupted ride, mounted to the top deck and sat alone in a front seat. There, feeling guilty but safe, I withdrew the sheet of notes.

The opening section contained the same instructions as the will I'd drafted for her: David was to inherit her share of the flat and her personal possessions (Springsteen poster, collection of forty-fives and all). What followed, however, was new:

1. To Astrid Asprey of New York, at 18: the funds held in the account of Amanda Finch at the Bank of Geneva (account no BGS4237651) less the sums below. Astrid to get letter.
2. To Claire Asprey (current name unknown) of Las Vegas: letter plus £500. If A Finch dies before niece Astrid is 18, Samuelson Stevens to appoint Claire as executor of a trust fund. She to earn £2000 per year. If she won't do it, we will.
3. To Jackie Newlands of London: £500.
4. To Natalie Giovanni (married name?) care of her parents in San Diego: letter and £2000.
5. To May White, San Francisco: £2000.

The next line had been crossed out and written over, with a note saying it had been amended by phone. It had originally said:

6. To the Campaign for Socialist Chile: £50,000.

Now it read:

To Carlos de la Fuente: £50,000.

After that I recall none of the journey, only the ache that developed as this new fact chased its tail around and around in my mind: a Swiss account. A Swiss account so large that she could give away fifty thousand pounds and still have enough left over to create a trust fund for her niece. A Swiss account that David – the husband who wasn't to know of its existence; the widower who, thank God, had established his alibi – the account that David would now automatically inherit.

When I arrived at the Diegos' flat, Connie was huddled in front of the TV pretending to watch an afternoon game show. Her eyes were red and puffed, and as I walked towards her they filled and overflowed and she broke into deep choked sobs. Juan went to her side to soothe her while I pulled up a chair and tried to help him. One way and another she finally quietened.

'You had no idea he'd escaped?' I asked softly.

Connie stared down at the ragged tissue she was twisting between her fingers and shook her head. A tear rolled along the side of her nose and landed on her hand. 'I'm sorry to be like this, Dee.' She daubed at her eyes. 'I can't believe it. I never imagined, even after everything that's happened to us, that things would not be okay for him. He was still so young. I have been praying for understanding, but it makes no sense to me. Do you know anything?'

I repeated to them David's version of events, then asked when they'd last spoken to Carlos.

Connie, who had been looking at me until then, now flinched and turned to her husband.

'We telephoned him at the hospital on Friday night,' Juan said. 'Connie wanted him to know what you had told her.'

'And he said nothing about escaping?'

Connie's gaze returned to the frayed paper rag in her hands.

'Nothing,' Juan said firmly.

'And did you notice anything peculiar about what he did say? Did he refer to his future, for example, or to Spain?'

He shook his head.

'This man whose house you borrowed – have you asked him if he minds vouching for you?'

Connie looked away, as if the very question confused her beyond bearing. Juan, however, turned on me abruptly with a resentful glare: 'Why? Why *should* we ask him? Why should we prove anything? Are we to blame? Isn't this a free country? A democracy? Whose business is it . . .'

'Juan,' Connie started, 'don't . . .'

'Don't, don't – don't say to me "don't" – it is wrong and I refuse to . . .'

'Please,' I interrupted, 'believe me, I understand how you must feel. It's a bad time and the police have made it worse with their insensitivity. That cannot be condoned and I'll raise it with the officer in charge. But in trying to find out who did this terrible thing, they must also satisfy themselves about who did not . . .'

'*We* didn't,' he said in a sharp, hostile tone.

'Of course not,' I continued. 'I know that and you know that, and now they must know it. Look, tell you what – give me your friend's name, let me get a statement from him and I will do everything possible to protect his identity. I appreciate that there are people like this, supporters of Chile who . . .'

'Of *free* Chile,' Juan erupted again. 'Our friends are friends of *free* Chile, of socialist Chile, the Chile that we lost when it was crushed by the war-mongering, capitalist, imperialist forces of *your* American government, which . . .'

Connie put her hands to her ears and cried out: 'Stop it – I beg of you, Juan, stop it. Dee is one of the good Americans and she is trying to help us. Do not offend her.'

At this his anger seemed to dissolve and, kneeling by her he enveloped her in his arms. I don't know a lot of Spanish, but what she mumbled into his shoulder sounded like 'Tell her – please – trust her.'

'Shush,' he whispered. 'Hush.'

I waited, wondering.

But when he turned to me again, Juan said only: 'Forgive us – forgive me. I will telephone our friend tonight.'

Four

David and I didn't see each other again until seven fifteen the following morning when we boarded the train back to Little Yarmouth for the inquest.

From Connie's I'd returned to my office and, from there, in the early evening, gone on to a meeting of the Women's Rights Group editorial committee. David was to have met me at my place around eleven, but instead he'd rung from a call box. And he didn't even need to say where he was: the background noise and the soupy lilt in his voice had told me.

'Good news,' he'd shouted. 'Turns out one of the other doctors parked next to my car on Sunday about one and noticed it was still there when he left at six. Isn't that a relief?'

'Now there is an understatement.'

'Say that again?'

'*Great!* Are you coming over?'

Cupping his hand over the mouthpiece, he'd whispered hoarsely: 'I hope you know I want to, but I'm with Phil and his car's packed up and he's stuck in town and he's asked if he can kip on my floor. I can't think of a way to say no.'

'You must have a grandmother like mine,' I murmured.

'What?'

'We must do it another time,' I said, much louder.

'I hoped you'd say that. Do *you* have any news?'

'Amanda didn't sign the other will.'

'Didn't? God, this noise is impossible.'

'Didn't,' I'd repeated. Then I'd yelled goodbye.

David of course had arrived on the platform with Phil, who'd given me a quick, bold, head-to-toe glance, stuck out his beefy right hand, smiled and, addressing me at about breast level, said: 'Hi! I understand you're a Yank too. Do you know, we're about five per cent of the population of Greater London? A genuine

64

minority group, how about that? . . . Now then, I've reserved us all seats in the breakfast car and the others are probably all there, so . . .'

'What others?' I'd asked, suddenly disinclined to move. 'Not journalists? Not at this time of the morning?' I'd turned to David and only just checked the impulse to touch him. 'I'd planned to run through your statement to the coroner with you.'

'Oh he'll be okay,' Phil had cut in. 'He knows his lines.' Then, bending down at me from his tall well-fed frame (played football in college, I thought; Midwest), he'd given me a paternal pat on the back. 'And as for this bunch' – he'd nodded towards the train – 'they're all tame. The real sharks are on the make for the latest on poor old Charles and Di.' He'd let out a self-satisfied laugh. 'So don't you worry your pretty little head, you hear? Just leave them to me.'

And true to his word, Phil Knight took charge of the all-male party, which he entertained for the next two hours with anecdotes about his own and other journalistic experiences and about printed *faux pas*. Most of his tales, like most party jokes, were either sexist, racist or climaxed in a punch-up, and that fact, together with the way he patronised me, made me classify him as an authentic example of *Homo machismo*, that once dominant species soon (please God) to join the dinosaurs.

But a murderer?

Somehow he was almost too obvious.

When we arrived at the hall, I left David with the other men and went to seek out Henning. I needed a few private words with him about a number of points, but especially about Connie's and Juan's alibi, for although Juan had kept his promise and prepared his 'friend' to expect my call, I'd been unable to get any reply so far.

'Forgive me Miss Street,' the Detective Superintendent remarked when I'd explained, 'but your clients do seem to be making a meal out of what you claim is very straightforward.'

'For heaven's sake, they're upset. And the way your men pressured them for the name hasn't helped.'

'Pressured?' he repeated ingenuously. 'I had no idea.'

'They were insulted,' I went on, 'and quite rightly. They're not dangerous terrorists, just campaigners – and that's the difficulty. They promise their contributors confidentiality.'

He looked pained. 'You *will* get this statement?'

'By the weekend.'

'All right,' he conceded. 'All right. If the coroner presses the point, I'll offer reassurances.'

'Another thing,' I continued. 'Amanda's will has been–'

'I know. A solicitor named Simpson –'

'Samuelson.'

'Yes – he rang me yesterday. I have his statement.'

'And?'

'Given his clientele, I'm not surprised he was burgled. And his evidence is soft, merely coincidental. I've learned of far more relevant break-ins nearer to hand.'

'Oh?'

'There were two others that same day in that same vicinity. Is there anything else? It's almost time . . .'

'Just one more . . . about Ms Finch's effects . . .'

'Didn't I make myself clear about that? One empty handbag, assorted cosmetics and a suitcase full of clothes. The tickets and forged passport were found on the young man. In retrospect, you know, her husband saved us several days' work: we'd have been hard pressed to identify her. Ah – here's the coroner . . . Not many in the press section are there? I expected a whole circus.'

There weren't many in the non-press section either: Craig; the Diegos; the doctor who'd dealt with Carlos at Michelmore's; a tall slender woman of about my age, in a tailored black linen suit, whom I took to be Amanda's friend Barbara from the intensely concerned way she was speaking to David; and a shorter, older, blonde woman in more casual black who appeared to be Barbara's companion but who hung back from the familiar conversation.

The proceedings began promptly with the opening questions, as usual, addressed to the police, whose role it was to clarify the where, when and how of the two deaths. Then David was called.

Could he confirm the circumstances as described? Could he review his activities prior to his arrival at the cottage? Could he say whether the word 'faithful' had applied to his late wife? How had he felt about her previous infidelities? Had he truly never struck her? Why hadn't he filed for divorce after leaving her? Why, if the reconciliation hadn't worked out, had he stayed? How had he felt on recognising Carlos? What would he inherit?

How he bore it I don't know, but he did. In fact he was considerably more controlled than Phil, who was subjected to fewer and less penetrating questions and who revealed, as far as I was concerned, only one new piece of information: that he'd been at Heathrow awaiting a parcel from about mid-morning through to late afternoon on the day of the murders.

Barbara was next, but unfortunately the coroner didn't share my interest in her. For his equal lack of interest in Connie and her husband, on the other hand, I was grateful: they needed some reason to relax, no matter how slight, and it seemed he was giving it to them. The trouble was that he then cruelly took it back again by insisting that the last witness, the doctor from Michelmore's, describe in detail Carlos' recent behaviour.

Sensing Connie's growing disquiet as the questioning touched on the failed tribunal hearing, I reached for her hand. 'Hold on,' I whispered, 'it's almost over.' And of course it should have been. This coroner, however, decided to take it upon himself to provide an original closing flourish.

'Ladies, gentlemen, officers,' he began. 'I am going to adjourn this inquest now pending further investigation by the police.' He looked towards Henning. 'But before I do, I have a recommendation for them. I have heard evidence this morning that one of the deceased suffered from mental illness, was known to be violent and had indeed demonstrated violence shortly before escaping from care. I have also heard evidence about the state of the cottage where the bodies were found. What I have *not* heard is any evidence which eliminates the possibility that this young man, Carlos de la Fuente, was *himself* the murderer. Nor, come to that, has it been proved that the two victims didn't kill each other.'

At this Connie, stiffening with shock, doubled over in her seat, put her arms around her ears and started to rock, murmuring 'No – no – no *posible*.' The coroner paused.

I moved to put my arm around her shoulders, but Juan, scowling first at the coroner, then at me, pushed me away, put his arm around her instead, lifted her gently from her seat and guided her down the aisle and out the back door of the hall. David, none too pleased himself by this twist, rose abruptly and followed them out.

The coroner waited until they'd gone, then closed his file and stood up. 'This is a line of inquiry which cannot be neglected . . . . This inquest is now adjourned for one month.'

Well, talk about uproar – *no*body liked it. Henning was affronted: as if, after all these years, he couldn't distinguish one type of killing from another. And as for evidence – pfaa! They had all they needed. But if he wanted more, he would get it. The cottage and grounds would be stripped!

He marched off muttering about the ratepayers' money.

Phil, looking sour and serious, drew his colleagues into a huddle. 'Keep it short,' I heard him direct them. 'For the moment it's enough to say it was adjourned.'

Craig, for all his 'she brought it on herself', apparently hadn't meant it quite this literally and fumed about suing for defamation. I'd have pointed out that this was a legal nonsense, but he brushed past me so curtly I didn't have a chance.

David, his dismay still obvious, was simultaneously trying to soothe Connie and placate Juan, who looked as if, handed a bomb, he'd know whose seat to put it under.

As for me, I just wanted to find a quiet corner where I could sit and think; instead, however, I wandered lamely from one person to the next, offering sympathy and wondering how to diffuse all the heated feelings that were being expelled in the foyer of that hall.

Suddenly the blonde woman I'd noticed earlier emerged and calmly set about organising the situation. She spoke a little Spanish, she said, and would like to accompany Connie and Juan back to London. Would David drive? Yes. His car keys had been returned to him. And yes, there would just be room for Craig. Juan had brought his car? She looked around. Phil volunteered to drive it back. Who needed a lift? Four or five journalists raised their hands. I started to say I'd take the train, but she shook her head and smiled past my shoulder. I turned.

'You're Dee, David's solicitor aren't you?' Barbara said in a rushed, breathless way as she clasped my hand and shook it quickly. 'I've been hoping I'd get a chance to talk to you. I'll give you a lift. Come on. Let's get out of this place.'

Forty miles and as many nods, grunts and 'oh really's later, I had realised that when this high-strung woman said talk, she meant it. I had also realised that she was easy to listen to – a warm, intense speaker with that dry, self-effacing manner typical of so many of my English friends – and that she had been terribly fond of Amanda. I'd lived in London long enough, too, to sense what was going on. Barbara wanted to tell me about their friendship, but she and I were new to each other: she had to get the measure of me. So while on the surface it seemed that she was holding forth and I was silent, I knew that underneath she was listening as closely as I was.

And eventually she made up her mind. She'd been telling me about her work when she stopped in mid-sentence and glanced

68

over at me. 'I'm sorry,' she said, 'this whole thing's got me incredibly wound up. That poor detective superintendent – I think I must have driven him up the wall. I reckon he must have slipped the coroner a note: "watch this one or you'll never shut her up".' She laughed carelessly but the sound carried a hurt edge.

'I wondered if you didn't have more to say,' I said.

She shrugged. 'Oh I've said it. I told the police in great detail all about the last time I saw Amanda. And they were polite and they listened and they wrote it down. If the coroner decided it was irrelevant, well, that's his job.'

'. . . but?'

She sighed, shaking her head as if to save me the trouble of dismissing what she was about to say. 'I know I'm probably looking too hard, trying to turn a short visit into something full of significance, and I know that's illogical and silly. But I can't help myself. I can't forget about it. And so I guess when David told me who you were I thought – crazily, I suppose – I thought that because you must know about this kind of thing, and because you're another woman –'

'There's another point too,' I interrupted. 'For some "illogical", "silly" reason of my own, I'm interested. So stop apologising,' I smiled, 'and just keep talking.'

Amanda had entered the studio hesitantly, as if the impulse that had prompted her to drop in hadn't fully persuaded her body that the visit was necessary. Barbara, however, had known instantly which side to take.

'My God,' she'd exclaimed, laughing as she stepped backwards and played at shielding her face. 'If my neighbour Alick the producer sees you, he'll cast you in a rum commercial and send you back to the Caribbean. You look fantastic!'

Amanda smiled and kissed her friend on the cheek. 'Babs,' she declared solemnly, 'I love you.' Then she looked across the room at the loom and sighed. 'I love your new work too – what a beautiful pattern – and I won't keep you from it too long, I promise. In fact, I wouldn't have barged in on you during the day like this at all, only I –'

But Barbara cut her off. 'No excuses. This is too rare a pleasure and I was about to take a break anyway. The coffee's even ready. Now tell me: how was El Salvador?'

'Indescribable so far, except in the kind of "subjective gush" as

69

he calls it that Phil can't stand,' she replied as she accepted a mug and sat down. 'The women I met were remarkable, totally dedicated to the revolution – and after seeing the way they live, I can understand why. Honestly, to think that my own country is subsidising the dictators who want to keep things as they are . . .' She shook her head. 'My biggest – well – "revelation" I suppose you could say, was that I felt much more like picking up a rifle and joining them than picking up a pen and writing about them . . . And then Nicaragua – my God! If proof were needed that the Salvadoreans are doing the right thing, there it is.' She stopped suddenly and smiled. 'See what I mean about the gush?'

'So? What's wrong with it? You were obviously touched by what you saw.'

'I'll say.'

'Well then? Treat yourself for a change.'

'Half the problem is that in Phil's opinion, that's what I have been doing – and he's being an absolute bastard about it. He's even hired a new freelance stringer to . . .'

'Again?' Barbara didn't hide her disgust. 'You'd think he'd come up with something different.' The two women had had many conversations about Phil before. Despite that, though, Barbara carried on, saying what she always said: 'I know you think he's been good to you, but he's such a boor – all that bully boy, macho stuff. You don't need him, you know.'

And this time, instead of offering the usual defences, Amanda nodded. 'You're right,' she said. 'I don't. Not any more.' She lit up a cigarette. 'It probably sounds weird, but I think I've been – no, I know I've been – afraid to take the big step. But that's over now. I'm going to quit, and this time I mean it. I'm going to go off on my own.'

Barbara raised her mug. 'Thank the Lord for that. To your future!'

Amanda smiled. 'I've got to finish the articles about my trip first. And there's something I have to write on the quiet – you know, while I've still got a salary. But I can't work in the office, and at home – well – it's pretty tense there too. That's why I've come. I wondered if . . . I mean, before I left you offered . . .'

'. . . the cottage,' Barbara finished, reaching into her bag for the keys. 'It's yours.' Then, seeing her friend's expression, she added: 'And don't worry. If Phil has the cheek to ring me, I'll growl at him.'

70

'Phil or anybody else – please. Now – how do I get there?'

They studied the map together for a few minutes, then both of them stood and walked to the door. There, finding the intensity of Amanda's thanks embarrassing, Barbara cut across them saying, 'By the way, I rang you last week when I thought you were due back. David said you'd tacked on some holiday. What did you do? Find a little beach somewhere?'

Amanda dropped her eyes the way she did when you asked too personal a question. Yet rather than doing what she often did and leaving the awkwardness, she finally lifted her eyes again and studied her friend's face. 'Part of "treating myself", as you put it before, was that I paid a couple of visits I should have paid years ago.'

Enigmatic as this statement was, it made one word rise in Barbara's mind: Cuba. She swallowed hard to keep herself from speaking it aloud, but couldn't refrain altogether. 'You went back?' she whispered.

She felt certain that slight inclination of Amanda's head was a nod.

'And?' she pushed.

Something that Barbara was later to think of as struggle pulled at her friend's noncommittal expression, as if habit were, for once, finding it difficult to quash the desire to confide. Then Amanda seemed to reach a compromise with herself. She shrugged in-differently but softened what might have a rejection by saying: 'I don't think my life – any of it – will seem the same again, *ever* . . .'

Barbara sighed. 'I'm such a romantic. I got it into my head that the piece she wanted to write "on the quiet" was about her childhood in Cuba and her return twenty-whatever-it-is years later. It was stupid really.'

'Why do you say that?'

'Because she must have lived in at least half a dozen other countries out there too – Panama, Venezuela, Brazil – and Chile. I mean, that could easily have been where she went. It makes sense when you think about it: she went there, came back to find David working with Carlos, saw a story, visited him – and fell for him.' She frowned to herself. 'Though God knows, there doesn't need to be a connection between her trip and her choice of a lover. It's not as if she'd never taken a young Hispanic man before . . . Still, I can't help but feel there was something exceptional about him.'

71

'Because she went to such lengths?'

'Yes, that. But also because – well because back when she and David were separated she came over to see me one day to ask me about my therapist. She told me that she'd suddenly had this awful sensation that her habit of having affairs might not be the sign of liberation it's meant to be. She wasn't choosing to have them she said; it was more like a compulsion, something she couldn't control. And the worst of it was, it wasn't making her happy. I put her on to Eve – the blonde woman I was with at the inquest – and it was my impression that she hadn't had a lover since. Only the other week in fact she made a joke about maybe giving up cigarettes next.'

'What did you make of the coroner's suggestion?'

Barbara's hands tightened on the steering wheel and she sat straight up. 'I thought it was absolute rubbish. Complete nonsense. She'd never have shot anyone except in self-defence and I watched the way Carlos' relatives reacted: they obviously don't believe for one minute that *he* attacked *her*. Also, it implies that Amanda got hold of the gun, which is completely out of character. I mean, I can't tell you how many times she said that one of the main reasons she liked this country was because guns are so hard to come by that people can't go around shooting each other all the time. She might know where to get a phoney passport, but I cannot conceive of her even trying to buy a gun. Why?'

'Maybe she was afraid. She was anxious enough to sort out her will when she got back.'

Barbara glanced over at me. 'Was she? That's interesting.'

'That's not all either,' I continued, telling her about the break-ins.

Gratifyingly, she whistled. 'The police know all this?'

'Oh yes, but of course it's merely "soft evidence" – not the type of thing they're fond of. Look at that case that was reported the other day. Six witnesses died before a big drugs trial and the police issued a statement saying there were "no suspicious circumstances". The question I can't answer is, who would have felt threatened by her – threatened enough to kill her? And to steal her personal papers?'

But Barbara just shook her head and we rode along in silence for a mile or two.

Finally, hesitantly, she said: 'I don't know if I should say this, but ever since I heard what had happened I've been wondering

72

about – well – about Phil. He can be unpleasant – vicious – when he's crossed. And he was in some kind of military commando unit in Vietnam. He's killed people. He says he got disenchanted, but . . .' And there she faltered. 'That's a terrible thing to think about anyone isn't it?'

'Well if it helps, I've been thinking it too. Trouble is, he's not trying to hide the fact that he can get aggressive. Look how frank he was with the coroner about his argument with Amanda. Besides, as you said yourself, he seemed to be quite good to her.'

'Mmm,' she frowned. 'Maybe too good. He's forever sacking people. He's just done it again, to that sweet young woman who was Amanda's secretary. Imagine! He didn't even have the decency to wait a week! But that's typical. The one exception was always Amanda. He seemed to go out of his way to keep her. It was as if, you know, he fancied her deep down – couldn't let her go. And what she said about being afraid to leave him – I'm probably reading too much in, but I have a feeling that it wasn't only because she was worried about surviving as a freelance. She could have been worried about how he'd react, and that could be why she wanted to leave London.'

'But do you really believe he would do it?'

'It's inconceivable to me, Dee,' she said, 'absolutely inconceivable . . . The problem is, I actually believe he would.'

When David arrived at my flat that night, by invitation, at eight fifteen, he bore a bouquet of summer flowers and a bottle of Moët & Chandon. Kissing me elegantly on the mouth, he sniffed the air appreciatively.

'Spaghetti?'

'Spare ribs. My own recipe.' Taking the flowers, I went into the kitchen to get a vase and some glasses. I heard him curse sharply and returned to the sitting room to find him sucking the edge of his thumb. 'What's the matter?'

'Bloody wire round the cork.'

I noticed then the dark shadows under his eyes. 'Is that all?'

He sighed. 'I've been feeling rough all afternoon. I thought I'd shaken it off on my way over.'

'Physical, mental or emotional?'

He tapped his brow. 'It's just tiredness really. It was a mistake letting myself get manoeuvred into driving the Diegos back to town. Juan went on and on about his offended honour and "so-called" British justice and how Carlos should have known better than to trust an American woman reporter. It was incredibly difficult not to react, you know? I mean, Amanda and I had our problems, but she *was* my wife. And it's not as if I fancy being the widower of a murderer any more than he fancies being the brother-in-law of one.' He brushed his fingers through his hair. 'But if that's the way it happened, we're all going to have to learn to live with it, not blame each other.'

'There are other possibilities. In fact I –'

'Well – whatever,' he cut in, sounding weary and resigned. 'Anyway, then I went back to the flat thinking it was time I cleared it up so I could move in again, but when I got there and saw all those week-old dirty dishes and the open desk drawers and all those things of hers everywhere, I thought: I not only don't want to be here now, I can't imagine wanting to be here ever.

'There's a new trainee doctor in my department, from India, who's been looking for a flat to rent, so I decided to ring him. And that's what capped it. Do you realise the goddamn police have tapped my phone? I couldn't believe it – there I was, just getting used to feeling relieved and I discover that! I practically ripped the thing out of the wall.' His frown had a sheepish quality. 'Instead I had a go at the answerphone.'

I couldn't help it. He looked so woebegone, I laughed. 'What did you do then?'

'Wrote Henning one stinker of a letter telling him where he could stuff his tap – *and* his coroner.' He felt in his pocket, humour returning to his expression. 'Here,' he said, thrusting it at me. 'I had the sense not to post it.'

He picked up the bottle and resumed his attack on the cork. 'The good news – there *is* some good news it may please you to hear,' he smiled, 'the good news is that my trainee doctor friend is delighted. He's coming over on Monday night – wants to move in as soon as possible. And my mate Charles in Wimbledon is going away on Saturday for a month, so I can stay at his place.'

The cork popped out undramatically and, after filling our glasses, he extended his towards me. 'To our first night together *not* discussing what shall hereafter remain unmentionable – and to freedom. Thank you Dee.'

Various things I'd been going to say got swallowed along with my champagne.

But two hours later, as he followed me into the kitchen to (he

74

claimed) study my coffee-making technique, I heard myself declare: 'Oh shit, David, there's something I really have to tell you.'

'I knew it,' he sighed, 'you use instant.'

'I confess,' I laughed, 'though not usually on special occasions.'

'Which this is?' he asked, stepping back as I opened the three-foot-high door of my fridge against his legs.

I grinned at him. 'Oh no. I get sloshed on champagne with a sexy shrink at least once a week. It's the secret of my good health.'

As I retrieved the bag of beans and shut the door, he looked up at the ceiling with goofy stupefaction. 'Did you hear that? She actually said "sexy". Did she mean me? Am I in here with a chance?'

We obsessives, however, are not so lightly deflected. True, I did have to turn away from him, but putting together the grinder parts gave me an excuse. 'Seriously,' I said, 'I think you ought to know that the Samuelson Stevens' office was burgled on Sunday as well. The copy of Amanda's will and the letters that went with it are gone.'

He cursed and when I looked around at him, he was leaning against the counter glaring at the points of his socks.

'The whole section of the D–E–F–G clients' valuables have vanished from the safe,' I added. 'And the files – well – half the upstairs rooms are still carpeted with papers.'

He not only straightened, he brightened. 'Ah. Now. That's different.'

I frowned. 'Different?'

'Different,' he nodded. 'As in probably a normal everyday act of vandalism and villainy. As in a curiously timed coincidence. As in something I don't really have to think about unless my solicitor raises it in our next meeting.'

His reaction wasn't the one I'd wanted, nor even the one I'd expected, and he must have sensed this as I turned away and reached up to unhook a couple of mugs. There was a step and suddenly his arms were encircling my waist. 'Sorry,' he said, blowing the word gently against the back of my ear lobe. 'Some of us aren't used to feeling bubble-headed.'

'Mmm,' I murmured. My neck began to stretch left of its own accord as lips massaged its opposite side. Talking became difficult, but as I've said, we obsessives don't break easily. 'I just think it's strange, that's all. The cottage. Your place. Samuelson Stevens . . .'

The lips revisited my ear where they whispered. '*And* two other cottages near Barbara's *and* five other flats in my terrace *and* I bet something like fifty other offices in central London. The way I understand it, there's only one kind of break-in that deserves worrying about and that's the kind where everything's been turned over on to the floor and nothing valuable is missing.'

I inched my way around so that I was facing him. His eyes were closed and he'd left his lips puckered while he'd waited for me to reposition myself.

I touched them with the inside flat of my fingers and they began to work again. Yet even with my hand tingling I managed to say: 'So you mean you honestly truly believe in coincidence?'

He stepped back and smiled at me from arm's length. 'Not always, no. Where there's even the slightest hint of politics, I usually have to be convinced that there isn't a guiding hand. But here there's no trace whatsoever of politics.' He resumed his administration of neck relaxation therapy. 'Besides,' he mumbled, '*you* must "honestly truly" believe in coincidence yourself. Why else are we standing together on this spot at this very moment?'

This seemed such a brilliantly inspired point that my obsession stood down. My wandering hand discovered a small gap where the back of David's shirt had come untucked from his belt, inserted itself and began to explore. 'Why,' I breathed, 'are we standing?'

I woke up thinking: I want to stay home today. I could easily stay here in bed with David all day.

Then I remembered the two urgent briefs and the file of correspondence I'd set aside in order to go to the inquest and had a sudden vision of the day's page in my diary. Hell, I couldn't even take the morning off.

In fact, if I were going to catch up with my work, I needed to get to the office early, before the phone calls and the clients' demands and the emergencies started.

Which meant that I had to get up immediately.

Telling myself that I must be a mad woman, I disentangled myself from David's arms, resisted his sleepy pleas and by eight forty-five was sitting at my desk feeling noble and virtuous.

Fifteen minutes later, the doorbell rang. I ignored it.

It rang again. Again I ignored it. (There was a sign for Christ's sake: Office Hours, 9.30–5.30.)

The third time I slammed my pen down in disgust, stood up, strode angrily through the reception area and impatiently opened the door, prepared to give whoever it was a brusque reading lesson.

It was Connie. And of course, she saw my glowering expression before I could adjust it.

'Oh! Dee!' she said with nervous surprise, as if I were the unwelcome caller. She took a step back. 'I'm sorry. I didn't mean to . . . but I . . . Juan thinks . . .' Then her eyes began to fill.

Uncertain as I felt about my ability to cope with her tears that early, I knew that whatever had brought her had to be important.

I smiled. I apologised. I explained. I coaxed her in and made her tea. The tears dried. Trust, that fragile thing I'd so nearly lost, returned.

'I won't stay long,' she began. 'Juan thinks I am at Oxford Street. Yesterday we argue, argue, argue – I want to come to see you; he forbids me. Finally he gets red and breaks some plates and makes me promise to obey him.' She sighed. 'It is a very big problem for me and I do not sleep all night. I understand Juan. He is very bitter, more full of hate than I am about Americans. He thinks that you are like others he knew of in Chile who said they were friends and were not. He is afraid. He says to me, see Consuela, your brother trusts an American woman and look. You trust this Dee and see – suddenly Carlos' name is nothing. I said to him, what could she do? She didn't know what the official would do. That is right, isn't it?'

I nodded.

'So – it is as I told Juan. You are my friend.' She frowned. 'Of course, Juan too is my friend – my better friend as you say. That is why I do not sleep. I have two friends and I am lying to one, which is bad, no? But to change and tell the truth, I am lying to the other.' She smiled. 'Finally I decide it is Juan's fault. He has asked me to lie with being stubborn. You have not. And if I tell you the truth, maybe it will help you prove who killed my brother.'

'Hold on,' I started, 'it's the police who are –'

'No,' she exclaimed, looking at me with horror. 'No. *This* is the point, this is Juan's fear – that the police will learn and deport him – deport us . . .' She shivered. 'You know what it would mean for us to be sent back to Chile now.'

Well, I did know, and knowing, it was impossible not to be touched by her appeal. Yet ethically I was being edged into a dubious position. 'And you know,' I tried feebly, 'that I'm only a solicitor, not a detective. I'm not sure that you'll really gain anything by telling me the truth.'

'I will gain two small but precious things,' she said softly. 'Hope – and sleep.'

'How could you Dee?' Suze groaned when I'd reviewed the past couple of days. 'You *stole* a page of notes from Ian's office? And now you're an accessory to illegal exit and entry of the country, forged travel documents *and* withholding information from the police?'

'It's not quite that bad,' I said in defence. 'This industrialist Armstrong *has* produced a statement saying he lent Connie and Juan his bungalow. They *are* covered.'

'Sure – by a lie.'

'By a half-truth. Be fair. He did lend it to them. They simply didn't use it. Juan left first thing Sunday morning to catch the coach to Barcelona . . .'

'. . . leaving Connie with the friend whose husband had forged *her* husband's Common Market transit visa. Jesus H Christ.' She shook her head, then dropped it into her hands. 'Let me just get all the background clear. How many phone calls were there?'

'Two.'

'And the first was the one you knew about.'

'Yes. Connie did ring Carlos at the hospital after she and I had talked. He didn't sound particularly upset though. And that's what depressed her: she thought he'd been put on another tranquilliser.'

'So they arranged to borrow Armstrong's bungalow.'

'Yes. And went to bed. Then Carlos rang them. Juan answered the phone and Connie heard him shouting. He came back into the bedroom, announced that Carlos had escaped and started getting dressed. Carlos was paranoid about their phone. He'd given Juan a call box number and told him to ring back from one.'

'Which he did.'

'Which he did. Connie stopped to get dressed and by the time she got there he was accusing her brother of really being crazy. She grabbed the phone and Carlos pleaded with her to understand. He said that this American woman . . .'

'Unnamed?'

'Apparently. He just said "this American woman" who had money and contacts was helping him and wanted to help them. He begged her to believe him – the woman was a true friend, an old friend of the cause who knew many secret things about what had happened in Chile. He said she'd told him that she'd always been ashamed of the way the American government had conspired to bring down Allende and that this was her way of making up for it. He said she knew they would find it hard to believe her on his say-so, so she wanted them to come to Barcelona too, so that she could explain things to them herself. They must be there, at some café Connie knew, at ten on Monday morning. Then Juan took the phone again and demanded to speak to this woman.'

'Amanda came on?'

'Yes, briefly. Juan laid into her too – insisted she take Carlos back to the hospital and when she refused, insisted she tell him where they were.'

'She presumably refused to do that too.'

'Presumably. The call ended when Juan started getting abusive. Amanda hung up on him.'

'Why on earth didn't Connie phone the police?'

'She intended to, but when they got home and began to talk about it, they began to worry that they or their group might get blamed for the escape. They also started wondering what "secret things" this woman knew about. One way and another they persuaded themselves that Juan should go over to Barcelona and try to get Carlos to come back with him. There was just one small problem.'

'Their passports are in the Home Office.'

'With their citizenship applications. But it seems that transit visas are easy to duplicate and this printer who did it is Juan's cousin twice removed and owes him one for something or other. It was panic logic, but I suppose it seemed a fair risk at the time.'

'They merely failed to reckon on one rather large problem.'

'And one small one: Armstrong rang the bungalow a few times and realised they weren't there.'

'And what does Connie think now?'

'Well, for a start, she's absolutely certain that the relationship between her brother and Amanda was platonic, that of bene-factress and beneficiary.'

'Which this,' Suze said, tapping the page of will notes, 'supports.'

'Yes,' I said, feeling uncomfortable. 'She also thinks that the mysterious "secret things" Carlos claimed Amanda knew might have provided the motive.'

'Does she have any suspects in mind? I mean,' she added facetiously, '*apart* from the CIA?'

'It's not a joke, Suze, not to her. Hell, ever since the Campaign for Socialist Chile got started they've suffered from tapped phones and opened mail. Connie thinks it's got to be either the CIA or the Chilean authorities.'

'Or some combination thereof, I daresay . . . I'm sorry, Dee. I didn't mean to be sarcastic. I can appreciate how Connie would believe that. It's you I'm surprised at. Don't you see the contradictions?'

'What, with my suspicions about Phil? If you want to know the truth, he's still my main candidate. I suppose Connie's theory appeals to me because it's impersonal – and it won't hurt David. Whereas the Phil idea . . .' I shook my head. 'How can I say that in my opinion the man's "support" could be part of a cover up? Hell, I can't even think of a way to tell him that he's a rich man . . .'

'That's easy. He hasn't cleared out his flat yet has he? Well, just make sure you're there when he does. You're bound to find a passbook or a statement to lead you to the point.' She growled and made fangs at me. 'You'd better or you know whose name comes off the door. But what I –'

'That's great. Why didn't I think of that? My God, I might even discover where she got all that money.' Then, suddenly calming: 'But look Suze, I want your honest opinion: do you think I should be pursuing this thing? I mean, let's face it, David isn't asking me to and while Connie wants my help and Barbara thinks the police are on the wrong track, I could stop.'

'Are you kidding?' she smiled. 'And have us miss the headlines? "Mystery Deaths of Journalist and Lover *Solved* by London Solicitor." I dream of the cases we'll be turning away after that.'

'We already know that your publicity fantasies are my nightmares. And I'm serious. Maybe I'm just trying to cover up my guilt for moving in vulture-like on her husband.'

'So? Don't underrate guilt. It's been responsible for untold worthy achievements. Anyway I don't believe that. It's something else.'

'Yes, well, I suppose I also kind of feel that if it happened to me I'd want *some*body to make sure all the questions got asked.'

'And you're Amanda's "somebody".'

'I think I might be.'

'Then there's no question of stopping. You can't and that's that.

My only worry is that you may already be getting too emotionally involved and that that could cause problems.'

I nodded. 'Like raising certain things with David.'

'Yes – and like not seeing what's right in front of you. What I've started to say a couple of times is that I think there's another possibility in what you've told me. There *is* someone else, Dee, who could have known where Carlos and Amanda were, could have got into a fatal row with them, could then have noticed the will and realised its implications, and could have broken into the Samuelson Stevens' office and David's flat. The problem is, can you even bear to let yourself suspect what Connie has to be blind to – that her husband, Juan Diego, committed these murders?'

Five

Craig Asprey's generosity to his grief showed in every aspect of the funeral, from the flower arrangements to the boys' choir to the selection of readings by the Bishop. The most important detail, however – the presence of the body of Amanda Finch inside the hand-carved oak coffin – was the work of Detective Superintendent Henning. And many people credited him with their peace of mind as well, for his second search of the cottage grounds and further forensic tests had cleared both Carlos and Amanda.

'I do know, you see,' he'd said to me on the phone the day before, 'genuine victims when I see them. And now that I've wasted all this time proving that, I'll get back to the real business of hunting the real killer.'

'Well,' I'd remarked, 'as you've satisfied yourself that Dr Blake isn't part of that real business, how about removing the tap from his phone.'

'My dear Miss Street,' he'd bristled, 'I know of no tap on the doctor's telephone, or indeed on anyone else's. Certainly you don't imagine for a moment that *I* –'

'He's heard it come on.'

'Ah yes, but people are constantly "hearing noises" on their phones. The cause invariably turns out to be works along the line.'

'Not this time. I've checked it with the engineers.'

At that there'd been a lengthy silence. Then he'd sighed and said: 'Although I'm virtually positive it's nothing, it does occur to me that perhaps, just perhaps, when Carlos de la Fuente escaped, the Home Office may, in its wisdom . . . Look, leave it with me, will you?'

Connie, of course, had been the first person I'd told about the forensic results, but troubled as I was by Suze's suggestion I'd added some advice to the good news. I'd asked her to collect up all the bits of paper from Juan's trip – the receipts, the ticket stubs and the forged visa, stamped with the date and time of his entry into Spain. Connie had immediately appreciated how crucial these would be if he were forced to explain himself and had agreed. I in turn had promised to push the authorities about the Diegos' citizenship applications.

That evening David had seemed tense and distant and during the night he'd got up a number of times; once he'd gone for a walk. I'd slept only intermittently myself, plagued by brooding thoughts of lives cut short too soon. Both of us could have used the other's company at the services – the pathos of him holding a shovelful of dirt over the grave was an especially sore test – but propriety dictated otherwise and we obeyed. We went separately to Craig's hotel suite for the reception afterwards too.

I'd hoped, I suppose, that someone in that crowd of strangers might tell me the magic word whereupon all would be revealed, but I was disappointed. I heard innumerable anecdotes and memories about Amanda, but all were fairly impersonal illustrations of her energy as a journalist.

I'd also hoped to get Phil Knight alone and ask him a few questions, but my plan was thwarted by that gregariousness he'd displayed on the train. Finally, I'd given up and joined the circle of men he was entertaining in front of the table of spirits.

On seeing me enter his orbit, he grabbed a bottle of Johnny Walker by the neck and waved it at me. 'Hiya sweetie,' he called, 'what can I do you for?'

But even as I was raising my full glass of wine and shaking my head, he was winking at his audience. 'Don't look now boys,' he said in a stage whisper, 'but this here little lady is a member of the world's oldest profession.'

Flushed smirks appeared on cue on all faces but mine. I felt the irritation swell even before he uttered the predictable punchline: 'Not *that* one you mothers – the law!'

The others laughed. I glared. And of course, of the two responses, it was mine he relished. 'Oops,' he said, coyly slapping his own mouth, 'the lady isn't amused. C'mon honey, your uncle Phil didn't mean nothin' by it. You tell her Simon,' he said, elbowing the man next to him, 'tell her how much I love women.'

The man called Simon started listing the women Phil had loved.

The noisy throbbing in my head muffled any humour I might – just might – have summoned. I began to edge away.

A stocky, balding man in wire-framed glasses began to edge away with me. He looked familiar; where had I seen him before?

'You seem doubtful about all this "love",' he remarked.

I glanced at him sharply. Another American? Or was he imitating my accent?

'I am,' I said. 'I can't understand how Amanda took such crap.'

He shrugged. 'I didn't know her, but from the little I witnessed in the office, she gave as good as she got.'

I placed him. 'Mark, isn't it? You went to the inquest.'

He put out his hand. 'Mike. I work for Phil, or rather I'm working for him temporarily. I'm the one he hired to put pressure on her when she got back from Latin America.'

I whistled. 'Did you . . . I mean, were you aware . . .?'

'Hell no. It was just incredibly poor timing.'

'And so not your fault.'

He looked away, his slight frown telling me that he wasn't sure about that and would prefer not to go into it.

'You must have heard some of their infamous rowing,' I prompted.

'A bit.' (He didn't want to discuss this either.) 'I was out a lot. I've only been at a desk – her old desk as a matter of fact – since she – ah – left.'

'Oh?'

' "Oh" what?' he smiled.

' "Oh" I wonder if she left anything interesting behind.'

Despite a quizzical glance, he shook his head. 'It had been cleared out. I even needed to order a pen and some paper.'

'A new secretary too from what I hear.'

'She starts Monday.'

'You approve? I mean, why was Amanda's sacked?'

Another shrug. 'The real question is how she lasted as long as she did. Phil's revolving door policy is legendary. Still, I agree. Firing Jackie was really un –'

'Jackie?' I repeated. 'Jackie who?'

'Newsome – Newcombe – New-something. Why?'

(Jackie Newlands – £500: the will notes. That was why.)

'I know a young secretary named Jackie,' I lied, 'and I was simply wondering if . . .'

'*Still* wondering are you? Good, good.' It was Barbara. I introduced her to Mike and she reached over and drew the woman I recognised as Amanda's therapist into the company. 'I've been

84

dying for the two of you to meet and have a chat. Eve is a "wonderer" too you see,' she winked. Eve smiled.

Mike looked from one of them to the other, then back at me. 'Is this an in-joke?' he asked politely.

Barbara laughed. 'In maybe, but a joke? Never. You see before you the founder members of question askers anonymous.'

This is not, I thought, the way to preserve anonymity. 'Mike's a journalist,' I said pointedly. 'He works for Phil.'

Barbara's smile stayed on her mouth but left her eyes.

Mike backed away. 'Well,' he said, 'nice to meet you all.' He saluted us and turned to go, then turned back and added softly: 'I'd go very carefully ladies if I were you.'

'Men,' Barbara muttered when he'd moved out of earshot. But even as the three of us shared a knowing laugh and turned to the problem of finding a time when Eve and I were both free to get together, all of us registered that a new item had just been added to the list of things to wonder about.

David was like a man just born. He arrived at my place at two wanting to play and his air of released exuberance was infectious. He and I went out and played.

We walked through Regent's Park admiring the flower beds and black swans and exotic ducks; talked politics over a pot of tea; paused to watch a game of baseball in the fields; took the path along the canal past the Zoo; browsed in Camden Lock market; decided to do what both of us had always fancied but never done and took the Jenny Wren waterway cruise; ate dinner at an Indonesian restaurant in Soho; and finished with a late-night film in Leicester Square.

Back at my flat, he dropped into an armchair and held out his arms, beckoning me into his lap. 'Now that,' he said, nibbling my ear, 'is what I call a successful exorcism. I thought I'd never shake this morning. Thank God it's over.'

'Mmm,' I managed, 'I'm surprised you got away from the reception so early.' Then, recalling the moment when I'd told him I was leaving, I asked: 'Did Craig say anything after I'd gone?'

He smiled, feigning innocence. 'Should he have?'

I biffed him on the shoulder. 'You did come up and plant a rather large wet kiss on my mouth and say "see you later". Talk about light dawning! You could see the pieces going clickety click behind what might charitably be described as a cold glare.'

'Maybe you could – my eyes were closed,' he laughed. 'And hell, it's not as though anyone else saw.'

I sat up and confronted him: 'You did it on purpose, didn't you?'

'Yes – yes, I suppose I did,' he said, still laughing. 'All that pretentiousness – I had to puncture it somehow. Besides, I don't need to care any more *what* Craig thinks. The one good part of this whole miserable ugly business is that he's now my *former* brother-in-law . . . What were the two of you talking about anyway? You asking for hot tips on oil shares or something?'

'No, just being nosy about the family history.'

'That won't have helped your standing. Learn anything?'

'Not a lot,' I hedged. In fact what I'd been trying to do was find out what Craig knew of his sister's mysterious private assets in Switzerland. The answer, buried in another lecture about her secretive tendencies, seemed to be nothing.

David and I returned to our playing and what I remember most vividly now is the way he turned to me sleepily a couple of hours later and whispered: 'Dee, do you know what I really fancy?'

'No,' I said huskily, 'what?'

'I really fancy you and me in a little bungalow next to a long white sandy beach thousands of miles from here.' He sighed, his words becoming almost unintelligible. 'I can see it now. Waves. Sun. Seafood. A pile of paperbacks . . . How'd you feel about that?'

The way I felt about that was uneasy: I hadn't yet found the moment to tell him I was going away for a fortnight at the end of the week.

Or was I?

The past few days I'd begun to wonder how I could bring myself to go, to leave David so soon. Yet when I thought about postponing the trip, I knew how much hurt it would cause.

Suddenly the solution came to me.

Not very gently I nudged my dozing companion in the rib cage.

He grunted and opened his eyes to find me leering at him. 'David,' I said, 'how would you like to meet my mother?'

The other problem that had been niggling at me was how to persuade David to let me help him sort through Amanda's study. Now, ironically, his own excitement about coming with me to California made my help essential.

We stayed up until nearly dawn that Saturday night talking about the trip, which of course meant that we got up hours late the

86

next day. Then he started in again. Was I certain my mother wouldn't mind? What sort of gift should he take her? I wanted to go to San Francisco too? (It transpired that the clinic on which he'd modelled his hostel idea was located there – as was my old friend Paula.) In that case, could we hire a car and drive up the coast road? No, not could we – we must. And en route we would stop in places like Big Sur and Monterey. We could even stay in one of those super-bourgeois motels, the ones with the waterbeds and the colour tellies that have a hundred channels and piped-in music and swimming pools. (He'd always, he confessed, had a secret yearning to see what those places were really like.) We also of course had to drink a real milkshake at a real drugstore counter, not to mention visit a state park.

David, as I was only coming to appreciate, was a rambler, one of those people whose idea of a good time is a three-day hike along the ridges in the Lake District. Now he grabbed my atlas. Yosemite. (He pronounced it Yohz-mite.) We could camp out for a couple of nights. He'd bring the tent, the sleeping bags, the gear. We could lie out under the stars listening to the crickets.

'Or listening to all the other campers' CBs, which is more likely,' I laughed. How had my dutiful daughter's journey to the arms of her caring mother been transformed into this action-packed pioneering sortie into the new world? (And would I actually find time to talk to the poor woman?)

Eventually, some time in the middle of the afternoon, David carried the breakfast dishes into the kitchen, where he intended to put the kettle on again. Instead there was a great clattering noise. 'Half past three!' he exclaimed. 'How can it be half past three? I've still got to sort out my whole bloody flat!'

(*Cue Dee – Dee is on.*)

'You have here before you,' I called out, 'a spare set of hands.'

He protested but not very wholeheartedly.

Nor, when we arrived at the flat, did he argue with my suggestion that he work on 'their' and 'his' areas while I tackled her study.

God was I pleased with myself.

As I opened the study door, however, my confidence faltered. Just standing on the threshold I felt like an intruder: this small, cluttered, book-lined room was so obviously a private place. And the angle of the bentwood chair in front of the open roll-top desk, combined with the butt-filled ashtray and mug on the writing surface and the partially drawn-back lace curtains, made it easy to imagine that the room's owner had simply spotted an acquaintance passing in the street and rushed out to have a quick word. Indeed the uncanny sensation of an imminent return was so acute that I even had a guilty thought about what I'd do if she found me there.

Could I really bring myself to pick through the personal keepsakes of this unknown woman and decide coolly what was 'important' and what wasn't?

I pulled myself up sharply. Of course I could. I had to.

Moving to the desk, I saw that various old bills and business letters were strewn across it and quickly determined that they belonged in the narrow slots above, where they'd presumably lived until the previous intruder had withdrawn them. Vicariously indignant, I neatened them before stooping to look through the lower side drawers, where again other hands seemed to have rifled carelessly through. I did find some bank statements, but they were all for her local account.

If not in the desk, where?

I reached for one of the albums on an adjacent shelf: Amanda's clippings collection. I flipped through, fascinated – air disasters and floods, royal visits and film festivals, EEC agricultural meetings and athletics contests – if there was an 'event' anywhere in Europe, she seemed to have been there. (God, no wonder she and David hardly saw each other.)

The closet was the only place left to look and it was here in fact that I finally struck it – the real chaos. What had been an extensive but ordered filing system was now just several messy shelves.

I stepped back to assess the extent of my task and in doing so bumped into the stereo.

Music. That would help.

I checked the tape deck, saw that Springsteen's 'Born to Run' was in place and switched it on. The title track was just ending and as I shouted along with the familiar chorus, I glanced up at the framed poster of the man himself hanging above the console. I'd learned one thing about Amanda: she and I liked the same music.

And it was lucky, too, because I needed to listen to quite a bit of it during the two hours or so it took me to work through that cupboard. I made myself sort without pausing until everything was in one of three categories: research materials (the largest pile), rough drafts (almost as large), and personal memorabilia (disappointingly small). Finally, when the shelves were satisfyingly bare, I picked up the personal stack, took it over to the armchair and sat down to examine what I'd found.

Most of it was loose photos, and even without the two envelopes labelled 'Family' and 'Berkeley' it was obvious which was which. There weren't more than a dozen of the first group, and all of them had tropical backdrops. Amanda, a naked infant on a white beach; Amanda, a toddler, staring at a pack mule on a dirt track; Amanda at about five hugging two small Spanish girls; Craig as a pimply boy holding his sister's hand in a market area; Amanda, now eleven or twelve, tall and barefoot beside a pretty smiling woman and a handsome man in front of a white stucco house shaded by palm trees. There were no dates or captions, but it took little imagination to fill in a story.

It took none at all to fill in the tale told by the other, larger group of pictures. All I needed was memory.

True, I hadn't been to very many of the demonstrations caught by this camera. I'd been too young (or so my mother had insisted) to go to the Free Speech rallies of 1964–65 and too caught up in what was going on around LA to make it away for the big Free Eldridge and Peoples Park marches of 1968 and 1969. But it seemed reasonable (if a little ridiculous) to search for my own among the faces of the Bay Area people protesting against the Vietnam War and the Cambodian bombings, and I did.

It's true too that it was impossible to tell whether most of the concerts she'd photographed were the same ones I'd attended: the Dead, Big Brother, the Airplane, the Youngbloods (ah, the Youngbloods) and others had appeared so many times in Golden Gate Park and at the Fillmore. But about Altamont and Hendrix at Berkeley I could have no doubts. They'd been one-offs and it both pleased and unnerved me to realise that it wasn't so fanciful after all to imagine that Amanda and I might have crossed paths back in the mists of the late sixties, early seventies. Here was proof that we had.

Wouldn't it be extraordinary, I thought, if we'd known some of the same people? This notion, though, *was* fanciful – studying the faces in the close-up shots, I had to admit that none was familiar. Yet their look, her look, had been the look of those times and my friends and I had worn it too.

An early picture, for example, showed a group sitting around a table at the Student Union café. The three men (men? no, boys) had what was then called long hair – Beatles inspired, it just covered their foreheads and ears – and wore bell-bottoms and Navy pea jackets. The girls beside them obviously still slept in rollers to get that bouffant, flip effect, still applied white over their lipstick, still wore pointy bras and were all leg, their mini-dresses barely covering their seats.

In a later photo, four young women posed with their arms around each other's waists in front of a brightly painted Victorian clapboard house in Haight Ashbury that had 'Free Huey' posters in the windows. Now they all had straight, long (presumably ironed) hair, parted in the middle. Two wore jeans, T-shirts and no bras, the other two wore granny dresses and sandals.

Amanda appeared in only a single shot. She was leaning against a tree in a wood staring gooily into the eyes of a young black man who had his arms draped over her shoulders and was grinning at her. This picture alone had a caption on the back. 'To a trippy chick,' it said, 'and a trippy day. Love ya – Tommy.' (So: she'd played around with drugs too.)

Now I'm not one of those people who yearn for the late sixties. In fact, I look back with some amusement on the illusions so many of us shared: that it was possible to drop out of 'the system'; that peaceful marches and free concerts would bring about world change (quick world change); that instant intimacy and sleeping around were somehow good for the female soul; that clearing away the cups and chairs after meetings of white male middle-class activists was 'radical'; that America was the hub of the universe and that our campus (whichever one we happened to be on) was the hub of America.

For all that though, the photographs stirred up a kind of wistfulness.

How could so much time have passed – and so fast? How could it be that all these years stood between me and the teenager who'd sworn she'd rather die than turn into the thirty-year-old who now sat there smiling at the thought of her?

I sighed as I picked up an envelope labelled 'Barb clips'. Yellowed cuttings fell into my lap, all bearing the 'Skye Finch' byline. An interview with Mario Savio; reports of the assassinations of Martin Luther King and Bobby Kennedy; accounts of be-ins and love-ins and sit-ins; descriptions of rallies for Angela Davis, Herbert Marcuse, Eugene McCarthy, the Black Panthers; coverage of events in Oakland, San Francisco, Chicago, Washington, Woodstock.

'She certainly went everywhere, didn't she?' David said.

Engrossed in the past, I hadn't heard him enter and started when he spoke. He managed to catch the clippings just as they were sliding to the floor and we both laughed.

'I hadn't appreciated how involved she'd been,' I said.

'Neither had I until she showed me all this last year.' He shook his head. 'I was really surprised too. I mean, I knew she'd been out there during all that – Phil had told me before he'd introduced us. In fact that was half the reason I'd wanted to meet her. Because in my mind, you know, Berkeley and Columbia were "it" in the sixties and early seventies, *the* places where the political future of the West was taking shape. All we had, all of us who were active in the WRP and the SWP and the YCL and the other groups we thought were so "revolutionary" in those days – all *we* had was this mountain of theory. Whereas over *there* people were actually out on the streets putting it into practice. God I can't tell you what I'd have given to be there . . .

'Go ahead, smile . . . no . . . I see you . . . but at the time it was no smiling matter.' Struggling to suppress his own grin, he put his fist to his heart. 'It was the single greatest frustration of my youth that I could never save enough money out of my grant to get to the States.' He sighed with what I'm sure was intended as self-mockery and when he didn't quite bring it off, he crossed to the desk and peered out of the window.

Over his shoulder, he went on: 'You can imagine how I felt when I found myself in the company of this beautiful woman who'd actually been there. I *assumed* that she had to be incredibly politically sussed. And because of that reserved manner of hers, and because she was so articulate and thoughtful and had all these other virtues I'd always fancied, it was easy for me to do that.'

He turned back around to me with a grim half-smile. 'When you get right down to it, of course, it was my own mood that was to blame. I'd never had a whole summer off before, not since school, and I was delighted that she was as contented as I was to ignore the big wide world. I know it must say a lot about the state of my ego, but I took it as another sign of our amazing compatibility.'

Shaking his head again, he frowned at the floorboards. 'It was only later, after we'd moved in together, that I realised my assumptions about her were wrong. My old political interests picked up again – that's what did it. I began to notice how uncomfortable she'd get when I made certain sorts of statements. It was difficult to get her to say anything much, you understand, but gradually, from the various things she did say, I discovered that although she seemed to have more or less liberal instincts, she had no political philosophy of any kind.

'But what was even more alarming, from my point of view, was that she also seemed to be carrying around these absolutely extraordinary misconceptions about socialism and Marxism – completely extraordinary. I decided there and then that she might have studied out at Berkeley, but she'd obviously not been the least bit involved in the radical movement.'

He gestured to the clippings. 'When I saw those I thought – well, I didn't know what to think. I still don't.'

'Why? Is it so inconceivable to you that she could have been out there where you were dying to be, doing what you were dying to do, and yet could have come away from it all so . . . so . . . what's the word you'd use? "Woolly"?'

'That will do,' he nodded, 'and yes, I suppose it is inconceivable to me. I mean, for the first few months after we got back together, when she was trying to write think pieces, what she was doing really was using me as some kind of political mentor, and while it was flattering and all that, every time we'd talk I'd think: how can this be? She must have five times the direct experience I have. She must have discussed issues like these with her comrades every day of the week . . . You're giving me that smile again. Have I said something funny?'

'Sorry. It's just odd – the idea of Americans regarding each other as "comrades". Hell, you know what a right-wing place it is.'

'Now it is, certainly, and in the fifties. But in the sixties and early seventies . . .'

'Don't kid yourself David. It was exactly the same. It couldn't help but be. There isn't one of us alive who wasn't raised on the Pledge of Allegiance to the Flag and the belief that we have the market on greatness cornered. Nationalism is right here in our gut along with the rest of our political attitudes and the general mass of sixties' kids weren't any different. We might have talked about the generation gap, grown long hair, taken to the streets, shouted slogans, even deluded ourselves that we helped get the military out of Vietnam, but believe me, deep down "Marxism" evoked the same paranoid vision in us as it did in our parents. It meant communism which meant the Soviets which meant the Bay of Pigs which meant the devil.

'There's no questioning that equation there, no sense that Marxism, like Christianity – or like democracy – is still an ideal that the different people who practise it maybe haven't got quite right. And it's very hard, virtually impossible, to appreciate that you've got that blind spot until you leave there. So it doesn't surprise me, in other words, that Amanda had one or even that you saw it before she did. I had one too and I didn't see it until Suze got hold of me – Suze and Michael.' I laughed. 'God help me, when I first met Michael and learned he was a Party member, I nearly asked him why he wasn't wearing a little red suit with pointy ears and a long tail.'

'You're exaggerating. You must be.'

'Only a little. And I think what I'm driving at is that the way I hear you, you weren't wrong in your assumptions about Amanda so much as you were wrong in your assumptions about the whole sixties' American student movement. It was just a fashion like everything else over there David. It was a reaction, a momentary spasm. That's why it died out so completely.'

'Oh come on . . .'

'Do you see any sign of it? . . . No, well neither do I. The difference is that I'm not mystified by that because I know that the other thing you noticed about Amanda is true of most of us: we don't have the philosophical basis to our politics that you take for granted. Here you have a long tradition of debate – you start with your heads. We come from the gut . . . Where are you going?'

'To fix myself a drink.' I thought he looked almost worryingly downcast until I caught the glint of humour in his eye. 'And to toast another delusion shot to hell. Join me? Or are you going to stay in here, poring over what might have been?'

Recalling again my other motives, I decided to pore.

An assortment of old letters remained, most of them from Claire, Amanda's ex-sister-in-law. From these I discovered that she and Craig had separated because she had insisted on returning to the dancing career she'd given up to marry him, even though he had protested that it was 'common' and would harm his political ambitions. The harm, however, had been done by the resulting divorce. ('Serves him right if you ask me,' Claire had written. 'He even tried to take back my lousy engagement ring.') Amanda, I deduced, had sided with her friend over her brother and the two women had stayed in close contact while Claire established a career in New York and afterwards, when she appalled her ex-husband even more by taking up a job in Las Vegas ('of all places').

The last of these letters was postmarked February 1971 and described how Claire had arrived a few days before at Mandy's place in Berkeley, evidently by pre-arrangement, and been surprised to learn that 'you'd gone away, no one seems to know where.' Then:

> Your friend Nat said the whole house was busted for drugs. She said there's a rumor that you turned everyone in. I wanted to tell her that Craig had probably just bought you out but I remembered that none of them knows about your connection with a certain well-known New York oil family. I didn't tell her that I thought you'd stayed away because you were so embarrassed either.
>
> The s.o.b. I'm amazed he waited this long to blow it for you.
>
> She asked me to give you this note. I hope that bastard Craig sends this on. Call me.

'Nat' turned out to be Natalie Giovanni, a name I recognised from Amanda's will notes, and what her letter revealed was that she was out on bail, pregnant, planning to move to her boyfriend's in San Francisco – and feeling badly let down. 'Skye,' she wrote,

> why did you split like that? Howie is saying you sold us out and let him and Tommy take the rap. He's b.s.-ing I know, the creep, but you know what a violent guy he is and he's been saying some scary things. Can't you come back and make him shut up?

A closing remark filled in yet another gap: the supposed will beneficiary named May White was Tommy's older sister.

Sliding the letters into their envelope, I stared unseeingly at the bottom row of books beside my feet, mulling over this new dimension to my picture of Amanda. I understood the need to play down family connections; I'd done it myself, and half the reason I liked living in England was that people took me for me. I also understood why she'd panicked and run rather than face trying to explain, for I, to my shame, did something similar at around the same age. The difference was that I'd done it to a young man I'd been seeing at college after I'd realised that he seriously believed I would stop work and become a housebound mother of two point

94

eight of his children once he got a lectureship. Worse, I'd known that I hadn't the vocabulary to make him comprehend my fear. (I probably hadn't the confidence either; his vision, after all, was 'normal' at the time.)

Had she, I wondered, still dreamed (as I did) of the people she'd hurt?

The title of the book I'd been staring at came into focus: the *I Ching*. I smiled. Here was something else in this room that took me back. Another of my younger selves had sought comfort in its pages, trying to adopt the attitude of 'no blame' counselled there so frequently.

Unfortunately, it wasn't that easy. I blame myself only too readily.

Amanda – she must have done that too. Why else, in sorting out her life's loose ends, would she leave will notes that were so obviously meant to atone for a youthful mistake?

I considered this person Howie and his threats. Could it be that his old hatred had hardened, the complement of her remorse? Could it be that he'd found her and had his vengeance? Or was it simply that I was so desperate I was getting silly?

I picked up the last item in my lap, an old address book. Yes, he was in there, under H: Howard Louder.

David switched the vacuum on in the sitting room, a signal that he was nearly finished. The phone rang. He switched off the machine.

Feeling dissatisfied, I sighed, stood up, stretched, looked around. My work had cleared up the room, but had failed to clear up the problem of the Swiss account.

I went over, knelt by the collection of forty-fives and began to flip through them, seeking a tune to inspire me. Elvis? No, I wasn't in the mood. (It was possible that she'd had her passbook and statements with her at the cottage.) The Teddy Bears? Too many memories of that horrible pimply boy. (If so, they were gone, like the will and passports.) 'Teen Angel'? Too maudlin. Oh but the Righteous Brothers – I'll have that out. (And if they were gone, I might as well give up.) I passed up the Everlies, Fabian, Frankie Avalon, Dion and the Belmonts. I pulled out 'Spanish Harlem', 'Under the Boardwalk', 'La Bamba'. (I'd just have to write to the Bank of Geneva, notify them of her death and explain.)

Crawling on my hands and knees between the console and the shelf, I reached into the far corner. The girl groups! My old favourites! God, she had all of them: 'He's So Fine', 'Sweet Talkin' Guy', 'He's a Rebel', everything. Excitedly, I lifted out a whole handful, bumped my head against the shelf above and dislodged a couple of paperbacks, which fell to the floor along with an assortment of papers.

None was of any interest – receipts, a shoe repair stub, a couple of takeaway menus – but I'd realised something. Swivelling, I looked along the shelves behind me. Yes. Here again Amanda Finch and I were similar: we both tucked bits of paper along the tops of our books. And she'd slipped most of hers into a spot so close to where I'd been sitting, I hadn't noticed it: the shelf next to the armchair.

It was a balmy evening, the harbinger of the first week of sunshine of that damp summer, and I found David in the garden stretched out on a deck chair, his shirt open and his feet bare, sipping a beer. When he glanced up and saw the papers I was clutching to my chest, he made a big thing of groaning 'Oh, no' and rolling his eyes.

'I've discovered some possible leads,' I said, regardless.

He sat up and tried to look interested. 'No kidding? Shit, all I discovered was a stash of her old letters to me.' He pulled a long grimace. 'Listen, are you hungry? I'm absolutely famished and there's this not-bad little French place not far from . . .'

'But David, these leads – they might be important.'

'Oh,' he said, 'right.' Then, after a hesitation: 'Will it take long? Those letters – I don't know – I feel a bit . . .'

I leaned down and kissed him. 'Better?' I smiled.

He laughed and gestured me to sit beside him, which I did.

'Did she ever mention a letter she received about four months ago from a Dr Alan Dexter?' I began.

He shook his head. 'Who's he? Not one of her old –'

'No. He's an academic political scientist, works in New Jersey. They met a couple of times out in Berkeley through a mutual friend named Natalie. He reminds her of that in the letter and then – well, I'll read it out. He says:

I'm contacting you again now to ask if you'll participate in a research project into that period when we met.

Its starting point is the widely accepted if scrupulously denied fact that in the decade leading up to Watergate the CIA exceeded its charter by engaging in covert surveillance of American citizens within the United States. And my thesis, it may not surprise you to hear, is that the Agency's special target on the domestic front was the alleged communist infiltration of the student anti-Vietnam-war movement.

My objective is to identify who their agents were, which I'm trying to do by piecing together the hints in the intelligence files of former activists such as yourself. These files are now of course obtainable under the Freedom of Information Act, and what I'm asking you to do is send for yours and forward a copy to me in confidence.

If it's typical, your file will have certain names whited out 'for security purposes' and these names are the important part of my project. You will need to tell me if you can remember and identify the individual(s) whose name(s) has been censored. Once everyone I'm writing to has done this, it will be possible to compare and deduce who was working from inside to betray the peace movement. When that's done, I'll try to persuade them into the open.

I enclose a letter from the Dean attesting to my credentials. My dissertation, which I'm preparing for publication, was on the CIA in Latin America from the Bay of Pigs through the overthrow of Allende. If you'd like a copy, let me know.

'Now,' I continued, 'clipped to the back of that were the State Department's acknowledgement of her letter; a copy of her reply to Dexter saying she'd participate and asking to see his dissertation; a short note from him enclosing it and welcoming her "ideas or comments on, or contributions to" its revision; and this –' I held up an eight by eleven inch manila envelope with airmail stickers on it. 'It's postmarked Washington and came ten days before she left for Latin America and there's a compliments slip inside that says, "Enclosed – the information you requested".

'On the back of it Amanda has scribbled: "Remind David to be very careful of Diana and Bruce" and then, below that, she's written "Jackie at home" followed by a phone number.

'I couldn't find the file itself anywhere, but I did find the dissertation behind her armchair on top of a pile of books about Latin American politics.' I opened it at random and held it up to him. 'Look. Page after page is underlined.'

David looked, then began to frown away into the distance, towards a rose bush in the far corner of the garden.

After I'd waited a moment, I asked: 'Are you still with me?'

He blinked and squinted down into his beer, avoiding my eye. 'I'm . . . not sure. Listen. Dee. Perhaps I shouldn't . . .'

I patted him on the knee. 'Hold on. I'm nearly done. You'll see what I'm driving at in a minute . . . Now, you know this mystery about where Amanda spent her holiday? Well, she told Barbara that she'd "gone back" somewhere. And Barbara believes, because of Carlos, that that somewhere might have been Chile. On top of that, Connie feels – and I'm afraid I can't tell you why; you'll have to take my word on this – Connie feels that the murders occurred to prevent an exchange of information. She's sure Amanda was trying to pass something secret to the Campaign for Socialist Chile via Carlos.'

I paused hopefully but although David began to turn the beer can around in his hands, his expression remained fixed and he said nothing. Puzzled (what *was* he thinking?) I none the less carried on.

'So. If you put these points together with Dr Dexter's invitation to Amanda to contribute to his research, what I'm thinking is that she just might have decided to take him up on it. After all, she wanted to change the direction of her career; you said so yourself. Even more importantly, she told Barbara she'd made up her mind once and for all to resign from Phil's agency. In fact, that was one of the reasons she borrowed the cottage: to work on a piece Phil didn't know about. And the possibility I see is that what she'd come up with was so secret that it was dangerous. *That* could be the reason she left town and *that* could be the reason she changed her will. She *knew* someone might try to stop her.'

Again I gave him an expectant look and again he didn't meet it. Instead he sighed, stood up and walked around behind me to the picnic table. Feeling even more confused and not a little let down, I listened to him tear into the cardboard wrapping and pop the lid off a fresh beer and I thought: I wish we'd known each other longer. If we had I might understand why he's become so remote. I might be able to tell whether it's been created by something I've said.

What could I have said though? All I'd done was string together a few ideas.

He cleared his throat. 'Is that – it?' He sounded far away.

'No,' I said. 'No. There's an alternative.'

'Oh.'

It was a flat noise, I'm sure of that now, but at the time I thought I heard a question mark. I guess the truth is that I was so uncertain of him that I didn't know what else to do but keep talking.

'Yes,' I went on, 'maybe she "went back" to the other place where she'd spent a lot of her life: America. Maybe the significance of Dr Dexter's letter lies in the part about his research into domestic espionage. This note to herself to remind you to be careful of Diana and Bruce – it could mean that the "couple of visits" she told Barbara she should have paid years ago were to the people she suspected of infiltrating the peace movement. I checked the old address book I found; there's no Diana but there's a Stephen Bruce. And remember – her own file from the State Department isn't here. Maybe she asked too many questions over there or pushed them too far; maybe they were determined not to be exposed. Maybe *they* were the source of her fear, and maybe she was right to be afraid of them.'

When, at this, he once again made no comment, I swivelled round to look at him. As before, he was gazing into the distance.

I set the papers down on the grass, got to my feet and went to his side, where I sensed his remoteness so acutely that I feared to touch him in case he took it as trespassing. 'David,' I said, 'where are you? What's wrong?'

He shook his head. 'I'm sorry,' he said quietly. 'My control isn't – what it might be. I don't . . . there are moments when I don't . . . know myself. I think it's just that, with you, when we talk about her, I find that I . . .' He broke off and turned to me. He smiled too, a slight, hesitant smile, and with that seemed to warm and come closer. In any case, he reached over and ran the back of his fingers lightly along my cheek, inhaling shakily as he did so. The smile worked its way into his eyes but couldn't hide his sadness.

He glanced back down at his feet. 'There's something I haven't told you Dee. Something about when I found the bodies. About me . . . I – it's not something I'm proud to admit, though God knows why. It's not as if it's unusual or unheard of or even shameful really. But I – *feel* ashamed. It sounds – cold. And I – the last thing I want is for you to think me – cold . . . Oh *damn*.'

Suddenly his arms were around me, pressing my face into his bare chest. 'I – didn't go straight to the phone and ring the police. I – my first thought, when I saw that the wounds weren't fresh, was to get out of there. I even – went to my car. I actually tried to push it out of the mud. That mud – it was the only reason I stayed, do you understand? The only reason. Because what I wanted to do was walk away. I *didn't want to know*.'

'It was shock,' I started, 'a natural re –'

'So I've been telling myself. But the trouble is that now – now that I've been through the questioning and the clearing myself, and now especially that the funeral is over, I feel that way even more. I want it solved as soon as possible of course – I want it yesterday – but I also, in another sense, a moment to moment sense, want to put it behind me – put her and us and all the problems that we never solved, behind me. I want to move on, or at least give some time to working out where I go from here. And you – what I can't get over is how you appeared and how you've become part of what I see in front of me . . . It's just that – oh God, I don't know how to say this to you without – without . . .'

'I do,' I whispered, 'and it's me who should be apologising to you. The trouble is that I can't leave it alone. I'm rooting around. I'm still asking questions . . . What you're trying to say is that you'd be happier if I didn't do it around you.'

He sighed and squeezed me tighter. 'Yes.'

'Consider it a promise,' I mumbled into his warm pectoral muscle. I felt terrible. How had I been so insensitive? Why hadn't I realised? Why had I thought I could treat the guy as if he were another lawyer? 'I'll take my bright ideas to Suze,' I added, 'where they belong.'

He nodded into my hair and we clung to each other in silence for a long moment. Then, so softly that I barely heard, he said: 'I'm not actually certain myself that it's worth bothering her with those two.'

I tensed. 'What do you mean?'

Cursing himself at the same almost inaudible level, he stepped backwards so that he was holding my shoulders in either hand and looked into my eyes. 'That was an unnecessary remark. Can you forget I said it? We've said we're not going to discuss all this; let's keep to that. Let's go to the restaurant . . .'

'But David, you've just dismissed in a sentence what I've spent the afternoon piecing together. It's only fair that you tell me *why*.'

He held my eye and I saw a question, a hesitation in his. It disappeared as he let go of my shoulders and shrugged. 'Of course it is.' He pulled the bench from beneath the table, sat down and gestured to me to join him, which I did.

'What I meant,' he said, looping his arm through mine, 'is that I think your hypotheses are interesting but highly unlikely. In fact, as far as I'm concerned, this time, for once, the police are pursuing the right lines. I believe, as they do, that the most likely motive was panic on the part of some extremely unstable, would-be burglar; jealousy is the only alternative. And I'm not saying this because I haven't thought about the other possibilities, because I have. I'm partial to conspiracy theories myself as you know. But I also knew *her* quite well – as well as anybody could – and it's because of what I knew that I'm so certain a political motive is out of the question ... Not that I blame you for romanticising her. How can I? I did it too.'

I was aware of having to work to speak calmly. 'So that's your opinion is it? That there's no actual substance to the ideas I outlined? That I've simply "romanticised" her for some mysterious reason?'

He frowned thoughtfully. 'I don't think it's all that mysterious. You've spent hours in that room of hers, sifting through things that have sentimental value to you as well as to her. It led you to identify.'

'Women do do that,' I said sharply.

'Yes and sometimes they do it mistakenly. Please,' he said, gripping my hand, 'I'm not trying to insult you *or* your ideas. All I'm saying is that, in my view, while they might be fine if we were talking about you or about Connie or about half a dozen other women I could name, they don't stand up if you apply them to Amanda.'

'How? *How* don't they stand up?'

'Dee – look – the last thing either of us needs is for you to get ups–'

'I won't if you'll answer my question.'

From the way he straightened it was apparent that he too was becoming irritated, but he merely nodded. 'Yes. Okay. Right.' He drew an imaginary figure one on the table. 'To begin with, there's the point we were talking about earlier: Amanda may have gone through a radical phase as a student, but all the time I knew her she was virtually apolitical. And while she may have had liberal leanings, she definitely didn't have the commitment to the left that she'd have needed to cast herself in the part you're attempting to cast her in. Second –'

'Hold on. You're overlooking the effect of her experiences in El Salvador and Nicaragua. She told you and Barbara both how moved she was.'

'True, and that may be the explanation for her impulsive behaviour with Carlos. His precise nationality may have been less relevant than the fact that he was a Latin American who'd suffered from the kind of struggle she'd witnessed so recently at first hand . . . Which leads me back to what I was starting to say.' He drew a figure two. 'Amanda wasn't an investigative journalist. She was a reporter and always had been, even in Berkeley.'

'But we know she wanted to change direction.'

'Dee, I'm sorry, but she'd been threatening to do that for an awfully long time.'

'But what if she –'

'All right, all right, just for the sake of argument, let's assume she'd reached the moment of decision. In that case, Chile would have been a ridiculous place to go expecting to find an exclusive. I mean, for heaven's sake, what's left to learn there that's news? Everyone knows it's corrupt and repressive and supported by American money. And after reading that dissertation you found in her study, Amanda would have known that too *and* realised that foreigners with press passes wouldn't be allowed to wander around freely asking questions.'

There was no denying it: David had just found a major hole in my precious theory. But reluctant to abandon it, I offered a last feeble possibility. 'Well, maybe she met a Chilean refugee somewhere else. Maybe that's how she came by dangerous secret information.'

'Maybe,' he shrugged. 'It's a thousand to one chance, but maybe. And the next question, in that case, is what would Amanda have done if she'd got hold of something she suspected might be useful to a left-wing group like the Campaign for Socialist Chile? . . . No, don't waste your time guessing. I'll tell you. She'd have asked my advice.'

I frowned and he saw me.

'That's not meant as arrogance,' he said. 'She was the one it suited.'

'I was thinking of your communication problems.'

'Ah yes, but whenever she needed a political sounding board, she saw to it that the channels opened and that was true right up until the end. I must have told you how she picked my brains about Carlos and his history? We discussed Chile at some length. If she'd been harbouring anything secret, never mind anything dangerously so, she'd have brought it up then. And that's what I see as the basic flaw in your second hypothesis as well. Maybe Amanda did think she knew who'd infiltrated the student anti-war movement, but if she'd been considering confronting them, she'd have talked it over with me. More to the point, though, why should she have bothered? All she had to do – all I expect she did do – was pass her suspicions on to Dexter and let him do the dirty work.'

'Yes, yes, but it's still possible that –'

His groaning laughter cut me off and as I turned to face him, he let out a huge mocking roar, grabbed me on my upper arms and pulled my mouth to his. I didn't quite forget what I'd been going to say – not quite. It was just that, somehow, I lost the urge to say it.

David lost the urge to go and sit in a restaurant.

Six

'Bloody hell,' Suze said when I walked into her office the following morning. 'You look dreadful.'

'Woke up at five,' I mumbled, slumping into the chair beside her desk. 'Couldn't get back to sleep. Finch case.'

She poured me out a mugful of coffee which I sipped at gratefully, feeling the caffeine coax my limp nerve ends into something like life. After waiting until I'd begun to revive, she said: 'So? What's the problem?'

I told her about the papers of Amanda's that I'd found and how David had responded to my ideas about them. 'It was hard to argue with him at the time, but the more I thought about it this morning, the more I wondered if *he* isn't the one who's romanticising. What the hell, you know, just because he's a shrink doesn't mean he's immune to psychological blind spots.'

She gave a short laugh. 'Quite the opposite from what I've heard. Go on. I'm intrigued.'

'Well, look, all he's really saying is that she wasn't a political thinker, but to him that also rules out political action. To me, on the other hand, it simply suggests that to act she'd have needed to be touched at gut level, like most Americans . . .'

'. . . and most women.'

'Yes, and I'm saying I think she *was* touched. I'm saying that she was moved to take a stand without consulting him. I'm saying, Suze, that she didn't *need* him in the one area where he was sure that she did. The poor guy was bound to get all defensive.' I shrugged. 'But what do you think?'

'I think it's impossible to eliminate anything yet – not until we've got a sharper picture of who she was. Have you had any further thoughts about where she might have got so much money for example?'

'She had a small inheritance. She could have saved it.'

'But why? She could equally have used it to set herself up freelance or buy her flat or do any number of other things.'

'Because she'd chosen to earn her own way. I respect her for that.'

'So do I – if it's true.'

'What do you mean "if"? It was one of the first things David told me about her.'

'Yes but like I said before, it seems to me that at the moment you're still obliged to treat all "could haves" with an open mind.'

I hesitated, aware that she was driving at something but uncertain what it was.

'Do me a favour,' she went on. 'Forget David's Amanda and her brother's Amanda and her best friend's Amanda and the Amanda you like and tell me honestly: what's the first thing you suspect when you hear that someone you've never met has a Swiss account?'

'Oh come on Suze,' I started.

'No *you* come on, Dee. What all the theories so far ignore are three little facts about this woman: she's known to have jumped a drugs charge, she helped a certified patient escape from a prison hospital, and she organised a forged passport.'

My first call was to Detective Superintendent Henning, whom I quizzed about Phil Knight's alibi. 'His wife and a neighbour have both confirmed that he was home at the time of the murders,' he told me. 'He left for the airport around lunchtime. We've also found a baggage attendant who remembers him.'

'And that evening?'

'He says he was working alone in his office and we haven't pursued it. Knight's not the one we're after – unfortunately.'

'What about the person who forged Carlos' passport? Are you trying to find him?'

Henning laughed. 'You angling for my job or something?'

'No, just doing mine. My clients are anxious about the progress of the investigation.'

'Are they now,' he declared, clearly amused by my equivocation. 'So Dr Blake is wondering about the extent of his wife's criminal contacts is he?'

'Not exactly,' I demurred.

'But you are?'

'It crossed my mind.'

105

He hesitated, then said: 'All right. Between you and me, we have the suspected forger in custody. I will keep you informed.'

My next call was to a client of mine who works as an investment consultant in the City. Could she, I asked, find out about the financial position of the Knight Agency for me? Could she trace the list of Asprey Oil shareholders? And if I gave her the number of a certain Swiss bank account, could she possibly discover when it had been opened and the frequency of subsequent deposits?

She said what I wanted to hear, which was that she'd do what she could.

Juan received me curtly when I arrived at the small Catholic church on the Harrow Road for Carlos' funeral. Connie looked strained. The service was conducted entirely in Spanish.

When it was over I took Connie to one side. 'Did you do it? Did you collect up all his . . .'

But she was biting her lip and shaking her head. She'd been unable to find her husband's travel receipts and worse, he'd caught her looking through his papers. He'd guessed that she'd confided in me.

She clutched desperately at my arm. Over her shoulder I could see him glaring at us. 'He says he's thrown them out Dee,' she whispered. 'And he's so angry with me he's hardly talking to me. He's not the same person since this happened to us. It frightens me. What I think frightens me.'

I was a bit unnerved myself but nevertheless murmured reassurances. She listened closely, nodding and straightening her shoulders, but her eyes said that she didn't quite believe me. I didn't quite believe me either.

My afternoon was lost in a series of appointments and emergencies, and to preparing for a case due for hearing the next morning. The evening disappeared in a meeting that lasted until eleven. In spare moments I made several false starts on a letter to Dr Alan Dexter and tried, unsuccessfully, to reach Amanda's former secretary Jackie. I didn't see David.

After I'd finished in court on Tuesday, I visited both the Chilean and American embassies and was fortunate enough in each to speak with sympathetic officials who agreed to find out for me whether Amanda had entered their respective countries on the dates I gave them. It would, though, take time, so I explained that I'd be going away soon and asked them to contact Suze.

When I returned to the office, there was a packet from my

investment consultant friend on my desk. Her cover note said:

Interesting link. Craig Asprey was a founder director of the Knight Agency; he resigned two years ago. He'd invested in its setting up and wrote off the amount as a tax loss the following year. He also helped with a cash flow problem in '79. The debt's since been paid off and the Agency's now showing a small profit.

I've spoken with my friend in Geneva this morning. She's tied up all day but will telex details tomorrow. We're closed as I expect you are. I'll ring you Thursday.

I looked for something sinister in the connection between Craig and Phil but didn't see anything. Amanda had presumably persuaded her brother to help create a job for her. If his money had still been in the firm just before she'd been killed, when she'd planned to resign, her boss might have had a financial motive for panicking. But it hadn't been.

The list of shareholders in Asprey Oil and its subsidiaries did not include Amanda's name.

I returned to my letter to Dr Dexter and was scowling at the piece of paper when Suze came in.

'Why write?' she said. 'Ring him from your mother's.' She leaned over and squinted at me. 'You haven't forgotten you're going away on holiday on Saturday, have you?'

I crumpled the sheet into a ball. I hadn't exactly forgotten; I just hadn't realised that Saturday was only three days off now.

'I tracked down that journalist friend of a friend. She could have spared you some time after lunch.'

'Shit.'

'I thought you'd be annoyed. However, as I happened to have a conference at Lincoln's Inn at twelve, I took the liberty of standing in for you.' She grinned. ' "Suze Aspinall, Private Detective". I rather like the way it curls around the tongue, don't you?'

'Stop tormenting me,' I laughed. 'What did she say about Phil?'

'You already know most of it I'm afraid. He's sociable but hard to work for. Men tend to like him except as a boss. Women journalists tend to think he's a pig. Did you get hold of a copy of his accounts?'

'Yes.'

'What's his salary?'

107

I looked it up and told her.

'Hmm,' she said. 'Maybe that's it. Apparently the gossip among his opposite numbers in other agencies is that he gets a lot more than that.'

'Why?'

'Expensive lifestyle, why else? Big house out in Bushey, two cars, wife doesn't work, three kids at the American School, deluxe hols . . . this woman Jackie who worked for Amanda – perhaps she'll know something about it.'

There was just this small problem called getting hold of Jackie. And even when I did at last get through to her flat, her flatmate would say only that she was away for an indefinite period and could not be reached. I left a message anyway.

David had spent the evening at his flat finishing off his packing up to move the next day. By the time he let himself into my place, I was dozing in front of the test pattern on the TV. Whatever we mumbled to each other, it didn't include the name Amanda.

When I arrived at Eve's Georgian terrace house in Hampstead that Wednesday afternoon, she guided me through a hallway lined with oriental hangings into a sunny conservatory. The royal pageant of the year, Charles and Diana's wedding, had been staged that morning and despite snide remarks from David about my ideological inconsistency, I'd watched the whole thing. So had Eve, so our getting to know you conversation over coffees was easy from the start. It carried on that way too and by the by I picked up that she'd qualified as a therapist five years earlier following the death of her husband and just as her sons were leaving home. She laughed. (I learned *that* quickly enough: she laughed a lot.) 'Now I keep cats.' On cue two Persians sloped in, examined us indifferently, chose the sunniest spots on the floor, stretched out and fell asleep. She called them (what else?) Sigmund and Karla.

Finally, as she refilled our mugs, Eve said: 'You know, don't you, that Barbara's got you cast as the Great Untangler of the Mysteries?'

'Oh dear, I was hoping that was you.'

'You evidently haven't consulted the police.'

I admitted I hadn't.

'Well,' she sighed, 'after I'd deliberated endlessly about my oath of confidentiality and decided it was best to offer up what I knew, they weren't interested. I hadn't seen her for a month, you see – and

108

I wasn't saying I was certain there was a link between her state of mind then and her murder. They told me very politely that they'd get back to me if they required any more "background information".' She shrugged. 'I guess they haven't.'

I took out my notebook. 'But I do.'

Amanda had waited as she often did until two minutes before the session was over, then she'd said: 'I had a dream about my parents the other night.' She'd glanced at the clock. 'I guess it'll have to wait though.'

But Eve had smiled. At long last it had happened. 'I've had a cancellation,' she was able to say. 'I've got plenty of time.'

Hostility had crossed Amanda's features: she'd felt tricked and didn't like it. Eve had wondered if she'd leave.

But no. Amanda used the business of lighting another cigarette to recover before reaching into her bag for her notebook. Then, once she found the page, she read from it as if it were a story that had nothing to do with her.

'I was standing by our old house outside Havana, looking for my parents' graves, when I noticed a basement entrance and decided to look down there. It was dim and eerie and very humid and there was such a terrible fetid smell that I started to turn back, but suddenly I heard a child crying and it was so sad that I held my breath and went towards it.

'At the end of the hall I came to a door with a small window in it, like in a hospital operating room. I looked in and saw all these people I knew standing on either side of a draped bier. Along the left were childhood friends like Estrella and her brother Miguel, my first boyfriend. Their parents were there too, with other local families, and next to them were Tommy and other men I've – ah – left, like José and Martin and – and Pedro.

'Opposite were people like Claire and Phil and Craig and Barbara and Alan Dexter.

'Suddenly they all began to shout across the bier, but I couldn't hear what they were saying – all I could hear was the crying – so I knocked. Miguel's mother began to come towards me. Craig waved at me to go away.

'I opened the door. The stench in there was unbelievable, but Miguel's mother dragged me in and I went to the bier, which I knew was my mother's. I shouted to everyone to shut up, but the only person who heard me was Alan, who said, "We've been waiting for you. She can't be buried unless you uncover her."

'I was horrified. Uncover her? A rotting corpse that I thought had been buried twenty years ago? I covered my eyes and refused. Then Pedro came and pushed me and said, "Look!"

'I did and there was this little girl, dressed as I was in one of the pictures I've got from the time. I sat beside her – she was the one who was crying – I hugged her and told her to stop. Then I started crying and she began to comfort me. She looked just like Astrid, which alarmed me. I couldn't stop crying and that's what woke me up.'

Shutting the notebook abruptly, Amanda looked up and shrugged. 'I picked up my Cuban visa yesterday. I suppose that's why, last night . . . it was obviously on my mind.'

'Are you having second thoughts about going back?'

'What if I am? I mean, Phil is really annoyed with me.'

'So? You expected that. You also reckoned he'd recover.'

'He won't if he finds out I plan to go to Cuba as well.'

'But that's the point of the rest of the trip, surely. Besides, it's your holiday time. What's it to him?'

Amanda mumbled inaudibly and looked away, ostensibly absorbed in stubbing out a butt in the ashtray.

Eve said: 'The problem isn't really Phil, is it?'

Amanda started turning her lighter over and over in her fingers, watching them move yet clearly preoccupied. 'No,' she said at last. 'No.'

'And visiting your parents' graves? Is that the problem?'

She shook her head.

'I see.' Eve paused and waited. Minutes passed. 'Well then, I guess you must be having qualms about poking around in the local records.'

A nod.

'Why?'

Amanda shrugged, glanced up, looked away again. 'It's stupid. What will it prove? I believed the evidence twenty years ago. Why open up the accident report again now?'

'You've told me, Amanda. You don't need to call it that in this room.'

Another shrug. 'What does it matter what I call it?'

'You deal with words. You know the importance of using the right one. Besides, this isn't semantics. There's a substantial

110

difference between an accident and a murder – and I mean, look: it's made a difference to you. It's only since your dream a few months ago, the one that made you tell me what really happened, that you've admitted that you may have accepted the official report twenty years ago, but you didn't like it.'

'Well it hurt for Christ's sake,' she said, suddenly angry. 'The two men who were convicted had been in and out of our house hundreds of times, *hundreds*.'

'Yes and part of your response to that hurt was to speak of what happened as an accident and bury your questions and doubts . . . I understand why you did that, you know I do. What I don't understand though is why you've returned to it now. Last week, when you let your doubts loose, they moved you to arrange this trip. This week . . .'

'This week I've come to my senses. Jesus, I've changed dozens of appointments, argued with Phil, put my job in jeopardy – and why? Because I had a few dreams that I persuaded myself had some bearing on reality.'

'Don't they?'

'No. The truth is there, in writing, and no wispy night phantoms can change that.'

Very softly Eve said: 'What are you so afraid of? Being right? Or being wrong?'

Amanda rolled her eyes upwards as if praying for help in communicating with an imbecile. 'I don't know why I come here. I can't say anything without you challenging my motives.' Then, eye to eye: 'I'm not – repeat not – "afraid" of anything. I've thought about it and I've decided it will be a waste of time. It's as simple and straightforward as that.' She glanced at her watch. 'I'm sorry. I've got to run.'

'Just one more point, please,' Eve said as her client made for the door. 'If what you've just told me is true, then explain this: in the dream, the only person you could hear was Alan Dexter, a man who specialises in uncovering secrets. Why don't you want to listen to him?'

Suze says that, knowing me, she's sure I'd have agreed to meet Amanda's former secretary Jackie that Friday evening even if Henning had rung me before I made the appointment with her instead of after. She says she remembers very clearly the way I told her that the police considered the case as good as solved.

'You were sceptical Dee. You walked into my office excreting doubt . . .'

'Don't you mean "exuding"?'

'No. Excreting. You excreted doubt the way you do when you tell me something in your "get a load of this" voice. And you were right. That's the point. God knows how or why either. It sounded like pretty solid circumstantial evidence to me: a tip-off about a derelict garage that turned out to be full of stolen goods, including all Barbara's things, all the things taken from the nearby houses, Amanda's typewriter for pity's sake *and* a van with a bootprint in the back that matched the bootprint outside the cottage. Hell, all things being equal, a careful stake-out like the one the police mounted could easily have netted them the random-burglar-turned-murderer they'd let themselves be convinced they were on to.

'Besides, let's face it, it's not as though the other ideas you had were leading anywhere. Phil's alibi looked firm. Your investment consultant friend found out that Amanda's Swiss account had been opened in '74, which didn't suggest anything at all. The Chilean Embassy worked fast and told you she hadn't been to their country. And while your conversation with Eve may have inspired you to request information from the Cuban Embassy as well, it left you completely bewildered otherwise.

'But for all that, when Henning rang you to say they'd definitely solved it, you didn't buy it. You went on about cover-ups and the police finding what they were supposed to find and thinking what they were supposed to think. Really, if Jackie had rung you then, you'd still have gone out of your way to meet her Friday night. Anyway, you like to finish what you start and she was a loose end.'

'Maybe I was just pissed off. That was David's opinion, remember? He said the only reason I was so determined to keep that appointment with her was because I was so annoyed at Henning.'

'A view which, as I recall, earned him his first taste of the full wrath of Dee Street.'

'Give me a break Suze. The mood I was in, the last thing I needed was him putting pressure on me.'

'I know, I know but the poor sod was *desperate* to believe it was all over and he'd spent *hours* organising that celebration cum farewell drinks party at the pub for Friday evening. He'd even arranged it early so you'd have time to do your washing and ironing and packing. He'd invited so many people too . . .'

112

'Yes but he could have had it at lunchtime. I mean, he was seeing Craig then anyway and he always said he hated seeing Craig alone. Jesus, if he'd only been willing to change it to the middle of the day I could have made it, and if I'd made it then perhaps . . .'

'Now Dee, don't be unfair. David was in the same position with Craig that you were in with Jackie: he couldn't get in touch with him. Besides, Phil was busy at lunch – several people were – but he particularly wanted Phil there to thank him for the way he'd handled the media. Come on: it was a reasonable decision at the time.

'And as for this business about you being pissed off, what does it matter if you were? Hell, I'd have been just as angry – *any* solicitor would have been. After all, we're not used to seeing ourselves as suspects . . . You've got to hand it to old Henning really. He may have missed a lot of things, but he didn't miss what was going on between you and David. . . Look at you: you still go all pink about it.'

'Well it embarrassed me! Imagine: they went around and asked Jack in the next allotment if I'd been there that Sunday she was killed.'

'So? You were. Goddammit, why am I lecturing you like this? You did what you had to do and it can't be helped now. Stop kicking yourself.'

It's easy for Suze to say that of course: she doesn't have my memories.

That was the year when everyone in the generation behind me seemed to have stepped out of the pages of the photo albums of the generation ahead of me, at least from the neck down, so I could tell that Jackie was young from her fifties' style. Her turquoise skirt flared to fullness at mid-calf from a waist cinched tight by a wide belt; her white blouse had padded shoulders; her emerald shoes were flat and pointy-toed. Hair styles, on the other hand, were visionary, and while it wasn't quite the period of razors and gells and day-glo colours, it was the run-up. Jackie's curls sat in a muff on top of her head; the sides and back were shaved.

Yet where the difference in our ages really told was in the deferential, almost wary look I saw in her kohl-ringed eyes as we approached each other on the pavement outside King's Cross. My self-image may have it that I'm a short, unprepossessing person usually at odds with the system, but she obviously viewed me as an older authority figure.

'I'm so sorry I've kept you waiting,' she started. She was about a minute late. 'I had to ring my boyfriend. He's picking me up here later and he's in a real state.'

I smiled, thinking ah, young love. 'How long have you been away?'

'Ten days.' Her jaw tightened. 'Since I was sacked.' Then she shook her head – she didn't want to talk about *that* – and said: 'But he's not in a state about *me*. It's his motorbike. He bought it a few days ago – second hand – and he's been fixing it up. He's a mechanic, terrific with cars and bikes. Anyway, he wanted to have it ready for when I got back, so when I rang yesterday and said I'd be coming a day earlier . . .'

'Oh dear,' I murmured. 'I didn't realise. Did I twist your arm that hard? Because if I did, I'm afraid that I . . .'

She seemed startled. 'But it was me who twisted your arm, wasn't it? I mean it's a Friday night – you're going away in the morning . . .'

'The police now believe they've solved the case though. They're certain it was a burglar.'

'Oh what?' she exclaimed. 'That's fantastic! What a relief for her family!' Then, with a puzzled frown: 'But I didn't want to see you because . . . I mean, you didn't think I'd have any ideas about *that* did you?'

I shrugged. 'I wasn't sure. You asked if I was solicitor for Amanda and her husband . . .'

Her hand fluttered to her cheek. She stared at me with her mouth open.

I gestured to her bag and smiled. 'Come on,' I said. 'I'll buy you a cup of tea.'

When we'd settled into seats in the Wendy Burger bar, cups in front of us, she began to apologise for misleading me. I cut her off. 'You did nothing of the kind. Forget it. Now – suppose you tell me why you wanted to see me.'

She sighed. 'It's simple really. I thought you could tell me how to contact her husband. I've been trying to reach him ever since – well, ever since it happened. First I got an answerphone and I hate those things; then I got no reply. Then I got an Indian-sounding man who gave me another number, but I got no reply there either. I began to worry that he'd gone away or something.'

'He's been around,' I told her, 'but he's off tomorrow – for two weeks.'

114

'Oh damn,' she muttered. 'I knew this would happen.'

'I can reach him for you tonight.'

She brightened. 'Can you? God, that would be wonderful.' She rummaged through her bag, pulled out her cheque book (what was this?) and a scrap of paper, wrote out the address of her bank and handed it to me. 'If he could send them a copy of his signature and say it's the one I said they could expect . . .'

'And can I tell him why he should do this?'

'Oh yes, sure, you see, the week Amanda got back – a couple of days before she left again – she asked me to go to the stationer's and buy her a deposit box. When I brought it back, she put a large manila envelope inside – she said it was research papers – and asked me to put it in my bank in my own name. The idea was that if she needed them quickly, she could ring me at home and have me post them on my way into work. Otherwise she'd have me fetch them for her when she got back. She gave me the afternoon off to do all this too. But then, the next day – Thursday it was – she came in and said that she wanted me to add her husband's name – make it a joint account – just in case.'

'In case of what?'

She looked at her hands. 'I didn't ask. She was in such a weird mood.' She straightened. 'Anyway, I told her that I knew the bank would need his signature and said should I ring him for her, but she said no, I should just write them the note and say his signature would follow. She said she'd get him to do it. I guess she forgot.'

'You've checked?'

'They sent me a reminder. It arrived the morning she . . . the morning I heard.'

'I see,' I said. 'Do I take it this was unusual? She'd never had you do this before?'

She nodded.

'And is it fair to assume you didn't tell the police?'

She wrinkled her nose and nodded again. 'Why should I tell *them*? They were her private papers. Besides, they didn't ask.' She smiled. 'Not that they could. I was hysterical. I don't think I've ever cried so much in my whole life.' Then: 'The truth is, though, that I did wonder if I should tell them. But I talked it over with B.J. – my boyfriend – before I went up to my parents, and we decided I should get in touch with her husband. The way we figured it, everything that was hers belongs to him now, including that envelope, so we thought: tell him about it, get him to collect it, and

115

leave it up to him whether to tell the police.' She shrugged. 'And if, like you say, they've solved it now, I guess we did right.'

'So you had a little doubt?'

'Yes,' she said. 'I think I did.'

'Well,' I admitted, 'I still do, I'm afraid. They haven't actually caught the murderer. There's no one behind bars, no confession. And now, even if David Blake writes to your bank, he won't know what's in the envelope for another fortnight.' I took a breath and said carefully: 'What I'm wondering is – how about this. If I can arrange it tonight, would you be willing to go into your bank Monday morning with one of my partners and open the box so she can examine the contents? She can note anything she thinks David should know and ring him if necessary. And if it is just full of innocuous research material, well – that will be that. At least everyone's mind will be at rest . . . What do you think?'

'If you think it's worth all that trouble, fine, I'll go along. It's not as though I have anywhere else to go on Monday morning. What shall I do? Ring you later?'

'I could ring you.'

She shook her head. 'We're going out and after that I'll probably stay at B.J.'s and he's not on the phone.'

I wrote out my home number and handed it to her. 'Give me till ten thirty or eleven.' Then, with that organised, I said: 'Does it upset you to talk about Amanda?'

'A bit.' But she smiled. 'Not that it stops me. I've bored the pants off my parents, and B.J. and my flatmate – well!'

'Would you like a fresh pair of ears? I'm interested. What was she like to work for?'

'Oh Jesus,' she declared, 'the best. *The* best. Kind. Patient. I mean, it was my first real job, you know? I was only eighteen when I started. I went in as a temp and I was hopeless. You wouldn't believe how hopeless I was. But for some reason she liked me, and she argued with Phil to keep me. She told me she thought women should help other women if they could, because it's so hard for us to get started. And then –' She leaned across the table and went on in a pleased whisper. 'The fact is Miss . . .'

'Dee.'

'Dee – the fact is, I don't care that I got the sack because I don't need Phil Knight. And do you know why? Because Amanda persuaded me to apply for a media course. I'm starting in six

116

weeks. I've even got my grant sorted out. I'd never dreamed of being a journalist myself – never. But she said, "well, why not?" She grinned.

'It sounds like she was awfully fond of you.'

'Not half so fond as I was of her. That's the real reason I got the sack, I'm certain. I was too "loyal" to her as far as Phil was concerned. I even know what the "last straw" was.'

'Oh?'

'Mmm. It was the day she rang to say she was going to add a bit of holiday on to her Latin American trip. She picked the time carefully so she wouldn't have to speak to him – the afternoon of the weekly journalists' meeting, when no one's meant to be disturbed for anything short of a coup somewhere. She asked me to leave him a note saying she'd be back a few days late and she was really apologetic – said she knew she was dropping me in it but figured I could handle it.

'Well! When he saw that note he came storming in so red-faced I thought he was going to have a heart attack on the spot – I mean, he must be at least forty and he'd been ill; that's why she went out there in the first place. That little manoeuvre didn't please him either, but that's another story. Anyway, he started in at me: was this all she'd said and didn't she leave a number and where was she and how could she be so irresponsible and how could I be so stupid and why hadn't I come into the meeting and said she was on the phone. It was just over the top, even for him, and he's got an incredibly short fuse. It didn't exactly make me feel like co-operating and I did something I'd never dared do before: I told him I'd appreciate it if he'd refrain from speaking to me as if I were a born idiot. You can imagine what that provoked.'

She laughed. 'And of course, the point was that if he'd been civil, I might – just might – have told him that I had a pretty good idea where she was. Fortunately there was no chance and I was bloody glad I'd kept my mouth shut when she got back and I realised she had no intention of telling him the truth.'

Questions had begun to queue up so fast in my mind that all I could manage was 'Oh?'

She nodded. 'She lied to him, I heard her – well, everyone heard her, only *I* knew she was lying. She didn't go to Barbados, Miss – Dee. Or if she did, that's not where she was the whole time. She rang from America; I know because the operator cut in to tell her the time and charges.'

117

My hands tightened around my cup. Somehow I got my voice to work. 'I don't understand. Why would she have lied about that? Do you have any idea?'

Jackie's young eyes turned old, careful, as she studied my face. 'Yes,' she said finally. 'Yes. I do. You see, Amanda once told me ... no. I'll begin at the right place. It wasn't only because she was such a wonderful boss that I'd have done anything for her. She ... that is, I ... oh hell. I got pregnant a little over two years ago. I'd been working for her all of about six months, I was nineteen, I was living alone in a bedsit and I'd got drunk at a party full of people I didn't really know.

'It was a stupid mistake, really stupid, and I got all screwed up about what to do. One day she took me out to lunch and told me she'd guessed I was in some kind of trouble, so I told her. She and I talked about all the options for me and finally – well – I had an abortion. She helped me get it, went with me, everything. I was only six weeks along – nine when I had it – and even though it was awful and I'd never do it again, I've always been glad.

'The point is though, when we were talking about it, she told me something she said she'd never told anyone: she'd been pregnant once too, only she'd had the baby and given it up for adoption. In America.

'I couldn't help it, I asked her if she wasn't curious. She said of course. And *then* she said she knew who had her too. Can you imagine? All those years, knowing? I mean, she didn't say, but I suppose her daughter could be, well, a teenager.'

'Are you saying you think she might have decided to visit this daughter?'

She nodded. 'Almost positive. It explains why she lied, and it explains that really weird mood she was in. Also, she was finding it impossible to write up that trip – that's why she went away again – and I think it was probably because she was so upset. Wouldn't you be? But there's something else too – proof. Her first day back, that awful Monday morning when she rowed with Phil and he hired that new freelancer Mike – well, after that row she went into her office, slammed the door and started typing. I thought it was a letter of resignation, you could tell it was something difficult because she kept ripping paper out of the machine. But then a little later she came out with an envelope under her arm and said she'd be gone an hour or so.'

'Was this around lunchtime?'

118

She looked thoughtful. 'It must have been. Why?'

'She came to see me. Anyway, what's this about proof? Did you rummage through her dustbin or something?'

'I didn't have to. She'd left one of her false starts on top of her out tray. She'd begun "To my darling daughter", but she'd made a typing mistake. I figured she hadn't meant to leave it there and I threw it away.' Jackie stopped and frowned. 'Look, I shouldn't have told you this. You won't tell anyone, will you?'

'Of course not. Who would I tell?'

She shrugged. 'Good point.' She glanced at her watch. 'I wonder where the hell B.J. is.'

'There's one more thing I wanted to ask you. Have you heard this rumour that Phil lives – well – above his means?'

She laughed. 'Ha. Who hasn't.'

'Any idea how he does it?'

She leaned towards me again. 'They say he gambles. Why? Do you think he's involved in something funny? I wouldn't put it past h – ' Suddenly there was a tap on the window next to us. 'B.J!' she cried, then jumped to her feet and rushed out. I watched the two of them hug and couldn't help smiling to myself. If she'd stepped out of a photo album, he'd stepped out of *Rebel Without a Cause*, right down to the pomp hairstyle and pack of cigarettes rolled up into the shoulder of his short-sleeved white T-shirt. The only flaw in his image was the expression of happiness on his face.

I picked up Jackie's bag, took it out to her, met him briefly, reminded her to ring me and watched them climb on to a BMW and drive off down the Euston Road.

Was I really in such a daze that I lost control of my body? So it seemed. For as I approached the kerb to cross and catch my bus, someone from the crowd around me gave a hard push, knocking me to my knees. As I let out a startled cry, I felt my bag being yanked from my shoulder. Two men stooped to help me up, but I pushed their arms away and pointed to the figure running towards St Pancras. One of the men set off after him. The other took my elbow, got me to my feet, gave me 50p to get home.

And once there, I had to make arrangements not only with David and Suze (both of whom were wonderfully sympathetic) but with my bank, American Express and other credit card bureaux.

Yet for all that, what upset me the most that night was that Jackie never phoned.

119

Seven

Nothing seemed to go right that Saturday morning. The locksmith arrived at eight fifteen instead of seven thirty, and with the wrong bits to change my front door locks. David's car refused to start and it was only after the AA had arrived that he discovered his card had expired. We decided to take a cab but had to walk almost to Marble Arch before getting one. The check-in queue at Heathrow was immense, so we jumped it, provoking black looks from the other passengers and a reprimand from the attendant. And after we'd run like crazy to board the flight before the gate closed (and just made it), the plane taxied out, stopped, turned around and went back.

Everyone was asked to disembark and for the next two hours we waited in a hot stuffy lounge which gradually filled with the distress cries of uncomfortable infants and the wingeing of five hundred adults. We joined in.

Finally, at one pm, our plane took off for Los Angeles.

I glanced through the flight magazine and had to smile. 'I've seen the film,' I said to David.

He laughed. 'So have I.'

The hot drinks and the papers eventually arrived, and after diverting myself with the *Guardian* crossword, I turned to the inside pages to scan the news. The item was on page four, in one of the 'News In Brief' columns.

Headlined 'Hit and Run', it said: 'Police are looking for witnesses to the accident which occurred around 10.30 pm last night on the Westway flyover and took the life of Jacqueline Newlands, 22, of Hackney. The driver of the motorcycle on which she was a passenger and which apparently collided with another vehicle has been identified as Benjamin James, 22, of Islington. He is now in a coma at St Mary's Hospital, Paddington.'

I must have made a strangling noise because when I threw the page at David and tried to say 'Look at that', he was already staring at me with concern. Somehow my hand found the bag in the pocket of the seat in front of me and I was sick.

There was commotion of course: David rubbing my back, the passenger across the aisle signalling the steward, a glass of cold water, a towel, soothing words that assumed I must be sensitive to external turbulence. I forced myself to smile and protest just so people would stop looking at me.

When they had, I said to David: 'Well?'

But he merely sighed, shook his head and gazed out the window.

'You see it now, don't you?' I persevered. 'This was no accident. And no "random burglar" killed Amanda and Carlos.'

He gave a slight, reluctant nod.

'These murders, your flat, Michael's office, my handbag,' I carried on, 'they're all connected. Someone was afraid of what Amanda knew about something, and now they're afraid that there's still some scrap of evidence that will reveal their identity. And goddammit, whoever they are, they must have been watching Jackie and me in that Wendy's. They must have taken my bag because they saw her hand me that slip of paper and maybe, when they saw the bank address she'd written down, they figured I was going to pay her for information . . . the bastards,' I fumed. 'Bloody evil bastards. A sweet kid like that . . . and her boyfriend . . . I mean, honestly. An "accident". That's ridiculous. He was a skilled mechanic, an experienced driver. And *I* had to be the one who got them into that position.' The feeling of sickness rose again and I struggled to quell it.

'I'd say you're lucky to have got away in one piece,' he said. 'They must have been following *you*.'

'Me? What do I know? I'm no risk to anyone. No, the really lucky thing if you ask me is that I'd already brought that address book and those letters home and put them in my suitcase. If they'd been in my bag . . .'

David faced me abruptly. 'What address book? What letters?'

'The ones I took from Amanda's study last Sunday.'

'Jesus, you mean you'd been intending to keep this up? Over in California? *After* the Norfolk police had solved it?'

'After they claimed they'd solved it . . . but yes, I have been intending to make a few phone calls. Her old friends deserve to know what's happened and I'm sure that Dr Alan Dexter can put me in touch with most of them. I expect Craig can be persuaded to

121

tell me how to reach this woman Claire, his ex- . . . And I thought, while I was talking to them, I'd try to find out if any of them had seen her after she left Nicaragua and before she got back to London.'

'What in heaven's name are you talking about?'

I squinted at him. 'Why are you being so sharp with me? You said you'd rather I didn't air my speculations around you and I've respected your feelings. The fact is though that Jackie said Amanda rang the office from America. What's more, she believed Amanda went back there for personal reasons.' I told him about the illegitimate child.

He looked pained but his expression didn't seem to be addressed to this new fact. 'And do you honestly think,' he said, 'that she confronted the adoptive parents and that they then followed her across an ocean and into the English countryside? Do you know how far-fetched that is?'

'Yes. Very. It means they're insane.'

'Exactly.'

I frowned at him. 'How can you say that so dismissively? Have you forgotten your own statement to the police? You yourself said the wrecking of Barbara's cottage had to be the work of a madman. And there was that note she left too – "be careful of Diana and Bruce". *They* might be the ones . . . and I *bet* there's some important clue about all this in the deposit box that Amanda had Jackie put in her bank.'

'Don't tell me. What you really want to do when the plane lands is go back to London.'

'It's tempting, and if I knew which bank the box were in, I'd seriously consider it. As it happens, you're the only one who can go in and open that box without a court order.'

'Which the police could get.'

'Yes. They don't know it exists yet of course, and they'll have the same problem – trying to discover which bank it's in.' I shrugged. 'Her flatmate might know, or her parents, but I don't imagine they'll feel much like discussing banks for a few days. And besides, if the police open the box without you present, we may never know what's really in it.'

There was a long silence. David stared at the clouds and I stared at the back of his head, thinking bleak pessimistic thoughts. My impulsive decision to invite him to California suddenly felt like a mistake. I wondered: were he and I a mistake? Had I just fallen (again) for a smile and an interesting ideological line, and let sympathy and guilt (and lust) push me too fast? (Me and my grandiose ideas about soul mates – honestly.)

And yet, I hadn't been disappointed by either the smile, the line or the lust. It was only this new side that made me uncertain of him, not least because I found myself reconsidering his urgent need to put Amanda's death behind him. Was it really, as I'd assumed, a response to the specific strains of this event? Or was there some – what? – some coldness beneath the surface that I would encounter more often as I came to know him better? And I wondered: had Amanda had secrets because sometimes he made it too damn difficult to confide in him?

Lunch arrived and as we ate he talked in a forced kind of way about sightseeing tours and camping, as if he were trying to persuade himself that the holiday would be what he'd imagined. I went along with it because – well, because what the hell, it might turn out that way.

I guess, though, that the pretence made him as uncomfortable as it made me. When the stewardess had removed our trays, he said: 'What if I were to suggest that you ring Henning, tell him about the people you want to speak to, and get him to work with the police in America – let them do the contacting?'

'I'd reject the idea. I doubt Henning could persuade any American police to co-operate at this point even if he wanted to. There's nothing concrete for them to do. That's why I want to ask a few questions – so I can see if there are any new facts Henning might use. Anyway David, you know as well as I do how people feel when the police come calling. That response would be counterproductive. I'm not so threatening.'

He rolled his eyes upwards sceptically.

That did it. 'Why the fuck does it bother you so much that I want to make a couple of phone calls? Have I asked you to help? Have I even hinted that you should give up so much as a minute of your goddamn holiday? Why do you have to act so bloody superior? What's wrong with you?'

'There's nothing wrong with *me*,' he answered coolly. 'You're the one with the problem. You seem to think this is "Cluedo" or something, just a parlour game where you can sit around deducing that the crime was committed in x room with y weapon by the butler and if you guess right, that's the end of it; we can pack up the board and go to the beach. Well allow me to disabuse you. This is serious – much, much more serious than I'd realised. Whoever this murderer is, he's killed three people already and I hardly think a fourth or a fifth will matter. Do you see what I'm saying? If you guess right, it's not the end of the game, it's the end of *you*.'

I stared at him, incredulous. 'You really must think I'm a fool.'

'You're sure as hell not Wonderwoman.'

'And you're sure as hell not Superman.'

'I know,' he said as the cabin went dark for the film, 'but I'm not trying to be.'

Because he was a foreign tourist, David cleared Customs quickly, whereas I had to make small talk with an official who assumed that I couldn't possibly have chosen to live abroad. 'You must be so relieved to be home,' she declared, staring right into my eyes. I stared back and nodded, but I guess my nod lacked the enthusiasm she expected, for she then unzipped my suitcase and spent several minutes satisfying herself that there weren't any Swiss watches or fresh vegetables concealed among my well worn Marks and Spencer T-shirts. I emerged into the terminal of LA Airport just in time to hear myself being paged.

Certain it was my mother calling to say welcome home (she hates the drive to the airport) I left David with the bags and hurried to the airline counter. But the contralto voice on the other end of the line had a Spanish accent which my mother's didn't.

'Is that Dee Street?' it asked.

'Yes. Who . . .?'

'You don't know me,' the woman went on. 'I am calling to warn you. You must not continue asking questions about the murders of Amanda Finch and Carlos de la Fuente . . .'

'Now wait a minute,' I cut in, 'who the hell . . .?'

'Please. Listen to me. You are in danger and you must stop for your own safety. If you do not believe me, ask the man at the counter why your flight was delayed leaving London.'

'Oh Jesus,' I muttered. 'If this is some kind of game . . .'

'Do it,' she said.

I cupped the receiver with my hand, leaned over the counter and spoke to the clerk. He shrugged. 'Bomb scare.'

Oh Lord, I thought. 'Real?' I managed. 'Or hoax?'

'I'm afraid I don't know, lady.'

'Okay,' I said to the caller. 'Now suppose you tell me –'

'Think about it,' she interrupted. 'For your own sake.' Then she hung up.

And I – well, I'm not a physically brave person, so I took her advice. I slid into the back seat of the taxi beside the bags and thought about it, all the way to Malibu.

Although my mother retired not long after my father died, she's held on to two things, at least, from her years as a legal secretary: her friends (she collects them, and has saved them all) and her ability to recognise trouble instantly. This meant that even as she was reaching out to give me a welcoming hug, her expression was saying that she'd already scented the strain between David and myself. It also meant that she'd told so many people about the arrival of her prodigal daughter and the real live Englishman that a steady turnover of company kept us from talking about it.

Finally, after we'd both watched David knock back his third neat whisky, my mother began to whisper to her neighbour the character actress Marcia; moments later Marcia put her well-tanned arm through David's, shouted at everyone to shut up and announced a guided tour of the beach. Suddenly the house emptied.

My mother, who was looking closer to fifty-five than to her actual sixty-eight anyway, gave me a pleased smile that took off another five years. 'Give,' she said.

I told her the whole story.

By the end she'd gotten up and was standing at the kitchen sink staring out into the back yard, and for a long while after I'd finished she just stared like that, saying nothing. When she eventually turned back around to face me, there was such an aching expression in her eyes that I automatically started up, but she got to me first and, leaning down, ran her hand along my cheek.

'I hoped you'd avoid the violence,' she said softly. 'I hoped you'd really stick to divorces and wills.' She straightened and laid her palm gently on the top of my head. 'But so be it.' Then she went to the refrigerator and took out a fresh pitcher of iced tea and sat down beside me again at the table.

'Do you have a plan?' she asked me. Despite the message in her eyes, her tone was matter of fact. I relaxed.

'Only to call Alan Dexter . . .' I glanced at the clock, '. . . preferably before it gets much later back East . . . What I do after that will depend on what he can tell me.'

'So if he says yes, she did know who these undercover people were – they were Diana and Bruce, or Jane and John Doe maybe – and I just happen to have their address right here . . .?'

'I'd want to go see them.'

'And you'd want to see this old friend of hers Natalie, too, I guess.'

'Yes. And anyone else in that crowd he can put me in touch with.'

'To ask about the possible Hispanic connections.'

I nodded. 'And about her teenage daughter.'

'And you definitely want to talk to them face to face.'

I nodded again. 'Now that I'm close enough to have someone worried, yes. Besides, you're the one who always used to say that you lose the most important subtleties over the telephone.'

'Sometimes you never even get to them.' She drank and set her glass down carefully. 'So. Sounds to me like you'll be needing to get yourself some protection.'

'I thought I'd drop in on Paula's dad.'

'In Palm Springs?'

'Oh hell, he hasn't gone and retired at last, has he?'

'I thought I told you. When he hit seventy-five, Flo said she'd had enough.'

I sighed. It would have been good to get some help from someone familiar – someone that professional . . . I said: 'Well with all your contacts, mom, you must know another private eye.'

She smiled. 'Yes. And so do you. The boys took over from Paul. Made a lot of changes too I hear. Expanded things. Modernised. They do a good – personal bodyguard service.' She shook her head in the way that meant she'd had enough of that. 'Are you going to tell me what's eating that poor man David?'

'I wish I knew. He's wanted to look straight ahead ever since he was cleared of suspicion, which I've just about been able to understand. But the way he immediately pushed Jackie's murder away – well – I couldn't help it, I thought: what if it happened to me? Would he want to ignore my death too?'

She frowned. 'Have you *asked* him what's going on?'

'Are you kidding? He's English. It would be an invasion of "privacy".' (I pronounced this to rhyme with 'give-acy'.)

'My my honey, you sure have mastered their rules.'

'When in . . .'

'Yes and when in California . . . he's on our turf now Dee, and so

126

are you. You've got to talk to him about it. You need to know whether he's in or out.'

I thought: and whether he and I are on or off. (And I realised they were the same.)

I said: 'First I need to find out exactly what I'm asking him to be in or out *of*.'

Dr Alan Dexter as I'd pictured him wasn't a man who would pick up the phone on half a ring and snap 'Yeah' into the receiver. Nor did I see him as the type who would say 'Who wants to know?' when I asked for the open, helpful, well-spoken university lecturer I was calling to talk to. And I certainly never expected that when he heard my name he'd blow his lips as if it had pushed him over the line into absolute exasperation.

'How did you get my number?' he wanted to know.

'From a letter you wrote Amanda Fin–'

'Jesus H Christ,' he cursed.

'Look,' I carried on, 'she's dead – she's been murdered. All I want to do is ask you a few questions.'

'You and who else.'

'I work for myself,' I protested, aware that my voice had moved into the upper octave. 'Her husband's my client. I just need –'

'I'll tell you what you need: a brain scan. Now listen to me,' he said, 'don't call this house again. In fact, do yourself a favour and stay off the telephone while you're over here.' And with that he hung up.

I placed the receiver back into its cradle and stared at it. Stay off the phone while I'm 'over here'?

How could he know I was in the States?

(Somebody sure as hell knew. A woman with a Spanish accent knew.)

And why had he been so curt with me?

I dug the letter from Natalie Giovanni out of my bag and dialled the number at the top a couple of times, using different area codes. No one anywhere had heard of her. The Las Vegas number Claire Asprey had given in her last letter also turned out to be out of date, as did the numbers for Howard Louder and Stephen Bruce listed in Amanda's old address book.

When I tried long-distance information for San Francisco, the operator just laughed at me. 'Sweetie,' he said, 'I'm staring at eight pages of Whites and not one of 'em's named May. There are loads of M. Whites and T. Whites and Thomas Whites, but unless you can give me some kind of address . . .'

Nice, Dee, I thought. Nice. People warn you to stop and you can't even get started.

I went out to the back yard where my mother was putting hamburgers and corn on the barbecue. 'Mom,' I said, 'you don't suppose "the boys" have a computer research facility do you?'

The combination of alcohol, sun, the jetlag, culture shock, and (presumably) strained communication with me dragged David off into a heavy sleep on the living room sofa at about eight thirty. I told myself I didn't care and didn't try too hard to wake him, but after mom and I had caught up on each other's news and I went up to bed alone, I felt the anger beginning to churn again in my stomach. An hour full of bitter resentful thoughts later, I cursed heterosexual love, cursed the couple dream in which I still seemed to share and took a sleeping pill.

I awoke abruptly the next morning at about seven. Sounds were drifting up from below: clattering pans, running water, a high laugh, a deep voice. Sun shone around the edges of the blinds. Was there hope? Maybe there was. We couldn't go through two weeks like this, that was for damn sure. We had to decide about us and we had to do it immediately.

(Yeah!

You tell him Dee!)

When I woke up the next time an hour and a half had passed and the house was quiet. I got up quickly, went over to the window, pulled back an edge of the blind and looked out. My mother and David were in the far corner of the garden kneeling by a small fruit tree and patting the soil around its base, a shovel lying between them. He was wearing short faded cut-offs and no shirt or shoes and as I watched he stood, brushed the dirt off his knees and extended a hand to help her rise. Together they turned and walked slowly across the grass, he talking earnestly, she listening and nodding. She gestured towards the patio, just beneath my room, and as they headed for the chairs, I ducked back.

He was telling her about his boyhood in South Yorkshire but going into much more detail than he'd gone into with me, especially about his mother. I'd known, for example, that she'd been widowed when David was seven (his father had had black lung) and that it had been her active membership in the Labour

128

Party that had inspired him to get so involved in politics himself. What he'd never said was that it hadn't been any old driver who had run into her during a snowstorm and left her in a coma from the time he was twelve until her death when he was fifteen. It had been the local property developer whose plans for a certain playing field she'd begun to campaign against. Nor had he ever mentioned that he'd applied for a Council scholarship to boarding school because he hadn't wanted to live with his mother's sister, who thought the property developer a decent, blameless man and David a silly impertinent lad. The anger that had made him do that (he said) had made him study so hard he'd got into medical college – and by the by carried out his late father's wish that he become anything but a miner.

My mother began to tell one of her favourite stories about her own mother, so I went off to shower and dress. When I raised the blind twenty minutes later she made a visor out of her hand, looked up and waved. David was lying on his back on the grass with his eyes closed and didn't see.

Mom and I met in the kitchen, where she announced that she had some shopping to do. She kissed me on each cheek, patted me on the back and wished me luck.

I took the coffee pot out with me and refilled his mug. He didn't move, just said thanks.

I noticed anew how tightly toned he was across the chest and shoulders, and how flat across the stomach. Where his love of long hikes really told though was in the shape of his calves, and suddenly I had a memory of them, of that body, wrapped around mine. Of its own accord my free hand reached out to touch him, but I pulled it back and instead sat down in my mother's chair.

'We have to talk,' I said. 'This is stupid.'

'Yes,' he said.

'Okay. My position is that I have to find out who these people are who killed Amanda and Carlos and Jackie. I have to know why they did it.'

'They'll bloody whip you off and tell you themselves if you carry on like this,' he said. He sat up and looked at me with an expression that made my desire turn tail. 'I know about the call at the airport. I cannot for the life of me understand why you don't go to the police. It's one of the few good reasons for having them, one of the jobs they're trained for. This person or people – they're professional killers. They need to be handled by professionals.'

129

'I agree. That's why –'

'That's why you should hand all the papers over to them.'

'No. I can't. Apart from anything else, I stole one of them.' I told him at long last about the will notes.

He looked as if he might be sick. 'This was a bad idea, wasn't it,' he managed to say. 'I shouldn't have come with you.'

I got to my feet feeling really annoyed. 'Yes. I wish I'd known you could be so cold before I invited you. But better late than never as they say. Better I'm not lying dead and discover you just want to *ignore* it and get on with your life.'

He stood up instantly. 'Is that what you think? Jesus. You don't listen, do you? Ignoring it – ha! I'm trying to stop you from getting yourself killed, can't you see? I'm trying to stop you doing what my mother did, which was take on more than she could bloody handle by herself. I'm trying to prevent you from going off half-cocked *on your own*.' He was shouting.

'I'm *not*,' I yelled back.

'You are!' he bellowed.

'I'm *not*. God almighty, you don't half make assumptions. I'm not your mother and I won't let you turn me into her either. Thanks to *my* mother, I've got the use of a goddamn bodyguard. I've got the services of an entire professional private detective agency!'

At this (to which he quite patently had no reply), he shoved on his sunglasses, hit some invisible bits of grass off his thighs, turned abruptly and made for the beach.

It took only moments for me to realise that I was completely on my own and a second to decide that I'd really feel much safer out in the open in the middle of people. I left a note on the door for mom and for the 'escort' who was due any time before lunch and went down to the beach myself.

I picked a spot within sight of the house, applied a layer of grease, and lay down to let the sun get to work on my pasty skin. I'd brought a novel but even if I'd been able to concentrate, on my back reading was no good. I shut my eyes and the darkness immediately filled with racing thoughts: Jackie – Amanda – Carlos – (David) – Amanda – Jackie – Amanda – (David). The sun's heat quickly stilled them however – or I presume it must have, because when the husky voice spoke into my ear, my heart and body both jumped.

Paula tried to laugh and say she was sorry at the same time but the laughter won and she was still shaking with it even as she sat down beside me on my towel and gave me a big hug. After that we just grinned at each other for a long moment. (It was always like this with us. Years passed but somehow, whenever we got together, we picked up as if we'd left off only yesterday.)

'This is amazing,' I said when my voice came back. 'I called your apartment last night to *ask* if there was any way you could fly down. My trip up to San Francisco – well, I don't know about it now. I've gotten myself all involved in this murder investigation, you see, and . . .'

'Paul's told me all about it. He said to tell you that Pete's had the computer going on the material overnight and has some results for you. In fact I thought he'd be here by now.'

I looked nervously over my shoulder. 'To tell you the truth I'm more concerned about this "bodyguard" I'm meant to be having. Did Paul happen to mention when . . .'

Paula stuck her arms out to either side. 'Ta dah,' she trumpeted.

At first I didn't get it. Then, suddenly, I did.

My voice failed again, leaving my mouth to work soundlessly for a while. '*You*,' I said at last. 'You, Paula? But you . . . but you're . . .'

'Watch it. Don't you be sexist. You went into your dad's line of work. What's wrong with me doing it?'

I looked at her five foot one inch frame. She and I had been the shortest girls in our high school graduating class, but the word 'gamine' had always applied to her in a way that it hadn't to me. More to the point though, she'd spent several months in the hospital the year before recovering from head injuries and broken bones.

'You're that fit?' I said.

'Listen,' she laughed, 'I am *so* fit . . . and I owe it all to the self-defence classes at the rape recovery centre. God was I depressed before those. Oh and thanks for all your cards by the way. I really meant to write.'

I didn't ask why she hadn't. Paula never wrote letters.

'Anyway,' she went on, 'I wasn't in any shape to go back to my old job –' She'd taught skiing, tennis and water sports at a resort north of Vancouver. '– and I was desperate to be active and really angry – just so angry – and the course seemed right. I turned out to be good at it . . .'

'Surprise surprise.'

131

She shrugged. 'I signed up for the teacher's course and when Paul found out – well, it all fit in with his plan to expand the San Francisco office. Weird, isn't it? If you'd told me last time we were together that I'd end up working with my brothers, I'd have told you you were bananas.'

She shook her head and began to brush the sand by her feet with the flat of her palm. 'That bastard – coming to terms with what he did to me – my life's changed in other ways too. Remember how frustrated I used to feel about never meeting a man I wanted to stay with? Well, that's all over now, that restlessness. I've found the person.'

'Oh Paula! That's wonderful! It's not anyone I know, is it?'

She glanced at me – hesitated – then looked away. 'No,' she said. 'Her name's Kathy.' Then she looked at me again.

I understood. How could I not? But at the same time an uncontrollable ripple of feeling, half anger, half sadness, made me shiver. (*Men*. Jesus.) As we held each other's gaze, I felt my eyes dampen.

She said: 'I'm contented now Dee, honestly contented.' She stared out at the waves again. 'In fact, my only worry at this moment is you.'

'Me? Jeez Paula, it doesn't make any difference to me what you . . .'

'I know it doesn't,' she cut in. 'That's not what I meant. What I meant was, I only faced one brute. You seem to have two after you.'

I flinched. 'Oh what?'

'I didn't think you knew,' she said, jumping to her feet and heading towards the water. 'Come on.'

By the time I caught up with her, she'd already squatted by the shoreline, dug out a couple of handfuls of mud, patted them into a mound, and was letting another handful trickle through her fingers. As I stooped beside her, she said: 'Remember the drip castles we used to build together? Some team, weren't we?'

'I'll say. I also remember the wicked gleam in Peewee's eye when he'd come charging at our carefully balanced turrets with his shovel, the little creep. But why the hell are you making one now? And what did you mean, two? And how do you know?'

She kept on digging, patting and trickling. 'This is called looking normal and I'm doing it because they're watching us. I saw them from your mother's. They look like Chicanos – which, as

132

you know, on *this* beach . . .'

'Oh God. At the airport, a woman with a Spanish accent . . .'

'I know. That's what made me notice these two.'

'Where are they?'

She nodded towards the ocean. 'One of them's out there on a surfboard, just beyond the breakers. No – don't look yet. We'll go for a walk in a minute. The other one's behind us, up by the dune in front of the big pink house with the cluster of palms by the gate. He's wearing black trunks and those mirror sunglasses and pretending to read a newspaper.' She dripped one last turret on to her castle, rinsed her hands in the moat and leaned back to admire her work. 'Ready?'

We both stood up and started walking.

'There are a couple of other things you ought to be aware of. I checked your mom's phone and had a general look around for bugs.'

Appalled, I stopped. 'Oh they haven't,' I groaned.

'Keep walking,' she smiled. Then, when I'd obeyed: 'I'm afraid they have, whoever "they" may be. But whoever they are, one thing's for sure – they're sloppy. I mean, the tap has set up a really noticeable echo. I had your mom listen. She's positive it's new today, so there's no harm done. And if I were you, I'd pretend I didn't know about it. If you play it right, you might persuade them you're going to stop. The same goes for the bug I found. It's in the back yard in one of the fruit trees. A directional microphone.' She wrinkled her nose. 'Honestly, it's so old fashioned, and so obvious, you know? Nearly useless outside like that too . . . Okay, this is far enough. Let's just pause and look at the sea.'

We did, and found ourselves staring right at the man on the surfboard. I noticed his Zapata-style moustache before he averted his face and paddled on.

'Get a load of that, eh?' Paula muttered. 'Talk about uncool.'

We turned and walked back towards the towel. The other man had also kept pace with us and now stood with his hands on his hips ostensibly studying the seagulls overhead. Although his skin was olive rather than brown and his features seemed to be Caucasian, the mirror shades made me think of the Ton Ton Macoute. Was my nerve, I wondered, up to this level of intimidation?

'*He*'s not very subtle either,' Paula remarked. 'Well? Ever seen them before?'

I shook my head and said with as much equanimity as I could

summon: 'But I have a terrible feeling that I know who they are – who they must be.' As I bent to pick up my clothes, I explained Connie's theory. 'David doesn't believe Amanda had enough political commitment to even think of passing information to a left-wing group, but judging by what's happened the past twenty-four hours . . .'

'Judging by what's happened the past twenty-four hours, I'd think twice before I paid these people the compliment of calling them "intelligence" agents.'

I glanced at her sharply. 'So you dismiss the idea too?'

'I'm not dismissing anything – not yet. I'm just saying that if what I've seen so far is a sample of the quality of the work of right-wing Latin American intelligence agents, the whole of the southern hemisphere would have turned communist twenty years ago.'

'Shit,' I grumbled. 'Then who the hell are they?'

'God knows,' she smiled, slipping her arm through mine. 'But one thing's for damn sure, you look like you could use a drink. Come on.'

We'd nearly reached my mother's house – were so close that she and Pete were looking at us expectantly from the patio – when I realised that David was walking up the sand towards us. I glanced at Paula, then back at him, then back at her. She smiled again and patted me on the shoulder. 'Your mom told me. See you up at the house.' And with that she joined the others, who all turned and went inside.

David was wearing a shirt again, unbuttoned, and had acquired freckles across his nose and forehead. The rest of him had begun to turn an even pinkish bronze. We stood three feet apart, facing each other, in silence for a long moment before he took off his sunglasses and showed me his sad eyes. He said: 'I want you to know how sorry I am, Dee. The last thing I meant to do was insult you. I just never expected . . . I just assumed . . .'

I held out my arms to him and he took a step forwards and suddenly we were holding each other. He sighed a deep relieved sigh and murmured into my hair, telling me how he'd only today realised the extent and depth of his fearfulness for me and understood that it had been making him act – well – 'odd' – not himself. He said he wanted to help – said he had to help, for his own peace of mind. He said more too – more about us and not wanting

Amanda to come between us and all manner of things which interested only me.

But midway through all the reassurances and the nuzzling and the soothing and making up I began to be aware of something pulling me away from this romantic scene. It was like ammonia – like an acrid burning something – not very nice – coming from David – from the sleeve of his shirt – where I was pressing my nose.

I began to cough then and had to step back.

He frowned and had a sniff. 'That's the trace of my news,' he said. 'I've been getting myself ready to help. I ran into Marcia and her husband this morning. He told me where to find it. I've been at the gun club, Dee. I'm going back later. And I've enrolled you for a couple of lessons too.'

Eight

Faced with a thick address book and not much time, Pete had limited himself to searching through the records for California only. He hadn't been able to go any further than the names as given either, which meant that women who'd assumed married names were as lost to us as people who lived out of state. And unfortunately, for whatever reason, both Natalie and Claire were missing.

On the other hand, the list of contacts he *had* found for us was long – twenty-five names – and it did include Stephen Bruce (of Hollywood), Howard Louder (of Big Sur) and May White (of Oakland). Another of its features was that two thirds of the people on it lived within reasonable distances of either Los Angeles or San Francisco, and if you included the people scattered in between, the percentage grew to three quarters. Including these scattered people also meant that we had a perfect excuse to do what David had wanted to do all along, which was drive north up the coast following in the treadmarks of Kerouac and Cassidy, and I'm sure it was that prospect that in the end overcame his reservations about the need for face to face interviews. (These reservations, I should point out, had been aggravated by Paula's suggestion that we view ourselves as decoys, out there on the road to lure into the open the people who were trying to intimidate me – an idea which, I must confess, nearly caused me to back out myself.)

Pete did us an extra, unexpected service too: he mulled over the pieces of the puzzle he'd been given. And he saw in one of them a possible significance the rest of us hadn't appreciated: if (he said) the only thing that Carlos and Jackie had had in common was their designation as beneficiaries in Amanda's unsigned will, might it not be that that list of beneficiaries was some kind of hit list (motive unknown)? Moreover, didn't the mere possibility imply that the other intended beneficiaries – May, Natalie, Craig's daughter

136

Astrid, his ex-wife Claire, and (oh God) David – might be in danger?

A shiver passed along my spine and I leapt at once to the obvious: they had to be warned immediately (or in Natalie and Claire's case, warned as soon as they could be traced). Pete, however, pointed out that the first rule in his personal 'Procedures Guide for the Paranoid' was to cover your back *in a stealthy fashion*. Applied to our situation, this translated as arranging protection for the remaining beneficiaries, but doing so without telling them about it or about the reasons for it. You never knew, he said; they could easily have been involved.

'Astrid couldn't,' David said. 'She's only seven. I'm going to ring Craig.'

Paula put her hand over the phone. 'Not from here you're not.'

Mom said: 'Use Marcia's. She won't mind.'

'Or come back to the office with me,' Pete offered. 'I'm driving over as soon as we finish sorting out your plan of action.'

But David in fact ended up placing the call (or trying) from the public booth at the gun club. When he failed to get through, he tried later – twice – from Marcia's, where again he met failure. And much, much later, after we'd healed our earlier differences and had been lying pressed against each other in the dark stillness of the bedroom listening to the distant waves roll and drag on the sand for so long that I'd nearly slipped into sleep, he let out a deep sigh and admitted that for some unknown, completely unfounded, highly irrational reason which he couldn't quite put his finger on, he was worrying about Astrid and Craig.

The next morning when we returned for another practice session at the gun club he put through a call to Asprey Oil and spoke with Craig's secretary.

'She hasn't seen him since he left for London,' he told me afterwards. 'She says he was due back Friday but he hasn't called in yet.'

'She's not worried?'

'No. Says it's normal in August. Says he goes up to his lodge in Vermont for long weekends – his wife and child live there during the summer.'

'And the phone number . . .?'

'. . . is unlisted. Private. Worth a fortune in the right hands. He doesn't give it to anyone. He calls in. She said the lodge is like a fortress it's so secure.'

'Well that's something.'

'Yes. If only I could be sure he's in it. I left a message asking him to call Marcia's.'

We left around lunchtime in a rented car – a convertible, to appease David's Dharma Bums fantasies – which Paula had kitted out with an array of electronic devices which were (she declared with great confidence) lightweight and easily removable in case we wanted to change cars. James Bond would have looked down his nose I expect, but it was enough technology to reassure me that help could be summoned if we ran into trouble.

And I needed that reassurance after my performance on the range. I was useless. Every time I'd take aim I'd think, what am I doing? I *abhor* violence. And despite the pragmatic arguments ranged on the other side (such as the fact that we were tracking someone who'd killed three people), this old emotional aversion utterly undermined my co-ordination.

God, did I feel ashamed.

'Ashamed?' Paula said as she headed towards Venice, where we hoped to interview our first subject (Hank Jacobs, screenwriter, forty-seven. Formerly a Berkeley Journalism Department lecturer and a one-time free speech movement activist). I was in the passenger seat keeping an eye on the rearview mirror and David was sitting in the back. 'Why on earth are you *ashamed*?'

'Because I've let the side down. I've behaved like a typical, fluttery, squeamish female.'

She laughed. 'Oh Dee, you're still this real perfectionist aren't you? You shouldn't be so hard on yourself.' Then, more seriously: 'But I understand how you feel. It's one of the problems with this equality business. A lot of the stuff we're supposed to be trying to be equal to is just brutal and violent and inhumane and I mean, who needs it, you know? It's *backwards*. Men should be trying to develop qualities like sensitivity and compassion so that we don't *have* to learn to defend ourselves against them.' She shrugged. 'Trouble is, some of them are so far gone that they can't hear you talkin' to them unless you speak in the same tongue ... Anyway, you've learned to tell one end of a pistol from the other, which is the important part. Don't worry, if you need to use it, you'll do it right, believe me.'

It wasn't Paula's say-so though that underlay the gradual easing of my anxiety. It was the absence of even so much as a hint of trouble the entire time we were driving in and around LA, stopping at various addresses, parking openly, and going inside (in the three instances where people were available anyway) for fairly long periods. And it was also, a bit, the rapport that built up between the three of us over that first day, the sense that we were a team.

It was good, that. I learned something new about both my friends. I discovered that David was the kind of person who, once he makes a choice, puts whatever else has happened behind him. And I realised that Paula's decision about her sexuality wasn't going to turn her into a social separatist, the way it had a number of my other women friends. On the contrary, it seemed to me that, freed from the pressure to flirt with men, Paula had become much more easy about being herself and saying exactly what she felt about the world men had made *to* a man more directly.

We'd had a number of fairly heated discussions about some of her views during the afternoon, in between analysing the scant fruits of our early interviews, but now, as we left LA along Route 1 north in the late twilight of that high summer evening, we switched to the more immediate issue of food. The top was down and Paula was driving again. David had his legs stretched out along the back seat and was toying lightly with the back of my hair and neck. I got caught up in describing a wonderful seafood place that I remembered from years before which I was sure was somewhere this side of Santa Barbara (if only I could recall *where*) and in my enthusiasm had turned my attention away from the rearview mirror towards Paula.

Suddenly she swung the car into a gas station we'd nearly passed. We'd filled the tank not three quarters of an hour earlier.

'Oh God,' I said.

'What is it?' David said.

'Blue Ford pick-up, looks like a farm truck; battered. Two guys, both dark, one with those mirror shades on. It might be nothing – a coincidence.' Then she pulled back out on to the road.

Two miles later we passed the blue pick-up waiting in a layby. It slipped in about eight cars behind us.

My tension returned abruptly, so abruptly that it overwhelmed my capacity to reason with it. I bit down hard on my lower lip, stared out into the surrounding night, trying not to give in or let on.

In the distance a neon sign announced a motel and restaurant complex. Paula turned in and pulled up in front of the office. Switching off the motor, she glanced back at the road, shrugged at

David, then gripped my arm. 'I'm just going to check us in,' she said. 'You'll be okay here.'

As she got out, David slid over into the front seat beside me and put his arm firmly around my shoulder. He kissed me on my forehead and on my cheeks and on my nose and my chin. I felt the knot loosen. He stroked my hair for a while.

'There's a swimming pool here,' he whispered, 'and jacuzzis. Also a bar. The bedrooms have colour tellies and waterbeds. The restaurant specialises in seafood . . . What do you say?'

I looked over his shoulder and up towards the road. As the neon flickered I saw the front bumper of a blue pick-up. Something inside me stiffened (something like indignation). The panic began to back down.

He was right. We were here. We might as well enjoy ourselves.

Some time after the wine and the meal and the brandies and the stories and reminiscences, and after we'd said goodnight and separated into our rooms, and probably while David and I were enjoying each other, Paula organised a different car for us.

The next morning she knocked on our door about seven and after I let her in, transformed herself by putting on a wig of long straight black hair and sunglasses with frames so large they covered half her face. Lipstick had turned her mouth into a large kiss-me pout. She looked like a starlet pretending she doesn't want to be noticed, which she said was the idea. David became portly and bald with a pipe and looked as if he'd crawled out from beneath a pile of leaves. I was their son.

The convertible was still out front and there was no sign of the pick-up. We carried through the charade anyway. I skipped to the dark blue Cadillac ahead of the other two.

Just before our first stop of the day in Santa Barbara (Candy Rogers, paediatrician, thirty-five, former relationship with Amanda unknown), we reverted to normal. As we pulled up in front of our second subject (Tony Santucci, thirty-five, teacher and anti-nuclear activist; served time for going AWOL while on leave from Vietnam), Paula said: 'They've changed cars. They're in a yellow Volks.' She reached for the binoculars and looked into the rearview mirror. Squinting, she slowly recited the plate number, which I wrote down. Then she punched some buttons on the electronic device under the dash. 'Pete should have that checked out by this afternoon,' she said.

'Why don't they move in on us – *do* something to us?' I said.

'What's the matter?' she laughed. 'Not exciting enough for you?'

'Not *clear* enough. I don't understand what's going on.'

After another two interviews (one with a woman who'd become a meditation instructor, the other with a man who now sold real estate), we stopped outside San Luis Obispo to have lunch and buy gas and use the telephone. I called Pete, who reported that the yellow Volks was a rental car from Santa Barbara, leased that morning to a Mr John Perez of Miami. More usefully, he'd also managed to trace Amanda's ex-sister-in-law Claire, who was still living in Las Vegas but now using the name Clara Clarke, and had put a bodyguard on her.

He had news for us too about another of Amanda's intended beneficiaries, May White: she'd been staying with her daughter in Chicago for the past six weeks – ever since her younger brother Tommy had died of a heroin overdose. I wrote the date of his death beside the short description of him on my list that said: 'Tommy White, 34, Fillmore; arrested numerous times (once for alleged rape, usually for theft) and been in and out of prison since his release from his first sentence, for drugs, in '73. One-time member of the Black Panthers. Formerly a scholarship student.' In the margin I noted that Amanda couldn't have visited him on her last trip but may well have heard that he'd died. From his sister? Could she have visited *her*? (She hadn't visited anyone *else* we'd interviewed so far.)

David called Marcia's to see if Craig had rung in there yet, but there'd been nothing. My mother was there at her friend's, waiting, and was obviously relieved to hear from us. David tried New York again, but Craig still hadn't contacted his office. David left a second message, emphasising the urgency.

When we finished, we found that Paula had swapped the car for a camper van. We slid into the back. She came out of the ladies' room dressed in jeans and a sweatshirt and track shoes, with her hair pulled back into a baseball cap. She was wearing aviator shades and had a cigarette hanging from a corner of her mouth.

We headed inland, seemingly free of the yellow car, and took the main highway most of the way to the home of our next subject, Jack Davis, thirty-seven, a junk dealer and sometime welfare recipient who was holding out for the sixties to come back (or perhaps was just unaware they'd ended). As we turned into the dirt lane leading to his small dusty bungalow, however, we all saw the

Volks parked a couple of hundred yards further on. And in case we were in any doubt, one of our pursuers was leaning against the trunk, smoking, his mirror glasses glinting fire in the bright sun.

I shivered. Paula swore. David muttered.

When we came away, they'd gone, and as we returned to the coast we seemed once more to be free of them. This again was an illusion for as we approached the Big Sur region and began the ascent, I picked them out about ten cars behind us. We were heading into cloud – it had been forecast and it was visible up ahead – and I felt my fear stir as I thought of the long narrow snaking road and the steep cliffs to either side. Could they have *compadres*? Might we be ambushed? And why, oh why couldn't I rid myself of all those cinema scenes where the car goes over the edge, bounces on the rock and ignites into a ball of flame before crashing into the sea.

I found David's hand as he was reaching for mine. With his other one, he felt around his torso. 'I keep thinking they must have put some kind of sonar device on our clothes.'

'Yes,' Paula said. 'Mmm.'

We entered the cloud and for the next interminable half hour concentrated on the red rear lights of the cars in front. I felt I must have held my breath the whole time, because when we finally broke clear into the sun and the cloud was beneath us like a sea of cotton fluff, I exhaled so deeply that the other two laughed. They were relieved too though – giddy with it really – and we were each more than ready to stop by the time we reached the clifftop inn where rooms had been reserved for us (thanks to a friend of a friend of my mother's, which is the level of contact needed in early August). There were no vacancies, the restaurant served only guests and the security was clearly excellent, so we could relax.

Over dinner on the terrace, which overlooked the shifting cloud and the world it would veil and reveal, we attempted to talk about what we'd culled from the interviews of the past two days. The trouble was, there wasn't a whole lot to say. No one had seen Amanda (or would admit to having seen her) since her flight from Berkeley in '71; no one knew anything about a child or even about a pregnancy and no one could think of any Hispanic link to Amanda or to anyone else in her immediate crowd. Six, it is true, remembered knowing a man or men named Bruce on campus and two recalled girls named Diana (three if I include Tony Santucci, whose long story about his brief affair with Amanda contained at least four references to 'their' song, 'Can't Hurry Love' by Diana Ross and the Supremes). And while all seemed to have been asked by Dr Alan Dexter to participate in his research project, none could say – or in some cases I am sure, *would* say – that they had identified someone as a government infiltrator, never mind confide who it might have been.

'None we've met *so far*,' Paula said.

'Exactly,' David said, 'look how many it took to find one who'd give us Natalie's married name and address. Six? Seven? But we've got it.' It turned out that Amanda's old friend, now going by the name Ellison, lived up in Oregon – or had as of three Christmases ago.

'I just hope she has something to say to us,' I said. 'It's a hell of a long way to go for more nothing.'

'The trip wouldn't be entirely wasted,' David smiled. 'We have brought the sleeping bags and tent with us.'

I wouldn't be jollied though. I was losing faith in my own premise, the premise that if we asked enough people enough questions about Amanda, the identity of her murderer and of Carlos' and Jackie's murderer would emerge with a kind of inevitability.

We turned to other topics (thankfully) and to the wine and once I stopped thinking about the case, I cheered up. And this feeling of well-being was enhanced when David and I realised we'd been booked into one of the so-called 'Honeymooners' suites'. Apparently there'd been a cancellation.

David said, 'A cancellation? In a honeymoon suite? Can that bode well?'

The answer turned out to be yes.

We awoke the next morning into the kind of pure sunlight that lifts one out of bed, and it lifted all three of us up into an early start, destination Howard Louder. There was no sign of the yellow car anywhere.

'Wow,' Paula said, reading the notes. (David was driving.) 'No wonder he's got such a flash address. He's in the "import" business – travels back and forth to *Bogotà* . . . You know what that's code for don't you?' She sniffed sharply to help us along. 'I bet you anything – anything – that the place'll be fenced in, covered in hi-tech equipment and guarded by Alsatians. You wait.'

She was right. Louder's house was a beautiful redwood and glass structure perfectly contoured into the landscape, but I only know this because I peered through the outer wire with Paula's strong binoculars in defiance of half a dozen growling dogs.

David did the talking into the elaborate entryphone while cameras scanned us all. Finally he alone was admitted. Paula and I found a good rock and prepared for a long wait, but a quarter of an hour later he returned. He was carrying a blue wallet file which contained a copy of Louder's submission to Alan Dexter – 'proof', he had told David, that Amanda had been a US federal *agent provocateur*.

'Oh God,' I said, 'the paranoid ravings of a coke head – that's really useful, really *constructive*.'

David sighed and nodded but had opened the file and was skimming its contents.

We walked back to the van and Paula suddenly swore and pointed. A yellow car tail was just visible around the next bend.

She switched on the ignition brusquely and revved the engine. 'That's it,' she said. 'I've had it. I'm sick of these boys and their nerve game. I am going to find out who the hell they are and what they want from us. David? How'd you feel about visiting that clinic of yours today?'

'You mean – go to San Francisco *now*?'

'That,' she said, 'is exactly what I mean.' Then she told us her idea.

The Morton Clinic is in the Haight, which on that warm hazy August day was as crowded as it had been on the warm hazy August day in 1968 when Paula and I had first arrived in our mini-skirts and beads. Then of course it had been a shabby inner-city area, the Mecca of the American hippy counter-culture, and the crowds had consisted of people like us – runaway middle-class kids who'd saved up their allowances, stuck out their thumbs on the freeways and invaded its streets to play drop out among the more authentic poor who'd been pushed there. Now, like those Meccas of the British counter-culture, Portobello Road and Camden High Street, it had become the epitome of what we'd earlier thought we could escape, a clean, up-market shopping precinct where well-heeled tourists browsed in smart boutiques and ate expensively prepared healthy foods in plant-filled restaurants.

I thought: we blend in just as well today as we did then.

Paula glanced at me as she circled the block searching for the right parking place. 'You know what I think?' she smiled. 'I think we were lucky to survive that summer.'

'You can say that again,' I sighed. 'Maybe it's because we weren't really very good hippies.'

'What do you mean?' she laughed, feigning indignation. 'We did all the right things – handed out flowers, strung necklaces, made candles, crashed around, caught scabies, boogied in the park, took drugs, got by without money . . .'

'Hang on,' I chided. 'Don't exaggerate. When we were broke, we called home.'

'Did we?'

'Twice. Your folks, then mine. We told everybody else we'd been panhandling.'

'Oh yeah, so we did. I never could bring myself to do that.'

'You couldn't bring yourself to drop a handful of acid tabs for breakfast either, *or* try smack, *or* drink those "instant enlightenment" cocktails.'

'Ha,' she snorted. 'Horse tranquilliser, rat poison and strychnine – some enlightenment.'

'I know, I wasn't interested either. In fact, the mere thought scared the shit out of me. And that's what I mean. If we'd been good hippies, we'd have figured it didn't matter what we took so long as it blasted open the old doors of perception and rid us of our evil egos. That was the whole point, remember? And measured against the purists, we were failures. We were just a bit too straight.'

'Thank God,' she murmured as she lined up to park. Then, pausing to look at me again: 'What do you suppose happened to the successes?'

'I know,' David volunteered. 'They either killed themselves, got committed to state institutions or ended up in the Morton. That's why it was set up, here, in '69: to cope with the "successes" . . . Is this it? Are they still with us?'

Paula squinted into the rearview mirror. 'Yup, they've stopped back there at the corner . . . Come on boys, no need to double park – there's that nice little place at the end of the street and you'll just fit . . . That's it, back up, go on . . .'

A horn blatted impatiently and she laughed with pleasure. 'That's what I like to see – rudeness. *Ignore the bastard*,' she rooted. As a souped-up fifties Chevy sped past us, she leaned over and gave me a prod. 'This is it, kiddo, act one. You're on.'

David and I opened our doors and stepped on to the sidewalk. I stretched ostentatiously to give the men watching us a clear view of my pink T-shirt and roseate jeans before the two of us walked slowly arm-in-arm to the clinic entrance. There we hugged for a long moment.

'Three o'clock,' he said into my hair. 'You won't forget to ring.'

I stretched to kiss him. 'I won't forget. Wish us luck.'

Paula smiled as I got back in beside her. 'Not quite Bogart and Bergman, but touching. You ready?'

This was, however, a rhetorical question, for even as I was swallowing to reply, she pulled out into the road, tyres squealing, and set off up the hill.

She'd warned me that she intended to drive just as she would if she were genuinely trying to lose our mysterious tail ('Why not? We want him to worry'), and she kept her word. During the next twenty minutes, she took every hair-raising chance she could, veering abruptly across oncoming traffic on downward slopes, jumping lights, passing blind on upward runs, and ignoring small details like cyclists and pedestrians and speed limits. In fact she was so expert that several times she had to contrive to get the van into a jam just to let the other driver catch up. But this manoeuvre, too, served our purposes, for it was only when she slowed down that I could focus the binoculars.

'He's definitely alone,' I said on my second attempt to confirm whether part one of our ploy had worked. 'Ton Ton must be watching David. We've got the one with the moustache.'

'Good, good,' she murmured. 'Now start praying that we can find a space to park or we'll have to try this somewhere else.'

I obeyed and for once seemed to catch the ear of a benevolent force: we arrived at Fisherman's Wharf during one of those ideal phases when more people were leaving than coming. Then we left the van and began to walk along the waterfront towards the shopping district. Paula chanced a glimpse back over her shoulder and cursed. 'We've lost him already, dammit – either that or he's going to be lazy and stay by his car.'

'But that means . . .'

'No. Come on. Let's not give up yet. Maybe he missed those spots. You look this time. Try the road side.'

I did. 'He's cruising about a hundred and fifty yards behind us . . . He saw me see him, I'm sure of it.'

'That's okay. We want him to know that we know he's there . . .

Oh boy, this could be our day. Someone's pulling out right here. Walk faster.'

When we arrived at the Cannery, she turned again. 'He took it; he's parked. I don't see him but he must be on foot by now – must be. Now remember, give me an hour. I'll meet you at two fifteen sharp by the cable car turning at Beach and Hyde.'

'Is that enough time? What will you do if he . . .'

'You just worry about yourself, you hear?' She squeezed my hand. 'See you later.' And with that she slipped between some passers-by and disappeared into the shopping area.

I will admit I felt acutely self-conscious as I continued on my own towards Ghiardelli Square. Surely it was obvious that I was a lawyer not an actress. Surely all eyes were on my back. Surely my occasional over-the-shoulder glances fooled none of the other pedestrians I bumped and jostled and dodged, nor could they possibly be fooling the man with the moustache.

And was he really behind me anyway? Was our logic right or had he followed Paula, or (just as bad) stayed in his car?

I will also admit to a renewed spasm of panic. Again, our reasoning had it that I was in no danger because if our pursuers had wanted to harm me (or us), they'd have found an opportunity already. On top of that, or so I'd let Paula persuade me, they certainly wouldn't attack me in the middle of the day in a crowded tourist section.

I hoped she was right.

I made it unscathed to the converted chocolate factory complex and, having made it, carried on following instructions. Checking my watch, I slowed and spent ten exceedingly long minutes browsing in the shops. Then, after buying a magazine, I went up the stairs to a restaurant-bar, hesitated at the entrance, looked around, forced an expression of disappointment, waited for a table, sat down and ordered.

It wasn't difficult to twitch and seem anxious after that. Neither the food nor the drink interested me, and although I pretended to read, I found it impossible to do: I was too concerned about Paula. Yet somehow I sat through the forty minutes I'd promised to spend there and more, completed the charade by making another quick tour of the square, this time glancing hastily into every restaurant and bar I passed. At two twelve I headed for the cable car turning point.

She was there and, as planned, waited until I'd almost joined her

147

before breaking into a run. I followed as she cut over the road and up the side street where she'd parked the new car she'd rented.

'This is it,' she grinned as she unlocked it, 'the moment when he realises that we're about to lose them. Ha! Little does he know. God, he must be kicking himself.'

'Just so long as he doesn't rush over here and try to kick *us* . . . Get this thing moving, will you?'

But she was already doing that. I turned to look out the back window and for the first time in an hour actually saw the man I'd been trying to divert. He was still running and he looked furious.

It had worked.

'It worked,' I said to Paula. 'I don't believe it – it *worked* . . . How about you? Did you do it all? Did you contact . . .'

'No problem. He gave me two lids of some bum Mexican stuff. I hid it in with the spare tyre. And I had no trouble at all with the squad either. My captain friend Harve Turner was even at his desk for a change and from the way he reacted I obviously caught him in a slack period. God, you'd have thought I'd tipped him off about some major smuggling ring. I have a hunch the clinic is already surrounded.'

'Surrounded? For two ounces?'

Her quick glance was mischievous. 'Do I know how much they're carrying? My informant told me dope dealers. I passed it on.'

'Oh Paula . . .'

She shrugged. 'This is a street game, Dee. The ethics are different. And anyway, two ounces will only get them twenty-four to forty-eight hours now and a fine later. I got the fingerprints, that's the important part. Both their sets. Off the briefcase in the trunk.'

I couldn't help but sigh. 'What a relief. Imagine: now we can drive to Oregon without worrying . . .'

'That's the next thing. We're not going to Oregon.'

'Not going? Why not?'

'Look in my bag. There – those typed pages in the front of my notebook.'

I got them out and needed only a brief glance through. 'Holy . . . this is the list of names we gave Pete – from Amanda's old address book – only they seem to have found *everyone*.'

She shook her head. 'Look again. It's not the *same* list. For one thing, theirs is longer than ours, though they don't have Diana or

Bruce either. For another, we've got one key name and address they don't have. Here's a hint: check out the 'A's and the 'C's.'

I did. 'Ah hah . . . No Claire. It must be her then. They must be waiting for us to lead them to her. What do you think? Should we go straight to Vegas now and leave Natalie for later?'

'No need. Like I say, this is our day. Run your eye down the 'E's.'

I found the listing and looked over at Paula. We both started laughing.

Natalie Ellison, née Giovanni, was back living in Berkeley.

Nine

We weren't the only ones with good news to tell. Pete had uncovered Natalie's Berkeley address through his own channels late the night before and had immediately sent someone out to keep an eye on it, and Craig had at last called in to Marcia's. My mother had been there at the time and had told him in a general way of our concern for his daughter. Once he'd calmed down he'd said he'd be back in New York the next day and asked that David ring him in his office around lunchtime.

David, for his part, was as relieved by the sound of my voice as by my messages. (What if we'd been wrong? he said. What if the two men had been waiting to get me on my own?) What's more, it had been a lucky day for him as well. Art Morton, founder of the clinic, had not only been in, he'd welcomed David with enthusiasm – it seemed that he had been following David's recent articles. The two doctors, in short, had found each other's conversation extemely useful.

'He's just offered to go through all kinds of details with me too,' David said. 'Patient costings, success rate statistics, follow-up, even the interview techniques he uses to find the right support staff. If we don't have to fly off to Oregon . . .'

'Oh stay,' I said, 'you must. We'll wait for you.'

He hesitated. 'I'd rather not feel under pressure to finish,' he said. 'Maybe . . . that is . . . look: would you object if I didn't come?'

I checked with Paula, who allowed as how we'd probably manage. Then, after stopping for a very belated lunch, we drove across the Oakland Bay Bridge and on into Berkeley.

'Good God,' I muttered as Paula signalled right and waited to turn off Telegraph Avenue by the Safeway. 'Natalie lives around *here*?'

'According to the map. What's so surprising about that?'

I shook my head. 'Only that it's the same part of town I used to stay in. I've always thought of the south side as the student side.'

'Maybe it was in those days.' She smiled. 'Or maybe, like most smart-ass college kids, you thought nobody else existed.'

'This is possible,' I nodded, gazing out at the busy parking lot. Then: 'I'll never forget the morning I rolled in here for some milk and found National Guard troops bivouacked in this lot – armed soldiers, tanks, jeeps, grenade launchers, the works . . . Reagan had called them in – because some locals had made a park where the authorities wanted to put something else.' I sighed. 'Who'd have dreamed he was only practising up for Latin America.'

She completed the turn but almost immediately got slowed by supermarket traffic. It was all so ordinary now. I said, 'The whole area was ringed by military. You had to show ID just to go home. And there was a six o'clock curfew.'

'There was a curfew on the time I came here,' Paula said, 'but it was patrolled by the police. There must have been six or eight kinds – Highway Patrol, State troopers, local police, Oakland police, San Francisco, all in different coloured padded jumpsuits and guns and holsters. We were inside watching them drive round and round, stoned out of our minds.' She laughed.

We were approaching a school playground and I pointed left. 'That's where Jay Jay and Roxie lived, down there.'

'You mean "Can you dig it, man, far out, far fucking out" – *that* Jay Jay?'

I laughed. 'That Jay Jay.'

'He went here? Jesus, I didn't think he had the vocabulary to order a take-out from the Jack-in-the Box.'

'That's what he wanted you to think. The fact is, behind that greasy shoulder-length hair and pimples there lurked the fevered brain of a mathematical genius. He got a Merit scholarship.'

She gave me a wry glance. 'Another secret grind you mean?'

I shrugged. 'I didn't keep it such a secret.'

'True,' she said. 'True.' She paused to make a left-hand turn and looked at me again. 'It's weird, isn't it, what happened between us after we left the Haight and went back to school.'

'Don't remind me. I'm still ashamed. Honestly, if you hadn't showed up at dad's funeral . . . I was never so glad to see anyone in my life.'

'It was mutual,' she said, driving on. 'Anyway, you make it sound like it was all your fault and it wasn't.'

'Nonsense. I'm the one who turned into such a little snot our senior year. All you did was become one of the jocks I despised so much.'

'We despised you every bit as much as you despised us, don't worry. I mean, the very idea – sitting around indoors, wasting all that time, and on reading, of all things.' She pulled over to park. 'And you especially – my old tennis partner. I remember wondering how you of all people could do that when the whole reason we'd gone back to school was because we'd decided that something was missing from the hippy trip. And there you were, ignoring your body just like they did.'

'And there *you* were, ignoring your head just like they did.'

Her grimace was pained. 'And that's why we barely spoke for three years – because each of us was so sure that we were right and the other was misguided. What the hell got into us anyway?'

Pretending to strum an invisible guitar, I wailed à la early Dylan: ' "Ah well, we were so much older then, we're younger than that now." '

'That must be it,' she laughed, squinting out at the road. Then she turned and peered out the back window. 'Whoever Pete's got watching the place seems to be well hidden.' She swung around again and nodded towards the house. 'What do you think?'

I smiled. Even from across the street it was obvious that appearances, or home maintenance at any rate, featured low on the Ellison family's list of priorities. The paintwork, where it hadn't peeled away completely, was faded and curling; the gate hung by a single hinge off the post of a picket fence which was itself collapsing under the weight of overgrown rose bushes; a screen door, presumably there to shield the entrance, was propped ajar at an angle that suggested permanence; a weathered Santa Claus drawn by battered reindeer stared down at us from the roof.

Closer to, it became equally obvious what came top of this household's list: kids. Lawn (or what had once been lawn) and pathway were indistinguishable beneath a thick layer of toys and bicycles. Pop music was coming from somewhere and over it, the high-pitched squeak of a tonette fumbling to play along. In the distance (the back yard?) children were cheering and shouting. Lots of children.

Unlikely as it seemed that anyone would hear us over the general din, we nevertheless knocked hard on the half-open front door. When this produced nothing, Paula shrugged, stepped across the threshold into the cluttered hallway and called out. Then, signalling to me to follow, she began to walk down the corridor, still calling.

I was about to go after her when suddenly a boy of nine or ten appeared, running, from around the side of the house. His arms were extended horizontally into wings and he was yelling 'zoom, zoom' at a pitch evidently intended to break the sound barrier. Seeing me there he made the noise of screeching brakes, slid to a stop, grinned up at me and said: 'Who d'you want, Mom or Chuck?'

'Mom,' I smiled.

'Attic,' he said. Then flew off again around the other side of the house.

We interpreted this as licence to carry on trespassing and made our way up four flights of stairs to the top of the house. Piano music filtered through the uppermost door, accompanied by light humming.

At my knock, a voice replied, 'Che honey, *please*. Go bug your dad.'

Paula and I exchanged a quick glance. 'Mrs Ellison,' I began, 'this isn't . . .'

'Oh dear,' said the voice, 'come on in. I'm afraid I can't get up.'

Entering the room my attention went at once to the tiny baby feeding from one of her breasts. The mother, who was seated behind a desk strewn with open books, smiled over at us from between the curtains of long thin blonde hair that framed her face. 'It's happened again,' she sighed, as if this were an old familiar story to us. 'It's not finished. The twins came down with colds. Tell the Professor that I'm sorry and I'll try to bring it to his office tomorrow, so he . . .' She stopped and stared uncertainly from one of us to the other. 'You have come to pick up my term paper, haven't you?'

I shook my head. 'My name is Dee Street – this is my friend Pau –'

She frowned at me. 'Do I know you? God, I can't believe how many people are still here.' She frowned harder. 'I don't want to be rude, but I can't place your face.'

'I never lived here – just visited . . . used to stay a couple of streets over in fact – but I doubt . . .'

'Who did you know?'

The possibility, frail as it was, that Natalie (and perhaps Amanda) might have known my old friends was so tantalising that

I let myself be drawn. I named names and when she didn't seem to recognise them, described the house.

'I'm sure I must have been in there,' she said. 'Where they political?'

'Jay Jay wasn't but most everyone else was. And because the house was so close to the campus they ended up dishing out masses of vaseline every time the police used tear gas on a demonstration or march.'

Paula said: 'If you did ever meet this guy Jay Jay, you'd never forget him. He looked like Icabod Crane.'

'Ah,' Natalie cried out, '*him*.'

We all laughed together.

Despite our noise, the baby had somehow managed to fall asleep and Natalie now swung it around gently and placed it in a basket. As she readjusted her T-shirt, she said, 'So why . . . ?'

'We've come to talk to you about Amanda Finch.'

The change in her expression was as dramatic as it was abrupt. Her eyes, until then friendly and open, clouded with wariness as she withdrew from us. Her smile vanished into a frown almost hostile in its severity. 'Who sent you?'

'No one sent us.'

'Do you know she's dead?' Paula asked her.

'Dead?'

'Murdered,' I put in, 'about two and a half weeks ago.'

She inhaled sharply but held on to her composure. I thought: she definitely didn't know.

'Where?' she asked.

'England. Norfolk.'

She closed her eyes as if in pain, then opened them again quickly. 'Who are you?'

'Her husband's lawyer. I live in London, where she did, *they* did. I'd just drawn up wills for them.'

She looked at me. 'She knew.'

'I think she must have had an idea. The most intriguing thing is that, after drafting a first will in my office with her husband, she went on a trip and stayed away longer than she was supposed to. Where she went during that extra time, no one knows, but when she got back, she came to see me again, alone, to do a second will. This has now disappeared but in it you were named as a beneficiary.'

Genuinely surprised, or so it seemed, she flinched. 'Me?'

'Yes. I wondered if she'd been to see you.'

Her eyes narrowed. 'Are you kidding?'

I shrugged. 'If you can think of some other reason why she had you in mind . . .'

Natalie stood up. 'Look, whoever you people are, I have nothing to say to you about Mandy Finch, nothing at all, so if you'll excuse me now, I'd like to get back to . . .'

'If you're worried that we're feds,' Paula interrupted, 'we're not.' She smiled. 'We both have ID. You can call and check it out.'

Natalie resented the pressure, it was obvious from her expression, but despite that she seemed to waver. Finally, grudgingly, she held out her hand.

We handed her our cards and as she studied them I said: 'While I was helping Amanda's husband sort through her effects I found a letter you wrote her just after she left here. I know she hurt you and I can appreciate that maybe you still feel bitter. But she met an incredibly brutal end – the kind no one deserves. So did the young Chilean refugee she was . . .'

'Excuse me,' she said again, leaning over to pick up the Moses basket. 'I won't be long.' And she swept past us and hurried down the stairs.

Paula turned to me.

I shook my head.

She crossed to the desk and began to browse through the books. I wandered over to the dormer window and stared down into the back yard. There were kids everywhere – little ones in a sandbox, slightly larger ones crawling in and out of a pup tent, others clambering over a jungle gym, still more tossing a ball around. In the far corner three adults, two men and a woman, were sitting in deck chairs under the shadow of a large tree. The men were engrossed in conversation. The woman's attention was on the children.

Suddenly she waved and a moment later Natalie appeared. She put the baby basket down, knelt by one of the men and started talking. Almost immediately he stood up and drew her aside. She continued talking. The man turned to the others, said something which made them nod, put his arm around her shoulders and led her towards the house.

Ten minutes passed; then footsteps approached up the stairs.

By this point both of us were nervously clutching our bags, ready for eviction, but the man who pushed open the door was carrying

155

three cans of beer. 'Hi,' he said, grinning down at us from a height so formidable that it forced him to stoop under the beams of the converted attic. 'I'm Chuck, Nat's husband.' He handed us each a drink and lowered himself on to one of the floor cushions beside us. I noticed his three-day beard, the smile in his eyes, the faint smell of marijuana that came from his skin and thought: I know you. I've never met you before, but you feel like an old friend.

He appeared to feel much the same about us. 'Well,' he said after he'd pulled back his pop-top and taken a large swallow, 'Nat sure as hell's upset.'

It was as if, from his point of view, we were as blameless for her state as he was. From mine, however, he was being far too generous.

'I'm sorry,' I said. 'It's hard to make that kind of news less disturbing.'

'Of course,' he nodded. Then: 'I detect an English twang. You must be Dee. Tell me something: why do you live over there?'

Somewhere in the back of my mind I wondered if Chuck Ellison was stoned. Why else such a weirdly casual, disconnected question? Still, I answered it anyway.

'Ah hah,' he smiled. 'So underneath you're another disillusioned sixties' drop-out. Why law though? Isn't that a pretty straight thing to do?'

'Not the way she does it,' Paula said.

He looked at me again. 'Oh?'

I gave him a quick description of the firm and of the Legal Aid system.

'And are all your clients women too?'

I shook my head. 'Look,' I started, 'we're here to . . .'

'Tell me about some of your cases.'

'Really,' I said, 'We haven't got an awful lot of time. Maybe after we've spoken to Na –'

'Tell me,' he repeated, the humour vanishing from his eyes.

(*Wow, what the hell was this all about?*)

As briefly as I could, I summarised a few recent trials, finishing with Carlos' mental health tribunal. 'He's the Chilean refugee who was killed with . . .'

'And what are your views about America's role in Chile?'

'I consider it deplorable that the CIA was allowed to destabilise an elected left-wing government. Please – Chuck – can't we discuss this another –'

'What about the Soviet-backed revolutionaries in Nicaragua and El Salvador?'

'Oh for Christ's sake,' I snapped, 'I'm not sure they are Soviet-backed, but if they are it's because they associate America with oppression. We've forced them to look to the Russians by propping up dictators like Samosa for forty years. Now honestly . . .'

But he'd turned to Paula. 'And you? What's your feeling?'

'My feeling is that I wish you'd asked us straight out what our politics are.'

His grin reappeared and he shrugged. 'I was hoping to catch you off guard, that's all.' Then, to me: 'I'm sorry. Nat wasn't sure where you two are coming from, or maybe I should say she was inclined to trust you but didn't trust herself. She has that problem with her instincts about people – they're all screwed up. I don't suppose that surprises you, though, does it?'

'Mmm,' I murmured, 'not if she spends most of her time cooped up at home with kids, no.'

He tilted his head and gave me a quizzical look.

'No offence meant,' I said hurriedly. 'I like kids.'

Paula said: 'Are you saying she has something to tell us or what?'

'If she did, would you believe her? Why should you trust her any more than she trusts you?'

'Maybe I have more faith in my gut.'

'Hold on,' I said, 'he has a point. I mean, I hate to say it, but for all we know . . .'

'God,' he laughed, 'you really are a lawyer aren't you?' Then, with a gratified flourish he reached into his shirt pocket, pulled out a piece of paper and handed it to me. It was a certificate signed by a witness showing that a girl had been born to the Ellisons on the fifteenth of July. 'There were complications,' he said. 'She was in the hospital for a week. And she doesn't have a passport anyway. And for what it's worth we're both active in the local gun control campaign, Parents for Peace, and Citizens for a Nuclear-Free Bay Area. Anything else you want to know?'

'Yes,' I smiled. 'What do we have to do to get Natalie to talk to us?'

He stood up. 'You've done it.'

The Ellisons' kitchen, like the outside of their house, had the air of a battle lost, or perhaps never fought at all. Comic books, piles of small clothes, blocks, crayons, colouring books, board games, cards, stuffed animals, dolls and their miniature accessories, half-finished cups of juice, abandoned bowls of food, stray pieces of train sets and farm sets and tea sets – nearly everywhere the eye rested, a child had claimed the spot.

Natalie was sitting at the table, her back to the door; her shoulders were hunched, her head bent forwards. Without turning she said: 'Is this your friend's house?'

I picked my way to her side. She pointed to a black and white snapshot in the album that was open in front of her.

'Yes, that's it.' I peered more closely. 'I think that's Roxie there on the far left.'

'Oh? I knew her as Deva.'

'Deva? Did she go orange? When?'

She shrugged. 'Beats me. I only met her once.' Then she lifted a cage of hamsters off the chair beside her and put it on the table next to an empty fish bowl. 'Sit down.'

Chuck said: 'Hon, wouldn't the living room be . . .'

'Che and Angela have been in. I promised you'd make tacos if they stayed outside with Bill and Betty a little longer.'

'Okay. Sure. That's fine. It'll only take a couple of minutes. If you want to go into the . . .'

She swivelled around and looked up past me at him. Her eyes were bloodshot.

Immediately he went to her, stooped and hugged her to his chest. She leaned her head against his shoulder while he rubbed her back and kissed her hair. Eventually she mumbled something; he rose and moved over to the refrigerator.

As Paula and I sat down, Natalie reached into her shirt pocket, took out a small box, a pack of cigarette papers and a matchbook, and set about rolling a thin grass joint. When she'd finished constructing it, she lit up, inhaled deeply, held her breath for a long moment and, on the exhale, said: 'What do you want to ask me?'

'Well for a start, do the names Bruce and Diana mean anything to you?'

'Sure, we know two or three of each.'

'Do any of them form couples?'

'No, though I think one of the Bruces fancies one of the other ones. What's this got to do with Mandy?'

'These Bruces and Dianas you know – did any of them know her?'

'Don't see how. They're all Oregon people.'

'Okay, how about this: did the two of you talk much about children?'

She took another drag and smiled. 'Now *that* is an under-statement.' Then, handing me the joint: 'We debated children. I was for, she was against . . . Now that you mention it, I'm curious: did she ever have any?'

'You don't know?'

'How would I know?' She glanced at Chuck and back to me. 'Are you trying to trick me? I told you I never saw her again.'

'Dee's not trying to trick you,' Paula said as she reached over to relieve me of the joint. 'She's just trying to find out if Amanda ever told you she'd had a child before you knew her.'

'No, definitely not. It can't be true. She was much too careful. Where did you hear that?'

'From a woman who worked for her.'

I meant to go on, but faltered at the thought of Jackie.

Paula said: 'The story is that Amanda had this child – a girl – in America, and as we know that she left America when she left here . . .'

'Did she?'

'That's what she told her husband,' I said, puzzled by her challenging tone. 'He has no reason to lie.'

'No,' she mumbled, looking down at the table top, '*he* probably doesn't.'

I stared at her curiously and was about to ask what she meant when Chuck said, 'Do you mind if I ask how you think this child is relevant?'

Still preoccupied, I was happy for Paula to answer. 'One of the many theories about her death is that she came back to the States three weeks ago to try to reclaim it. There may have been an illegal adoption . . .'

'I see,' he nodded, tapping the spatula thoughtfully on the counter. 'So if Nat did know the whereabouts of this child – who is presumably pretty grown up now – she might be in danger too.'

'Yes. That's one of the reasons why we took the precaution of having a guard put on your house.'

He smiled. 'But not the only reason.'

She smiled back noncommittally and passed him what was left of the joint. He took a clip out of the pocket of his shorts and, slipping it on the roach, said to me: 'What are your other theories?'

'A couple arise from the fact that the young man killed with

Amanda was a political refugee from Chile.'

Natalie made a tsk'ing noise and I looked at her, but her face was still averted. Chuck said: 'Go on.'

'Do either of you have a link to any Chilean groups here?'

'Nothing direct.' He shrugged. 'Can't do everything.'

'But if you were sent, say, a parcel of information that might be useful to a group like that . . .'

'I'd know who to give it to, sure. I haven't seen anything like that though. You Nat?'

She shook her head and looked over at him. 'Honey,' she said, 'why are we dragging this out? They obviously don't know . . .'

'Let's let them finish,' he answered. 'I'm interested.'

'Look,' I said, 'why waste time? Whatever you've got to say, for God's sake . . .'

'We'll tell you,' he promised, 'don't worry. What else did you want to ask?'

I sighed. I'd had just about enough of Chuck's games. 'Only one more thing really. I believe it was through you, Natalie, that Amanda first met a man called Alan Dexter.'

The name appeared to startle her. She looked at me at least, which made a change. 'You know about Alan?'

'Why yes. I found a letter he sent Amanda last spring. He asked her for help with his research.'

'Jesus,' she whispered, holding my eye with such intensity I began to wish she'd look away again.

Chuck said: 'And this letter – it suggested a connection to you, yeah?'

I nodded. (Why was she staring at me like this?)

'Namely?' he prompted.

Forcing myself to turn towards him, I said: 'Namely – well, it's obvious, isn't it? She must have worked out the identity of the person this Dexter's been looking for and maybe decided to pay them a call herself. She *was* a journalist, so . . .'

Natalie slid her chair back and stood up. 'I think I'd better go check on the baby.'

Chuck gestured to her to sit back down. 'The baby's fine.'

'I'm not,' she murmured, crossing to the door.

He went after her and the two of them stood just outside the room for a few minutes, talking quietly. When he came back and sat back down where she'd been sitting, she continued to stand, half in the room, half out.

'So you think she may have been murdered because she uncovered a federal agent?'

'It may have been unintentional, but yes, that's what I think.'

'I see . . . I take it you haven't spoken to Alan.'

'I tried. He wouldn't speak to me.'

'He never speaks to strangers over the phone,' Natalie said. 'He hardly even speaks to his family.'

'If that's a polite way of telling me I was naive, I realise that. All I wanted was some names and addresses.'

'All!' she snorted.

I shrugged off the criticism. 'Sometimes it pays to go for the obvious.'

'So are we the only people you've seen?' Chuck asked.

'No. I found Amanda's old address book and we've managed to trace a lot of the people who still live in-state. On the way up from LA we dropped in on about half of them.'

'Oh?' Natalie said. 'Like who?'

I named the people we'd interviewed.

'Howie Louder?' she repeated. 'He let you in?'

'He let David in. Is he a friend of yours?'

'The word isn't in his vocabulary.'

'Mmm, that was the impression we got. I suppose acute paranoia must come with his job, though.' I described the elaborate security. 'And as for his opinion of Amanda . . .' I shook my head. 'Do you know what *he* thinks?'

'I've heard,' she said softly, gazing out of the door. 'Incredible, isn't it.'

'Wow,' I laughed, 'I'll say . . . problem is, it did make me wonder.'

She turned towards me again, a question in her eyes.

'Apparently he has an alibi,' I said, 'but what if he poisoned someone else with his crazy ideas? Imagine . . .'

'No,' she said flatly. 'No. Howie didn't . . .'

'Is it so inconceivable?' I pressed. 'Alan Dexter seems to have written to lots of people. All Howie had to find was one . . .'

'But why?' Chuck cut in. 'I've never met the guy and from what I've heard I don't want to, but I mean, why should he lie about something as serious as this?'

'Because he believes that Amanda set him up for a drugs bust he got sent down for back in '71.'

Nat said: 'He also believes that she planted explosives in his

161

house. After he'd been charged with the dealing, they also charged him with conspiracy to commit a terrorist act.'

'My God,' I said, 'that quadruples his motive ... Look – please – if there's someone – anyone – from your old crowd who's suggestible – malleable – someone Louder might have manipulated into . . .'

'Howie never sees anyone from the old days. Never.'

I nodded. 'Okay. Fine. I can stop worrying that some deluded maniac did her in by mistake.'

'Oh,' she said, coming back into the room, 'I'm sure it wasn't a mistake.'

'Are you? How?'

Ignoring me, she reached up into an upper cupboard and got down a bottle of bourbon, then took a shot glass from the drying rack. Her back still to us, she filled the glass and stood for a long moment, staring down at it intently.

'Please,' I said, 'I'm finished. No more questions. I wish you'd tell us whatever it is you know.'

She turned and peered at me, her eyes damp. 'You're a real idealist, aren't you?'

'Sure,' I smiled, feeling I had to humour her. 'Aren't you?'

She walked over to the table; Chuck slid out of the chair and she sat back down next to me. 'Not about people . . . not about Mandy Finch . . . Here,' she said, handing me the glass, 'you'd better drink this.'

I glanced over at Paula. She had her head in her hands and seemed absorbed by the crumbs on the table. I looked up at Chuck, who made a drinking motion. I turned again to Natalie. A tear was rolling down one of her cheeks and she was gnawing at the knuckle of her right index finger.

'Please,' I repeated. 'What is it? Tell me.'

Paula slipped her arm around my shoulders. 'Dee,' she said to me gently, 'I think they've told us.'

Even after my persistent incomprehension forced poor Natalie to speak the truth out loud to me in short words I couldn't seem to hear it. That happened only after first Chuck then Paula had been compelled to repeat it. And when at long last I finally did register the message, I immediately began to laugh.

Amanda Finch – David Blake's wife – an undercover agent, an *agent provocateur*, a spy for US Intelligence during the late sixties,

162

early seventies . . .? Why, that meant she'd spent years pretending to be someone she wasn't – befriending people whose beliefs she despised – betraying their confidences – setting them up . . . And not in Moscow or Warsaw or Havana but in California – in America – in the land of the free, home of the brave.

It was inconceivable.

Preposterous.

What kind of fool did they take me for?

Surely it was the Ellisons who weren't what they appeared?

Indignation welled and I suspect I said a lot of things I'd regret if only I could remember what they were. Fortunately I can't and memory cuts back in with the sensation of Paula gripping my forearm and cooing and clucking at me as if I were an hysteric who needed to be coaxed back from the precipice of a nervous breakdown. I hate being soothed in that tone – even by a close friend who's just trying to be helpful – and felt if anything even more offended. I did, however, shut up.

With perfect timing, Chuck (whom I hadn't even noticed go out) came back into the kitchen bearing a thick folder, which he deposited momentously before me on the table. 'This,' he announced, 'is Alan's research through March of this year – the statements of over fifty people. And as you'll see, ninety-nine per cent of them went into the exercise with no preconceptions about who it was.'

'In fact,' Nat put in, 'certain people didn't even believe there *was* anyone.'

' "Certain people",' Chuck said, 'were prejudiced about the researcher.'

'Certain people had damn good reasons,' she snapped.

Paula cleared her throat. 'I see,' she said mildly. 'So what was it that prompted them to get involved?'

Chuck smiled. 'Certain other people came along and pointed out that if the researcher was really so misguided as all that, it would be doing him a favour to contribute and prove it.'

'I fell for the challenge,' Nat sighed. ' "And if he were right, why was I so afraid of that?" ' She placed her palm on the manuscript and looked at me. '*This* is why I was so afraid . . . the kids will be in soon. I think you'll find it quieter in the living room.'

Alan Dexter had put all the people he'd interviewed at their ease by casually asking them each to talk about what they'd found in their

State Department intelligence files, and then, when a person had exorcised the almost universal sense of 'really it was a long time ago, how can it matter now', he'd persuaded them all to try what he termed a 'visualisation exercise'. He evidently used a more soothing, less surly tone with them than he'd used down the phone with me for they all seemed willing enough to cast their minds back to the incidents noted in their records and view them from the fly on the wall position he urged them to try.

The effect was almost obscenely compulsive, like those horror films you watch through a slit between your fingers. Again and again, over and over what came across was how unquestioned a part of the fabric of the Berkeley scene Amanda Finch had been – how beyond suspicion – to virtually everyone who knew her. She was arrested in the demos they were arrested in, played her part in dope deals, made her share of meals and cups of coffee and produced her share of leaflets, and consistently developed better contacts for munitions than anyone else. But the fact that lent her most credibility in most minds was the way she had once stood up to some mean little rumours about her establishment background back east and the kinds of friends it might have given her. The woman who'd put them around had the ill fortune to be a junkie who'd visited the house while Amanda was away and trespassed in her room on the scrounge for drugs and money. She'd found instead what she'd decided were coded notes and taken them to Howard Louder, who'd been so certain they had some other explanation that he'd returned them to Amanda. She'd given him the reason to believe her and more, had ended up with her reputation for integrity enhanced by her sick accuser's paranoia.

'God,' Paula said after she'd read the interview with this unnamed woman, now recovered from drugs and working in an ashram in the Hawaiian islands somewhere. 'God. No wonder Louder hated Amanda so much. The stupid bastard had been warned and had walked into a set-up anyway.'

'Yes – well –' I mumbled, pulling myself out of the statement I was reading, 'he got his revenge by passing the word to Alan Dexter... Wait till you see what this plumber from Pittsburgh has to say. He'd be a lawyer now if she hadn't seen to it that he was busted.'

She pointed to her own growing pile of pages. 'I've just finished the story of a waitress who's a trained remedial teacher.' She made a gruesome face. 'Amanda not only turned her on to Marxism in

the first place, she introduced her into a "revolutionary underground cell" – the one that had the original idea to kidnap Patty
Hearst – *and* gave her and her boyfriend the address of a so-called
safe house for deserters which happened to have guns and grenades
stashed in the cellar and was under surveillance. The boyfriend
went to Sweden – lived there for ten years. Now he's a gardener.'
She sighed. 'It had never crossed her mind that Amanda was
responsible. Not once.'

'She wasn't the only one.' And many who had been deceived had
been far less gullible and far more street wise. Amanda's own
boyfriend Tommy for example. Tommy who had been so determined to get out of the 1967 version of the black ghetto of Oakland
that he'd won a scholarship to San Francisco State. Tommy who
had quickly come to see himself and his race in ideological terms
but who couldn't drop out because if he did he would end up on the
wide black frontline in Vietnam pointing a gun at his 'revolutionary communist comrades'. Tommy who after being busted
for drugs along with Amanda and Natalie and Howie and some
other white radicals had been presented with an alleged hit list
allegedly in his handwriting – a list of racist (or 'prejudiced' as the
term then was) politicians. Tommy who had admitted to this list
instead of revealing what little he knew of the internal structure of
the Black Panthers.

We went back to reading for another while, then Paula said: 'I
really understand why they all felt so outraged, don't you? I'm sure
I'd have felt the same, just on principle.'

'Yeah, but which one?'

She looked over to see if I was being facetious but I wasn't.

'That's what the plumber goes into that I think is so good.' I
sought his chapter again, then searched for the page. When I found
it, I read aloud to her: ' "Our starting point was disillusionment,"
he says. "We'd been brought up to believe America was the greatest
nation on earth, but when we got out there and looked we saw this
gulf between what it preached and what it practised. We exercised
our right to point this out and were instantly and summarily
branded as part of the communist conspiracy." That's what really
pissed him off, Paula: the fact that his own government so
distrusted the ideas of certain of its own citizens that it was secretly
depriving them of their constitutional right to speak freely.'

'But how did he know?'

'Too many activists kept getting pulled in by the police on

suspicion of this or that only to find themselves being interrogated – hell, and warned – about their political activities. And of course the irony was that this behaviour led even more students into the exact kind of extremist politics the government so feared. After all, like this guy says, if the government could break the rules, why couldn't they? Especially as they believed that their individual crimes might draw attention to the government's greater crime. That was certainly the plumber's reasoning when he decided to blow up that court house.'

'Does he still advocate the use of violence?'

'No. He's changed his mind about that.'

'Well then? Maybe Amanda getting him busted saved him from himself.'

'Yes, he says that, but as he also makes the point, at what cost? He may have changed about his own reaction to hypocrisy, but he's still angered by the hypocrisy itself. Don't you see? When the American government sends out agents to spy on its own citizens in the name of its holy war against communism, it's putting that war first and the constitution second. Worse, it's behaving in exactly the same way as it accuses the Soviets of behaving when they send out the KGB to spy on dissidents. The difference is, the Russians expect it. Americans don't. Amanda didn't simply betray the confidences of a few individuals, Paula; she betrayed a fundamental democratic principle. And by doing that, she took America one step closer to becoming everything it claims to oppose.'

Much later, after I'd pushed myself through the last paragraph of the last page of the last statement, I slouched into the sofa in the Ellisons' living room and closed my eyes.

How would I ever break it to David?

How would he take it?

Did it matter to me any more who'd killed her?

I couldn't excuse murder – no – definitely not. But after reading the fifty stories of fifty victims of deception, I could understand the desire to get even. Despite myself, I could understand that.

And if Amanda's espionage activities had continued over the past decade, wasn't it conceivable that another fifty or a hundred people might also want to get even?

Should I pass everything over to Henning and let him do what he liked with it?

Paula said: 'I suppose there's an outside chance it's fiction.'

'Ha,' I muttered, 'I wish.'

'Yeah, but it is funny that Dexter's left out the witnesses' names. I mean, why are the chapters just numbered?'

'So he's paranoid. What does it matter? I recognised Louder's section and Santucci's section and Natalie's section easy enough. Are you suggesting she's part of some complicated plot to con us? Why would she do that?'

She sighed. 'Just trying.' There was a pause. Then: 'I wonder why Amanda did it?'

But at that moment I didn't give a damn.

'Money?' she said.

I grunted. Money? Amanda? With a brother as rich as Craig?

A stray fact asserted itself through my feelings. The Swiss account. Opened in '74. (Not '71. She'd left Berkeley in '71.) Untouched since.

And there was the will, the added beneficiaries, the division of the money between her niece and Claire (family ties), Natalie and Tommy's sister . . .

Tommy's *sister*. Amanda had known he was dead. (*Agents know that kind of thing.*)

Was she trying to make amends to two of the people she'd hurt?

Paula said: 'About David . . .'

I thought: This is why Amanda hadn't wanted David to know about the Swiss account. She'd said, 'If I love and trust anyone, it's David.'

Had she been lying?

Did it matter now?

I said: 'I don't know how I'm going to tell him.'

'I have a feeling he knows, Dee. He read Louder's testimony in the car. He didn't come with us. I think he knows.'

I shook my head.

Behind my closed eyes, I heard her stand up. 'Maybe they'll let us borrow the manuscript overnight – to show it to him.'

She left me to my ruminations, which began again where they had started before and repeated themselves over and over un-endingly for half an hour without progression. Finally it occurred to me that it was getting late, that David might be getting concerned. I pulled myself together (more or less) and found my way back to the kitchen. The children had obviously been and gone and the three grown-ups seemed to be engrossed in an intense conversation.

167

As I entered, Chuck was saying, '... that's the deal. I don't know what your fees are, but . . .' Seeing me, he broke off. 'Recovered?'

I shrugged.

Natalie gave me a sympathetic look, a look of kinship, and gestured to a chair. 'There's a spare of the manuscript in Chuck's office – God knows why visiting professors of ancient history get safes, but they do – so you can take this one.'

'I called David,' Paula said. 'He's going for a drink with that doctor. He'll meet us at my place. I told him where the spare key is just in case.' Then, to my quizzical glance: 'He didn't ask, I didn't offer.'

'Perhaps we should leave these people to their . . .' I started.

Paula said: 'Dee, we've just been talking about the possibility of . . . well –' She hesitated and turned to Chuck. 'Maybe I should call you tomorrow. I don't know if she'll want to . . .'

'Want to what?' I asked.

Chuck said: 'We want to hire you.'

'Hire us?'

Paula said: 'I merely asked if they thought any of those fifty people might have committed homicide.'

'And we said – I said – yes,' Nat put in. 'While you were off reading, I talked it over with Chuck and decided to tell you that much even if you didn't ask. Beyond that – well, I'm prepared to say who only if you're prepared to prove, or try to prove, that I'm wrong. I want you to check up on *everyone* in that manuscript – find out if anyone flew to England at the right time. That's all.'

'My brother can do it on the computer,' Paula said. 'Easy.'

'But we don't know their names,' I began.

'The names are on a separate list which is coded to the book. They'll let us have that.'

Natalie touched my arm. 'Please. I'd be incredibly grateful.'

'It's just a mechanical operation, Dee,' Paula urged. 'What can it hurt?'

What can it hurt? I thought. Me? David? Someone who's been hurting so badly for so long that he or she killed because of it?

'You really want to know?' I said.

'I have to know,' Nat said.

Then she told me what had been left out of her statement in the manuscript – left out because it was too familiar to the interviewer to need mentioning. I learned about her move to San Francisco after Amanda had vanished; about the child she'd been carrying –

her son Che; about the day she'd taken the child's father along to visit Howie Louder in prison; about how the child's father, already fascinated by espionage theories, had become obsessed with uncovering the agent who'd been operating in Berkeley.

'He wasn't convinced it was Mandy,' she told me. 'What got him was the sheer idea that there had been *some*one. To him it was as if the McCarthy hearings hadn't ended, they'd just moved underground.'

I also learned about how this obsession had ruined the relationship for her. 'I'd moved away from Berkeley to get away from politics and intrigue. All I wanted to do was have some fun before the baby came. But oh no. He kept nagging me to go back with him – look people up – chase records. Problem was, he needed my contacts and I wasn't into giving them to him. When I caught him trying to steal my address book, that was it. I walked out.'

I discovered other things as well about Alan Dexter – that after he'd traced Amanda's London address the previous March ('God knows how'), he'd been summoned by the head of his department and told that if he continued this particular line of research, even though he was doing it in his spare time, he would find himself without a job; that he had sent the manuscript to Nat via Che when the boy had gone to spend the Easter holidays in New Jersey; that he had chosen her to send it to because he still, after all these years, regarded persuading her as his biggest challenge.

Chuck muttered: 'He still loves her.'

'Nonsense,' Nat said. 'He's remarried.' Then, to me: 'I like his wife a lot. She's Haitian – he met her down there when he was finishing off his doctorate – and she's what I could never be, never wanted to be.' She laughed. 'Another obsessive . . . No, I don't mean that. She *is* very committed politically though, very single-minded – works as an organiser for some pan-Latin American group that helps get left-wing refugees out of right-wing countries.'

Paula raised an eyebrow at me. Neither of us said a word.

During the drive back to San Francisco, Paula said: 'Take a look at that list of names, the one that's coded to the manuscript.'

I dug it out of her bag and looked. Then I slunk down into my seat.

(Did I care? Did I really care?)

It was a duplicate of the list Paula had stolen from the car of our Hispanic pursuers earlier that afternoon.

Ten

Paula had been right: David knew, or at any rate, showed no surprise. In fact, he showed no emotion at all, just nodded and said 'I see' a few times while I told him. Then he asked to see the manuscript, which he weighed in his hands for a moment before clearing his throat to suggest that it might be best if we went out for a meal without him. Badly as I wanted to touch him, it was evident from his manner that he had closed off, withdrawn, and more, that if I tried to invite him out with affection or sympathy, he would refuse the invitation.

Paula and I lingered over dinner as long as we could, yet spoke very little. There seemed to be only one thing to talk about, and neither of us had the desire to go that way again.

When we got back to her place, there was a message from Pete on the answerphone. It said: 'The security guard's just called. Somebody hit him on the head and broke into our office . . . . Gone to check the damage. Give me a call in the morning.'

I swore.

Paula said: 'Maybe it's coincidence.'

'You're kidding.'

'Yeah,' she said, 'I am.'

On the kitchen table there was a second message propped against the pepper grinder. It read: 'Gone for a walk. Will use the spare key to let myself in. Don't wait up.'

We watched TV for a while, but it only reminded me that here was another small reason for living in Britain. I showered and changed, got Paula to show me how to unfold the sofa bed in her den, wished her goodnight, dug out my book and tried to read.

David came back at about one-thirty smelling faintly of whisky but acting sober. He sat down on the edge of the bed and took my hand, which he stroked as he told me that he'd decided to do now what he'd realised tonight he should have done immediately after

Amanda's death: he'd decided to go off up to Yosemite on his own for a few days with his tent and sleeping bag. He felt that a couple of nights or so under the stars – some long hikes – some fresh country air – some solitude (especially that) – he felt this was what he needed. He'd fly back to LA on Sunday or Monday. 'That will leave us almost a week together,' he said finally. Then he stopped and waited. He didn't ask if I minded or if I understood, but the questions hung between us as palpably as his hope that my answers would be 'no' and 'yes'.

I thought: we've shared a lot in a short time but we're still new to each other, still unpredictable. And I thought: I could use some time on my own myself.

I told him that I understood and that while I'd much rather he stayed with me, I thought I could bear a short separation. He smiled and shook his head and reached for me.

After we'd held each other for a long moment, he let out a deep sigh. 'What I can't understand,' he said into my hair, 'is why she went around hiding her real views. Why not simply be straight about them like her brother? Why didn't she just take him up on his offer and join the board of Asprey Oil? If she was so mad keen to further the cause of reactionary capitalism, surely that would have been the way. Or if she genuinely wanted to be a journalist, why not bandy the Asprey name and let Craig pull a few strings?'

And how had she justified her deception to herself? That's what he really couldn't comprehend. There was no logic to it, no rationale, no thought.

... Which led him to the conclusion that she (she whose name he clearly found unspeakable) she had to have been well to the right of people like her brother, 'out there in the wilds with all those ... all those ...'

His voice broke and he let it rest a moment. Then he looked over towards Dexter's manuscript, which he'd left on top of the chest of drawers. 'She even goaded people into violence,' he said with disgust. 'She put them up to it. Jesus Christ, any normal person, anyone with any respect at all for other people, would have had the decency to try to persuade them out of it. She was bloody entrapping people.'

And he had lived with her – loved her – married her; he, a psychiatrist whose everyday work took him into the border zone between mental health and mental illness. 'If my professional judgment is so bad that I can't even read the condition of my own wife,' he said, 'how can I carry on at the hospital, never mind go ahead with the hostel?'

Perhaps worse, there was his political work. He had friends in all kinds of different Marxist groups that got branded 'extreme left' – hell, even the bunch of guys he went rambling with were all long-term activists. How would he face them? How would he begin to explain what had happened?

I merely listened (what could I say?) and from time to time mumbled soothing noises which seemed to me to be inadequate and unmemorable and utterly feeble but which nevertheless made him look at me gratefully.

Later, as I lay against his shoulder in bed, I told him what Natalie and Chuck had asked us to do. He raised himself up on one elbow and looked into my eyes. 'Can't you leave it? Alan Dexter – Dee, he's one of us. And most of those people he interviewed are like us too. They've made their mistakes and they've learned from them and now they're just getting on with it. Whatever they did, they've paid for it. Besides, don't you see? If one of them did it and you prove it, it'll bring about exactly what she wanted: it'll discredit another leftie.'

'Yes,' I said, 'but is that reason enough to condone murder?'

Collapsing back down on to the pillow, he seemed to speak to the ceiling. 'Is that what I'm doing? I thought I was merely suggesting that you stay out of it, not get any dirtier, not let her turn you into an agent too.' There was a pause and then he said: 'Has it occurred to you that Juan might have done it?'

I nearly laughed but was stopped by the sudden memory of Suze saying exactly the same thing.

David went on: 'If he figured out what she was up to and realised that what she was really doing was recruiting Carlos – well, he had the opportunity.'

'The police don't know that – yet.'

'No and are you going to tell them? And are you going to add that curiously enough we've been followed around by two Hispanic men?'

I wanted to answer but somehow couldn't. Instead I told him about Alan Dexter's wife.

'Oh that is wonderful. That is bloody marvellous. Now it's a choice between two people who've both escaped from fascist regimes and have put God-knows-how-many years into helping other people do the same. Jesus Dee, between them they're worth a

172

hundred of her. And I'll tell you something else too: if I'd been in their position – hell, if I'd realised at any point over the past five years the position I was in – I'd have been tempted to kill her myself. I'd be lying if I denied it, just like I'd be lying if I pretended that I don't think she deserved it.' He leaned over and kissed me. 'Sorry,' he said, 'but it's true.'

David was up, dressed, shaved and packed by seven the next morning and by half past had arranged another rented car, got hold of a good map and worked out his route. Then, just as he was on the point of leaving, both of us started to waver. A lot of it was the prospect of missing each other, but there was also, at least in me, a sudden knot of anxiety about our two friends in the drug squad cells and when they'd be released and whether they had other friends who might, if they saw David drive away alone . . .

Paula observed me beginning to cling and look worried and immediately came up with the remedy: she went to the phone and called Harve Turner's office. It turned out to be as she'd predicted: the two wouldn't be let out until late afternoon at the earliest (because they were carrying immigration papers stamped in Miami which needed to be verified). But just to be absolutely safe, she decided we should follow David at a distance of several cars out of the city, across the Golden Gate Bridge and into Marin county. And I must say, watching his car disappear into the northbound traffic, I wished I'd stayed behind: it felt even worse than ending the goodbye kiss.

It was only when we were back in her neighbourhood and had found a spot to park and were locking up the car that Paula said to me: 'Well? What's the plan? I mean, are you still game for Las Vegas or what?'

Here it was, the moment of decision. I sighed. 'I think I've had enough, Paula. I think I'd like to put it away for a day or two. Let's wait until Pete's checked through all those . . .'

'Pete!' she cried out, 'my God! I completely forgot to call him.' And gesturing to me to hurry, she rushed towards her apartment.

An hour later we were on a flight to Las Vegas.

Pete could not and had not assumed that our investigation was the cause for the break-in to his office. The agency was large and reputable and had dozens of sensitive cases in progress and tens of dozens of closed cases in storage. Every bit of information about all of them was on the computer and the one sign of the intrusion was that the computer had been turned on. So although he stayed up all night searching through discs hoping to figure out the connection, it had been a telephone call from the man who'd been keeping an eye on Amanda's ex-sister-in-law Claire that had made the link.

This man, BB, had already reported in to Pete that Claire no longer danced; some overenthusiastic admirer in some audience some years before had thrown something that had hit her right leg in such a way as to damage the nerves in the tendon. Now she called herself a hostess but seemed in fact to hang out at the gaming table where he'd traced her.

He'd been following her home at about eight am for the second morning in a row when two men had appeared on the other side of the street and lunged at her. He unfortunately hadn't been fast enough to prevent the first blow, which had dislocated her shoulder, nor had he managed to catch either of her assailants. But judging by the hunting dagger one of them had dropped, BB was pretty sure he had saved her life. What he knew for certain was that the attackers had been Hispanic.

'Oh no,' I said to Paula, 'there *are* more of them. David . . .'

'Don't do it to yourself,' she said. 'He's got a gun with him. We know he wasn't followed. Don't think about it.'

Had I passed Claire Asprey Clarke under the artificial light of a casino, I doubt I'd have noticed the split, dried-out ends of her dyed red hair any more than I'd have taken in the smudged black circles around her eyes, the thick smear of blusher on her gaunt cheeks or the shakily drawn line of artificial fullness around her mouth. Coming upon her as I did in mid-morning sunlight, propped up against crisp, fresh, white linen, these features were impossible to miss. And while I quickly told myself that hospitals only ever flatter the healthy, I was just as quickly forced to conclude that, in that case, she still had a long way to go.

She glared over at us. 'Jesus – reinforcements. Look, I swear, I have nothing to say. First I was on my feet, then I was on the ground. That's all I remember. Now let me out of here, will you?'

'We're not police,' Paula said.

She frowned. 'Not police? Well then who the hell are you?'

I told her our names and started to explain why we'd come, but I only got as far as Amanda's name.

'Mandy?' she repeated, struggling to push herself up. 'Mandy?' Then, suddenly, she smiled, and just as suddenly I saw in her eyes another Claire, a spirited and younger woman who had somehow got herself trapped in that dishevelled, undernourished body. That Claire bubbled out for about thirty seconds: 'My God – *Mandy*! I don't believe it. Shit, sit down, sit down. Tell me how she is. *Mandy*. How did she find me? Is she coming too? When can I see her?'

Abruptly she looked down and saw the trap around herself. Her expression collapsed into anxiety. 'No . . . no, she mustn't see me. Tell her you couldn't find me . . . tell her I was away . . . yes, that's it, tell her I was in a show in Monte Carlo for a month. I'll get myself together – I will. I'll eat and I'll . . .'

Wondering why I kept having to do this to people, I interrupted and explained to her as gently as possible why she needn't worry about a visit. She sank back into the pillow and, turning her head away, closed her eyes and bit her upper teeth hard into her lower lip. Paula and I gave each other helpless looks and waited until finally, able to wait no longer, Paula crossed to Claire's bedside and touched her on the shoulder. Claire shrugged her off. Then she extended her bony thin arm and flicked her hand vaguely towards the floor. 'The bottle,' she said. 'In my bag.'

We found the bag but no bottle. Paula went out to the corridor to see what BB could do and came back almost at once with a fifth of brandy. I didn't ask any questions and neither did Claire, who grabbed at it, unscrewed the top, tilted it back and sucked hungrily. My head ached like tomorrow morning just watching her.

'Look,' I said, 'we're sure there has to be a connection between the assault on you and Amanda's death.'

Letting the bottle slip down her chest, she laughed a short, derisive laugh. 'I'll say. It's called a curse.'

'Please,' I said. 'I'm serious.'

'So am I. Hell, Mandy believed in it too. Why do you think she changed her name? I'll tell you: because every woman who gets landed with Asprey pays for it, that's why. Her great grandmother fell down a mine in South Africa; her grandmother, the one whose old man found the oil – she walked off into the jungle one day and never came back; and her mother, well – the heat and all went to her head too, only her damn silly ideas got her *and* her husband killed. I mean, what more do you want?

' 'Course it's true, there hadn't been any daughters in so long

175

that we weren't sure if you could inherit it or if you just caught it by marrying into it . . . Guess I've got the answer now.'

She stared at the foot of the bed, her eyes forlorn and distant, but as I opened my mouth to ask what she'd meant about Amanda's mother, she sighed: 'Poor kid. I told her too, I said, fat lot of good it'll do you, takin' your mother's maiden name. Pick a brand new one, I said; start clean. But she liked the sound of Finch.' She shook her head. 'There'd never been any divorces in the Asprey family either and we used to wonder if you could get rid of the curse that way. Heh – no chance. Learned that ages ago . . . Still, what the hell, I'm alive at least.'

Paula said: 'I think you had a close call this morning.'

Claire's glance was sharp. 'What do you mean?'

I said: 'Didn't the police tell you about the knife? One of the assailants dropped a knife.'

Her eyes widened and she swore. 'I don't understand. Why would anybody want to kill *me*?'

'For what you know – about her.'

'But that's crazy. I haven't seen Mandy in years.'

'Maybe not, but from what we've learned it seems quite possible that it's someone she had dealings with years ago who's behind all this.'

'Political dealings,' Paula added. 'With some kind of Latin American angle.'

At that, and despite the layer of blusher, Claire's face went instantly and obviously pallid; perspiration rose on her forehead and her hands shook so badly as she fumbled for the bottle that she spilled some drink on her chin. She didn't notice.

Paula and I looked at each other again. We both knew we'd hit; some new revelation was imminent if we could just persuade this poor woman to impart it to us before she passed out.

Paula said: 'Did you know your assailants were Hispanic?'

The other woman closed her eyes. Her jaw slackened. The answer was no.

'Last Saturday,' Paula continued, 'Dee got a call from a woman with a Spanish accent who warned her off this case. The next afternoon two Hispanic-looking men appeared on the beach near her mother's and when we drove up to San Francisco they followed us. We had a list of names, including yours. We've since discovered that they also had a list of names, but theirs didn't include yours. We had those two arrested yesterday afternoon. We *know* they

176

were inside last night, yet last night my brother's office was broken into. He's the one who traced your address for us and it was on his computer and his computer was turned on. There's something else too, another detail: Mandy didn't die alone. She was murdered with a twenty-three-year-old Chilean man.'

Claire moaned and began to shake her head from side to side as if struggling to fend off some nightmare phantom.

'Please,' Paula said gently, 'I'm not trying to torture you. We simply have to know what she did – what happened that caught up with her.'

'No,' Claire mumbled, her eyes still closed, her head still shaking, 'can't . . . gave her my word . . . never tell . . .'

Paula şighed. 'Look,' she said, 'we saved your life. The man who ran your attackers off – he works for my brother.'

That did it. Claire pushed herself up, her frail arms strengthened by her indignation, and glared at us. 'You knew?' she spat. 'Jesus Christ, why the fuck didn't you . . .'

'Calm down,' Paula said. 'We didn't *know* anything. We were just going on . . .'

' "We didn't know anything",' Claire cut in, mimicking my friend's words in a snide sing-song. 'Oh sure, that's fat. How'd you get my name then, huh? And who's paying your brother, eh? It's that bastard Craig isn't it? . . . Well? Isn't it?'

'No. And we got your name from Amanda's will. You're one of 'the beneficiaries.'

Claire's anger vanished as abruptly as it had welled. 'Me? She named *me*? She remembered *me*? She left me money?' She looked down at the blanket. 'My leg. I can try that new surgery.' She set the bottle on the bedside table and, hugging herself, looked upwards. 'I can take the cure. I can get out of Vegas. I can start again . . . Oh God, Mandy, wherever you are, thank you.'

Paula cleared her throat. 'There is a complication. The final draft of the will was stolen by whoever killed her. No signed copy exists.'

'Oh,' Claire said in a small, deflated voice. She reached for the bottle again, but this time drank more slowly, obviously pondering what this meant.

'There's a rider as well,' I remarked. 'You're basically to earn your part of the money by overseeing the trust fund she wanted set up for her niece.'

'Niece?' she frowned. 'Niece?' There was alarm in her tone as she protested: 'But Craig's sterile. He caught smallpox in Panama when he was three.'

I frowned too, dimly aware that something was wrong here, something I'd assumed, something I'd never questioned. I said: 'Well he's got a little seven-year-old daughter named Astrid. I'm surprised you didn't . . .'

But Claire had risen up on to her knees and now heaved the bottle at the far wall. 'Damn his soul,' she cried out, 'damn it, damn it, damn it. Christ almighty, I knew he was an evil son-of-a-bitch but I never thought – never dreamed in a million years . . . That child,' she said, turning to us furiously, 'that child is Mandy's.'

And then she told us about the last time she'd seen Amanda Finch.

It was when Claire had turned the corner of East 86th Street, glanced up out of old habit and seen the familiar outlines of the penthouse that her nerve had suddenly wobbled. In fact she had such an excruciatingly jelly-like moment that she'd had to stop still in the gusting cold mid-November wind and give herself a sharp talking to. So what (it went) that she'd sworn never to set foot in her former home again? That had been seven years ago. And as for her hurt feelings over the way Mandy had disappeared from Berkeley without so much as an apology that time two years before, well, surely what was more important was that she was needed again now.

She looked at her watch, pulled up her collar and forced herself to carry on. She had to hurry. Bella – dear Bella – Bella who had held on to her decency despite fifteen years as Craig's housekeeper – Bella had urged her to come this particular afternoon because it was the one in the week when the current Mrs Asprey could be counted on to be out. . . . Trouble was, the doctor was due in just under two hours and the not very pleasant man in a suit who called himself John and who seemed to Bella to be more in charge of Mandy's care than Craig invariably arrived about five.

Bella was there when the elevator doors parted and the two women fell on each other. Both would have loved to talk – the last time had been a year earlier – but they accepted that they couldn't. Bella took Claire's coat with one hand and with the other handed her the tray full of coffee things. Claire didn't need directing: she automatically turned towards Mandy's old room. She also shivered with the uncanny sense of slipping back fifteen years.

This sense was heightened when she pushed open the door and saw the familiar pink-print wallpaper and frilly curtains and football pennants and photographs – so much so that she had to stop herself from calling out to the heap under the large quilt on the bed that she'd be late for school if she didn't get a move on. Then she realised that the head peeking out from beneath the bedclothes was dark. She went closer. Yes: Mandy's hair, once long and blonde, was cropped and black.

Claire took one of the cups off the tray and, as she juggled to set it on the bedside table, inadvertently knocked the edge of a framed photo. It didn't quite fall but it moved and she noticed with some surprise that it was a picture of Mandy's late mother Lucy. *Some*thing had changed: in the old days, pictures of Lucy Asprey lived in bottom drawers.

The figure in the bed, disturbed by the slight noise, moaned and rolled over. Crouching, Claire put the tray on the floor and said: 'Mandy? Are you awake? It's me Mandy, it's Claire.'

The figure's forehead pinched into a frown but the eyes stayed shut.

'Honey, look at me.'

The figure, still frowning, shook its head.

'Well then, will you at least give me your hand?'

Nothing happened.

Claire stroked her friend's cheek. 'Please?'

After a long moment, the bedclothes slowly stirred and fingers slid out the side. Claire took them in her own.

The eyes opened and stared at her vacantly, as if the person behind them were too weak or too wary to commit herself to focusing. Instinctively Claire leaned over so that her nose was inches from Mandy's and smiled. The other woman's head jerked backwards and her eyelids shut once more; then they opened again, struggled to focus and finally widened. 'Claire,' she whispered, 'oh Claire, it *is* you.'

' 'Course it's me. Would I lie? Come on now, drink this here coffee and talk to me. Where you been keepin' yourself the last couple of years anyhow?'

Mandy bit her lip and swung her head away. 'I can't tell you.'

Right, Claire thought, and pretending to ignore both the statement and the lassitude behind it, reached over, fluffed the spare pillows into a back rest, helped her friend sit up, gave her a cup and chided her until she drank from it. Then she took several paper wallets full of photos out of her bag and spent about ten minutes showing them to Mandy and telling her stories about life in Las Vegas – the breaks she'd had, the clubs she'd been playing, the people she'd met. Gradually the tactic worked. Mandy became interested, began to ask questions, even laughed.

'And this,' Claire said, handing over the last picture, 'is my new house. See this window? That's going to be your room. And this little window – well, I figure that room'll do just fine for the baby.'

Mandy blanched. 'How did you know?'

'You told me.'

'I?' There was alarm in the syllable.

'Yes. You wrote me. From Miami.'

'No. No. I wasn't supposed to do that.'

'Well maybe you weren't but you did. Look, here's the . . .'

But Mandy closed her eyes again.

'You said you'd tried to call me,' Claire persevered. 'You'd wanted to ask if you could come and live with me. You said that you felt awful – didn't know what to do, where to turn. You told me that the father . . .'

Mandy put her hands over her ears. 'Stop,' she pleaded. 'I remember, but you must destroy that note. I was being weak. I was still sick and deluded. If anyone finds out . . . Rip it up, Claire, please. It was wrong.'

'Sweetheart, the only thing wrong about that note was the address – and the fact that I was away when it *did* get delivered. That's why I didn't come sooner.'

'And you have to go away again – now.'

Claire stared at her. 'Is that what you really want?'

Mandy looked uncertain. 'Yes.'

'Okay.' She stood up. 'I just thought you might need a friend. It sounded that way and I mean, I know what it's like to be depressed. Hell and I owe you – for all those years you listened to me.'

Mandy was gazing down at her stomach. Softly, so softly that Claire barely heard, she said: 'It's my fault. I betrayed him.'

Claire sat back down. 'Oh sugar, we all make mistakes. Did you love him?'

Mandy nodded.

'Did he love you?'

Another nod.

'Well how about this: why don't I go and find him; talk to him; tell him you're sorry; ask him to . . .'

'You can't. He's dead.'

'Oh shit. Darlin', I didn't realise.'

She reached over to hug her friend, but Mandy pulled back. Then she looked into Claire's eyes, looked in deep, and seemed after a moment to decide something. She sighed a long and shaky sigh. 'You must promise never to tell anyone.'

'On my honour.'

There was another pause. Then: 'I got even. I went there to get even and I got even.' She picked at a string on the quilt. 'And I hate myself. I should have died with him. I wanted to die but I . . . they . . .'

Claire said: 'Got even? Oh my God – for . . . ?'

Mandy glanced at the picture of her mother. 'Yes.' She shut her eyes. 'I've been in South America, Claire, in Chile. I've been working for . . .' – her voice had caught – '. . . working for the government.'

'*Our* government?'

'Yes. The communists, they took over in Chile two and a half years ago like they took over in Cuba in '58. They did it a different way but it came to the same thing: the same kind of people were in control. Or that's what I thought; that's how they put it to me. So when they asked me to help, play a little part in a plan to get rid of them, I said yes. I did something similar in Berkeley; that's the real reason I left so fast. I screwed up. So this time they trained me better. I pretended to be Spanish, not that it was difficult. I worked as a translator for a British news agency. I acted like a sympathiser, a comrade. That's how I met – how I met Pedro. He was a journalist, an activist; he worshipped Allende. I wasn't supposed to fall in love with him and I wasn't supposed to see any sense in what he believed. He was the, ah, the enemy.' She sighed another deep sigh and fell silent.

Claire, never a political person, wasn't exactly sure what to make of this confession. She'd heard of Chile, of course she had; she wasn't stupid. But the place had so little relevance to her life that she'd always just assumed it was where they grew the small red peppers she used in taco sauce. She didn't know anything about who ruled in the country. And as for Mandy's work there, well, frankly, she'd never even considered that real people did that kind of thing, not in the 1970s. Spying (for she could see that that's what her friend was admitting to) – spying was something men did in war movies.

Nor did she understand what Berkeley had to do with it. Mandy's letters from there had always been full of news about her courses and boyfriends, about concerts and drugs and weird bean diets, and it had been the same whenever Mandy had visited her in New York. Politics had never come into their conversations, not really.

On the other hand, Claire, like every decent American, had a gut-level loathing for communism and she knew that Mandy possessed more of that loathing than most people for the simple reason that it had made her an orphan.

She squinted thoughtfully at her friend and mentally upbraided herself. She should have realised that sooner or later that hatred would need an outlet. And now, regardless of the exact political details, she could see the dilemma. Mandy's revenge had backfired. She'd been charmed the same way her mother had been charmed. For of course even Claire knew about the real tragedy of Lucy Asprey's death: somehow this wealthy American woman had been persuaded that communism would be right in Cuba. She'd befriended some 'revolutionaries', even talked of giving them some money, and then – then they'd turned around and killed her and her husband.

Delicately, Claire said: 'At least you got out in time. You did what you'd gone to do and you got out.'

'I didn't want to leave. I was pulled out against my will. That letter I sent you, that shows how crazy I was.'

'Well,' Claire tried uneasily, 'you're obviously recovering . . .'

'Am I? Then why do I still love him? I'll tell you why, because I'm a bad person.'

'Oh honey . . .'

'No, don't deny it. I am. I have no control over myself either. My head betrays my heart, my heart betrays my head and I end up looking two ways at once and betraying everyone and everything: my parents' memories, my country, myself, my lover, his country' – she glanced at her stomach – 'and now my child.'

'What do you mean? The child isn't even . . .'

'I mean, if I can't live with myself, how can I live with it?'

Appalled, Claire protested: 'You're not saying . . . but Mandy, the child is your chance to put things right.'

'Yes. That's why I'm going to make sure it gets a good home and doesn't have me around to provide an unstable influence. I'm going to give it away, Claire – no, don't look at me like that. I've decided.'

Claire studied her friend's face. 'I don't believe you,' she said quietly. 'I'm hearing Craig, not Mandy.'

Mandy closed her eyes.

'Please,' Claire urged, 'listen to me. I know you. I remember the conversations we used to have. If you hadn't wanted this baby, you wouldn't have chosen to get pregnant in the first place.'

'I made a mistake. I can't have a child whose father was a . . . was a . . .'

'For God's sake, politics aren't in the genes! Look, come out to Vegas with me. Pack a bag now and we'll go. Give yourself a chance to think about this away from Craig and . . .'

But shaking her head, Mandy rolled over. 'No, Claire,' she whispered. 'No. You're too late. It's all arranged.'

The next day when she called she learned that Bella had been fired for letting her in. Amanda had been sent away.

After we'd filled my mother in on all the details we'd gathered over the three days we'd been away, she said: 'Well it sounds to me like you girls've done every single thing you possibly can. There's nothing else you can do now until Pete's finished tracking down all the loose ends you've asked him to find out about, so you might just as well put the whole thing right out of your minds and try to relax and have a good time.'

I had a sudden image of David's face, followed by a surge of panic. 'If only,' I sighed.

She put her arm around my shoulder and squeezed.

Paula put her hand over her heart. '*I* won't talk about it if you two don't – scout's honour.'

Despite sad eyes, my mother pledged and I forced myself to agree as well. Then we planned ourselves a busy programme of shopping and visiting old friends and lying in the sun and eating out which we stuck to grimly in the name of Fun for the next two excruciatingly slow days.

None of us, in fact, managed to hold to the vow. We'd go for a while – an hour, an afternoon, ten minutes – and then one of us would break and give voice to our current surmise. And what gradually emerged from this was that each of us was nurturing a different Amanda.

My mother's, for example, was a poor mixed-up young woman who'd given up politics after giving away her child, put her golden handshake into a Swiss account which she'd afterwards felt too guilty to touch, and married a psychiatrist because she needed one. 'I can believe,' she said at one point, 'that she really didn't know about David's politics at the beginning.'

Paula, whose Amanda was an American intelligence agent right up to her last breath, said: 'So why didn't she divorce him when she found out?'

'For the same reason,' my mother said, 'that she didn't change her name when she moved to London. Part of her desperately wanted to get caught.'

For Paula, however, the confusion theory ignored the emotion with which she herself had spent the entire previous year trying (and none too successfully, she insisted) to come to terms: hatred and the taste for revenge. This, in her opinion, had driven Amanda along – and sometimes driven her into such tight corners that all she could do was bolt.

For myself I couldn't see why the US Central Intelligence Agency would be particularly interested in David Blake *or* his friends – surely they were much too fond of public argument to be dangerous? And I attached great importance to the missing second will, which it seemed to me signified her remorse. In fact, I fancied that she'd decided to tell all to Alan Dexter – or I fancied it when I thought about her, which wasn't too frequently given what she was competing with.

For instance the Chilean connection.

After all, whichever Amanda any of us pictured, she had undeniably betrayed the Chilean left. Who had this simple reason, this frighteningly simple reason, for killing her.

Who definitely counted Juan and Connie Diego among their numbers, and may have counted as well the people who had called to threaten me at LA Airport, followed us up the coast, broken into Pete's, harmed Claire.

And there was the worry about David – this most of all. Why didn't he ring? Why didn't the Ranger Station in Yosemite that we'd contacted call us back? Where in the hell was that useless associate of Pete's up there who'd said he'd look for him? Why didn't something *happen*!

By Saturday evening all of us were tense with the pretending, with the strain of ignoring the unresolved mess suspended inches above our heads. Even my mother, who has good nerves and doesn't drink a lot, was filling her wine glass pretty full pretty often. We decided to go out for a Japanese meal and follow it with drinks at a fashionable beachside bar where we could distract ourselves by spotting famous people.

We spotted a lot and reminisced and drank too many Tequila Sunrises and to tell you the truth I think that if Paula and I had been on our own we'd have happily stayed there until dawn just because we'd at last attained exactly the right level of mindlessness. My mother, however, although energetic and healthy for her age, was nevertheless in her late sixties; we had been pretty active the past two days and between that and the tension and the drink she began to nod off at about ten thirty.

Twenty minutes later, as we cut up the sand towards my mother's bungalow after a revivifying arm-in-arm stroll along the tideline, we heard the telephone ringing in the distance. Mom's look said 'fat chance' but she handed me her keys and I attempted a semi-inebriated run. (David. Surely it would be David.) Typically, though, the ringing stopped the moment I opened the door. Hopeful that whoever it was would try again, I switched on the percolator and was throwing some water on my face when my hope was rewarded.

'Thank God,' said my partner Suze. 'I had this horrible feeling that you'd gone away for the weekend.'

'Gee,' I answered, 'I'm fine. Been having a great time.'

'Sorry,' she sighed, 'sorry. It's too early for the niceties. Are you sitting?'

'No but I can.' I sat. 'What is it?'

'Juan. He's been charged with the murders of Amanda and Carlos.'

My mother's eyes filled with tears and I waited for her to give way and say the harsh things about my work that I knew she was feeling (I was feeling them too). But she made do with venting her disappointment on the mugs and the refrigerator door and with muttering to herself about how it wasn't my fault and my father had been the same. Then she began to talk about the next time and when it might be and the places we could go that didn't have telephones, places where my work would have no chance of finding me.

We also discussed the next day: although she'd had something planned for ages, she felt suddenly torn about going to it because of David. How could she leave him to an empty house? My task was to persuade her to go and, with Paula's help, by the time we went up to bed I'd more or less succeeded.

Yet desperate as I now was for sleep, my thoughts wouldn't lie down. I needed to talk to Pete – see about a stand-by ticket on a flight – decide whether to stop over in New York and confront Alan Dexter on my own.

And then there was David. Could I really bring myself to leave California without knowing if he was all right?

Dawn entered through the blinds. The insomnia won.

I got up again, picked up my notebook and case file, went down to the kitchen, reheated the coffee and began to read all the papers once more from the beginning.

Some time later, as I was reconsidering whether it would help or hurt to have a couple of hours rest, someone started tapping quietly on the back door.

David!

I leapt up excitedly and just as quickly became fearful.

Does the bogeyman knock first?

Should I waken Paula?

Cautiously I peeked out through the curtain, then hurriedly unlatched the chain and opened the door.

'Jeez Dee,' Pete smiled, 'what are *you* doing up at this hour?'

'Isn't that my question?'

He laughed. 'My answer's "not by choice". I got a call from New York about half an hour ago. There's been some funny business, the kind I thought you'd want to know about at once.' He leaned inwards and sniffed the air, which made me realise we were still at the door. I gestured him in, pointed him to a chair and poured him out some black coffee. He took a long swallow.

'Craig Asprey,' he said, 'is at this very moment on a British Airways Concorde flight to London due to arrive at six o'clock tonight their time. And right behind him on a Pan Am 747 flight due to arrive about three hours later is your Dr Alan Dexter.'

'He's *tailing* Craig?'

'Yup. Has been for a couple of days. The guy I sent over to Asprey's apartment to make sure the little girl is okay has been doing the digging about Dexter for me too, so he recognised him as soon as he saw him hanging around there. Boy was he surprised – the guy's got this squeaky clean record, you know? I was surprised myself. That's why I decided not to bother you about it till I'd finished my check of the airlines, which I did last night. I called but you weren't in.'

'So?' I said. 'Well?'

'Dr Alan Dexter,' he said, 'flew to London the day before Amanda and Carlos were murdered – and flew back the day after.'

Eleven

George Appleby Investigations of Whitechapel is a humble little operation compared to Paula's and her brothers'. I have a feeling that it's similar to what their father's outfit must have been like back in the thirties when my father first used it: a more or less one-person set-up run out of a spare bedroom (in this case in a flat above an East End betting shop). And as for 'hi-tech', well, in George's context that amounts to a reconditioned telex machine and a second-hand answerphone with a radio-pager hook-up device. Still, he's good, especially at the kind of footwork I needed at that point, and besides, I knew he wouldn't mind me disturbing him on a Sunday.

He was even in and after a quick précis of the case I gave him two instructions: to meet Craig Asprey at Heathrow, warn him and make sure he was protected, and to follow Alan Dexter and find out what he was up to. I also promised that Pete would wire him photos of the two men within the hour.

Then I did the hard things: I saw my mother off with her friend Marcia and I wrote a long letter to David which started with my worries about his safety (neither Pete's associate nor the Ranger Station had yet located him) and ended with a plea for him to call me in London immediately. I left this and a key to Mom's with one of her neighbours and left a note on the inside window of the back door directing David to her place.

Paula drove me to the airport and saw me off on the series of interconnecting flights which I'd been forced to accept in order to get myself home. Somehow I slept and despite a recurring dream about (of all things) a murder trial, I arrived feeling readier for whatever I was getting myself into.

This was a good thing, for after hiring a taxi to rush me straight to Brixton Prison, I was greeted by the first of the many unexpected events that were to mark that long Monday: Juan Diego refused to see me.

'But he's my client,' I protested to the guard. 'I'm his solicitor.'

'Not according to him you're not,' he stated. Then, looking me up and down, he shrugged and added: 'If you ask me, Miss, it's your accent. He's been raving about American women and CIA plots ever since they brought him in.'

Wonderful, I thought as I dialled Connie's number. For this I'd cut short my holiday and flown six thousand miles. For *this*. I calmed down a little though when I realised that she was as distressed as I was.

'Can you come over now?' she asked me. 'I'll get the others here.'

'Do that,' I said. 'Give me half an hour.' And stopping only to ring messages through to George's office and my own, I flagged another taxi.

The small Willesden flat was, by the time I entered it, crowded with men and women all talking to each other in Spanish with an impassioned urgency that suggested dispute. Connie, who looked as if she'd had just about as much strain as she could handle, gripped my arm in the hallway, apologised, didn't seem to hear me tell her not to bother, and led me nervously into the sitting room. Everyone quietened as she began the introductions, but it took little sensitivity to notice that while half the group smiled and nodded at me with interest, the other half begrudged my presence with assorted levels of hostility.

Terrific, I mused. Their comrade's up for murder and they're arguing about whether my American background makes me too ideologically dubious to conduct his defence. I was weighing up how best to cut through this situation (ignore it? deal with it straight?) when the telephone rang. Fortunately it was for me.

'Sorry to interrupt, luv,' George started in his scraping chain-smoker's bass.

'Don't be,' I sighed.

'Good, good. Look, I thought I better report in. First off, your man Asprey. My lad Jamieson had him paged as per plan and guess what? The bleeder didn't come to the desk.'

'Oh Jesus, you don't mean he wasn't on the flight?'

'No, he was on it all right and Jamieson picked him out okay. But he jumped when he heard his name over the tannoy, then took off at a run into the car park. Jamieson stayed with him and saw him get into a grey Mercedes. Trouble was, it took Jamieson a while to get his own car out. He lost him I'm afraid.'

'Shit.'

'Mmm, I didn't think you'd be too pleased, so what I did was, I rang round all the likely hotels.'

'I think his usual's Claridges.'

'That's where I started. He isn't due till Thursday. Do you want the whole run down on where he isn't?'

'No thanks. How about flights out?'

'Tried that too. Nothing booked. Want my opinion? I reckon he knows something funny's going on. I mean, it's too bad 'n all that he didn't figure out we're on his side, but he seems to have the nous to keep his head down.'

'What about Dexter?'

'Ah well, *that* you'll be glad to hear was a piece of cake. He walked right out and got into a Cortina parked a couple in front of mine. I got a nice look at the bloke in the driver's seat and scribbled down the registration. Traced it this morning. Motor and owner live at the same address I tailed 'em to last night, over here in the Bello. I'm just near the place at the moment.'

'Fantastic.'

'Yeah. Now for the bad news. It's the ground floor flat in one of those terrace houses that backs on to a communal garden. There are gates at each end and all the houses on the other side back on to it too. You hear what I'm saying Dee? I'd need another three, four men to guarantee he doesn't get out without me knowing. Can your client stretch to that?'

I thought: *what* client?

'Look,' I said, 'add one more for now and ring me at the office this afternoon.'

'Will do . . . oh, and one more thing. You want background on this Mike Berry bloke who owns the flat?'

The hallway suddenly seemed to shimmy around me and I put my hand on the wall to steady it. 'Mike Berry?' I repeated hoarsely as a vague image grew clearer: the reception after Amanda's funeral – the short balding American with the wire frame glasses who'd introduced himself to me – the journalist Phil had hired to put pressure on Amanda.

What had he said to me? 'I'd go very carefully if I were you.'

I told George to find out what he could.

The next surprise of the day was the note sitting on top of my pile of messages when I finally got back to my office. It said: 'Dr Alan Dexter rang. Will ring back around four.'

I was still staring at the piece of paper, willing it to tell me if it could really be true that the professor had someone watching me at the same time as I had someone watching him, when I heard a familiar whoop behind me and found myself being hugged.

'My, my,' Suze grinned, holding me at arm's length and peering at the pink tinge on my face, 'is that the best you could do?' Then, after we'd checked each other's health and state of mind, she nodded at the note. 'I saw that sitting there. Any idea what he's doing in town?'

'He's not on holiday, that's for damn sure,' I grunted, reaching down to lift my suitcase one more time. 'Come on.' I headed for her office. 'For the price of a cup of tea I'll tell you everything I know.'

But in fact we'd gone through two pots before I'd even approached the end and Suze was leaning down to switch the kettle on yet again as she said: 'So Pete managed to establish that Amanda actually did go back to Cuba.'

'Yes. And on to New York. She flew back here from there two days later. Little Astrid was in the hospital being treated for her asthma that week and the reckoning is that Amanda could easily have gone to see her without Craig knowing anything about it.'

'She could have gone to see Alan Dexter too presumably.'

'Presumably. I can ask him when he calls back . . . though I may leave it till after we've gotten through "Please tell me what is your exact role in the death of Amanda Finch?" and "How did the list of the names of the people you interviewed for your book end up in the boot of a car which followed us up the West Coast and whose driver turned out to be a Chilean refugee?" '

'Oh *what!*'

'Sorry, did I leave that out? We had tests done on the fingerprints Paula lifted from the car in San Francisco. We also had them done on the knife dropped by one of Claire's assailants in Las Vegas and guess what? He's a Chilean as well. That's not all either. It gets worse. *Both* of them entered the United States through a refugee agency in Miami which has links with the agency where Dexter's wife works in New York *and* with the campaign group Juan and Connie are so active in here, the CSC.'

Her forehead dropped into her hands. Her frown was pained.

I sympathised. I felt the same.

'Remember,' I said, 'Alan Dexter did research down in Chile for his doctorate – which was before his Berkeley research . . . I am sure he is the one person in this whole thing who could conceivably have pieced together Amanda's entire career as an agent.'

The frown was still there when Suze looked up. 'So where does Juan fit in? As Alan's "co-conspirator"?'

I shrugged. 'The CSC are adamant that he's been set up by the CIA.'

She smiled.

'Well,' I said, 'the evidence *is* of the easy-to-plant variety. All the police have is a boot which they claim was under some rubbish in Juan and Connie's back yard and which makes a print like the one found at the cottage; and a photo. This was at the bottom of the pile Connie's been collecting for about two years to put into the Campaign's book on Allende and is – or so they allege – a group shot taken in Santiago in the summer of '73. Someone has apparently circled the head of one of the women and on the back of the print, in what they purport is Juan's handwriting, it says in Spanish: "Amanda Finch and her lover, the late Pedro Rivera."

'Connie, needless to say, swears she's never seen this photo before. She *did* know Pedro – I guess everyone knew Pedro – and it sounds as if the story of his betrayal is so legendary it's practically a folk tale. It's even *the* reason why Juan and so many of the others distrust American women. But Connie is positive that it would never ever have even occurred to any of the British Chilean community to suspect that the wife of the consultant psychiatrist who helped their comrade Carlos at his tribunal hearing was the woman of the legend. As she says, why would anyone suspect that? It's too bizarre a coincidence. Besides which, the woman of the legend had no real name and to virtually all of them here in London, no face until the police produced that photo.'

'Incredible,' she murmured. 'Brilliant . . . Juan's defence can be built around the technicalities.'

I shook my head. 'You've forgotten about Armstrong. He's come forward and admitted that Juan and Connie hadn't actually stayed in his bungalow that weekend, even though he'd lent it to them. What isn't clear to me is whether he went to the police before or after they finally got a search warrant for the Diegos' flat – I mean to ask Henning that when I ring him. But whatever happened, once Juan was charged – well – anyone who knows his history could have predicted that he'd do what he's done, which is dig his heels in and refuse to tell the police where he really was.'

'It is still possible that his story about going off to Barcelona on forged papers is just a story.'

'Yes and it's equally possible that someone is taking advantage of the inevitable fact that Juan will let himself be sent down for murder before he'll let himself be convicted on some lesser charge that might get him deported.'

Suze nodded absently and stared out the window for a minute or two. 'So,' she said finally, 'Alan Dexter is either here to save Juan, his *compadre* who got caught, or he's let Juan become the scapegoat for some unknown and totally uncomradely reason, or . . .'

'. . . or both he and Juan are complete innocents and the whole thing is really some vast conspiracy being perpetrated by the intelligence services.'

Her eyes widened. 'And *that's* what he's going to claim regardless of what's true.'

'Yes,' I sighed.

When George rang in again at three, I told him I was expecting a call from Alan Dexter. He said: 'There's only one safe place to meet a geezer like him and that's by the main entrance of New Scotland Yard.'

I laughed.

'No,' he said, 'I'm serious.'

I said I was sure that Dexter would never agree.

'He will,' George answered, 'if you tell him you'll go inside and hand over everything you've got if he doesn't show.'

I decided to try it.

'I know you suspect me,' Alan Dexter said when we spoke at four, 'but I swear to you, I'm innocent. Look, I don't want to go into the details over the phone, but believe me, I have evidence that this whole thing is a vast conspiracy being perpetrated by the intel –'

'Sure, sure,' I said, 'bring it with you and we'll talk about it. Six o'clock. Can you find New Scotland Yard?'

He tried to argue about the venue but stopped when I explained the other option.

By half past five, when George and the muscular man–boy he introduced as Jamieson arrived to pick me up, my nerves were about as tight as they ever get. This was mostly, I'm sure, because David still hadn't rung, but there had been other frustrations: no one answered at my mother's or at her friend Marcia's and Pete and Paula were both unobtainable as well; Henning had been in some important meeting all afternoon; Jackie's flatmate wasn't home and her boyfriend was still, I learned, in a coma; and Connie phoned to say that the Campaign were at such a divide about hiring me that they were going to call an emergency general meeting to vote on it.

George obviously sensed how tense I was and, interpreting the source his own way, patted his pocket. 'I've got me trusty shooter,' he smiled, '*and* me licence to carry. I've got friends inside those Yard doors too – friends who owe me. So don't worry, luv. You'll be all right.'

More disturbed than reassured by the thought of his hidden weapon, I couldn't help sighing. (What I wouldn't have given for a hot bath.) 'Thanks,' I said. 'I think what really worries me is that he won't turn up.'

'Of course he will – I've done this before – *trust* me.'

'But what if . . .'

'Enough.' He opened the door and waved me out. 'Come on or we'll be late.'

Now much as I admire sanguine people like George for their ability to live in the moment, I do get annoyed when they dismiss the pessimistic projections of people like me. Whether they know it or not, they are implying that we worriers are 'merely' suffering from some wholly unfounded paranoia. They hardly ever seem to appreciate that we'd probably stop if only events didn't so often match up to our fantasies.

Take that meeting. I was right after all: Dexter didn't come.

Which brings me to the other trait I've noticed in people whose routine thought processes don't include a quotient of worrying: when they *do* worry, they do it in a big way.

Take George after we'd waited an hour and a half. He'd begun pacing up and down the pavement about half past six anyway – pacing and chain-smoking his funny-shaped little roll-ups – and now he stubbed out the most recent of these and kicked it over the kerb. It was a windy day and I think he was almost as peeved by this as by our situation: he's a balding man in his early fifties whose only obvious vanity is that he grows his remaining hair long on the right side and plasters the strands across the top of his head. They had, of course, come thoroughly unstuck.

'It tells us something – it bloody well tells us something,' he muttered as he pushed his fingers hard through the the tangled bits of loosened hair yet again.

'It tells *me* that he was more worried than I was.'

He put his hands on his hips. 'Yes, and ask yourself why and what *that* means.'

'I've been trying not to.'

'I haven't. It suggests that he actually is the murderer and that you are in danger. He's got to be desperate to catch you alone and I'll bet you anything he'll try it at your flat.'

A shiver passed between my shoulder blades. As a worrier myself, I have great respect for other people's worries, big or small.

'Shit,' I said. 'I could stay with Suze.'

'Hell no, we've got to stop the bastard. Look, we have to go back to your office to collect your suitcase, right? I'll go in with you and check he isn't there, then leave Jamieson with you while I go over to your place. I'll ring and tell you if the coast's clear and tonight I'll start keeping an eye on *you*. Ten to one I'll have him in the next twenty-four hours.'

'You don't think it's a ploy to divert us do you? Maybe he doesn't want me but simply wants me out of the way so he can . . .'

'Too big a risk,' he said, hailing a cab. 'Much too big.'

The next surprise of the day came in the note Suze had left for me. It said:

6.45 – David rang. He's *in town*! And was he ever sozzled – Jesus! The main thing I managed to extract is that he's got the envelope Amanda gave Jackie. I tried to get out of him what's in it but he just kept going on about 'with friends like his he didn't need enemies'. When I pointed out that he knows he can count on you at least he said he bloody well hoped so because he was going to need a lawyer when got through with (wait for it) *Phil*. How about that though? Wouldn't it be ironic if your first suspicions were right?

He's staying at that friend of his in Wimbledon and was about to go out to eat. And guess who with? Craig Asprey. It sounds like the two of them talked in America and Craig decided to come over early to see what was in the envelope.

I say 'early' because Henning phoned too and confirmed that he'd asked Craig to make a statement and was expecting him Wednesday.

(You may not believe this Dee, but after that call and before David rang I suddenly realised that the one person no one's ever suspected is Amanda's brother. I even went through your notes checking out the chronology. The big snag is that he was in New York at the time of the murders, but ever undaunted I had begun to wonder if we should verify the source of his call to David that day. When David then declared to me in his sloppy voice that Craig might be a capitalist pig but at least he was straight about it, I felt thoroughly ashamed of myself.)

I made David promise to ring you before he goes over to Phil's. Craig's going to drive him there, so hopefully he'll make sure the scene stays civilised.

I said you'd be home by eight or half past. Ring me, okay?

Oh – nearly forgot Henning's most important message. You know what started him nosing around Juan again? It wasn't Armstrong, it was that tap on David's phone. Remember how he swore it wasn't his doing and said he'd look into it? Well, when he did he learned that Special Branch had put it on at the request of the American Embassy. He wondered why but instead of speculating into the wind about it the way we'd have done, he hopped on a train, came down to town and had lunch with an old friend. (That's quote/unquote of course. Can't you just picture the significant handshake when they met? . . . God, wouldn't I just love a case that cracked the old boys' network.) The upshot was that he 'appreciated' that Amanda Finch 'might' have been involved in American espionage work and hop, skip, jump – Juan Diego.

I refrained from mentioning Dexter.

Ta.

I have asked myself if there was some way I could have heard anything other than the assurance I'd expected to hear in George's voice when he rang from my flat at about ten to eight, and the answer is no. To my ears his relatively subdued tone merely indicated tiredness and this, unlike other occurrences that long Monday, didn't surprise me. I retrieved my suitcase for the last time and summoned my young minder Jamieson.

Neither of us spoke on the drive across town, me because I was dreaming of a hot bath and wondering about my food supplies and Jamieson because – well, Jamieson because he seemed to be of an age and a type which found women of my age and type impossible to talk to. I'd noticed this earlier when I'd spoken to him: he'd sort of shuffled and looked away, as if I were a being so far outside his normal experience that his normal responses simply seized up. And while I could, I know, have made use of this opportunity to try to break through the divide of sexual and national and class stereotypes, at that point I was enjoying the silence too much to make the effort.

If I had, would he have come up to the flat with me for coffee? I think not. George, or so Jamieson told me with discomfited diffidence when I recalled my manners and invited him in, George had instructed him to stay in the car ('Ma'am'). I tell myself that his presence wouldn't have changed anything anyway.

Through the familiar gate and up the stairs I went, dragging my case. Why was it so heavy? Why did I live three floors up? Why was I so fond of old buildings with no lifts?

I hesitated by the door of my neighbour opposite. I could just go in for a minute – say a quick hello, see how she'd fared with my plants, admire the baby's newest tricks. But no. I could hear the little one crying. Besides, a 'minute' in there meant half an hour and George was waiting. I'd deal with him first – get my bag into my bedroom – have a drink – wait for David to . . .

And then I heard the phone. Perfect, I thought, hurrying along the corridor. Perfect. (So why the hell didn't George answer it? God, had he fallen asleep? He had my keys! Had he left the door on the latch?)

I turned the knob impatiently and when it gave, pushed the door and rushed in. A hand caught my arm and pulled me backwards; another went across my mouth, staunching my scream. Panic-stricken, I dropped my bag and tried to flail but couldn't. Unable to move, I stared straight ahead into the sitting room and focused suddenly on George. He was tied up in my armchair, his mouth gagged with a dishcloth.

As the phone ceased ringing, a calm, sad American voice spoke into my ear. 'I'm sorry about this, but you see, you left me no choice. The police station – honestly. But I don't want to hurt you and I won't, believe me. I'm not a violent type of guy. I'm here to help. We need each other. Now if I let you go, will you promise to listen quietly? Or am I going to have to force you to listen?'

I blinked at George, who looked utterly humiliated. Dexter – for it was of course he – released his palm from my lips ever so slightly.

'I'll listen,' I said angrily, 'but I'll tell you, it better be good.'

It was.

What's more, I believed every word. How could I not? This dark-haired man of thirty-five or so with his fixed frown and urgent, matter-of-fact speaking style seemed entirely genuine. Nor was it just his manner which inspired trust. Forbidding questions ('so you don't start wondering if you've fed me any leads'), he briskly wove together all the facts I'd either learned or surmised, adding several crucial details I'd yet to uncover.

It all fitted, but then, it would: he'd heard most of it from Amanda herself in the twenty-four hours he'd spent with her after she'd arrived at his home, without warning and in a traumatised state, ready to talk, on the afternoon of July the third.

'Afterwards, I offered to help her disappear but she said she had to come back here to London. She thought it would be best for both of us if she acted as expected. I had my doubts that she could keep it up – not after the kind of shock she'd had – but she insisted. Said she'd had plenty of acting experience, thanks very much. I could hardly argue with that.' He shook his head.

'She was on this huge high by the time she left on the fourth. She kept joking about how Independence Day suddenly had this whole new meaning. It was only because I was so worried about what she'd do when she came down that I called Mike Berry and asked him to keep an eye on her. It was damn stupid of me, damn stupid. Jesus, when I think of everything she told me about him – how could I have done it? How could I have gone and underestimated Phil Knight?' He broke into a string of adjectives, some aimed at himself, most aimed at Phil ('scheming', 'unscrupulous', 'devious').

George, who'd been freed once he too had agreed to listen, grunted impatiently and made a 'get on with it' sign.

'Sorry,' Dexter said. 'I just feel so guilty about it all.' Then he explained that he'd come to London the day before Amanda's murder in order to collect the written version of what she'd told him two weeks earlier in New Jersey. She'd refused to let him tape it at the time; she'd felt it would be too dangerous for him to keep it in his house. And besides, she was saying things she'd never said before and knew they were coming out all jumbled. What she needed to do – insisted on doing – was to go off alone, reflect, and refine her story on paper. She also needed to consider whether to tell (and if so, how to tell) the people who would be most affected. People like her husband.

Alan had agreed. After all, he had dreamed for years about such a moment, such a revelation – years and years. If he had to wait another few weeks for the written, signed, complete statement, he would.

They'd decided that she would leave the material for him in a locker at Heathrow Airport. He was to pick up the key at the counter of a small South American airline, which she chose for 'symbolic reasons'.

'The plan was that she'd drop her typescript there on the way out of the country, though she hadn't yet made up her mind where to go. We had a code worked out in case she missed the deadline; otherwise we wouldn't contact each other again. I asked her, didn't she think she might have second thoughts? I mean, the risk was so great, and not just to her. But she insisted that the risk was only to her. She was sure of that.'

Alarmed by Mike's reports, Alan had waited for a sign from Amanda, a new plan, and when it hadn't come, he'd left for London as scheduled the day before the pick-up. He was worried, for her and for himself, and when there had been no key for him at Heathrow, his premonitions of trouble had grown. As soon as he'd heard that she'd been murdered, and with whom, he'd immediately flown home.

'I felt awful – I can't begin to tell you how bad. I knew there was only one person who could have done it, and it made me sick. I also knew that if I wasn't careful, the whole thing might turn on me. Which it did.'

Waiting back in his living room in New Jersey to question him were two federal government 'security officers'. 'They used the fact that I'd been in England to intimidate me and it worked. I knew how vulnerable I was to being framed.' Surveillance had followed. 'Even my little girl was watched.' Then, when their random burglary cover-up had failed to persuade everyone (he glanced at me), the 'officers' had moved into the Dexter household.

'They called it "protective custody". Protective custody! In America! Land of the free, home of the brave!' Then, describing again how easy it would be for them to arrange for the murder charges to fall on Alan, they forced the Dexters to help them implicate Juan Diego. 'They made my wife Maria call and warn you at LA Airport knowing you wouldn't be able to tell her Haitian

199

accent from a Chilean one, and they confiscated my manuscript *and* the list of names of everyone I'd interviewed. I had a feeling they were going to use it somehow to make you believe you'd come across a Chilean socialist conspiracy.'

'So that, when Juan was arrested . . .'

'. . . you wouldn't feel able to defend him. Yes . . . And of course meanwhile they were getting us more deeply involved, so that we were damned either way. God did I hate myself too. I felt so cowardly but so helpless at the same time. You should have seen the "meaningful" looks they gave our little daughter.

'Maria of course, she felt as torn up as I did, but like she kept saying, if we tried anything, I'd end up in prison – maybe both of us would. Hell, maybe whoever these Chileans were that we were being used to set up would land up there *too*. They'd get as many of us as they could. Worse, if we tried to come out and accuse them of setting us up to cover up for one of their own, they'd make sure no one listened to a word we said. They'd implied that hundreds of times. Whipping up a communist smear campaign would have been a real cinch. On the other hand, if we played along, there would be no charges – that was the deal – and if I were spared those, I'd eventually be free to help the guy they pinned it on.'

Following a phone call the previous Thursday, the two official 'lodgers' ('who'd never gotten everything out of me') had put Alan and Maria through one more session which seemed to have satisfied them, again, that the couple had submitted to the blackmail and understood the risks. Then, instructing them to pack, they'd driven them and their daughter up to Maine and ensconced them in a resort cottage where they were to stay for two weeks.

'We were supposedly under surveillance but we didn't believe it. They'd indicated they'd finished with us and they were so complacent we felt we'd been pretty convincing. I took one or two experimental forays out and decided the surveillance really was bullshit – they make mistakes too, thank God – and went back home to New Jersey that night. I get the feeling you're aware of my movements since.'

What he wanted to know from me was whether I knew the whereabouts of what Amanda had given her secretary Jackie. 'She must have had something that points the finger. Why else did he kill her?' He was also hoping that there might be other papers scattered here and there.

'I tried to persuade Amanda to make several copies of the description of her life and espionage career that she was writing up for me, and of any back-up documentation, and scatter them, just in case. She was pretty dismissive – I think the "in case" got to her and anyway, like she said, leaving a trail was what she'd been trained *not* to do. But after Mike told me that her apartment was broken into and that her will was stolen from some law office, I started thinking that maybe, just maybe, she'd changed her mind. I mean, knowing who did it's one thing; proving it without a written statement from her – well, that's the big problem at this point.'

My larynx having constricted with alarm, I broke my silence with a hoarse protest.

'What?' he said.

'No it isn't,' I repeated, reaching for my bag. 'The big problem at this point is stopping him from killing again.' (Where was my damned address book?) 'That call you didn't answer as I came in – that was David. Craig's driving him over to Phil's *now*. David's learned some of it – he must just know that Phil was Amanda's "control".' (Found it.) 'What he doesn't realise is that . . .'

'Stop him,' both men said together in panicky unison.

'What do you think I'm trying to do?' I snapped, lifting the phone to ring David's friend's place.

'Tell him to come here,' George hissed. 'Tell him . . .'

I waved at him impatiently and he shut up. I let the phone ring and ring, willing David to reply, but there was no answer.

George, now on his feet and pacing, turned to me as I set the receiver back in the cradle. 'Where the hell is Phil's?'

I put my face in my hands. 'God knows.'

'I know too,' Alan said, feeling around in his jacket pocket. 'Mike got himself invited out there a while back – had a real good recce. We'd been thinking of going there again tonight or tomorrow for a closer look. Now I'm sure I wrote the address down when he told me . . . ah yes, I've got it here. It's in a place called Bushey. Mike told me it's way out in the 'burbs.'

'Crikey, I'll say,' George muttered. Then, to me: 'Where the fuck is David's friend's?'

'Wimbledon.'

He looked up, wide eyed, at the ceiling and sighed deeply. 'A break. Sweet Jesus, I don't believe it. We're closer to Bushey than they are.' He glanced at Dexter. 'That *was* a real shooter you stuck in my ribs?'

' 'Fraid so. Mike forced it on me. I'm not the greatest sh–'

George, however, had clearly heard all he wanted to hear and cut Alan off by looking upwards again and blowing a kiss at the unseen. 'Come on mate,' he ordered, 'we're going to have to burn up some rubber as they say over on your side. Dee my luv, you stay here and . . .'

'Screw that,' I said, heading for the door.

'But the back seat of the car – it's full of –'

'Then we'll have to leave Jamieson behind, won't we?' I turned back and caught his disgruntled expression. 'Look – George – David's in danger, yeah? I'll be happy to refresh your memory about what sexism means during the drive, but let's just get going, okay?'

I guess George must have been annoyed with me because he spent the first quarter hour of our journey chewing his lip and staring straight ahead at the road. A thick dark cloud of mixed-up feeling seemed to hover over his reddened face. And tempting as it was to put this display of petulance down to tiredness, his driving was so alert and so concentrated that it seemed an unlikely excuse. It was as if everything he couldn't find the words to say was being channelled into communication with the gearbox of his ageing Rover. But even when the mood finally passed and he rejoined our conversation about what the hell we were going to do when we got to Phil's, his skilfulness didn't slacken. All in all, we made good time.

Unfortunately, though, it wasn't quite good enough. Parked at the foot of the Knights' drive, blocking the two rather more sedate vehicles which presumably lived there, was Craig Asprey's silver Mercedes sports car. Cutting the engine, George rolled to a stop behind it and cursed.

Lights shone from several windows of the first and second storeys of the house, but the ground floor front windows were dark. Alan pointed to the garage and whispered: 'I remembered that right, look – there's the gate leading to the back yard. I'm sure now about the rest: the living room runs along the left side, the kitchen and dining room are on the right, the bedrooms are upstairs. He's added a conservatory at the back which he uses as his study. At this "soirée" Mike came to, the men adjourned there for drinks. Mike figures that's where he's hidden the confession document that was meant for me, along with her signed will and the letters that go with it. The three of them must be in there.' He looked over at me. 'You ready for this?'

'Not so fast,' George said. 'We've got to check. We could land on our arses if we storm the wrong place.'

'Right,' I nodded, swallowing hard as I quietly opened my door. Now that we were here, my nerve was beginning to turn, but having set on George about sexism, I could hardly wait demurely in the car.

Alan in the lead, me in the middle, we crept, barely breathing, up the drive, through the gate and along the side of the house. About two thirds of the way to the back, Alan stopped, put a finger to his lips, pointed, then cupped his right ear. A yellowish glow was filtering through the blind of the next window, faintly illuminating a flower bed. Voices drifted out, indistinct and muffled. Alan now made a 'wait here' motion, hunched down and continued on the path to the garden.

Moments later he returned and gestured us back towards the garage. There, exhaling, he murmured: 'It's exactly like Mike said: there are french doors. They're curtained but listen to this: one of them's slightly ajar. From the sound of it, things are starting to heat up. I think your David's just about to put two and two together.'

I gagged softly.

George said: 'That skeleton key Alan gave you – you can manage . . . ?'

I got the long slender device out of my pocket and recited the instructions: 'Try the knob first in case. If the door's locked, put this in like so –' I demonstrated – 'turn it *this* way, then *that* way and jiggle it. Frankly I'm more worried that his wife or one of his kids will appear than I am about getting in.'

George shrugged. 'If that does happen, scream like hell. Any sudden distraction, after all . . .' He stooped over, groped the ground, stood again and handed me a small rock. 'Use this if you don't want to get too close.'

Alan said, 'You can take the gun if you want, or we can . . .'

I shook my head. 'You wouldn't say that if you saw the way I hold a gun.'

'I'm no better. And anyway, no one's going to get shot –' he looked at George – '*are* they?'

George smiled. 'Not by me, mate. Christ, can't you just imagine the lip I'd get if I deprived Dee here of the courtroom drama of her career?'

I thought: don't forget the love of my life. I don't want to be deprived of him either. I said: 'What worries me is . . .'

'What worries *me*,' George cut in, 'is that we're standing around worrying.' He patted my shoulder. 'Get going. Remember: we should all be in position by the count of a hundred. Give it another twenty, then do your stuff, okay?'

Sighing my agreement, I turned and retraced my way to the front of the house. (One thousand one, one thousand two . . .)

The door was locked. (One thousand fifteen, one thousand sixteen . . .) My fingers oily with sweat, I retrieved the key and went through the routine. Nothing. (Forty-five, forty-six . . .) I tried again. Still nothing. The third time I felt the feeling of rightness I'd been told to expect. The lock clicked. (Sixty-one, sixty-two . . .) I slid inside and put my hand over the latch to muffle the sound of its shutting. Pausing to let my eyes adjust to the darkened hall (. . . eighty . . .), I tiptoed down the central corridor towards the study door. It wasn't, in fact, difficult to find – light seeped out around the edges and the voices were quite loud. No one interrupted me. (Ninety-one, ninety-two . . .)

I was about to put my ear to the door when I had a sudden, panicked realisation. Apart from ducking down, I had no cover or line of retreat.

Completely losing track of my counting, I looked along the walls I'd just passed. Yes, there were two doors, one on either side. Disregarding noise, I tried them both. The first was a cupboard, a full cupboard. The second led down some stairs. The smell of dampness was pronounced, but I left it open and returned to the study door.

David was saying: 'I don't believe this. I honestly do not believe this. You can't mean that *you* killed her – *you*. My God, are you insane?'

Phil said: 'You're looking down the barrel of a .38 and you can ask about sanity? Take it easy or you'll be next.'

Craig said: 'Listen to him old buddy, listen real good. Now that we all know, though, I suppose there isn't much choice, is there?'

This, I decided, was the moment.

I pushed open the door, threw the rock, yelled to David to get down and quickly ducked. As all three men turned towards me, guns poised, George (fulfilling, I'm sure, his every boyhood fantasy) shouted: 'Drop it or I'll shoot.'

But he was a desperate man, a cornered, desperate man who

must in that half second have decided that he had nothing to lose. More, there was, it seemed, one person whom he blamed above all others for his predicament – one person who'd refused to stop asking questions or to accept the cover-ups.

Me.

He didn't drop the gun. Instead, as I saw David's face crease with further alarm, sensed what might come, scuttled backwards towards the open cellar door, he swivelled round to face me – extended his arm – aimed the gun . . .

There were three shots: George's, which hit him on the arm; his, which went wild and lodged in the architrave over my head; and Alan's. Alan's hit him in the middle of the back.

The bullet tore out the front through his heart and Craig Asprey fell to the floor, clutching his chest.

Twelve

No one moved for what seemed a very long time. Then, through the stillness, I heard the sound of a pair of feet above and behind me, running down carpeted stairs. A woman in a Chinese dressing gown, her hair wrapped in a towel, rushed past me and into the room, paused, looked around, whispered 'Oh my God' and went to Phil's side.

With that, the rest of us suddenly became animate again. Alan let go of his gun, which fell heavily on to the hardwood floor, squinted disgustedly at his hand and began to shake it as if trying to drop it too. Apparently mystified by its tenacity, he turned, open mouthed and frowning, to George, who fortunately knows shock when he sees it and responded immediately: he put his arm around the professor's shoulders, guided him to a chair and picked up a half-empty glass that was sitting on a nearby nest of tables. Sniffing it, he took a quick sip before putting it to Alan's lips. On cue, Phil reached into the cabinet next to his desk and got out a stack of clean glasses and a bottle of Bell's.

David meanwhile had been hurrying across the room towards me and reached down and cautiously lifted me to my feet. Reassured, he gave me a long steadying hug followed by a long kiss that tasted of deep relief. Then, our arms still entangled, we began to move in the direction of the open french doors.

The nameless woman who was Phil's wife was by this point kneeling at Craig's side. Disregarding the blood, she'd loosened his tie and collar, covered him with the crocheted antimacassar from the sofa, and was feeling for his pulse.

'He's still there,' she sighed, 'but not for much longer.'

Phil shrugged and picked up the telephone.

David and I carried on out to the garden where we both dropped cross-legged on to the grass. We had to adjust our arms to sit comfortably, but managed not to let go of one another.

'He nearly killed you,' David said, his eyes only the length of our noses from mine.

I kissed him. ' "Nearly" is the operative word.'

He put his head on my shoulder, so that I couldn't see his face. 'Yes,' he said. 'Luckily, yes.'

There was a pause. It was, I realised, a warm clear night.

'What gets me,' David said, 'is that I'm supposed to be a professional judge of character and here I not only go and totally misjudge two people I've known for years, I decide that someone I've never trusted might not be such a sodding bastard after all.'

I stroked his hair. 'And there was your reason right there I'm sure. After learning about Amanda . . .'

'Yes, that was *a* reason. But there was another one too. Or at least I thought there was.' He pulled away from me and stared out into the starlit night.

'I was nearly to Yosemite on Thursday,' he said, 'when I remembered that I was meant to ring him. I stopped to phone and it was the conversation we had – that's what did it. He was so incredibly thankful to me for trying to warn him, so concerned . . . And I guess – no, I know – that I was feeling a bit strange at that point, a bit – cut off – sorry I'd left you behind – sorry I hadn't stayed with you. Driving by myself through all that extraordinary landscape I found that I wasn't actually particularly good company. It was so big, all of it, so big and so foreign. Craig – well, Craig was familiar. He was a connection.

'We talked a long time and somehow I ended up telling him about everything that had happened to us, including what we'd learned about Amanda's "activities" in Berkeley.' He brushed the flat palm of his hand across the grass a few times. 'That wasn't entirely uncalculated if I'm honest about it. I wanted to hear what he'd say. . . . What the hell, if he'd told me he knew all about it, I'd have had someone to shout at.

'What I hadn't counted on was that he'd get so upset. I mean, apart from the night the three of us went to dinner – the night we *thought* was Craig's first night in town – I've only ever known him to get ruffled a couple of times. He's usually in complete control of himself. And here he was, upset. And so spontaneously too. He didn't believe it. He reacted just like I had, just like you had. He was shocked. He felt completely betrayed.

'Of course his reasons were the diametrical opposite of ours: what *he* couldn't get over was why she hadn't joined the family firm, or better still, let him help her into politics where she could have "really done some good". He told me something I'd never realised – that he'd once planned to go into politics. He said it had been his dream while he was at Harvard to one day become Ambassador to the Court of St James's. That had ended when Claire had divorced him – that's the real reason he hated her, he said. The point, though, was that Amanda was one of the few people who'd known about this dream. The way he saw it, if she'd been on his side, truly on his side, she'd have done the proper thing and gone in the direction he couldn't.

'Then he began to deny what I'd told him. He began to come up with all these arguments about why it couldn't be true, why it didn't make any sense. He was so certain – as certain as I'd been when you'd suggested new ideas about her to me – so certain it was impossible. "She'd have told me," he said, "me of all people." . . . I couldn't help it, I felt sorry for him. I thought I knew exactly what he was going through. I said so too, but he kept on and on and finally he said he could prove it to me. He said there'd been an "incident" years ago that proved what a "silly pro-communist sympathiser" she was. He insisted, though, that he couldn't tell me over the phone. He offered me a ticket to New York and pleaded with me, really pleaded with me, to come there and then.

'Well, I didn't feel *that* sympathetic. If I had – if I'd gone there . . .'

There was a sudden upsurge of noise in the room behind us, the voice commotion of perhaps a dozen people. I squeezed David's arm, got up, went inside, identified the officer in charge and told him who and where we were. He had plenty to do and agreed to leave us until last.

Sitting back down, I leaned against David's shoulder. 'Go on,' I said.

'There's not a lot more. I told him that I didn't fancy driving all the way back to San Francisco – it may be a short trip to one of you natives, but I was tired. And anyway, like I said to him, if I was going to get on a plane and fly anywhere, I probably ought to fly back to London. That damned envelope Amanda'd given her secretary Jackie – ever since I'd left you, I'd had it on my mind. I kept thinking that if I went and opened it, it might put an end to the whole business.'

'And you mentioned the envelope to Craig?'

'I made that small mistake, yes. And of course, he got all stirred up again, but in an excited kind of way. Before I knew it, we were to be sleuths together, although we didn't decide when – or I didn't at least – for another day and a half. He had what he termed a few business odds and ends to tie up and that suited me. I was there to camp and I wanted to do a *bit* of lying out under the stars in the peace and quiet of Nature.' He laughed drily. 'I hadn't appreciated how many other people would have the same idea, or how many of them would bring radios and TVs and CBs with them. Jesus! I woke up Saturday morning and thought, admit it, this is a bad idea. The first phone I got to, I tried to get hold of you – I did that off and on until I caught the flight and kept trying after I got back here – and then I rang Craig. He said he could be here by Sunday night, which left me a day to do the legwork on my own. I was pleased about that. For all our new-found camaraderie, I honestly *can* only take Craig in small doses. He got my friend's number off me, said he'd book into a hotel in Wimbledon and promised to call me when he got in. Which he did.

'By that point, I was glad I'd decided to come back. Apart from the big problem of not being able to connect with *you*, everything had gone smoothly. I'd got a stand-by seat on the flight, no problem; I'd slept; and I had no trouble getting through to Jackie's flatmate yesterday morning. She told me that Jackie's parents had only taken away about half her stuff so far and that I was welcome to come and have a look through what was left. In fact, we did it together and she was as disappointed as I was when we didn't find anything. She said she knew that Jackie's parents were still pretty shaken up, but she had their number and she rang them and very tactfully paved the way for me. They obviously hadn't been able to bring themselves to go through her things yet, but they agreed to let me come and look through them myself today.

'Craig drove me up to Birmingham this morning and on the way he told me about his "proof" that Amanda was "really an extremist left-winger". This was a long story about how she'd left Berkeley to work for the socialist cause in Chile and how she'd nearly been killed by the military there during the coup in '73 and how he'd had to kick shit with the US authorities to get her out, only to discover when she arrived on his doorstep that she was pregnant. He told me that Astrid was the result and that he'd adopted her because Amanda had had a nervous breakdown and tried to abort herself and he'd realised that she couldn't cope. It seems he even sent his wife away for about five months so that all their friends would believe the baby was hers.

'Well old easy-shock Blake here conformed to pattern and got thrown again. Good God, I thought, Chile! She'd had a hand in that *too*.'

'You mean Craig's angle didn't sway you?'

He shook his head. 'That isn't to say though that it so much as crossed my mind to suspect that *he* was lying, because it didn't. I just assumed that she'd lied to her brother the same way she'd lied to everyone else – the way she'd had to lie because that was her job and he had to be made to believe her cover just like all the rest of us. Once I'd started to calm down, I said that to him and we argued about nothing else the rest of the way . . . I'll tell you Dee, I'm a stupid bugger but he's a bloody good actor, bloody good.'

'So it seems. He was also working with the truth.'

'Yes, I picked that up earlier, before you arrived.' He sighed again. 'Anyway, finding Jackie's correspondence with the bank seemed like an unimportant minor detail after that, even when I was holding it in my hand and thanking those nice people. How Craig had the nerve to face them – Jesus! Talk about cheek. But I wasn't thinking about him *or* them at the time. It was still the Chilean connection that I couldn't get over. And the more it went round in my mind, the more certain I was that she must have been an American intelligence agent the whole time we'd been married and that her manoeuvre with Carlos had been in aid of catching another recruit.

'I worked myself into such a state of anger – I was outraged. And Craig's refusal to see it my way just made me angrier. We spent the entire journey back to town arguing like we had on the way up. In fact, we were still at it when we got to the bank at twenty-nine and a half past three or whatever it was this afternoon. We made it right before it closed. But I was so preoccupied that I didn't care. I virtually let Craig take the envelope and open it – that's how out of it I was.

'Then – suddenly – Craig started cursing and swearing and handed me a typed sheet marked "Confidential – Released Under the Freedom of Information Act". And there, in a blank, she'd scribbled in Phil's name: he was her "control" in London.

'I kicked the lamppost outside the bank so hard I practically crippled myself. I mean, that really capped it. To think! Phil Knight – my mate Phil – *he* was a party to this dirty, filthy business too! I tell you, if I weren't a healthy man I'd have probably had a heart attack on the spot, I was that apoplectic.

'Craig's tack, once he'd got me back into the car, was to come on almost as indignant as I was. "Phil Knight may have been your friend," he said to me, "but I'm the one he conned into investing in his damn business. He could have had the decency to tell me it was a front."

'We stopped at the first off-licence we came to, picked up a few bottles and went back to my friend's in Wimbledon to plan the confrontation. We were on the same side again, see – brothers in disgust. Craig had at last begun to concede that my interpretation might be right. He had also begun to pour out these great huge glasses of neat whisky and after that – well – the rest I guess you know.'

He turned back to me and folded me once more in his arms. 'God,' he said over my head, 'espionage. What a sick little world it must be. I wish to Christ she'd trusted me enough to tell me about it, tell me what she'd been through. I like to think that I'd have understood – especially if she'd explained to me how she got into it in the first place. I mean, one thing that Craig said was true: it would have made far more sense for her to go into politics. I'd give anything to know why she chose to become an agent.'

'Ah – David – Alan Dexter . . .'

But he didn't hear me. 'The other thing I'd give anything to know is why she waited so long to write an exposé.' If she had a change of heart in Chile, as it seems she did, why hang on all these years? And why pretend with me? All I can think is that something happened recently, some catalyst, some . . .'

'David,' I said, sitting back from him abruptly, 'Alan Dexter knows. Amanda went to see him in New Jersey. She'd just had this huge row with her brother. She told Alan everything and he told me. That's why we're here. When he realised you were with . . .'

'Dexter?' he interrupted. 'You don't mean . . . was that Dexter who shot Craig? Holy . . . and he knows why? Where is he? Why are we sitting out here? Let's go in and . . .'

Suddenly, across the path, there was a flicker of light coming from the house. We both looked up as a figure appeared beside us, dressed in blue. It was the officer in charge and he was ready for our statements.

It was a long night, full of complexities I could have done without.

211

When we returned to the study, the crowd had grown. In amongst the swelled numbers of uniformed police, forensics people were scrutinising the furniture; two were on their hands and knees picking at the floor. Over by the desk, several men in suits were clustered around Phil's wife, who'd removed the towel from her wet, dishevelled hair and was holding it to her chest like a security blanket. They were doing all the talking and she was looking grim.

Other men, not in suits, were huddled together by the door smoking and muttering to each other as they watched the team of ambulance personnel finish adjusting Craig's body on to a stretcher. There was an oxygen mask over his face and one of the team was holding up a bottle of blood, which was connected to Craig's arm by a plastic tube. As we passed the person who seemed most like a doctor, I paused to ask for his prognosis.

'Well,' he said, 'I'll tell you, he's lost a lot of blood and his heart had stopped twice by the time I got here. It's stopped twice since. There's bound to be extensive brain damage and quite frankly, under other circumstances I'd be inclined to let him go. But I'm under orders to do everything I can to pull him through, so that's what I'm doing. We've got a life support system in the ambulance and we'll put him straight into intensive care. If he lives the night, and that's a big if, he'll be there a long long time.'

'So his chances of coming around, of speaking . . . ?'

He shook his head the way doctors do when they don't want to encourage you but don't want to be too blunt either.

I thanked him and moved aside to let the stretcher pass. So much, I thought resentfully, for my day in court.

I'd lost David and the uniformed officer in charge and was looking around the room for them when I noticed that Phil's wife had started to cry. I went over to her. 'What's the problem?' I asked.

One of the besuited men looked me up and down. 'Who are you?' he said to me.

I didn't like his patronising manner so instead of answering I returned the question. Quickly summoning up some charm, he smiled and held out his hand. 'John's the name. US Embassy. "Security".'

Already! How had they moved in already?

Ignoring the hand, I gave him an equally cryptic description of myself and nodded towards the woman. 'Where's her husband?'

212

'I'm afraid I'm not at liberty to reveal that, ma'am.'

Phil's wife sniffed. 'They're . . . he's . . . we're . . . back to America,' she managed.

I got the idea. 'Now hold on,' I said to the men as I attempted to pull my five feet two and a half inches into something more imposing. 'One of my clients is in Brixton Prison charged with two of the three murders that Phil Knight knows were committed by Craig Asprey. In fact, Phil Knight could well be an accessory to those murders, if not a material witness, and he almost certainly knows how and why my client was set up. In addition, there is a distinct likelihood that Phil Knight is in possession of vital papers left by Amanda which will establish Craig Asprey's motive. *All* of these papers were stolen and, according to my information, at least some of them were stolen by Phil himself.'

Talk about taking chances – God Almighty! But I'd started, so I had to finish. 'Of course,' I went on, 'I'll be happy to discuss these points with Mr Knight's lawyer in return for some co-operation, but . . .'

'You're talking to him,' said another of the men.

My mouth went slack.

Looking down at me with amusement, he shrugged. 'Special Branch were kind enough to provide a helicopter.' Then, reaching into his pocket, he pulled out his card and handed it to me. 'I must advise you, Miss Street, that Mr Knight is an employee of the United States government who has been working here, for us, with top security clearance. As you'll know, there is a mutual agreement between our government and that of the United Kingdom which regulates the legal status of such personnel. For all intents and purposes, they are treated much like diplomats. In short, there's no way that Phil Knight will be appearing in a British court in any capacity.'

'But my client,' I protested, 'surely . . .'

'Yes,' he said, 'I appreciate the difficulty. I'll do what I can.'

'Immediately?'

'As soon as possible.' He glanced at his watch, smiled an apology and, turning to Phil's wife, asked if there were another room where they could talk 'without being disturbed'.

Thus dismissed, I backed away, thinking angry thoughts. I'd be damned if I was going to let what seemed to be happening happen without a fight – damned. On the other hand, this was real big boys' territory, so how the hell I was going to get in there and tackle

213

them at their own level . . . Ah, but wait. I did know of a QC who specialised in international agreements and extradition proceedings. He would help; he had to. Now who was it I knew who'd worked with him? Larry? Or was it . . .

But my musings were here interrupted by the reappearance at my elbow of the officer I'd so blithely credited with being in charge. 'Miss Street,' he started, 'I wonder . . .'

'My statement – I know. I was just coming.'

But he shook his head. 'Actually, that can wait. I believe you said you're a solicitor?'

I nodded.

'Qualified in this country?'

'Yes. Why?'

He gestured towards the door. 'I've been asked to tell you that you've just been hired.'

He'd lost me – I was that far away – and I frowned.

'Dr Alan Dexter,' he said. 'We gather that he arrived with a "borrowed" gun and that it was that gun which was used in the shooting here tonight, but Dr Dexter refuses to let us question him without you present. And of course, it goes without saying that if Mr Asprey should die . . .'

I need this? I thought. Do I really need this? But I followed him out the door.

What became too clear to me over the next half hour or so was that the uniformed police saw their role as a limited one. They were the technical assistants, there to take down names and addresses, collect fingerprints and other forensic evidence, and record such logistical details as where we'd each been standing at the time of the 'accident'. That there were more fundamental questions, that the shooting of Craig Asprey had a context, that the incident was the culmination of a more complicated saga – none of this did they want to hear. 'All of that,' we were advised, was a 'security matter' which the 'appropriate authorities' would be dealing with 'in due course'.

Well, I suppose it must be a measure of the world that we'd entered that 'in due course' turned out to mean something verging on immediately rather than what it usually means. In any case, after the police had finished extracting from us the kind of brief statements they wanted, they led David and Alan and George and me outside, put us into patrol cars and drove us not to the local station but back down town to Paddington Green. There we were handed coffee-coloured tea in styrofoam cups and escorted to a back room with pale green walls and dusty venetian blinds which contained a trestle table, a telephone, a tape recorder and a stack of orange plastic chairs in which we were invited to make ourselves comfortable.

We were still wondering how to do that when four familiar-looking men wearing neither uniforms nor suits came in and the police officers left. They were the same four I'd noticed earlier huddled together by the study door at Phil's and it now emerged that three of them were 'connected with' American Intelligence and one with British. What they didn't say was that it was they who were in charge – but then, they didn't really need to.

Once we'd settled around the table, the one who looked like an ex-Marine drill sergeant put our 'choice' to us without preliminaries. 'You all can either forget this whole thing,' he said, 'just forget it and go back to your lives as if it never happened, or –' (he glanced at Alan, then at me) – 'or you can keep on trying to stir things up.'

If we opted for the former course, he went on, they would be prepared to do certain things to make the lives to which we'd be returning easier. For example, no charges would be pressed against Alan for the shooting or against his friend Mike Berry, whose gun wasn't, as I'd already learned, licensed in Britain. Alan would, in addition, get his job back if he wanted it. If he didn't, good references would be arranged. And finally, Juan Diego would be released immediately.

'What about my manuscript?' Alan asked.

The man turned to his nearest associate. 'John?'

John frowned and shook his head. 'Gee, John, that's not our department, is it? State's in charge of that kind of thing. He'd have to take it up with them.' He smiled at Alan. 'Could take a long time. Be pretty expensive too, pretty damned expensive. Not really worth your while, you know?'

I said: 'What about Amanda Finch's stolen papers?'

He let us see him struggling for a puzzled expression. 'Papers?' he repeated. 'I know of no stolen papers.'

'Ask Phil,' I said. 'Search his house. They're there. I'm sure of it.'

The British agent spoke up. 'We've seen the notes of the police search. I can assure you, there was nothing found that would be of any interest to you.'

I sighed. We'd been outmanoeuvred and I knew it. If there were a copy of the exposé Amanda had been planning to give Alan, these people had it. And without it we'd get no further.

I looked at David and George and Alan and saw my own sense of defeat staring back at me. Why did I bother with law when there were human beings like this – employees, for Christ's sake, of the governments who'd created that law – who were beyond it?

But I'm an arguer and the argument, no matter how hopeless, hadn't finished. For its sake, I asked what would happen if we 'chose' not to 'forget it', if we 'chose' instead to 'keep trying to stir things up'?

The military-looking John shifted his muscular bulk so that he was facing Alan. 'He knows,' he said. 'He'll tell you . . . Go on, professor. Tell them.'

Alan closed his eyes and leaned back. There was a long silence. Eventually, softly, he said: 'It's obvious that they were prepared to have it suggested in open court that Amanda worked as an intelligence agent. They were willing to do that to establish the motive for her murder, and Juan's mistakes, like mine, left him open to charges based on that motive. The difference was that he was over here in England, so it was less messy to pin it on him. If they pinned it on me, all that stuff about Berkeley would have come out and some Americans at least would have made a big deal out of it. Chile they know about. The fuss would have been smaller. But I was their reserve and they've very astutely and very carefully worked it so that my mistakes and Juan's can be made to seem linked. I reckon that if we don't go along with this, that link will now be exploited. Juan will learn that he had a conspirator in New Jersey.'

He opened his eyes and, addressing the ceiling, went on: 'They must have *let* me follow Craig over here from New York. He must have been disobeying their orders as much as I was. They probably anticipated what happened tonight. I imagine they were ready to make it happen if it didn't happen naturally. And now that it has happened, I'm in that much worse a position over Amanda's murder. I mean, I can hardly drag out my reputation as a non-violent man, can I?'

He paused and then looked over at me, his eyes sunken into their bony sockets. 'I've succumbed to their blackmail once already; I'm not exactly a paragon when it comes to resisting, and I think it would be pointless to resist now. Even if Craig recovers, he'll never be allowed to stand trial, never, and besides, we don't have any hard proof. I may hate myself for shooting him, but I have a feeling it's the only way that justice was ever going to be served. The only way.' He turned to John. 'I accept your terms.'

It was about three am when we found ourselves back outside on the pavement. George, who alone among us had any spirit, stretched his arms, beat his chest with his fists a couple of times and declared: 'Well I don't know about you lot, but I'm starving. This is Old Bill territory – there must be an all-night caff somewhere close by.'

'I'm not exactly hungry,' David said, 'but at this point I couldn't sleep if I was paid.'

We were within walking distance of my flat and I was opening my mouth to say 'Come to my place' when I remembered that I hadn't even unpacked, never mind replenished the fridge. As I said so, Alan shrugged and began to step away from our group.

'I think I'd better head back to Mike's anyway,' he mumbled. 'I'm feeling like such a shit . . . (inaudible mumble) . . . be alone . . . (inaudible) . . . not very good company.'

David turned to him with disbelief. 'You! Good God man, if there's a shit, you're looking at him. Hell, you just shot the bastard; *you* saved Dee's life. *I'm* the damned idiot who trusted him. I got you into that position . . . Besides, you can't simply walk away, not *now*. I mean, I'm the one person who hasn't heard what Amanda told you.'

Alan's eyes widened: he hadn't realised – he'd forgotten this was true – and reminded, his moroseness fell away. 'Maybe,' he smiled, 'maybe a cup of coffee wouldn't be such a bad idea after all.'

Alan had happened to be home working on his book the Friday afternoon that Amanda arrived. He had also happened to be alone, but despite that, she had refused to talk to him there, claiming that the risk for him would be too great. Instead they'd arranged to meet half an hour later at The Cellar, a cocktail bar on the other side of the campus.

She'd gone ahead of him by all of about ten minutes but was already on her second drink when he joined her. A cigarette was burning in the ashtray but she lit up another as he sat down. Then *she* started asking *him* questions: why had it taken him so long to prove it had been her? Which people had he talked to? What were they doing now (or not doing – she hadn't known until then about

about Tommy dying) and – the one that seemed to intrigue her most – how had he finally found her?

This, inevitably, was a quirky tale, complete with the essential lucky break – in this case, an article about Asprey Oil which Alan's wife Maria had come across in the course of an unrelated piece of research she'd been doing at work. The tell-tale clue had been a reference to Craig Asprey's mother, Lucille Gardner Finch. One of the sources Alan's wife had helped him check through had been a recent edition of *Who's Who* and she'd come away from it convinced that Amanda must have chosen 'Finch' at random. Now she'd realised how close she'd actually been.

'And London?' she asked. 'How did you trace me there?'

He studied her face, or tried. It was dark for examining features and she was wearing tinted glasses. 'You know,' he said. 'Surely you know.'

She arched one brow and shook her head. He decided to play along. After all, he had to get her to trust him, had to make sure she confided what she'd come there to confide. And so he told her all about it with a straight face, as if he believed she'd never heard any of it: about how he'd recruited his wife's niece, who worked as a temp in Manhattan, and got her to get herself assigned to Asprey Oil; about how she'd done as he'd hoped she would and got herself specially requested back a week later; about how she'd further met his hopes by ending up in the office of Himself; about how she'd rooted in his files, located Amanda's address, memorised it, and had been putting it away when he'd caught her; about how unpleasant an interrogator he had been but how well she'd held out; and about how, regardless, the Dean of his department had summoned him a week later and instructed him to cease his work on this project.

'And you assumed,' she said, 'that I'd been told of the incident and had arranged this?'

'I assumed that, yes.'

'So when I answered your letter the way I did, what? You thought I was playing for time?'

'Yup. And I wasn't surprised either. Before I wrote I had a friend in London do some research for me. I'd wanted to know how settled you were, how easy – or not – it would be for you to pull up quickly and disappear. When I learned how long you'd been there and heard you were married and making mortgage payments, I wrote. I thought if I let you know about me and gave you a chance

218

to think about co-operating, you might come around of your own accord, you know? I'd planned to wait a couple of weeks and then just show up . . . In fact, I've booked and cancelled on so many flights that the woman at the travel agency laughs when she hears my voice on the phone. You sure have been on the move.' He paused before adding: 'I don't imagine that's been a coincidence.'

She shrugged and looked away and reached for her glass, which was empty. When she discovered that she'd run out of cigarettes too, she got up and went over to the bar.

On her way back she paused to look at the juke box, dropped in some change, pressed some buttons and leaned against the machine listening intently to nearly all of the song she'd selected. It was a song he knew off by heart himself – but then, so did probably half the state of New Jersey. After all, Springsteen was one of theirs.

Now they'd come so far and they'd waited so long
Just to end up caught in a dream where everything goes wrong
Where the dark of the night holds back the light of the day
And you've got to stand and fight for the price you pay . . .

As the chorus was repeated, '. . . now you can't walk away from the price you pay . . .', Amanda pushed herself forwards and came back to the table.

She'd been weeping – he could see the tear tracks of mascara.

'Are you. . . ?' he started.

'Don't,' she murmured, rubbing her cheek. ('Little girl down on the strand/With that pretty little baby in your hands . . .') 'Don't.'

When the song was over she sighed and took out a cigarette which she turned end over end in her fingers before slowly putting it to her lips and carefully lighting it. Then, apparently steadied by this ritual, she said: 'I'm prepared to give you all the operational details of my work in Berkeley – where and how I was trained, who controlled my activities there, the groups and individuals I was instructed to report on, and the names of the other undercover agents. I can also tell you about the intelligence operations at Columbia and Kent State and other campuses up through '71. And if you want, I'll go through the statements you've collected and verify which arrests were really down to me.'

'Ace,' Alan started. 'That's great. That's everything I –'

'Beyond that,' she went on, 'it's important for us both that I tell

219

you what I did next – where I was assigned after I was pulled out of Berkeley and what kind of work I did there and why I had a so-called breakdown in '74. I thought, when I got your first letter, that you just possibly might have known about all this too. That's why I wanted to read your dissertation. But I realised after I'd been through it that I was being too paranoid. You obviously didn't know . . . Or maybe I should say, you knew but didn't connect.'

He frowned. 'Connect?'

But already the air around his ears was beginning to vibrate and rush.

'Think,' she whispered. 'Chapter two.'

He shut his eyes hard and saw the newsreels playing again on the backs of his lids. The news about Allende. The troops in the streets. The disappearances. The chaos in Santiago. The proclamations on American television that the 'socialist menace' had been eradicated.

He'd seen the 'before' only fleetingly. After all, at the time he'd been preoccupied researching right-wing suppression. He'd gone to Chile for a vacation; for inspiration; for contrast. He'd heard rumours of course. Certain large American conglomerates weren't happy, especially about the inflation rate. The American government was muttering about Soviet influence. But he'd met so many Chilean people and been so impressed by their determination that he'd left feeling confident that they could make their new system work. Later, afterwards, when he'd applied to go back, the military authorities had refused him a visa. He'd written the Chilean section of his dissertation largely on the basis of interviews with political exiles.

'Not Pedro Rivera,' he said.

She nodded, adding in the Spanish dialect of the Santiago streets: 'The legend of his betrayal by a woman, a woman he loved, a woman his sister Astrid never trusted . . .' She switched back to English. 'Your version – it isn't quite true.'

He gripped the edges of the seat of his chair, afraid of his own hands. She watched him and seemed to see his fear.

'I understand,' she said. 'It can't be easy for you to sit there like that. In your position, I'd probably hit me . . . I deserve it, that's for sure. But if it's any use to you, I'm also sure that you can't possibly hate me as much as I hate myself.'

'Then why the fuck did you do it?' he shouted, not caring a damn that every head in the bar had turned. '*Why?*'

220

'That's what I've come to tell you,' Amanda said quietly, 'although I'm afraid that I have to ask you for something in return.'

'For Christ's sake,' he snapped, 'I've lost my *job*. I haven't got the money to . . .'

'Not money. I want you to promise to tell another story as well, the story that explains why I decided to come to see you . . . No, don't shrug, not until you've considered the consequences. Think about it, Alan: all you've done to my brother so far is plant a temp in his office for a few days; if he'd destroy your career for that, imagine what he'll do when he realises you're going to ruin his precious reputation. Because that's what I want this second story to do: ruin that. I'd love it if it brought down Asprey Oil too of course, but I'm unfortunately not as naive about the marketplace as I've tried to be. It doesn't care much about the ethics of its investors.

'I do still have faith, though, in the moral integrity of the ordinary people of this country. I want to make them feel outraged – so outraged that they will never allow him to receive any political appointment, ever. I want a scandal, do you understand? And I want you to create it.' She looked at him. 'Well?'

Without hesitating, he extended his hand to her across the table.

Apart from the two weeks following her birth, which she spent in a New York maternity ward, Amanda lived nearly all of her first twelve years outside America. In fact, during her first seven years her parents moved so often that sometimes when her father asked her to recite the list of countries to grown-ups at parties she left a couple out.

To be fair though, those were the ones she'd been too little to remember: Costa Rica, where they stayed until she was about nine months old, and Panama, where they went next. She was able to recall Venezuela easily because of the big ginger cat she had to leave behind at three, and Chile because of the time she fell off the porch and had to have stitches in her chin.

After that was Argentina, where a lot of the kids spoke in a hard funny language which her mother told her was German, and after that, Brazil. Brazil was her favourite: they lived right by the beach in Rio de Janeiro and she started going to school in the mornings. The announcement that they were leaving there didn't please her at all, but when she cried and hit her father's knees with her five-year-old fists, he looked down his nose and said the words she always found so scary: 'Maybe it's time we sent you to Connecticut.'

She wailed and turned to her mother, who stroked her hair and said: 'Now Edward, we agreed.'

'But Craig is much happier there.'

'Yes, well, they are very different children. Craig wanted to go to prep school. He hated the heat and the flies and he never cared much for the local children. You know what work it was to get him to speak anything but English. Besides, he takes life so seriously.'

'So he should. He knows what he's going to inherit. I'm proud of him.'

'Of course, of course, so am I. I'm simply saying that Mandy is more adaptable and there's no point in sending her away; she won't be carrying the burden of the business. Anyway, you promised me. I waited ten years for her, ten years and three miscarriages . . .'

She stopped there, knowing that she needn't mention the constant depression of that difficult decade. After all, her husband had paid the medical bills. And they both recognised how important their small daughter had been to her recovery. It wasn't total – she still had what he termed her 'bad patches' – but the focus had changed. Now, instead of getting depressed about herself, she got depressed about the conditions of the people in the countries where they lived.

Edward gave in. 'We're going on a big boat this time, Mandy,' he said. 'You'll like that.'

She had. She also liked New Guinea, especially after her mother and two Australian women had started the little school. But that era ended too and they moved on to the Philippines.

They hadn't been there long, just a few months, when a telegram arrived and her father went away. He'd never left them before and Amanda found it kind of frightening, even after her mother explained all those things to her about the illness of her grandfather Asprey and about money and about how her own father, grandfather Finch, would have to help out again if the business was to survive. Amanda listened very closely and at the end she said: 'But won't Grandpa Finch help Daddy? Doesn't he love us?'

'Yes,' her mother sighed, 'he loves us more than anything. We're his whole family. But he isn't rich and he wanted what money he has to go to you two. Instead he's had to keep buying shares in Asprey Oil, although, because he loves me so much, he's put these in my name. The problem is that I now own forty-nine per cent. If

Grandpa Finch invests any more, I will be in control and even though that's just a technicality – I'd never dream of telling Daddy what to do – well, your father is like most men: he's extremely proud. He's had a run of bad luck, that's all, but he doesn't see it that way.' Her mother's pale eyes filled and she stooped to hug her daughter. 'Forgive me darling. I shouldn't be telling you all this.'

A few weeks later a letter arrived and within days they once more set off across the ocean on another big boat. The morning that the island of Cuba appeared on the horizon, her mother turned to her on the deck and said: 'How would you feel about settling down for two or three years, honey?'

Amanda clapped her hands.

Her mother smiled. 'That's how I feel. I've been thinking . . . maybe I'll try to exercise just a little control after all. No promises, okay? But I'll see what I can do.'

She had, too. To begin with, she refused to live in Havana, even in the so-called 'safe' area. 'It's full of gangsters and prostitutes and gamblers and drug dealers,' she said after walking around it. 'It's no place to bring up a child . . . And don't start about Connecticut. I want to live in the countryside, *with* my daughter.'

'But only peasants live out there,' her father argued. 'It's squalid in a different way.'

'Maybe, but it's a squalor I can at least try to do something about.'

She won, even though it had meant waiting for a hacienda to be built. Then, almost immediately after they moved in, Amanda's mother organised some classes in reading and writing for the local children and these proved so successful that a number of their parents began to come as well. At the end of the first year, just after Lucy returned from her father's funeral, a school house was erected; at the end of the second year, about the time that Grandpa Asprey died, two qualified teachers asked if they could help.

Lucy cut back her hours and turned her energies to the water supply and to health care; here too things quickly began to change, so much so that by the end of the third year Lucy Asprey was being treated virtually as a local, popular with everyone – or with everyone, that is, except her husband. For despite the fact that by staying in one country longer than a year Edward Asprey was at last making money (or so Amanda's mother told her), it was obvious even to his ten-year-old daughter that he was uncomfortable in his normally crowded house. He'd taken to staying

223

away overnight, sometimes several nights, which he'd never done before; and he'd taken to arguing with his wife, loudly and often, which was also new.

Amanda's mother claimed that all that was new was that she'd started arguing back.

'But why does he always say you're crazy? Why does he think the school is dangerous? And why does he shake his head like that when he sees me?'

'Darling,' her mother said, 'Edward preferred being married to a forty-five-year-old girl. He doesn't like it that I'm finally growing up into a woman. But he'll get used to the idea.' She winked. 'He'll have to if he wants to keep on running Asprey Oil.'

Craig had come that year, a tall stranger in a suit who was polite but distant with their mother and overtly disapproving of Amanda's friends. His fourth night in the hacienda, after Amanda had gone to bed, she'd been awoken by angry voices in the kitchen; when she rushed in, her brother pointed at her: 'There,' he declared. 'Look at her. She's a mess. And why is her English so poor? Why does she speak to me in Spanish?'

He left the following morning.

Lucy Asprey had of course been hurt – Amanda had seen the pain in her mother's eyes for weeks afterwards – yet despite her feelings, it was Lucy who insisted that all three of them fly to New York for Craig's wedding ten months later. 'He's my only son,' she said, 'and family is family. It's my fault he's ashamed of me; I shouldn't have sent him away so soon. Still, what's done is done. Come on: I'll make us some new clothes and we'll work on your English.'

Whether it was their efforts or just the occasion, Craig was charming to them both. In fact, the day before the service, he took Amanda to Fifth Avenue, helped her pick out a wonderful yellow chiffon dress and matching high-heeled shoes and left her (on her *own*) in a beauty parlour where she had her hair washed and trimmed and set in curls on top of her head. When he offered her an ice-cream sundae on the way home, he won her little eleven-year-old heart.

Then he started talking to her. 'I don't know if you realise,' he said, 'but our mother is very sick. She has a disease called manic depression, which means she goes up and down in a way she can't control. One of the reasons I went away to school was that she was down. Lately she's been up. The heat isn't good for her, but at least

224

in the past she's lived in cities where she could get medical treatment. Out where you are she hasn't had it and her condition has been getting worse and worse.'

Amanda struggled with this idea for a moment and decided it didn't sound right to her. 'I think she's great. Everyone loves her. I don't see what's wrong.'

'I'll try to put it simply. She's being used by some very clever, very evil people who are pretending to like her. They are followers of a man called Fidel Castro, who wants to take over the government of Cuba by force. He is a communist, which is a bad thing to be. What they want from mother is Asprey Oil and mother is so ill that she has been talking to father about giving them her shares in the Cuban operation, which is where all our profits come from now. She thinks that father should organise training sessions so that they learn how to run the business . . .'

'But . . .'

'No, listen to me. I know you believe they're your friends, but they aren't, not really. And by treating them as if they are, she's put the three of you in a very risky situation. You see, the company is supported by the government down there – by Batista himself – and if he hears of mother's plan, well, he'll probably withdraw that support. He'll kick us out and get in another American company and we'll lose a lot of money. On the other hand, if Castro's people begin to suspect that she might back out, they could kidnap her or you or father.'

Amanda, totally confused and frightened, started to cry.

He patted her hand. 'I'm sorry. I know this must be hard for you to understand, but I had to tell you. Father's going to try to persuade her to stay here, go into a – place – and if she agrees, you'll go to a nice school in Connecticut. The problem is, we can't make her stay, not yet, so if she doesn't agree, all three of you will have to go back. It won't be for long though, just long enough for me to sort out the legal side of things. And if that's what happens, I want you to promise me something: I want you to promise me that when father suggests a trip to Miami, you'll make sure that you and mother go. Will you do that?'

Amanda nodded but for some reason had crossed her fingers.

Later she repeated everything except the part about Miami to her mother, who did a rare thing and took the Lord's name in vain. Then she hugged Amanda tightly to her chest and said: 'They're the ones who are crazy. But don't you worry. I know how to play it.'

The day after the wedding they went back to Cuba where on the surface, at least, life continued much as before. The difference was that underneath Amanda felt torn apart with guilt and fear: guilt because she ought to tell her mother about Miami and fear in case her father suggested the trip. What would happen if they went? What would happen if they didn't? It seemed to her that if she influenced the decision either way, she'd lose the love of one of her parents.

Finally, when they'd been home about six weeks, her father uttered the dreaded invitation. Amanda instantly panicked but neither parent noticed for as soon as he spoke, Lucy looked at him and laughed.

'Edward,' she said, 'whatever I may be, I'm not a fool. I'll go to Miami when you stop intercepting my correspondence with our lawyers. Now please, if you want to talk about this, for God's sake, talk. But not in front of Amanda.'

The two of them had talked all night and the next day Amanda's mother said to her: 'I've bought some time. I've agreed to see a doctor in Havana once a week – I'll try to find a new lawyer while I'm in there – and I've also agreed to stop going to evening meetings at the school.' She smiled. 'Good thing most of the meetings are in the afternoons, isn't it?'

Over the next three months, Amanda started to relax; within six she was beginning to wonder why she'd ever gotten so upset in the first place; after nine she was so absorbed in her new feelings for her friend Estrella's fifteen-year-old brother Miguel that she'd nearly forgotten the whole episode.

The reminder had come on 12 July 1958.

She'd succeeded once more in inveigling an invitation to supper from Estrella and had lingered later than usual afterwards on the porch, watching Miguel whittling. At last, reluctantly responding to his mother's hints, she'd set off on the short walk home, preoccupied by her fantasies. (He'd liked her dress – he'd smiled four times – he'd mentioned the football game – he'd brushed her knee . . .) They'd lasted until she'd reached the front stoop of the hacienda when she'd stepped in something squishy and looked down, thinking it was cat's poo. A red sticky substance had oozed between her toes.

She'd known immediately – had been in no doubt – yet somehow she'd stayed calm enough to look inside. After she'd seen the bodies, she'd run back down the track, told Estrella's father, and collapsed.

Two days later, numb and sedated and with no memory of the intervening time, she'd found herself in a bed in her brother's apartment in New York.

When Amanda paused there to rub her eyes, Alan called the waitress over and ordered doubles. Amanda smiled at him and reached for another cigarette. He just waited and after she'd smoked for a while and sipped at her fresh drink, she continued in a sad, faraway voice.

'Once I started to eat and move around – I guess I must have been in New York a week or two – Craig sat me down and told me that two young men had been arrested and charged with murdering our parents. I knew them; they were just boys, barely twenty, cousins of Miguel and Estrella – people who'd been in and out of our house every day for five years. My mother had taught them to read and write; they'd helped build the school; they went to the same meetings she went to. I – couldn't believe it. And Craig – he seemed to understand that. He promised I'd be shown evidence when I was well.

'A month or so later the two of us flew down to Washington where we were met by a limousine and driven through the city to the State Department. I was only twelve, remember, so I suppose I was easily impressed by the size and grandeur of the buildings we passed. I know I was impressed by the one we went into, and as for the office where we spent the afternoon – well, you can imagine: presidents' portraits all over the walls, the flag just inside the door, mahogany panelling and glassed-in bookcases everywhere – I was overawed by it.

'The man in this office was an Assistant Secretary of some kind, and he came over as this incredibly warm, fatherly person. Over lunch he asked me all these tactful questions about what I'd been through – he used the word "brave" a lot – and by the end of the meal I swear to you I'd have trusted him with my life.

'Then he said he understood that I had a few questions of my own and pulled out a drawerful of files that he said he hoped would answer them. My memory's hazy on the details, but as I recall, the files and his explanation fell into three sections. The first was about the two men who'd been charged and, apart from showing me their confessions, he showed me proof that they'd been followers of Castro – just like everyone else we'd known it turned out. There was quite a bit about Castro too – enough to persuade a little girl that he was some kind of arch-fiend who'd manipulated and taken advantage of the "greed" and "naive faith" of the "peasants" so successfully that the spell had lingered even after he'd been caught and imprisoned by America's friend, the hero Batista.

'The second section contained notes of the conversations my mother had had with the lawyer she'd found in Havana. She'd been trying, I learned, to get him to draft a document that would allow her to sell her stake in Asprey's Cuba works to a co-operative of locals at below the market price and without my father's consent. She'd also talked to several of the banks about putting up the money.

'The third section consisted of my mother's medical records beginning with her depression after Craig's birth and going right up through the session she'd had with her doctor two days before she'd died. This "proved" all sorts of things about her: that she was unbalanced, subject to delusions, gullible by reason of illness, depressive, a danger to herself. I can't say I took it all in – it hurt too much, conflicted too much with my own image of her. But I got the picture. Logically I had to accept what Craig had told me the day before his wedding: my parents were now dead because my mother had been deceived by evil people.

'My feelings weren't so easy to move. It took a year's therapy, three sessions a week, before they even began to come around to the "facts". And at first I was so ashamed and so guilty that I was listening to someone who said bad things about my mother that I didn't even tell Claire, who was my only friend besides Craig, that I was doing it. I've never told anyone since either.

'Anyway, after two years, my memories of my own experience of my mother had been well and truly "shrunk" and by the time of the Bay of Pigs invasion, during my third year, I'd disciplined myself to think of her as Craig did: rarely and with embarrassment. I'd also had it so thoroughly instilled in me that if I wasn't careful I'd end up going the way she had that by fifteen I was petrified of mental illness – took the smallest hint of emotion as a symptom of weakness. I decided then that my best defence would be to do the one thing my mother'd never done: study hard, get a degree, understand the world before I went out into it.

'It was a natural path really – studying was my main escape until I discovered sex – and my junior year in high school I added a special tutorial in communism. It was a private school so you could do that sort of thing, though of course it never occurred to me that my reading programme would be biased. Still, the bias I got was the only one I would have accepted and it was neatly reinforced by the books Craig gave me from his own library.

'All that reading had one big important side-effect too: it kind of redeemed my mother. I could console myself that she hadn't been taken in by just any old thing: this was a system so subtle and devious that it had taken in hundreds of thousands of other people whose minds were far sounder than hers had been.'

'Jeez,' Alan whispered, 'the perfect recruit.'

She smiled wanly. 'That's what they said too, the two men who came up from Washington to see me at the beginning of my senior year. I'd already gotten into Radcliffe early admission, but after they invited me to "join the team" that was fighting to keep that system from taking over America's young people, I changed my plans. I can't tell you how flattered I was. I felt like one of the chosen.'

'Did your brother know?'

'Hell yes. He was my guardian, they had to get his approval. And he'd hardly not give it when he was "part of the team" himself.'

'And did you find it – easy?'

She shook her head. 'I should have after the training I was given, but out there "in the field" I turned out to have certain – weaknesses. I may not have trusted the people I was instructed to live and mix with, but some of them were – very appealing. Naive, foolish, gullible – but appealing. The sort I wanted to save . . . God, that sounds awful, doesn't it? But –' she shrugged – 'that was my perspective from the age of eighteen to the age of twenty-three.

'The trouble was that I'd been warned over and over during my training against such feelings. My role was to root out evil, not transform it. The urge to get involved, to be straight with people, to lecture them on the errors of their ways – well, these temptations were indicators of my own susceptibility to the power of what I was supposed to be fighting. My "control" had to remind me of this so many times and arrange so many arrests earlier than he wanted to that in late '68 he recommended I be dropped. Instead they had me in for "reinforcement re-programming". Basically they spent a summer pushing all the buttons about my mother again.

'After that I lasted more or less okay until I met Tommy. I had to have three more "re-psyching" sessions while we were together and eventually they arranged that bust behind my back to get me out of there. They figured I was that close to blowing it, and maybe I was.

229

Tommy'd gotten to me, that's for sure. He distrusted people even more than I did and his anger – I don't know, I guess it seemed deeper than the anger of the white students I'd hung around with. Maybe it sounds odd, but I'd never thought about racism. I mean, a childhood like mine, it makes you colour blind and even though Craig had always given me a hard time about my Puerto Rican boyfriends when I was in high school, I'd put that down to snobbery. I'd assumed my attitude was far more universal and the discovery that it wasn't really disturbed me.

'On top of that, I'd been told to enrol in a course in Free Speech and First Amendment Theory – it was supposed to be this "radical hotbed" – and after going for a while I began to wonder about the morality of working undercover in America. It struck me as almost an act of bad faith and I said as much to my "control". In fact I told him I was thinking about resigning.

'Being pulled out set me right back. Whatever relief I might have felt got wiped out by my feeling of failure, which of course they milked for all it was worth. I was in serious danger of going the same way as my mother – that was the message. I'd let down not only my country but myself.

'I got – incredibly depressed. Craig took me back in – he and Claire had split up and he'd remarried – and paid for me to start therapy again. Then, a few months later, he said that if I wanted another chance he thought he'd be able to arrange it. I wasn't sure I did, though I was more worried about disappointing everyone again than about anything else. Still, I listened and when I understood the situation in Chile, I accepted. It seemed a clean, straightforward opportunity to stop another Castro-style leader from perverting democracy and increasing Soviet influence in America's back yard. It seemed a way to prove myself – to make up for my mother – to make up for Berkeley – to avenge my parents' deaths directly.

'I was put through intensive re-training – insisted on it – and was posted to Santiago as a news agency translator.

'The first six months or so everything was fine – I felt good about myself for the first time in my life practically – and then I met Pedro. He was such a fine man – had so much intelligence and integrity – that despite myself I began to look at his culture the way he did. I saw respect for Allende – saw improvements taking place – saw hard-working honest people. It was my first experience of socialism in practice and it seemed – humane. It seemed democratic

230

too. But I – it wasn't easy, not after fourteen years of having it instilled in me that the system they were playing with was evil in its subtlety. I believed it to be like heroin: pleasant and seductive in its initial stages and when people are hooked, destructive. I knew its "addicts" had killed my parents, yet there I was, in love with the kind of person who'd murdered them. And I knew that Pedro and his friends were ultimately going to be destroyed because of what they were. After all, I was an agent of that destruction.

'It – screwed me up pretty bad. I kept on filing my reports, but when we were in bed together, the temptation to confess – to warn him – it was almost overpowering. And my "control" wasn't blind; he realised. I was pulled in for yet more "re-psyching" and when that didn't last was told that I had a choice: stop seeing Pedro or be sent home. I agreed to split up with him, which I did, but I couldn't keep it up. I started seeing him secretly, or so I thought, and I decided there was only one way out for me. I couldn't live with my guilt, my sense that I was betraying my parents and my country, but I couldn't live without this man. I decided to die with him when the time came.

'As always, however, a "control" is there to make the most of whatever happens and mine simply had me watched – so I realised later. God, what a fool I was, what a stupid fool. The day of the coup, when I went over to Pedro's, my "control" was there waiting for me. Pedro and his family and friends had already been arrested. I was taken to the airport and sent home. I was – three months pregnant.'

'Oh no.'

'Oh yes. I'd hardly admitted it to myself till then, but on the plane the baby was all I could think about, it and Pedro. I worked out this mad plan to go and hide with Claire in Las Vegas but – well – it didn't work. Instead I spent the next year in a sanitarium.' She looked down. 'Craig and his wife wanted the baby and I said yes. I'd come around to a "full appreciation of my treacherous, susceptible and unstable nature" – that's what I wrote in my letter of resignation – and I didn't want her. Just didn't want to know. If I'd realised . . . if I'd had any idea . . .'

She broke off there and reached for her glass, hurriedly swallowing what was left in it before going on. 'I received a "generous settlement" as they say – not that I've ever been able to bring myself to touch it – and went to Europe to bum around and sort myself out. I travelled a long time but eventually began to feel like working again. Craig said he'd speak with his contacts and one of them introduced me to Phil.'

'Were you aware that he was . . . ?'

'Yes, of course. I knew that no one with as mixed a record as mine is ever allowed an independent life again just like that. It has to be earned. And Phil wasn't to be a "control" in the strict sense. All he was supposed to do was keep an eye on me and regulate my assignments so that I finished up with a new career as a features writer. An apolitical features writer.'

'Who was to be the judge? I mean, that you'd finished?'

'Phil unfortunately. I probably should have slept with him the first week when I had the chance, too. I'd have been out of there years ago. But I couldn't do it and he's never forgiven me for that – never. Still, apart from his games, I was reasonably free for about eighteen months. If I picked up on any stories with "suspect" political overtones, for example, all I was expected to do was note it. And they let me cover women's issues.' She smiled. 'In their system – which I'm ashamed to say was mine as well when I started – the women's movement isn't "political". It's classed as "human interest" and isn't considered in the slightest threatening to the established order. Isn't that pompous? Do you believe it?

'But anyway, the point is, I did well in London, so well that not only did I stop thinking about politics, I came that close' – she pinched her thumb and forefinger together – 'that close to my release. Then I met David Blake.'

'Who sounds, I hope you don't mind me saying, like a pretty weird choice given what you've just been telling me.'

'Yeah, well, as far as I was concerned he was the first white man I'd felt attracted to in ages and it was this beautiful, hot, sunny summer. I knew he'd been active in the Labour Party for a long time and that something had happened to disaffect him somehow, but when he talked about it at all, which he didn't do too often, he just tended to make kind of snide, dismissive remarks about "so-called socialists". And I misread him – assumed without thinking about it that he was going through the rightward shift most people go through in their thirties. I didn't understand that it was a phase and that he would inevitably feel compelled to *fight* the conservative element that's finally broken away. I didn't want to understand either. I was having far too good a time.' She sighed.

'We were almost at the end of our honeymoon – we were sitting on this hillside in the south of France having a picnic, I'll never

232

forget it – when he started telling me this long story about some incident when he was an undergraduate. I couldn't believe what I was hearing: he'd been involved in both the Young Communists *and* the group that's become the Socialist Workers' Party. And it got worse when I suddenly realised that the bunch of guys he went off rambling with were all his old mates from that era – and that most of them are still active in a whole range of lefty organisations.

'Well of course the day I went back to work, there was Phil grinning this sickeningly smug self-satisfied grin. "Welcome back chicadee," he says to me. "Everyone at HQ is delighted." Needless to say he'd known all about David and, seeing the mood I was in, he'd decided to set it up for me to meet him *hoping* that something like what happened would happen. Why I didn't expect it – I mean, I *knew* that keeping me on the string gave him the money to pay his kids' school fees. And now they were guaranteed for quite a while – because, as we both knew, he had me. There was no way I could appeal to our bosses, claim it was an accident. In that world, that vocabulary, there's no such thing as an accident when it comes to encounters with socialists and communists. They're either intentional or they're not, and if they're not and it's someone like me having the encounter, it's a symptom of instability.'

She stopped to light a cigarette with shaking hands. 'I – you have to understand. This is hindsight. I've – had a shock, several shocks, the past week. I spent all day yesterday and all last night rearranging the pieces, seeing the true picture and the lies. At the time it wasn't how I'm telling it. At the time it was just a button being pushed. They'd made me and I saw myself as they did. I believed myself hopeless. My "inherited tendencies" would betray me no matter what I did or how hard I tried to control them. And Phil being the bastard he is was ready to take advantage of the position he'd contrived for me. He offered me a deal: he'd do the work and collect the fees I'd supposedly be earning. I just had to play along – not interfere in his friendship with David – "front" for him.

'Looking back,' she sighed. 'I guess what amazes me more than anything is that I didn't simply kill myself. I know it occurred to me, but somehow – somehow I was too angry to die. I was full of this enormous rage that was like nothing I'd ever felt before and it gave me this perverse desire to live. It gave me a reason for living too: I wanted to get even with everyone who'd put me in that situation: myself, them, Phil and most of all – most of all – David. And it gave me clarity. I woke up the next morning knowing

233

exactly what to do. I'd been trained in how to play people off against each other and I saw that I could use the principles I'd been taught. I went along with Phil's bent little scheme – that took care of our employers – and I proceeded to screw David around so badly he hardly had time for his political friends. Phil didn't have much to report. It was all incredibly easy. In fact, the hardest part was actually ending my marriage. Good old David – he's such a romantic, poor guy. It took three years before he finally gave up and left me. My God, what a relief *that* was. I . . . are you all right? You look a bit . . .'

'I don't know,' he mumbled. 'The way you said that . . . it sounded so – so cold blooded.'

'Yes, well it was. You're not surprised are you? How can you be surprised after you've spent all these years talking to people I set up?' Suddenly she smiled. 'Ah – I get it. Beneath that stern investigator's mask there beats a soft heart. You've listened to the story of my troubled soul and been taken in by it.'

He sat back defensively. Had she been playing with him? Had he been so gullible? Had he . . .

She reached across and placed her hand over his. 'Don't,' she said quietly. 'I'm really – very touched. I've – been as straight with you as I know how to be and I'd like to feel I deserve your sympathy. I'd like to feel I genuinely deserve it and haven't just been manipulating you into giving it to me. There's a slight problem though. I did undeniably do the work. Maybe not too well and maybe not with certainty always, but I did do it. And make no mistake: it took ruthlessness and calculation and duplicity and a coldness of outlook that would have been way beyond the means of any normal person – any normal woman. If I'd been tried at Nuremberg, Alan, I'd have been found guilty . . . I need another drink. You? Same again?'

After they ordered, she retrieved the broken end of her story. 'So – my marriage. I knew, you see, that if I could force David to walk out on me, the operation would have to be terminated and it was. On top of that, thanks to Phil's double dealing, I'd at last earned good behaviour marks. I requested release, got it and handed in my notice to Phil. The little shit insisted I work out the three months' period stipulated in my contract, but I was so euphoric even that didn't bother me. With holiday time knocked off, it was really only seven weeks. And I wasn't especially bothered either by the suspicion that he'd probably try to trick me into staying on somehow. It was practically inevitable given his need for the money I represented to him. I just thought: let him. I felt so strong, you know, so in control of myself.

'Nothing unusual happened for about two weeks and then he assigned me to do a piece about the common-law wife of a young man who'd been killed in a race riot. I wasn't sure what his angle was, but I knew there had to be one. I mean, the case had had a lot of publicity because of its political overtones. In fact, it was one of David's favourites. He and I, you understand, did occasionally talk to each other like ordinary people; it wasn't all trauma. But I'd very systematically – I thought – used the lectures he was so fond of delivering to me as practice. That's how I'd mastered my "tendencies" – by secretly resisting David's arguments.

'Anyway, it was a challenge I had to take so I took it. And I – well, what can I say? I lost.'

'Jesus,' Alan said, 'but how?'

She shook her head. 'The same way I lost all the other times: because I am who I am. I'd been to the inquest and like everybody else there I felt the jury's verdict was wrong: all the evidence pointed to the police's guilt. And I said so in my article. It would have been irresponsible journalism to have said anything else. I considered that I'd simply done a straight professional job and that by doing that I'd avoided whatever strange pitfalls Phil had hoped I'd fall into. And I – misjudged.

'Phil took one look at what I'd written and gave me the classic twisted grin. Not only was it "gushing", it was littered with what he termed "half-digested Davidisms". "Seems to me," he said, "that we should redeploy you in the lefty-liberal press corps. That's what they'll assume you're asking for if they see this. And maybe it's not such a bad idea when you think about it. It's where you belong – it's where you'd be most comfortable with gut reactions like yours. We've both known that for years: deep down you're a born radical. Besides, any way you slice it, they'll have to be informed of your "new interests", so why not do what I'm saying? Hell, look on the bright side: it'll take you a couple of years to build up a cover in that scene; the boys back home won't expect reports for a long long time.'

'I slapped him across the face, which amused him no end, but while he was holding my hands and watching me struggle, he said something so surprisingly human for him that I remember it. He said "I know you blame me. You think I'm a bastard and you're right. You have to be a shit to work for those shits as long as I have. But the only reason I can take advantage of you is because you let me. You could stop me any time – any time. All you have to do is stop worrying about yourself."

' "Or I could quit journalism," I yelled. He found that funnier than the slap. "And waste your *whole* life?" he said.

'I headed for the door and he called after me in this snidey-snide voice that I hate. "Go back to therapy – you need it kid. But for God's sake, pick someone good. Pick your own."

'Well I spent I don't know how long – over a week – at home trying to re-write that piece and thinking about the world and my life and my mother and feeling just so torn and guilty and depressed that I got so I couldn't even function. I knew, though, that if I didn't do something for myself I'd end up back in a sanitarium. I'd lose another year, have to start all over and I thought: damn it, no. I can't give them the satisfaction.'

'Sounds to me like they win no matter what.'

'Yes. True. But Phil's idea stuck – I could buy more time. Try therapy. Give it one more go, just one more. Not that I was particularly rational. I was just desperate. That's why I called David. I had to see somebody who'd talk to me like I was normal. Obviously I couldn't tell him the real problem; I had to tell him half-truths like I'd always done. But I did it again because there was no one else. There seemed to be no choice. And – that's how we got back together. Because I was frightened that if I were left on my own I'd fall apart.'

'I take it you agreed to Phil's strategy again too.'

Amanda looked down at her hands. 'I've fucked it up of course. My articles – aren't up to it. I can't get away with the super-ficial kind of stuff I cranked out in Berkeley; not in London. So I'm back – back where I was eighteen months ago, trying to force David to leave me – to spare him Phil's reports. I'm nearly there . . .'

She looked up again. 'I've just lied to you. I'm sorry. My life hasn't been exactly the same. There's been one difference: my therapist. If it weren't for her, I wouldn't be sitting here talking to you. It mystifies me when I think about it too because, scared as I say I was, I'm sure I went to her more for show and for comfort than for anything serious. How could I have expected anything serious when I wasn't prepared to be honest, you know? God, I've even edited certain dreams. But in spite of the way I've hidden

236

things from her and played games, she began to get through to me about my parents.

'When she heard they'd been murdered and learned that I'd been flown out before the funeral, she launched into a little spiel about rituals and "unfinished business". The way she put it was that I "hadn't given them a proper burial", which they deserved and I needed in order to "close that chapter". I'd never thought about that before and started fantasising about going back and paying my respects.

'I – it was your letter that made me decide that I had to go sooner rather than later. Knowing you knew – it felt like the lid on the box.'

'Did you consider talking to me?'

'No. Yes. I don't know. It would have – betrayed so much.'

'But you didn't tell Phil or your brother that I'd written?'

She bit her lip and glanced away.

Alan sighed. This woman's guilts surrounded her, let her get away with nothing.

Her mouth moved but he caught only an inaudible whisper.

'What?' he asked her.

'I think,' she repeated, 'that I intended to kill myself. Part of me – I've often felt I should have died with my parents. Often wished I had. I think maybe I imagined acting out some secret mythic melodrama by their graves. But maybe – maybe I didn't. Getting there became – an end in itself. There was no "after" in my thoughts. I suppose, deep down, I must have hoped – not for revelation exactly, but for direction.' As tears reappeared in her eyes, she smiled. 'I got it too. That's the incredible thing. I got it. And in a museum of all places. I mean, who expects their life to be turned upside down in a museum?' Then she began to laugh.

Alan waited anxiously, anticipating hysteria. It was that kind of laughter: close to the edge. But she saw his worried look and brought herself under control – or at any rate, she stopped laughing. The streaming tears were apparently beyond her, so she simply talked through them.

'When I arrived in Havana last Sunday, the public records office was closed, so I hired a cab to drive me out to our old house. I don't know how I found it; it's painted pink now and it's surrounded by other houses. Somehow, though, I recognised it and got the driver to wait while I went to the door. When a woman answered, I told her I was looking for some graves and she stared at me real hard

237

and suddenly threw her arms around my neck. It was Estrella. I couldn't believe it. She used to be this skinny little kid and she's this big stocky woman. Of course, she's had six children, so I guess it isn't surprising.

'Anyway, it turned out that the whole family was in the other room having dinner – her parents, Miguel and his wife and their kids, and all manner of other relatives; the whole tribe. She was determined that I join them – just beside herself with excitement that I was there – so I sent the cab away and let myself be dragged in. What a commotion, honestly. And God knows what I said. It can't have been much, though, because I'd hardly sat down when I realised that one of the men opposite me was Alfonso, Alfonso her cousin who'd murdered my parents.

'I stood up and started shouting at him – shouting at all of them. I just went – berserk. All those years, all that hurt – it all came out of me. Two of them had to catch my arms to stop me throwing plates of food. I was so angry. I mean, I'd assumed he'd been executed twenty-two years before.

'Estrella's mother poured water over my head, which shut me up long enough for Miguel to say to me: "You've been lied to. Alfonso was pardoned by Castro. We know that two of Batista's men murdered your parents. It was proved years ago, years and years ago. The story is that the CIA put them up to it."

'Well naturally I wasn't about to swallow that. Nothing in the world could have made me swallow that. I screamed at him that he was crazy. *I'd* seen the proof. *I* knew the truth.

'Miguel looked at his father, who nodded and said: "I have a truck. Miguel and Estrella will drive you back to Havana. They will show you proof."

' "You do that," I said. And they did. They took me – pushed me – forced me – into the truck, into the city, into the Museum of the Revolution and into the rear section where there's a sign over the door labelled Foreign Comrades. And there, on one wall, blown up and framed, was this old grainy black and white photo of my mother standing in front of the school surrounded by all her old friends. Beneath it there was a caption that said "Lucille Asprey, 1912–1958, Benefactress of the People. Awarded honorary citizenship posthumously in 1965 by Fidel Castro for her outstanding efforts on behalf of her comrades."

'Miguel said to me: "Castro isn't a murderer – that's an American imperialist lie – but even if he were, why would he give such a rare honour to an enemy he'd killed? It makes no sense."

'I'd sat down on the floor by this point and Estrella knelt beside me. "We know they tried to say your mother was a crazy person. We know that's what Americans call people who have different politics. We know it is a sin there to be communistic.'

' "They showed me files," I said. "I saw her medical records saying she was sick. I saw Alfonso and Ramon's confessions."

' "We heard that she was made to see a fake doctor. Alfonso and Ramon were tortured. Ramon wasn't at my house for dinner because he lives in a special hospital. Alfonso's back is one big scar."

'I wept so hard I felt I'd never stop.

'Miguel said: "We can take you to the grave now if you want. The monument is modest but made of marble, an unusual privilege. After that I would like to make some telephone calls for you. My father and I have a friend who is a member of the Central Committee. Through him we will get you an appointment with the Chief Archivist of the People's Revolution."

'I met with the Chief Archivist Wednesday afternoon – can it be only two days ago? It seems a lifetime. The next morning I caught a flight to New York. All I could think about was telling Craig. Craig had to know. I could picture his indignation, pictured us going to the State Department together, imagined the scene we would create. By the time I got to his apartment, I tell you, I'd planned the whole speech. The damages suit too: "Your Honour, I have lost twenty-two years of my life; I have hurt countless people. And all because I was misled." Then of course there was the Senate investigation and the networked coast-to-coast exposé.' She shook her head and wiped her eyes. 'How naive can you get. Jesus.'

'Your brother – he knew?'

'*Knew* – ha! He was involved in the planning – he and father.'

'But your father was *killed*.'

' "A mistake, my dear, a mistake," ' she said, haughtily flicking her hand in what Alan took for an imitation of Craig. Then: 'He didn't add that it had served his interests for father to die, but he didn't need to. Instead he tried to tell me – had the nerve to try to tell me – that it was "really all our mother's fault", that if she'd listened to father and taken any one of half a dozen "opportunities" he'd given her to enter a sanitarium, it wouldn't have happened. "They waited until they could wait no longer," he said to me. "She forced them to use Plan B, she and she alone. She was

239

acting contrary to the national interest, Mandy; she was a sick, disturbed, dangerous woman who'd been manipulated by the . . ."

'I said, "I know the story, I've been hearing it all my life. But couldn't you at least have told me the truth? Couldn't you have told me that she was killed by our side? Didn't I deserve *that*?" It was of course an idiotic question to put to a man whose greed and ambition have allowed him to collude in matricide. Lying to his younger sister and permitting – fostering – the perpetuation of that lie so that it perverts all her natural human feeling has to be a small thing to live with by comparison. And sure enough, that's how he treated it – as a minor matter barely worthy of discussion. "You had the same tendencies, my dear. They had to be exorcised – for your own sake – and that seemed the most sensible method."

' "And how much did they pay for all this?" I shouted at him. "Thirty pieces of silver?" He put his hands over his sensitive little ears and pursed his lips at me. "Please," he said, "don't blaspheme. Some of us are Christians . . . I send you Asprey Oil's Annual Report every year. You know what I've achieved. And you know as well as I do how I've achieved it. Fortunately, *my* schooling taught me to value old-fashioned virtues like patriotism. I understand my obligations to my country and have always willingly co-operated."

'I think by this point the idea of talking to you had come into my mind. I think it must have because I decided to try to draw him into bragging – I was hoping for a fuller picture of what he's been involved in the past twenty years – but he wouldn't be drawn. Still, I've deduced quite a lot over time. I have a good idea where he fits in the chain of command above people like Phil and my earlier "controls" and I've met several of his colleagues. I'll write down all the names and interconnections for you when I get home.'

She shrugged. 'There isn't much more to say about yesterday. Our communication deteriorated into accusations: he began to point out the "symptoms of instability" in my behaviour and I did the same to him, believe me. Eventually he informed me that he had a business engagement and left.

'I stayed in the apartment last night to go through family papers. He told me to take what I wanted, so I have.'

'Wasn't he concerned about what you might do?'

'Not until a little while ago. On the way to Kennedy, he said to me: "I'm pleased you haven't brought Astrid in to this. You must realise how silly it would be to use our disagreement as an excuse to raise that issue."

' "She hardly knows me," I said. "There's no point." It's true too, I'm afraid. He's been her father for her whole life and she loves him, poor kid.

'He said, "Excellent. I'm glad you're taking the sensible view. I'll naturally have to file a report on our discussions but I'm certain that I can safely omit the personal issues. On top of that, if you leave it with me, I believe I'll be able to sort out full release for you. Needless to say, I'll expect silence from you in return, but that's the price you pay; the price we all pay."

' "Do as you like," I said to him. "I make you no promises."

'He gave me one of his more patronising smiles. "Yes, you'll want a few days to think about it. I'll call you toward the end of the week."

'I couldn't help it. I had to stick the knife in somehow, crack that smug, saintly, all-knowing façade. I waited until a suitable interval had passed and then I said, real nice and casual: "By the way, how's the long-term political strategy going? You must have lived down your divorces by now, and with the Republicans in . . ."

'He gripped the steering wheel so tight I thought he'd snap it. It was a neck substitute – my neck. His teeth were clenched too but he managed to say, "I told you in the spring. I'm on the A list for prospective diplomatic appointees."

' "Oh yes," I said, "so you did. Well well well."

'He was shaking so hard he had to pull the car over. "Amanda," he said to me, "if you do anything – if you so much as consider doing anything to jeopardise my career in any way whatsoever – if you so much as say peep about our conversation – if you do not go back and pick up your life as if nothing unusual had occurred – I will ensure that you will regret it. Do you understand?"

'God, was that satisfying! I'd scored one – ruffled him. It was only when I sat down in the departure lounge that I realised what I'd probably done, saw that I'd probably gone and misjudged just like I've been doing my whole life. That's what made me decide to come and see you. *It* might be a mistake too, but I figure the two will cancel each other out.' She smiled. 'And even if they don't, I sure do feel better.'

Regulars were hovering around our table in the caff, staring at our empty cups and plates. David was too engrossed to notice. 'Why did she come back here? For God's sake, she must have known that Phil would report her return date. Once she'd got off that plane – I mean, it was suicidal. She should have just disappeared.'

'That or taken a later flight,' Alan said. 'She could have pretended she'd gotten sick. But she refused to hear of it. She wanted to go through the interviews I'd collected, tell me the details of each set-up. Look – she was euphoric. She'd confessed. And like she said, it was the first time in twenty-two years that she was free to admit to herself that she was who she was and that that was okay. It made her a little wild and who could blame her. Trouble was, there was no penetrating that mood. She was going to do what she was going to do and that was that. Shit, I had a hard time getting her to agree a code in case she ran into trouble writing out her story by the deadline she'd set. That's why I called Mike after she'd gone and asked him to nose around the Knight Agency – because I was worried about her.'

David put his head in his hands. 'Why the fuck didn't she tell me,' he muttered to himself. 'Jesus, if only she'd . . .'

'What was the code?' George asked. 'I'm always on the market for new ideas.'

Alan shrugged. 'She left it up to me and I'm the amateur, as you know. All I could come up with was the college kids' trick, you know the one: she'd call me collect and ask for a non-existent person. I'd say he wasn't in and get the operator to give me the caller's number. Then I'd go to a phone booth, call, get another real number off her, wait and try that . . . Not very foolproof really. Her one contribution was the phoney name. She chose Ross Springsteen. Got quite a kick out of that – laughed and laughed.'

David looked up. 'Ross Springsteen? *Ross – Springsteen*?'

'Sure, well you get it don't you? Springsteen for Bruce and Ross for Diana. When we were talking about it at the bar, someone put an old Supremes track on the juke . . .'

But David was on his feet.

George said: 'What the . . . I was about to order some more . . .'

I stood up too and grabbed David's arm. 'Diana and Bruce,' I repeated excitedly. 'Diana and Bruce.'

Alan said: 'What's going on?'

'Come on,' David said. 'There's a poster and a record collection in my flat that we need to have a closer look at. I think she may have left something for me. I think she really may have left something for me after all.'

242

Epilogue

I knew that Suze would never forgive me if I disappeared into my bed for twenty-four hours without telling her what had happened, so David and I stopped in at the office on our way back to my place from his flat in Kentish Town. It was still a little early, so we went in to wait on her sofa.

As soon as he sat down on the soft cushions, David gave a deep, satisfied sigh, smiled into my eyes with that smile of his, made a kissing motion towards my lips and, still clutching my hand, fell asleep. My own eyelids suddenly felt terribly heavy too, but as they were flickering for what might have been the last time, Suze began to shake my shoulder as she whispered: 'Dee – oh thank God. I've been worrying about you all night. What the hell happened to you?'

After I'd told her, I handed her the envelope that had been slipped into the sleeve of the single of 'Where Did Our Love Go' by Diana Ross and the Supremes, then watched as she pulled out the contents: the snapshot of the picture of Lucy Asprey which hangs in the Museum of the Revolution; Amanda's British passport stamped to show her entrance into Cuba; a recent statement of her account at the Bank of Geneva; and Alan Dexter's phone number.

Suze couldn't seem to speak so I gave her the other envelope, the one that had been tucked into the back panel of the 'Born to Run' poster. Inside was a note which, as I knew, said: 'David – I wish I had the words to apologise to you. I'll always remember that first summer. If a man named Alan Dexter hasn't yet contacted you, call him.' The number again followed.

Still dumb (or perhaps only numbed), Suze stared out into the morning mist. 'Imagine,' she said at last, 'what might have happened if you'd found these before you went to California.'

'Yes,' I said, feeling a chill. I had imagined that and had realised, as she had, that David and I would probably have been dead, either because David would have contacted Alan on a tapped line, or because David would have mentioned it to Craig during the same lunch when he inadvertently told him about Jackie.

Suze said: 'What do you suppose the real story is?'

'Your guess is as good as mine,' I shrugged.

But in fact her guess was to turn out to be so much fuller and more likely-sounding that the rest of us – me and David and Paula and Pete and my mother and Alan – adopted it as the orthodox version of the final surmise. It goes like this:

Craig must have become more and more irrational after his argument with his sister, a condition which his colleagues themselves may have aggravated by their failure to take his report of her threats seriously enough. They may even have proposed to let her say what she liked and discredit it by producing her medical records, a prospect which would have done nothing to tamp his fears about the shape and consequences of her vengeance.

In any case, he'd so 'lost touch with reality' (after the manner of his hero Richard Nixon) that he'd come to England, placed an unauthorised Embassy tap on David's phone and manipulated him into tracking Amanda.

After he'd killed his sister, his efforts to divert the blame to a random burglar probably seemed quite good to his employers. Whatever, Craig was pretty senior – senior enough to be given a second chance.

This he'd used up by killing Jackie. His colleagues had been forced to stage all that palaver in the States – all that setting up of Juan and Alan to cover up for him – because their budget was about to go before a key Congressional committee. They were on the verge of becoming a strong autonomous power again after years of public scrutiny. They didn't need scandal any more than he did.

If David hadn't called Craig from California and mentioned the envelope in the bank deposit box – well, Juan might be in Brixton Prison even today.

Ages later, months and months, after I'd written to countless Senators and Congressional Representatives and State Department and Embassy officials, a plain-wrapped airmail packet arrived from Washington for David. In it was the revised will, unsigned and therefore legally useless.

244

Despite this, David decided to distribute her money as she'd wished.

A year later, the Campaign for Socialist Chile held the opening party for the community centre they'd bought and renovated with the £60,000 they'd inherited. As I walked up the stairs of the hall towards the front door, I saw that a small brass plaque had been mounted under the bell.

'In memory,' it said, 'of our comrade and benefactress, Amanda Finch.'

I think she would have liked that.

Mary Wings
She Came Too Late

'She was a warm body . . . I didn't want to know her. And
I didn't want to notice the small black charred hole in the
back of her trench coat. I grabbed a wrist. It was warm
but there was no pulse. Not that I could feel'

Emma, at work at The Women's Hotline, receives a message from
an unknown caller: 'Emma Victor, I need you'. She arranges a
meeting, but stumbles upon a corpse, and is soon caught up in a
web of mystery linking a women's clinic and a yachting accident,
drug trafficking and a high-society home . . .

This is a fast-moving and contentious whodunnit in the Chandler
tradition. Mary Wings is at work on a second Emma Victor novel.

Fiction/The Women's Press Crime   £3.95
ISBN: 0 7043 3995 1
Hardcover   £8.95
ISBN: 0 7043 2879 8

Barbara Wilson
Murder in the Collective

Two print collectives, one left-wing and one radical lesbian, plan to merge. But hidden tensions explode when one of the collective members is found – murdered.

Pam is determined to uncover the truth, however disturbing. No one is free of suspicion. The Filipino resistance movement, the CIA, a drunken feminist on a binge, a fugitive in the attic, arms running, blackmail and a pair of unusual contact lenses are all involved before the mystery can be solved.

'A paragon whodunnit' *The Times*

Fiction/The Women's Press Crime   £3.50
ISBN: 0 7043 3943 9
Hardcover   £7.50
ISBN: 0 7043 2854 2

Barbara Wilson
Sisters of the Road

Pam Nilson, the feminist sleuth of *Murder in the Collective*, is back
again, this time looking for teenager Trish Margolin – and the
murderer of Trish's best friend. Her search introduces her to the
world of teenage prostitution and runaways on the streets of
Seattle and Portland.

As the suspense builds up in this excellent psychological thriller,
we are made aware of the issues of prostitution and violence
against women.

Barbara Wilson is the author of *Ambitious Women* and *Walking on
the Moon*, published by The Women's Press in 1983 and 1986.

Fiction/The Women's Press Crime   £3.95
ISBN: 0 7043 4073 9
Hardcover: £9.95
ISBN: 0 7043 5028 9

Gillian Slovo
Death by Analysis

'The female detective of the eighties has truly arrived'
Globe and Mail, Canada

Psychoanalyst Paul Holland is found dead in mysterious
circumstances, apparently killed by a hit-and-run driver.
Saxophonist Kate Baeier is hired by her own ex-therapist to
investigate. The hunt for the killer leads from the couches of
elegant Belsize Park to the streets of Hackney at a time of high
racial tension, and into a web of intrigue and police cover-up.

Kate finds herself on a journey into the past lives of Holland's oh
so respectable clients and into the depths of her own psyche. She
is forced to examine the nature of the therapeutic relationship and
ultimately the importance of therapy itself.

The Women's Press Crime   £3.95
ISBN: 0 7043 4018 6
Hardcover   £7.95
ISBN: 0 7043 5008 4